The Guardians of Karma

Mohan Vizhakat

Srishti
PUBLISHERS & DISTRIBUTORS

Srishti Publishers & Distributors
N-16, C. R. Park
New Delhi 110 019
editorial@srishtipublishers.com

First published by
Srishti Publishers & Distributors in 2013

Copyright © Mohan Vizhakat, 2013

Typeset by EGP at Srishti

Printed and bound in India

This is a work of fiction. Names, characters, places and incidents are the product of author's imagination, within the context of popular mythology. Resemblance, if any, to actual persons, living or dead, events or locals is entirely coincidental.

All rights reserved. This work is being published subject to the condition that it shall not, by any way of trade or otherwise, be lent, resold, hired out or otherwise circulated without the author's explicit legal consent, in any form of binding or cover other than in which it is published and without a similar condition being imposed on the subsequent purchaser and without limiting the rights under copyright reserved above. No part of this publication shall be reproduced, stored in or introduced into retrieval systems, or transmitted in any form or by any means (electronic, mechanical, photocopying, recording or otherwise), without the prior explicit legal permission of the copyright owner, except in case of brief quotations or reviews with appropriate citations.

To ANTIMAHAKALAN *and* TRIPURANTAKA
the two great aspects of Lord Shiva

CONTENTS

	Acknowledgements	*ix*
	Prologue	*xi*
1	Land of the Vetals	1
2	Legend of the Bheeshma	18
3	City of the Gods	33
4	Indra Sabha	49
5	Magical Somvan	57
6	Daityan Dilemma	71
7	An Empire in Crisis	77
8	Bheeshma Mission	84
9	Frontier Town of Kambhoj	96
10	Citadels of Tripura	110
11	Equation of Karma	117
12	Daityan Society	132
13	Confrontation	141
14	Sojourn at Gandharv	153
15	Ashram of Parashu	164
16	Daityan Council	172
17	The Ultimatum	182

18	Vicious Proposal	188
19	Devious Deceit at Patala	202
20	The Assassination Attempt	210
21	Tragedy of Lonar	217
22	Advice from the Mūrthi	223
23	Sarparanya	235
24	Takshak	248
25	Pinaka	255
26	Invasion of Bharat	262
27	Rudrapeeth	269
28	Devarth's Final Hope	278
29	Battle of Atalantpuri	282
30	The Mighty Tripurantaka	286
31	Notion of Dharma	292
32	Lake of the Mind	305
	Epilogue	*309*

ACKNOWLEDGEMENTS

The author thanks:

His wife Swapna and daughter Viyona for their continued inspiration and suggestions.

His publisher for showing faith in the potential of this work.

His dad for initiating him into the mythological legacies of the great Indian civilisation.

And above all, his Karma which led him to begin this journey.

PROLOGUE

The ancient Indian epics like the *Ramayana* and the *Mahabharata* describe a prehistoric age which was far more advanced from technological, sociological and spiritual perspectives in comparison to many millennia that followed, till the advent of 20th century. We are often fascinated and surprised by the level of sophistication of these mythological records in terms of their complexity and philosophical insights. Some parts of these epics seem almost like science fiction, even by the contemporary standards.

Is it possible that many of the ancient Indian myths do have some elements of truth behind them? Maybe an advanced civilisation with ethnic groups like *Devas, Daityas, Rakshas, Manavs*, etc., did exist in our distant past? Maybe the *Lokas, Talas* and other exotic places where they lived were actually the geographical land masses that used to exist during the Ice Age? Perhaps some of the legendary events described in our scriptures were interpretations of real incidents, gleaned from fragmentary cultural memories of a prehistoric era. Or maybe there is a common lineage to the ancient legends of many cultures across the world. For example, is the Indian legend about the free-floating triple cities of Tripura and the Greek one about Atlantis, both reconstructions of the same event?

The fact that very little is known about human history before 5000 B.C.E needn't preclude that those were the times of stone Age cave dwellers. Earth had been within the grip of Ice Age for a major part of human existence on the planet.

With sea levels much lower than today, there were numerous large islands all across the tropics. Since the average global temperature was much lower than today, these large archipelagos had salubrious weather and fertile terrain conditions, ideal for sustaining abundant life. Ice covered substantial portions of the mainland continents, but the lush green tropical islands might have served as the cradle for early human settlements to develop and prosper into advanced civilisations. After all, the human intellect and body form was no different then, when compared to now, so many millennia later.

Towards the end of the Ice Age, the rising sea water levels triggered by melting ice caps, had inundated and eventually submerged many of the tropical islands below the ocean surface as we see it today. Perhaps all the major archaeological evidence of the earlier era was lost during such a cataclysmic worldwide deluge or *pralay* that the scriptures describe of. Perhaps we are still not technologically advanced enough to discover them, especially from beneath the oceans.

From the fictional context of this book, the period towards the end of Ice Age marked the decline of the 'first wave' of advanced human civilisations on earth; which might have even rivalled the 'second wave' that we're experiencing now, in terms of sociological, spiritual and technological sophistication.

1

LAND OF THE VETALS

Hara woke up with a start. It was dark, but the rocky overhang under which they were sleeping provided sufficient shelter from the elements. He looked over at Acharya Parashu, who seemed peacefully asleep. This was reassuring since the Acharya was often the first to sense if there was to be any danger. He took out his water pouch, downed a few gulps and walked over to the ledge of the sheer cliff on top of a hill, where they had taken refuge the previous evening. The moon was past zenith within the sky, so morning must be still a few *muhurtas* away. He looked over the rugged valley below them. Everything seemed to be calm for now.

Why did Acharya Parashu choose to travel through this dreaded region known as the Brashtaranya, Land of the Vetals? Was there no other alternative? Perhaps it would have been better if they had taken a longer route around this region. Then again he recalled the words of Maharishi Vashist — "There is nothing like good or bad decisions. Incidents happen as they are meant to; no one can change them. We can only attempt to improve them, but even that is often part of the cosmic plan". In any case, it was a pointless chain of thought since they were already well within the Brashtaranya region.

It was just two days ago when Acharya Parashu, the veteran Bheeshma warrior monk and mentor of Hara, had broached the mission to him after returning from a meeting with Maharishi Vashist at Brahmagiri.

"Hara, I know you've been restless for some action." Acharya Parashu had said, as if reading his thoughts. "Maharishi Vashist says that it is now time for unfolding a chain of events that would lead us towards our path of right Karma."

The Bheeshma warrior monks were expected to be ready for action any time but Hara was particularly looking forward to it. After all, it had been quite a few months since the last mission was completed. "Yes Acharya, I've been looking forward to our next mission. When shall we embark on it?" Hara had asked earnestly.

"We're to undertake a Bheeshma mission to rescue Rishi Agastya and his wife from Atalantpuri, the capital of the Daityan Empire. We'll leave before sunrise tomorrow." Acharya Parashu had said.

"Thank you, Acharya. It would be an honour for me to be a part of this mission. After all that Agastya Rishi did for me, I am forever indebted to him." Hara had replied, recalling that it was only the timely intervention by Rishi Agastya that had saved his sister a few years back from the debilitating Kshaya.

Acharya Parashu had looked at him intently, "Hara, you must know that Bheeshma monks are bound by righteous Karma, not debt. Anyway, this mission is not about any debt. Rishi Agastya is under forced confinement at Atalantpuri, where he is being compelled to provide coercive support for one of their genetic drug development programmes called 'Kayakalp'."

Hara had kept quiet. After all, Acharya Parashu was his revered guru who had inducted him as a Bheeshma warrior apprentice years ago.

"We can reach the port town of Kambhoj within next three days if we take the shorter land route through the Brashtaranya jungles. It is better that not too many get to hear of two Bheeshma monks embarking on a mission towards Atalantpuri." Acharya Parashu had said.

Now, looking over the broken landscape of the valley ahead of him, Hara knew that this was going to be a tough mission. Even if they can somehow get past this Vetal-infested land, crossing the seas and passing through Daityan security to reach Atalantpuri would be difficult. But, as always, he was sure Acharya must have some plan or karmic insight regarding the way events may unfold during this mission.

The slight movement of their horses picketed close-by brought his attention back to the present. They seemed to be quietly nibbling on some fresh grass nearby. This was indeed a quiet and peaceful night—too quiet for comfort. "Is it a precursor to some upcoming crisis?" Hara wondered. He returned to their shelter to lie down.

⊤ Ш ⚥

They were up before sunrise and after some breakfast, started off down the hill. It seemed to have rained during the night and the path was somewhat slippery. The track that they were following soon entered a gully along an ancient river bed. This was a vulnerable position to be in as it was easy to get ambushed from either side. Acharya Parashu seemed conscious of the same and signalled Hara to be alert and watch out for trouble of any sort. The gully soon gave way to a straight-looking corridor, right through the midst of the grasslands ahead. The horses were fresh from overnight's rest, so they nudged them into a steady trot.

"At this pace, we should be able to reach the outskirts of Kambhoj by nightfall," Acharya Parashu said.

"Yes, Acharya. But are you confident that the Vetals wouldn't intervene?" Hara was still uncomfortable that the journey so far had been without any particular incident. This was unusual. Anyone venturing into this region would have by now been attacked by the Vetals, who were psychologically conditioned to hunt and destroy. He was sure that the Vetals must have spotted them.

"The Vetals know we are here Hara. I've seen their tracks ahead of us when we passed through the gully. Don't think they would attack us though. There is not much they can gain from two monks passing by. They may even know that we are the Bheeshmas, and are not likely to confront us directly. Even so, we'll need to be careful not to make any mistakes and pass through this region as fast as possible," Acharya Parashu replied, trying to assuage Hara's concerns.

The Acharya was right. The Vetals had spotted them as soon as they had entered the Brashtaranya region. They wondered as to why two Bheeshma monks had chosen to travel along this route, usually dreaded by all. If it had been anyone else, they would have launched an attack on them by now. Past experience had, however, taught them that attacking Bheeshma warrior monks could be a big mistake. These guys looked very capable of standing their ground. Even just a pair of Bheeshmas can be formidable opponents. Whatever little they could take from these monks didn't seem worth the trouble.

After riding for five muhurtas continuously, they got down near a stream so that the horses could drink and take some rest. Hara continued to keep a wary eye, looking out for any signs of impending danger. "Acharya Parashu was probably right that the Vetals wouldn't confront them directly," Hara thought. These creatures may wait for any signs of weakness, and only attack when their victims are in their most vulnerable state. He hoped that if they remained vigilant, it may well be possible to pass through this region without attracting too much attention.

Their confidence didn't last long. Just as they were preparing to remount the horses, they heard a faint scream from somewhere upstream. Acharya Parashu looked at Hara and nodded. In an instant they started off on foot towards the direction of the sound. Hara was actually surprised to hear anything in this region, let alone a human voice screaming. It seemed like an urgent cry for help and sounded feminine. What was a woman doing this deep within the Vetal land? Hara wondered.

The going was tough through the thick undergrowth, but they moved as fast as possible. Suddenly, there was another desperate shout for help, this time from somewhere nearby. They must be close! Acharya Parashu stopped and silently signalled Hara. They then moved slowly and stealthily towards the sound. Hara's hand was already on the handle of the Spatishūl secured on his waistband. On reaching a clearing right ahead, they stopped, trying to comprehend the scene.

There were seven of them. Most were of average six feet in height but one or two were well over seven feet tall. They wore some sort of black attire, mainly leather. Even though humanoid, their deep-set eyes and the leathery face looked fierce. Body was mostly muscle but many parts seemed clearly artificial. The sight of even one of them could take the breath away from any human. All seven were circling around the object of their attention – a young woman. She seemed terrified but was attempting to hold guard with a knife in her right hand. Acharya Parashu noted the Devan regalia on her dress. The Vetals had probably tried, but came short of capturing her. Or were they simply having fun with her? They had closed in on her from all sides and it seemed unlikely that the current impasse would last much longer.

Acharya Parashu signalled Hara to circle around the clearing. Then he drew out his Spatishūl, came out into the clearing and shouted, "Leave her alone, you vermin!"

The Vetal party suddenly turned around, totally surprised at this intrusion. Standing in front of them was a Bheeshma warrior monk with a fully morphed Spatishūl in hand. This was not something they had anticipated. Some of them knew that two monks had been spotted, but never expected them to be so close. Besides this, their attention was mostly on the woman and her companion who lay dead nearby. They looked at each other and four of them advanced towards Acharya Parashu, drawing out their swords. With an advantage of four to one, they seemed confident to deal with a middle-aged monk.

Acharya Parashu looked at the tall Vetal who seemed to be the group leader and said in the ancient language of Brahmi, "Save your lives and leave now."

The Vetal leader grinned back—if the expression that came up on its face could be called that and responded in a coarse, low-pitched sound, "You've walked to your death, Bheeshma."

Suddenly the Vetal approaching from the left launched an attack on Acharya Parashu's flank. Parashu had expected it but remained composed till the attacker came in close range. Then suddenly, he took a single step back with his left leg and made a complete circle with his right, simultaneously swinging the Spatishūl at a low angle. The Vetal who had attacked at a high vertical angle didn't understand the classical move from the Bheeshma veteran. It was totally surprised by the sudden, explosive but measured action at the precise moment. The crystalline sharp edge of the Spatishūl cleaved the Vetal in half and it collapsed into a pile without any sound, even as Acharya Parashu stepped aside to avoid impact.

The grin had suddenly vanished from the face of the Vetal leader and it hesitated for a moment. The confidence it felt earlier turned first into fear, and then anger and fury. It made a horrifying sound, and together with the two other Vetals, launched a multi-front attack at Acharya Parashu. As earlier, the veteran Bheeshma was calm as he saw them coming.

In the meanwhile, the three Vetals holding up against the young woman were forced to turn their attention to confront Hara who too had emerged from the trees behind them. Hara had seen the four Vetals attacking his guru, and moved in quickly to block the remaining, thereby effectively splitting them into two groups. Through the corner of his eye he could see that the young woman was looking at them in total amazement. Perhaps the actions happened too fast for her to fully comprehend what was actually going on.

As he moved in, Hara slid low on the ground and landed right below the Vetal nearest to the young woman. In the same motion, he thrust his Spatishūl straight into the Vetal's belly. As he got up, he saw that the second Vetal had turned towards him. The Vetal feigned an attack to Hara's left, and simultaneously taking out another sword with its left hand, swung it hard against his neck.

As the other attackers closed in on Acharya Parashu, he suddenly leapt upwards, while at the same time swinging his sabre arm, thereby slicing a deep gash on the shoulder of one Vetal. As he landed, the two Vetals had to turn around to confront him. The Vetal on the left had already got its sword into a striking position which he pushed towards the chest of the senior monk.

As a Bheeshma master of close combat, Acharya Parashu knew that unexpected moves from an opponent are to be used more as an opportunity rather than just counter it in defence. Even when a defensive or evasive movement is carried out, it should have the elements of a counter-attack. These movements were, however, never to be planned or thought. In fact, thought is the hindrance which can slow you down. The reactions had to come from beyond thoughts—even the ones never practised before. In the state of meditative *Stithapragya* during combat, he had complete awareness of the movements within and around him. In such a super-conscious state of awareness, time itself slowed down and reactions happened from within his very being.

His body instinctively stepped sideways to avoid the Vetal's thrust. As the Vetal's sword arm extended, Parashu moved the Spatishūl below it, only to thrust it straight into the opponent's open armpit. As the Vetal collapsed, the last one standing took out another sword to face him. Slicing the air around at impossible angles at incredible speed, it launched itself at the Bheeshma monk. Acharya Parashu had heard of this trick by Vetals who could move both arms with similar ease, making it impossible for their opponent to guess their line of motion. Instead of defending himself against the slicing movement of both swords, he lifted his left arm and gestured at the neck of the Vetal rushing towards him. The Vetal stopped suddenly as if it had slammed into an invisible tree trunk. Both the swords dropped from its hands as they went up to support the throat, crushed by the invisible telekinetic force-field projected by the Bheeshma. It made a loud groan and dropped to the ground, gasping for breath.

Hara blocked the sword swing from the Vetal with his Spatishūl and using his left arm punched hard at the opponent's rib cage. This was a mistake since the genetically engineered Vetals didn't have any vital organs there. However, the blow threw the Vetal off balance. By the time the creature recovered, Hara had moved the point of Spatishūl into its path. The leading tip of the sparkling crystal weapon dug deep into its eye socket and the brain behind it. The Vetal dropped like a dead stone. Meanwhile, the third Vetal, realising defeat, chose to exploit the weak spot of their opponents. It swung its sword at the young woman who was still attempting to comprehend the fast-paced action happening around her. Before Hara could do anything, the Vetal was close enough to strike her down.

What happened next feared would always be remembered by the young woman. As she realised imminent death, the Vetal's body got swung aside violently as if it was a rag doll. It seemed as if an enormous invisible projectile had slammed into it with great force. The Vetal was lifted up by at least nine feet into the air before crashing down, its body crumpled beyond recognition. Hara and the young woman turned over to see Acharya Parashu, in the meditative yogic posture of *Mārak Mudra*. Hara had seen it only once before, since this tantric combat technique was used by advanced Bheeshma warrior monks very rarely. It projected the complete *Jwalaprabha*—the *kundalini* energy coiled up within a Bheeshma monk—into a single telekinetic force-field that can be delivered from any distance.

The fight had lasted less than a minute. Six Vetals lay dead. They couldn't find the seventh one. In fact, Acharya Parashu had seen the injured Vetal run away as he invoked *Mārak Mudra* to save the young woman. He had let it go since there was no point in further pursuit. He turned towards the young woman who still seemed to be recovering from the shock of what had happened a few moments ago.

"Who are you, young lady? What are you doing here in the midst of Vetal land? How did you reach here?" Acharya Parashu asked politely.

She didn't reply, still unsure about these newcomers on the scene. Acharya Parashu smiled while slowly stroking his grey beard and said, "Don't be afraid of us, girl. I am the Bheeshma monk Parashu, and this is Hara, my apprentice."

"I'm Uma, the daughter of Dev Lok King Indra." She replied as some of her confidence seemed to return. Uma was dressed in fairly simple attire for a princess. She was of medium height with a somewhat delicate body structure. The pure white robe of fine linen, well secured by a fabric belt with Devan royal insignia on the waist accentuated the tone of her smooth, fair skin. Her extraordinarily large eyes above a short, slightly upturned nose and generous lips, set on the frame of a nearly oval face, were wide with apprehension. The long straight hair, framing her high forehead had got loose and were flowing down well below her long neckline. The only other things distinguishing were a pair of diamond-studded gold bracelets on her wrists, and an ornately crafted knife in her hand, with which she had attempted to defend herself.

Hara looked at her in total surprise. "You're a long way from Dev Lok, princess. How did you reach here?" he asked.

When she sensed that there was no immediate danger, most of her original poise returned. She replied looking back at Hara, "The *vimān* that I was flying in encountered some difficulty mid-flight and we were forced to crash-land here. The vetals seemed to be waiting for us and as soon as we landed, attacked us. The pilot put up a good fight but was killed. I tried to run away but they caught up with me in this clearing. If you hadn't reached just in time…"

"The pilot should've known that it is forbidden to fly over Vetal land precisely because of this reason. Vetals may not have built advanced weapon systems but they are good enough to scramble up interceptors for ordinary vimāns." Acharya Parashu said.

"I am to blame. The pilot had warned me but I was in a hurry to return to the Apsara Academy at Lonar, and so ordered him to take this shortcut." She seemed pained while replying.

"Where is your vimān?" Hara asked, as he helped her stand up.

"Must be around half *krosha* away. I don't think it is in a shape to fly. We hit a few rocks while landing and the crystal hull cracked."

"Can we attempt to repair it? Or at least salvage something useful?" Hara looked at Acharya Parashu.

Acharya Parashu looked worried, "No Hara. In any case, that spot must already be swarming with Vetals by now. They may also reach here any moment. The two of us won't be able to handle them if they come in large numbers." Then looking towards the edge of the clearing he said, "We'll take a circuitous way back to our horses. I'm hoping that they have been able to stay away from the Vetal eyes so far."

Hara understood his guru's concerns. Vetals would soon be pursuing them in strength. This was their land and they were fully familiar with its layout. They were known to be particularly single-minded and vicious while seeking revenge. He turned to Uma and asked, "Hope you can run along with us princess? We must leave this place immediately. There is no time to lose." Acharya Parashu had already started running towards the opposite edge of the clearing, and they followed him.

Fortunately, they didn't meet any resistance on their way back. On reaching the point where the horses were standing, they stopped for some breath.

Hara noted that Uma had not complained about having to run on the rough ground through the jungle. Obviously this was not easy for her, but maybe the fear was still more predominant than discomfort. It was only now that he was able to take a good look at her. Clearly, he had no opportunity to have seen Uma before. After all, he had neither visited Amaravati nor any such place where a Dev Lok princess may frequent. Yet, he felt a sense of familiarity and affinity towards her. It was not just her divine beauty but also the graceful manner in which she moved. Does this have anything to do with his Karma? Or was it just a fascination, characteristic of his youth? He brushed aside the thought.

They found the horses grazing on some fresh grass near the stream. Acharya Parashu and Hara mounted the animals and Hara helped Uma climb onto his horse. With Acharya Parashu leading, they started off cross-country towards south. It was the most sensible thing to do since the Vetals would soon block all tracks. The cross-country going was tough but their horses seemed to understand the urgency and galloped through the thick undergrowth. After about half-krosha through the thicket, Parashu signalled them to halt. He then closed his eyes and seemed to meditate for a few minutes. Hara had seen him doing this in the past and knew that he was summoning the universal Akashic vibrations to deduce the best course to move forward. Acharya Parashu opened his eyes, and indicated them to advance in the 10 o'clock direction.

It must've been another muhurta or so before the Vetals caught up with them again. Considering the pace at which they were moving, it was impossible to outrun them. Fortunately, it was only a small patrol party of five. It would have to be a fight.

Unlike the last encounter, this time they had the terrain to their advantage. The clearing that lay between the attacking Vetals and them was wide and even, which made it easy for them to manoeuvre.

When Parashu moved forward, Hara requested "Acharya, please let me handle them? There may be another party attempting to outflank us. They may reach Uma from any side, and she may need your protection."

Acharya Parashu started to protest but then thought better of it. Hara was right and it was useful to hold some reserve to meet any unexpected attack. Hara was perfectly capable of handling the five Vetals. While Uma looked on wide-eyed, Hara moved into the clearing, walking towards the Vetals, totally calm.

The attacking Vetals saw the young Bheeshma monk come out into the clearing. What was this foolish guy up to? He didn't seem to have even taken out his weapon and yet wanted to stop five Vetals? Their leader signalled others to encircle their opponent from all four sides. It was confident that they would rip him apart without even having to use any weapons.

Uma turned towards Acharya Parashu with pleading eyes and said, "Please help him, Acharya. Five to one against these monsters is no fair match. Don't worry about me. I can defend myself for some time." She drew out her own knife, as if to emphasise the point.

"Hara is perfectly capable of handling this on his own. If you must, have pity on the Vetals who want to attack him." Acharya Parashu said.

That was true enough. Hara had been trained by Acharya Parashu in all martial combat styles, including his favourite – *Tāndav*. Very few could beat Hara in this unique combat form. Tāndav required perfect alignment of the extraordinary power source of all Bheeshma warrior monks – their integral aura of kundalini force reserves known as Jwalaprabha. A monk needed to reach a certain spiritual level before he could channelise such universal *shakti* into the objective world. Hara had a bright aura of Jwalaprabha, which was one of the reasons why Acharya Parashu had inducted him into the Bheeshma order years ago.

Hara got into the characteristic Tāndav position. To an onlooker, the pose looked almost like that of a graceful dancer preparing himself to give a performance. With his arms held in precise mudras and well-prepared to strike at any angle around him, Hara had willed himself into a meditative state of Stithapragya with the Jwalaprabha coiled up and ready within his body. In such a borderland of *Samadhi*, when he was both in conceptual and non-conceptual worlds, all senses acted as one entity. Even before it really happened, he had sensed how the Vetals were going to attack.

The first Vetal, attacking from the back, was totally surprised as Hara twisted around and drove his foot straight into its neck. The kick, delivered with the full force of Jwalaprabha behind it, broke the creature's neck and it dropped down like a battered statue. Then two Vetals attacked him together, one from each side. Without even looking at them, Hara's arms extended like twin thunderbolts into their midriffs. With such a high-powered impact, even the tough genetically engineered bodies of the Vetals had no chance. They were propelled away to either side. By the time they hit the ground, massive damage to their internal organs had already extinguished the life out of them. The remaining two Vetals looked at Hara in total shock as his eyes suddenly opened at them. To the Vetals, the eyes looked like exploding stars that pierced into the very depths of their being. Even before they realised it, Hara's arms had come up from both sides and smashed their heads together.

Luckily, there was no second Vetal party circumventing them, as initially suspected. Together they mounted their horses and galloped towards the direction pointed by Acharya Parashu. Very soon, they had reached a marshy terrain and had to dismount and walk on foot with horses trailing in tandem. Acharya Parashu and Hara kept a keen watch as they traversed the low-lying area. Vetals hated water; that was the main reason for Acharya to have led them though this swamp. The soil was soggy and the going was tough. There was a foul smell emanating from the boggy terrain all around, probably a combination of rotting vegetation and other living tissues.

If attacked in large numbers, it would be very difficult to manoeuvre here. The Bheeshma duo could handle many Vetals but with Uma in tow, they may soon be overwhelmed. Vetals were known to be very persistent and would hunt them down till the end, even through the swamps. Their best chance lay in staying hidden and being unpredictable. Acharya Parashu had already changed the course many times and now they were moving in an entirely different direction to the one they had originally started. Uma seemed exhausted but tried to keep pace with them. After briefly stopping at a stream to refresh themselves, they moved through the water for around two kroshas before carefully climbing up a rocky embankment, trying not to leave any foot or hoof marks.

Nearing nightfall, Acharya Parashu led them to a hilly area. "We'll camp here tonight," he said. The location had been chosen well. It was a depression in the middle of an elevated plateau, making it impossible for anyone to see them from the surrounding terrain. At the same time, they had an excellent view and could be forewarned of any approaching danger. Hara recalled Acharya Parashu saying during one of his training sessions in the past, "The cause of success in any kind of conflict is not based on strength or skills alone. It depends greatly on the intelligent use of the environment around you, including the land and resources it can provide."

Hara knew that with their keen sense of perception, strength and intelligence, enhanced by genetic as well as artificial modifications, the Vetals were formidable opponents. In fact, the Vetals were known to have decimated entire army battalions unfortunate to have ventured into these lands. Even so, he felt great relief that his guru was himself there to lead in this critical situation.

He made a makeshift shelter using some branches and leaves for Uma to rest on. He then collected some moss pads from nearby and made a fairly comfortable bedding for her to lie down. Uma had noticed the extra attention being bestowed on her and smiled at Hara, "Please don't treat me any differently Hara. I'm grateful enough for being rescued from those Vetal creatures. You should take care of your own sleeping arrangements."

Acharya Parashu had just returned after a lookout and heard Uma. "No sleeping for Hara and me tonight. We'll need to keep a vigilant lookout. It would be most unfortunate if the Vetals are able to sneak in close before we are ready."

Uma looked at him in surprise. Here was a man in his middle age, yet stronger than any youth she had seen. Bheeshma warrior monks were well-known throughout the Dev Lok and she had seen a few in the past. But somehow this *guru-shishya* pair seemed very different. Acharya Parashu, towering at a height of 6.5 feet, with his flowing grey beard and hair tied to the back was clearly a veteran. He wore the characteristic white robes of a monk, well-secured on an athletic body that seemed to be ready for action in any instant. His piercing, brown eyes, above a rather long nose and strong jaw line were totally focused on the present moment. They were also somewhat gentle when he looked directly, with a depth she couldn't fathom.

Hara, on the other hand, was younger and more exuberant. Clearly, he admired Acharya Parashu greatly and obeyed him without question. Around six feet tall, Hara was himself dressed in white, mostly around the waist up to the knees. He had a broad chest which was covered diagonally across one shoulder with a yellow *angavastram*. He was clean-shaven but his hair was even longer than Parashu's, and flowed down well below his shoulders. With a roughly oval, chiselled jaw-line and slightly aquiline nose set under sharp eyes, he presented the image of a handsome yet rugged hunter. Both the monks had a fabric holster tied to their waist, with the Bheeshma weapon Spatishūl secured within.

Hara had gone out to take the first shift of guard after they had a brief meal of porridge and some herbs. The moon was high in the sky. Acharya Parashu was resting, reclined against a large rock with his eyes closed. Uma looked at him but couldn't be certain whether he was sleeping or meditating. She wondered what kind of life the Bheeshma warriors led. She had seen their incredible prowess and martial skills while in close combat with the Vetals. Even so, they had been on continuous guard ever since she was rescued.

"Acharya Parashu, who are these Vetals?" Uma asked. The brief encounter with Vetals was enough for her to surmise that they were not ordinary marauders. She had witnessed the extraordinary strength, aggression and viciousness of these humanoid creatures when they ripped apart the *vimān*'s pilot as if he was some soft linen.

Acharya Parashu opened his eyes and turned to look at her, "Vetals are the abominations created during genetic engineering projects within the Daityan Empire."

"Genetic engineering, Acharya?" Uma asked doubtfully.

"Yes. Daityas have been attempting to create a perfect breed of specialised soldiers using the genetic engineering technology passed on to them by the Mūrthi. I'm told that they have an army formation of similar humanoids called Yantraksh stationed at the Daityan capital city of Atalantpuri." He sighed and then went on after a while, "Vetals are the result of many of their experiments gone wrong. These creatures had perhaps acquired either some inappropriate characteristics or couldn't be controlled properly. Instead of terminating these flawed beings, Daityas carted them off to this rugged, wild land. Physiologically, Vetals are very strong and can endure enormous strain, pain and go on for weeks without food or water. Some say they're cannibals and even feed on human flesh, but this has not been confirmed. Here they survive by pillaging surrounding lands or waylaying unsuspecting travellers. Eventually, this piece of land became forbidden for most. Vetals have some indirect support from the Daityan Empire and trade with them surreptitiously. There have been instances where Daityan royalty is known to have used the Vetals' services for conducting clandestine operations. Vetal suicide squad assassins are infamous and feared around the world." Then he turned towards her again and said reassuringly, "Don't worry, Uma. You are under the Bheeshma protection now. I'm hoping that we wouldn't have to confront any more Vetals and will get out of their range of influence soon."

2

LEGEND OF THE BHEESHMA

The King of Dev Lok, Indra, was in his private chamber when one of his guards came up to him "Your highness, Dev Guru Brihaspati has requested your audience." Brihaspati was the guru and chief advisor to Indra. He was well known for his statesmanship across Devarth.

"Please usher him in," Indra said.

As Brihaspati entered in, Indra stood up and folded his arms in the characteristic *Namastute* to pay his respect, "Pranam Guru Dev. You're welcome."

Brihaspati waved acknowledgment and said, "Devraj, we have some news about Uma."

"Has she been rescued? Is my daughter well?" Indra asked anxiously.

Brihaspati was silent for some time before replying, "We're not sure Devendra. The search party found debris of the vimān in which she was travelling to Gandharv. Unfortunately, it had crash-landed within Brashtaranya territory – the land of the Vetals."

Indra's face turned grave as he realised what that meant, "Guru Dev is...is she alive?"

"You must not lose heart, Indra. We can't be totally sure yet. It is clear that the fallen vimān was attacked by the Vetals. The search party found the pilot's remains near the crash site. However, they could not see a trace or sign of Uma," Brihaspati replied.

"Does this mean she might have been abducted by the Vetals?" Indra queried apprehensively.

"I've considered that possibility, but it seems unlikely. In fact, the search party found bodies of six Vetals nearby. I was wondering who could have killed them? Then I recalled hearing from Maharishi Vashist about a Bheeshma mission for which two monks were expected to pass through the Brashtaranya territory around the same time when the vimān must have crash-landed. It is safe to surmise that Uma might have been rescued, by these very monks."

Bheeshma warrior monks were considered in highest esteem within Dev Lok. "Have we been able to trace their whereabouts thereafter?" Indra asked in a voice full of concern.

"Not yet. It is a thick jungle and the foggy weather condition is not helping either. Two of our search vimāns have returned without any sight of them. We'll continue the search."

"Guru Dev, do you feel these Bheeshma monks can evade the Vetals till we trace them and send reinforcements?"

"That is difficult to predict, Devraj. All I can say is that we are extremely lucky that Uma is with the Bheeshma monks. If there is anyone who can get out of such a difficult situation, it is the Bheeshma. The senior monk Acharya Parashu is a veteran Bheeshma and I'm told his shishya Hara is equally capable."

Indra looked out of the window of his chamber on the Meru tower. He could see the city of Amaravati below, and the turbulent sea beyond the coastline. 'It has become so rare to see a calm sea these days,' he thought. Then, turning his gaze back to Brihaspati, he asked, "Dev Guru, I know that the 'Order of Righteous Karma' was formed by the legendary Prince Bheeshma from the Bhārat kingdom many centuries ago and successive generations have been keeping up with the tradition."

"That is correct, Devraj. Prince Bheeshma, who founded this order of warrior monks was the son of King Shantanu of Bhārat and princess Ganga from Dev Lok. In order to respect one of his father's whims, he surrendered all the royal privileges and withdrew to seclusion and meditation. However, his Karma kept leading him back to the path of combat and action. Being adept in all the arts of war, he won many battles for the Bhārat kingdom. It was in the later years of his life that he established the 'Order of Righteous Karma,' which eventually came to be known as the 'Warrior Monks of Bheeshma'."

"Dev Guru, do they still wield the kind of influence they once did?" It was well known in Dev Lok that in his younger days, Brihaspati had been a Bheeshma monk himself, till he decided to surrender the *Bheeshmatv* and let his Karma lead him into the world of politics and statesmanship.

Brihaspati smiled while answering, "Yes, Devraj. The prime directive of a Bheeshma is to maintain spiritual harmony within human society and on most occasions, they prefer to remain in seclusion, out of public notice. We don't even come to know about many of the Bheeshma missions that might have actually changed the course of history. Their contribution to human society is vital and indispensable, even in the present times."

"I'm aware that they prefer to remain out of limelight. But if the main motive behind their missions is to maintain righteous Karma, wouldn't their allegiance to Devas or Daityas depend on the situation?"

"That is correct, Devraj. The Bheeshma monks owe their allegiance to no one. It is their code of conduct to work for the right cause and, indeed, the right Karma." Brihaspati replied.

"So, is it possible that they may even be working against the interests of Dev Lok? Can they be trusted with Uma's safety?" Indra asked uneasily.

"In theory, yes. If indeed Devas are not righteous in their actions, Bheeshma monks won't support them. However, in Uma's case, I'm quite sure they will protect her with their lives, if necessary. There is no reason to deduce that righteous Karma should be anything but otherwise."

"Dev Guru, how does a Bheeshma monk come to know that he is on the righteous path or correct Karma?"

"That is an interesting question, Devraj. Prince Bheeshma himself is said to have gained the art of knowing the path of correct Karmic action through meditative insight from his *guru* Parashurama, who was also a renowned warrior monk. For successive generations of Bheeshma monks, this art has been passed on from gurus to shishyas."

"It is well known that the Vetals are skilful, aggressive and vicious fighters, especially in close combat. Even our elite, battle-hardened *Maruth* soldiers dread to confront them. And you just mentioned that our search party reported six Vetal bodies. You think just two Bheeshma monks could have killed them all?"

"Dev Raj, due to their characteristic humility, it is easy to underestimate a Bheeshma monk. Apart from their expertise in martial combat skills, their primary strength comes from the kundalini force that they are able to evoke through meditation. Control of such powers requires a high degree of self-discipline and immense practice; it takes years of training and meditative purification to even qualify to become a monk. They are also known to be able to store some kundalini force coiled up within their body. Generally called Jwalaprabha, this force provides them with heightened spiritual perception as well as capability to project it into physical action. An advanced Bheeshma could use these energies in a variety of forms including telekinetic projection or extend it into their main weapon – the Spatishūl. Crafted at Brahmagiri, the alma-mater of Bheeshma, these weapons are made of highest quality of self-morphing live crystals, using a secret process passed on directly from the

Mūrthi Lord Rudra. The Spatishūl can only be activated by the Jwalaprabha of the monk. When in disuse, it is shaped almost like a small, short-handled Trident. Once fully-morphed, it is not unlike a straight sword with a crystalline, double-edged blade so strong and sharp that it can cut through any known material, like a hot knife through butter. When an advanced Bheeshma channelises his Jwalaprabha through it, the weapon becomes virtually unstoppable."

"Thank you for this reassurance, Dev Guru. It must be the play of Karma that these Bheeshma monks happened to be near the crash site. It is a great relief to know that we might still have a fighting chance to rescue Uma," Indra said softly.

𐤕 Ш ☥

Next morning, Uma woke up as Hara shook her shoulders gently. It was still dark, with a few muhurtas left before day break. Acharya Parashu wanted them to move down the hill without being seen and be on their way well before sunrise. Upon reaching the base of the hill, they mounted the horses and started off. The terrain was still marshy at places with thick vegetation all around and the horses strained to trudge along. Acharya Parashu led the way, followed by Uma on Hara's horse. Hara himself walked behind, protecting the rear of their column. He noted that Uma was fairly good at riding the horse and was keeping good pace. Whenever Hara lagged behind she would stop, look back and smile at him. After passing through the heavy jungle for better part of the day, they reached near a small lake. Parashu bid them to halt and went ahead to check the surrounding terrain and look out for a place to settle for the night. Hara was busy filling some water into his canteen from a nearby stream when he heard Uma gasp in fear.

The size of the snake was enormous and it was, almost upon Uma. She had probably walked toward the lake, mesmerised by the cool breeze blowing in from that direction. Running was futile since the snake, with its fangs fully distended would catch up with her in no time. Uma had her knife in her hand, but obviously it was not likely to be of any use against the monstrous serpent. The snake moved in for the final kill and she closed her eyes, seemingly reconciled to her fate.

The snake moved in for the final kill, but was forced to stop momentarily when Hara rushed in and pushed Uma aside. He now stood within the serpent's direct line of attack. Seeing another prey in front, the snake launched its attack on Hara even before he could attempt to take out the Spatishūl. He was totally taken aback by the speed with which the serpent coiled itself like a spring and catapulted straight at his head. He attempted to deflect it off with his left hand but it was too late. Wrapping itself around Hara's arm, the snake bit hard and deep into his throat. Reeling under the excruciating pain, Hara held up the body of the snake and using his right hand, took out the Spatishūl and cut the serpent's head off.

Even when decapitated, the serpent's head didn't let go of its grip on Hara's throat. He could see Uma's image fading in front of his eyes as the deadly poison started its effect. He went down on his knees and slowly collapsed unconscious.

By the time Acharya Parashu returned, Hara's body was already very still. The snake's head had opened and dropped off besides his body. Uma sat by his side, attempting to awkwardly cover the bite wound using a piece of linen torn from her dress.

"What happened?" Acharya Parashu asked as he tried to understand the situation.

"He saved me from the snake's attack, and got bitten in the process." Uma had tears welling in her eyes.

Acharya Parashu's expression was sombre as he looked at Hara's unconscious body. He inspected the fallen head of the snake. It was the dreaded serpent known as the Karkotakan. Its deadly poison had no antidote. If anything could save Hara, it would be his Jwalaprabha but to awaken it, he needed to come back to consciousness. Acharya Parashu got down on his knees and placed his palm on Hara's forehead, to link up with his Jwalaprabha.

After a while of intense meditation by Acharya Parashu, Hara woke up slowly. Extremely groggy, he tried to get up but Acharya Parashu signalled him not to. "You've taken a full bite of the Karkotakan snake on your throat. The poison has already started spreading. Once your body gets completely paralysed by the poison, nothing can be done. You have to stop the poison's damage using your Jwalaprabha. I'll put you into a meditative posture. Focus on your Jwalaprabha and channel the kundalini energy into your body." He lifted Hara's body into an erect sitting position.

Acharya Parashu went up to his saddle bag and brought back a small jar of medicine. He poured a few drops on the bite marks. The drops spread around the wound and formed a gel-like covering around it. Then looking at Uma, he said, "We'll establish a camp here itself, till Hara is able to walk." Acharya Parashu made a seat of leaves for Hara to sit on, next to the nearby tree. Grimacing under the agonising pain, Hara got into a meditative sitting posture. Holding his fingers in *dhyan mudra*, he focused on channelising the Jwalaprabha into his burning body."

"Is he going to be all right, Acharya?" Uma asked, concern obvious within her wavering voice.

"Hara needs to remain awake and meditate for a long time. I'm hoping that he is able to use the kundalini energy to negate the poison." Acharya Parashu said, trying to avoid any clear answers. He knew that this had never been attempted before and was at best a gamble. He was also hoping that they don't have to deal with another Vetal attack while in such a vulnerable state.

The sun was already setting and it would soon be pitch dark. As they settled down, Acharya Parashu continued, "Once Hara is better and the moon rises up, we'll move up to that higher ground over there. It has much better defence potential. Tomorrow morning, we may need to cross the open grassland bordering Brashtaranya before reaching the nearest coastal town of Kolwa, hopefully by the night fall. Once there, the next day we can hire a boat to take us up to the port town of Kambhoj. I'm worried about getting exposed at the open grasslands though. If Vetals have been able to discern my intentions, they would be observing any approach towards Kolwa."

Hara's body was already burning with high fever. The deadly poison had started taking its toll on his tissues. The toes and outer extremities of his limbs were already paralysed. Even Acharya Parashu seemed worried that the spread of poison was quick and his chances of survival very slim. Yet, he was confident that if anyone could battle against the poison and win, it was Hara. It would be a tough fight within his body and may take several hours before they know the outcome.

This recent turn of events had changed their original plan to a great extent. Now, rather than focusing on surviving within Brashtaranya and crossing over to a safer area, they had to wait for Hara to recover first. And if he succeeded, they would need to get out of this dangerous environment as early as possible. It had taken the best of his experience and spiritual perceptions to keep them out of trouble so far. Yet, there were too many variables to consider before predicting any viable course of action. Hara's encounter with the snake was an example. With Hara weakened and he himself tired, they'd be vulnerable against another encounter with the Vetals, if it were to happen anytime soon. If they were to be defeated by Vetals, that would be the end of it all. He was not worried about his own life. After all, what was there to save in his life, anyway? Hara, however, was young and had a promising future. He was like a son he never had.

Acharya Parashu watched Hara and Uma as he rested against a fallen tree trunk nearby. Uma seemed still shaken from the encounter with the snake and the precarious condition Hara was in. She sat beside him and using her dampened angavastram wiped his forehead regularly, attempting to control the high fever.

Acharya Parashu noted the clearly growing fondness between the young pair. It was quite obvious in the manner Uma looked at Hara whenever she could. Hara, however, was more reserved in his expressions; but Acharya Parashu knew him too well not to understand his attraction towards the girl. It was refreshing to see the developing affection between the two of them. It brought in memories of the brief period of his own love.

The only thing she had requested him was to settle down at her village. Parashu had almost taken that decision when he was called upon to undertake a mission by Maharishi Vashist himself. By the time he returned few months later, it was too late. The girl's parents—who were against their relationship from the very beginning—had told her he had died on the mission and got her married. Parashu never met her again, more for her sake than his. Perhaps this was what was meant to be. Was this indeed his Karma? Could it have been any other way?

Man lives his life mostly in the objective environment of his sense and memories. The mind constructs the objects, thoughts and concepts within this world based on the sensory inputs on a fragmented template of memory. This fragile template reinforces an illusion of continuity in terms of past, present and future course of events—the very concept of time and space.

Is the concept of our own personality or ego also just a mirage—reflection of objective conditionings, concepts and memories projected backwards into the subjective mind, just for the purpose of making sense of the world? Is the world we create within our mind actually real? Is the mind really independent or itself sustained by our inner self?

Do we or our virtual self or ego really take any decision? Or is it that we simply take ownership of such decisions after they automatically happen? Is it then any different from the manner our hand may take ownership of the decisions that has been passed on to it by a distant brain. Since the hand can't perceive the presence of a conscious brain who commands it, does it simply assume itself to be the originator of such commands? Is it that this whole cosmos is a single consciousness that controls everything but our limited ego takes ownership of the pieces of action that happen through our medium? Who are we actually? If we have no control over either our decision that leads to action or the outcomes that follow it, don't we have any responsibility either? What is our Karma?

Acharya Parashu woke up hearing an urgent call from Uma. She was still sitting next to Hara and tending to him, but now there was a look of desperation on her face. "What is happening to Hara? He has become totally cold. And look at the colour of his throat. It is totally blue!"

Acharya Parashu got up and examined Hara. Even in the dim moonlight he could see that the throat was indeed bright blue, especially around the place where the serpent had bitten. He held his palm against Hara's forehead and focused. Slowly a smile spread over his face and he turned to Uma and said, "Don't worry, Uma. Hara is in deep meditation. He has been able to resist the poison and limit its impact to his throat tissues alone. He will survive. His neck may retain this bluish colour for rest of his life though."

Uma looked visibly relieved. "But his body is still very cold," she asked doubtfully.

"Yes. The internal battle has depleted most of his energy reserves. It will be a while before he recovers fully." Acharya Parashu realised that this could be a problem, especially since they still had to walk quite a distance to reach Kolwa.

When the moonlight had become considerably bright, Acharya Parashu examined Hara's condition again. "Uma, I'm going to wake up Hara. He is going to be very thirsty and hungry. It is unlikely that he can consume anything but semi-fluid food for many days. Can you make some hot soup, please? Though we'll have to risk a fire, try to keep it as small as possible. There is a pouch of cereal, dried herbs and fire-making tool within the saddle bag of my horse."

By the time Uma returned, holding a bowl of hot herbal soup, Hara had woken up fully. He looked very tired but still attempted to sit erect to continue the kundalini flow within his body.

After Acharya Parashu went off to check their surroundings once again, Uma sat with Hara, offering him spoonfuls of soup. "Why did you risk your life for me, Hara?" She asked softly.

Hara smiled back weakly, "Obviously it's the snake that was actually at risk." Hara smiled back weakly. "Anyway, this incident seems to be offering some rewards too. It's not often that a monk gets the privilege of being nursed by a beautiful princess."

Uma turned away, attempting to hide the expression on her face, "I'll go get some hot water for you to drink." Hara watched her go. Over the past few days, he had actually felt a close bond developing with this girl. Was it because of the strange sense of familiarity he felt with her? He tried to believe that this was a passing fancy that two young people in such situations tend to feel for each other. Yet, it was not just her physical beauty and spirit that drew him towards her; there was something serene about her personality that Hara found irresistible. If they were able to get out of this situation, he would be most happy to get to know her more. He wondered if she'd want that too. After all, she was the princess of Dev Lok and daughter of Indra – one of the most powerful monarchs in the world. He was himself a sworn monk. As a Sanyasi he was forbidden to even think of getting involved in any emotional relationship. Although he knew Acharya Parashu would support him, surely the Bheeshma community would not approve of it. It is not that Bheeshma monks had not developed emotional bonds in the past, they had; and many had even got married and settled into domestic life. But not without having to forgo the *Bheeshmatv* and all the spiritual support that came with it. This meant that till their *grihastya* life lasted, there would be very little opportunity for spiritual advancement.

Hara could read it in the eyes of Acharya Parashu as he returned that they were in big trouble. "How many are there, Acharya?" He asked stoically.

"At least a hundred Vetals. They have this place covered from all sides, and will be upon us within another half *ghati* or so," Acharya Parashu explained in brief.

Hara knew what this meant. Without further words, he took his guru's hands and got up slowly. Uma had returned and Parashu told her about the situation. "There is nothing that we can do now, Uma, except fighting back. But considering the army of Vetals out there, we stand little chance."

"I'm sorry to have got you into this situation. It's all my fault." Uma was looking at Hara, as she realised the hopelessness of their situation.

"It is not your fault, Uma. This is the path of our Karma and we all have to face it."

It was still quite dark. Morning was at least three muhurtas away but the Vetals wouldn't wait for that long. With their acute nocturnal vision, they held a definite advantage during night and wouldn't want to lose it. They could already hear the rustle of Vetal footsteps on dry leaves in the distance.

Acharya Parashu helped Uma climb up to the lower branch of the tree under which they had been resting. Then, the two Bheeshma monks stood back-to-back in the middle of the clearing with the tree and the lake behind them. Maybe, by attracting the attention of the Vetals towards them, they could stave off the attack as long as possible? The lake on one side of their location helped, as it reduced the number of directions from which Vetals could mount their attack.

Acharya Parashu and Hara locked in their Jwalaprabha together. Its aura linked them with each another and activated the

Spatishūls now held in their hands. The Spatishūls had morphed into their full sabre form and glowed with a fiery blue luminance. Both the monks had taken up the classical back-to-back defensive duet-combat posture with legs apart and their weapons held high over the head. Even though Hara was physically very tired, their mutually supported Jwalaprabha coursed through his body, and his focus was totally on the present moment.

The first few Vetals paused for a moment, looking at the Bheeshma monks through their beady eyes. Then shouting loud war cries, they attacked them. Both the warriors wielded their Spatishūls in perfectly synchronised sequence and cut down all the attackers within a few seconds. The Vetals however kept leaping in to their certain death in front of the Bheeshma monks. Soon enough, the Vetal bodies started piling up and the monks shifted their stance to another part of the clearing.

Standing on the tree branch, Uma witnessed the precisely coordinated martial waltz of the Bheeshma pair, as they held up against the attacking hoard of Vetals. But she knew that despite the formidable fighting skills of the Bheeshma monks, it was only a matter of time before the sheer number of the attacking Vetals overwhelmed them.

The high-paced fight continued for more than a ghati. Having dispatched at least twenty Vetals, both Acharya Parashu and Hara stood exhausted. Hara's throat was bleeding profusely as the snake bite wound had opened up once again due to excessive exertion. It was only the combined power of their Jwalaprabha that had sustained him for so long. Some Vetals had spotted Uma standing on the low branch of the tree and tried to attack her. They hoped to divert the attention of the monks and simultaneously outflank them from behind through the shores of the lake. Acharya Parashu and Hara—instinctively realising their tactic—blocked and cut them down before getting into another back-to-back stand around the tree itself. They braced themselves for the next wave of assault.

When the next wave of attack didn't happen, they looked around to see whether it was a trick from the Vetals to distract them away from the tree. They were surprised to see some of the Vetals retreating. As they wondered what had spooked them, they saw the coherent pulse-rays emanating from the vimān hovering overhead. The lethal and powerful pulse-rays spewing out from the vimān had broken up the Vetal frontline. Many of them were now seeking protection behind any fold on the ground to escape from it. Some tried to even cover themselves with the dead bodies of other Vetals piled around them. The vimān landed vertically in the clearing close to the tree and at least twenty-five Maruth commandos got out, wielding crystal swords. They despatched most of the remaining Vetals within the clearing and formed a protective perimeter around the vimān and the tree where Parashu, Hara and Uma had taken their last stand.

The Dev Lok General Kshetrajna got out of the vimān and walked up to Uma who had just climbed down from the tree. He bowed and asked in concern, "Hope you are fine Princess."

"Yes. Thanks to Acharya Parashu and Hara, I'm still alive." Uma said, attempting a weak smile.

Kshetrajna looked at the Bheeshma monks in admiration, "On behalf of the Dev Lok, I extend our profound thanks for protecting the princess for so long. We don't have too much time. Please come on board the vimān."

Acharya Parashu nodded at Hara and they followed Uma into the airplane. The defensive perimeter had been held up well by the Maruth soldiers against intense renewed assault from the Vetals. Three Maruths had already succumbed to the Vetal fury, but were quickly replaced by the reserves. Kshetrajna decided to leave immediately and sounded the alarm. The vimān took to a height, and launched seven high incendiary missiles in multiple directions around the perimeter. As they impacted, the Vetals on the frontlines surrounding the Maruths were burnt to crisp from the intense heat. Others were badly scalded and retreated to more than fifty *dhanus* behind. Taking advantage of this brief respite, the vimān landed again to pick up the Maruth soldiers. In less than thirty more *kalas*, they were once again airborne and moving on a flight path towards the south.

Kshetrajna was seated along with Uma, opposite to Acharya Parashu and Haŕa, within an elevated enclosure inside the vimān. They had left the Brashtaranya airspace and were now cruising over the oceans. It was surprisingly quiet inside the crystalline shell of the vimān. The Maruth soldiers were in a separate chamber below them.

"It was very lucky that we were able to spot you. Indra had sent many search missions over last two days. One of them found the vimān wreck. There was no sign of Uma and they assumed that she must have been captured by the Vetals," Kshetrajna explained.

Uma was not paying much attention as she was dressing up Haŕa's snake-bite wound using the medical kit from the vimān. Then realising that she was expected to respond, said, "I escaped safely only because of Acharya Parashu and Haŕa."

"Kshetrajna, your arrival was just in time. Another half kala and it would have been too late. Haŕa and I were at our last stand. Bheeshma or not, we would have been easily overwhelmed by the sheer number of Vetals pouncing on us." Acharya Parashu said, sitting in meditative posture to recuperate from all the exertion over the past few hours. "Haŕa would need professional medical support. There is a danger that the poison may spread again unless it is neutralised properly." He then described the ordeal of the serpent attack earlier.

Kshetrajna looked towards Haŕa in admiration, "I'm really surprised that you could survive the direct bite of a Karkotakan serpent on the throat." Then turning to Acharya Parashu he said, "Acharya, we'll make sure he gets the best medical attention at Amaravati."

3

CITY OF THE GODS

They call Amaravati the "City of the Gods" due to its legacy of being one of the main habitation centres of the Mūrthi when they used to live on Earth. As they approached for landing, Haŕa looked down at the city. He was truly fascinated to see the intricate and beautiful patterns that defined the fine architectural design of the Dev Lok capital. It was early dawn and the first rays of the sun impinging on the crystal city gave it a surreal appearance. It looked almost like a diamond jewel glistening across the tropical island of 'Swarga Dweep'.

Looking at Uma, he asked, "When will I get to meet you again, Uma?" He felt a pang of sadness as the time for them to separate came near. Even though these past few days had been full of dangers, the presence of Uma with him had been exciting.

Uma smiled back, "I'm sure you are likely to be stationed at the palace itself under close supervision of the *Vaidyas* till the wound on your neck is healed completely. I'll definitely visit you ... and Acharya." She corrected on realising her extraordinary attention on Haŕa. Then looking at both the monks doubtfully, she asked again, "Hope you will stay for sometime at Amaravati?"

"Yes, we'll ensure that all of your comforts are attended to." Kshetrajna agreed, complementing her request.

It was Acharya Parashu who answered, "We're on a Bheeshma mission, and may need to move on soon."

Uma seemed visibly disappointed. She was about to say something when Kshetrajna intervened, "Acharya, you must allow us to fully extend our hospitality. Please do take some time out to see the city of Amaravati. I'm sure Indra Dev would arrange it himself but if you need any help from me, I'll remain ever at your service."

"Thank you, Kshetrajna. We'll definitely stay at Amaravati for a few days—at least till Hara's injury is reasonably healed. Who knows, coming here may be part of the karmic plan and perhaps a factor contributing to our mission as well," Acharya Parashu assured them.

They landed at the main palace grounds. There was a Devan entourage waiting to greet them. Uma's mother Sachi rushed in to hug her daughter and broke into tears, "Only God knows how relieved I was to hear about your rescue." She was followed by Indra. Uma attempted to touch his feet but he held her close and kissed her forehead, "My most enchanting daughter, you don't know what we've gone through since your disappearance. But I'm sure it must have been much more difficult for you out there." Then looking at the Bheeshma monks, he bowed and said, "I think it was because of the grace of our past Karma that you were there to save my daughter from the Vetals. Please accept my profound gratitude."

"Thank you, Indra Dev. It was all Karma and we were mere instruments," Acharya Parashu replied.

The palace Vaidyas attending to Hara cleaned his wound, applied medication and then covered it with a fresh layer of protective gel. They also gave him some additional oral prescription to heal the wound. When the treatment was nearly complete, the lead Vaidya brought in a vial of the medicine *Amruth*, which was known to heal anything from battle wounds to age-related deteriorations. The Amruth—also known throughout the world as the 'miracle medicine' — was yet another gift of pharmaceutical technology to humans from the Mūrthi. The medicine was concocted in various forms, but its potency depended on purity of the ingredient base. One of its special ingredients—the herbal extract called Mrithasanjeevani, came from an extra terrestrial plant brought in from the home-worlds of the Mūrthi. Even though these plants had been genetically hybridised to survive on Earth, it needed special techniques of cultivation, only known to a very few. Due to the rarity of its ingredients, the medicine was extremely expensive and, therefore, used very sparingly. In fact one vial of Amruth could cost many times its weight in pure gold.

This was the first time that Hafa got to taste this precious and exotic elixir-like medicine. The lead Vaidya said, "Take your time to drink it, Hafa. I'll be giving you many more doses over the course of next one or two days to help neutralise the effects of the poison. Soon after you consume it, the medicine may induce drowsiness and sometimes even hallucinations. It is best to take rest and sleep for a few hours. As you did earlier, please continue with your meditative efforts to restrict the poison to the throat region."

Hafa was in bed for most of the next day, alternating between few hours of meditation and long drug-induced sleep. By the morning of the third day of their arrival at Amaravati, his neck was almost healed and he felt surprisingly rejuvenated. Gone was the tiredness from running through the Vetal land, the last ditch battle with the Vetals, and even the pain on his throat. Soon after he completed his morning meditation, a messenger came and informed him that Indra had assigned his royal vimān Airāvat for their tour over and around the city of Amaravati. He dressed up quickly to meet Acharya Parashu who was waiting near the palace grounds.

The morning was pleasant and sunny when they embarked on the aerial tour from the palace grounds. Airāvat was one of the few vimāns built completely on the Mūrthi technology. It was very comfortable and spacious inside compared to the other vimāns in service of Dev Lok. With a hull made of ivory-coloured white crystals, the vimān was remarkably swift, considering its rather elephantine profile.

Once they were well above the city, the pilot manoeuvred the vimān around various interesting structures within the city. The most prominent building was the Meru towers located at its centre. Fifty-four storeys high, the conical tower housed the main administrative centre of Dev Lok. The entire palace complex was built within and around this crystalline tower itself. Acharya Parashu had been to Amaravati many times before and was quite familiar with the significance of the various structures within it. For Hara, however, it was a totally fascinating experience. From the elevated platform of the vimān, he was totally spellbound looking at the fabulous and out-worldly views unfolding beneath him. No wonder the city was called the 'City of the Gods'. Looking down at the sparkling city from high above, he felt it would have been more apt to call it the 'City of Crystals'.

"Acharya, how did Devas get to live in such a fantastic city? It seems almost beyond the capability of humans?" he asked.

Acharya Parashu continued to look at various sites spread out below them as he replied, "This city and, indeed, most of the infrastructure of Dev Lok were originally built by the Mūrthi as one of their main centres of living when they were here on Earth. Dev Lok is actually a collection of seven island groups namely Swarga Lok, Bhuvar Lok, Svar Lok, Mahar Lok, Jana Lok, Tapa Lok and Satya Lok. It so happens that these were the best tropical islands on the planet with plentiful of sunshine and salubrious climate. After the Mūrthi left the planet, Devas settled down at Dev Lok and chose Amaravati as their capital city. So in many ways, the Devan civilisation is a true reflection of how humans adapted to the Mūrthi way of life on earth."

"Acharya, most of us know that we owe our existence to the Mūrthi. Who are they and where are they now?"

"Mūrthi are the extra-terrestrial super-beings who arrived on the earth many eons ago. We're not sure as to what prompted them to stay away from their home-worlds at that point of time. One can only presume that it might have been due to the pressures of over-population or other difficulties that advanced beings tend to face, especially when they achieve extraordinarily long life-spans. Even then, as a species they were at one of the highest levels of spiritual and intellectual advancement. They settled down at various parts around the world and lived for many millennia with the aid of advanced technologies. The scientific insight of the Mūrthi made no distinction between natural and artificial systems. They saw nature itself as a highly advanced self-sustaining technological platform. So, much of their systems were based on tweaking the existing natural tendencies of materials and life forms. Even with direct access to advanced science and the powers that come with it, their simple and spiritual lifestyle reflected a belief of minimal interference with the natural order of the planet. They had also understood that all the physical forms of manifestation within the cosmos had astral umbilical connections with the 'universal potentiality' or 'cosmic consciousness' or *Brahmn*. Spiritual advancement and better scientific understanding of these astral connections between all manifested entities within the cosmos made it feasible for them to engage with the lower life-forms directly. Such techniques of 'astral engineering' enabled them to maintain a symbiotic existence with nature. It also meant that they could enjoy all the comforts and conveniences of modern technologies, yet maintain the fine balance of nature across the planet."

"So they are the originators of the human civilisations," Hafa asked.

"Yes. Being ardent believers of spiritual balance in nature, they knew that long-term intelligent life on the earth could only be propagated by the living creatures evolved from the planet itself and more suited to prosper within its raw native environment. Thus, they embarked on the mission of creating a species that had the advantage of native natural evolution as well as enough intelligence and spiritual propensity for advancement. Extensive experiments of genetic modifications on many suitable native species were conducted. As in case of much of the Mūrthi technology, such genetic manipulations happened in tune with natural evolutionary patterns already existent within earth at that point of time. In fact, most of the tweaking on their part was done primarily through astral engagement with the native life-forms. Since the astral identity of all life-forms define the nature of their physical structures, this was enough for the genetic realignment to happen on the lines desired by the Mūrthi. Over many centuries' efforts, they could develop a genome model containing both intrinsic native evolutionary structure as well as the Mūrthi genes. The small group they created grew into fairly large tribes and clans, mostly living on the temperate island groups along the planet's tropical islands where life flourished more abundantly. With due help from the Mūrthi scientists, humans developed techniques of self-sustained agriculture and industry which eventually lead to organised nation states."

"Acharya, this must mean that we are in many ways similar to the Mūrthi?"

"Yes, humans do share many of the Mūrthi traits. Our physical form is also believed to be similar to theirs but more adapted to the planetary dynamic of earth like gravity, air composition, food availability, etc."

"Why did they eventually leave the Earth?"

"As I said earlier, the Mūrthi were already at a very high level of spiritual advancement when they lived in their home-worlds as well as many other adopted planets. Over the course of time, they were able to advance even further, enabling them to maintain immortal super-conscious existence within their astral forms alone. So, many of them—especially those who were living on different planets within the cosmos—chose to return and continue their existence within numerous astral worlds, created in the true image of their original home planets. Physical travel between planets was no longer necessary. They could maintain connection with any planets that they had patronised, by way of astral links alone. To maintain astral connection with Earth, they had trained many humans in the art of meditation the – Rishis who continue this knowledge on the Earth. In fact, anyone can connect with the Mūrthi if they're able to attain a certain level of meditative advancement. These engagements, as necessary for monitoring the evolutionary progression of human species, are maintained by three Mūrthi Lords – Brahma, Vishnu and Rudra. The Rishis, along with a privileged class of priests, also inherited the repository of Mūrthi spiritual and scientific knowledge in the form of *Gyan Vedas* and *Vigyan Vedas* before their return."

"Acharya, we know that the Vedas contain the most fundamental information for sustenance of our civilisation. If so, why is it that it is only available to a few?"

"That is mainly because of the manner in which human societies got fragmented into various tribes, castes, classes and nations. As it exists today, the Vedas are the exclusive domain of the oldest nations like the Dev Lok and Daityan Empire. Even among these nations, the ruling class can only maintain their dominance through the support of the up-keepers of Vedas, i.e. the priestly class. The ruling class and the priestly class have equal status and interchange their roles frequently. Mūrthi knowledge, the domain of the priestly class, is kept secret and under strict control. Vigyan Vedas were considered so sacred that they got passed on from generation to generation within a very small control group of priests alone. In Dev Lok, these priestly classes are called the *Vasus*. So, even though Mūrthi had left behind vast scientific knowledge as well as technological systems, they are only available to a privileged few among Devas and Daityas, each having different aspects of it. Most common people across the world rarely understand such highly advanced technologies anyway and often consider them to be esoteric magic or sorcery of the gods. This is also the main reason for so many in mainland nations to view Devas and Daityas as gods and demons having extraordinary powers. For a long time, the ruling and priestly class among Devas have actually encouraged the god-like image of themselves, as this helped them maintain their special status and power over others."

"Acharya, you mentioned that the Mūrthi still maintain their interests towards humanity. How can they get to know the situation here on Earth when they are so far away in their own astral worlds?" Hara asked.

"They remain informed of the general course of events through the medium of spiritually-advanced humans located in various parts of the world. Apart from this, they're also able to directly observe the generic astral aura and overall karmic balance of all the life-forms on Earth. As I explained earlier, they had put the evolution of terrestrial life on a fast track through subtle astral suggestions. They do this even now, though direct interventions for corrections are extremely rare and only happen when their plan for this planet is in extreme peril."

"Acharya, how do they intervene if physical interaction is not possible?"

"When they need to intervene, it usually happens through one of the humans having extra-sensory spiritual perceptions. They are able to evoke any powers or influence through such resident humans," Acharya replied.

"Have there been any such interventions in the past?"

"Yes Hara, we've known many such interventions through spiritually-enlightened humans who came to be revered as avatars, Buddhas, saints, prophets, etc."

Airāvat had moved away for the main centre of the city and they were now close to the second most prominent feature of the city, the Devayana. It was shaped like a perfect pyramid and built with an interesting combination of crystals and metals.

Gleaming in the morning sun, the whole structure looked like a huge golden gem.

"The Devayana structure that you see over there is the spiritual heart of the complete Devan civilisation and remains one of the greatest legacies of the Mūrthi. During their stay at Amaravati, the Mūrthi had used the Devayana for astral-level interactions with each other as well as a host of lower life-forms. The Devas are now able to use it for similar purpose as well as direct astral interactions with the Mūrthi home-worlds," Acharya Parashu said.

"Acharya, if direct astral link-up is also possible through meditation, then why do they need this station at all?" Hara asked.

"For most humans, direct meditative link with the Mūrthi or for that matter even with their own higher astral selves is very difficult. It needs very high degree of meditative skills that takes years to develop. Even the Rishis find it difficult to accomplish it on their own. Very few Maharishis have achieved such high levels of self-sustained meditative skills. In fact, for many early millennia of their stay on earth, most of the Mūrthi themselves needed the aid of such external support systems for engagement with their astral selves. So the Devayana was originally built by the Mūrthi for the benefit of their own citizens having minimal meditative skills. Before returning to their home-worlds, they had re-tuned it to the level of humans. Even so, some astral images of their home-worlds still remain inaccessible through this method," Acharya Parashu replied.

"So this structure being located at Amaravati must provide a special benefit to the Devas. Does this mean Devas are closer to the Mūrthi?"

"Yes. Due to their more intimate astral connections with the Devas in general, the Mūrthi are closest to them."

"Acharya, isn't it correct that most of the technological advancements of Devan civilisation are also based on their skills to interact with higher and lower realms of existence through such astral connections?" Hafa asked doubtfully.

"Yes, the nature of Devan advancement is well-aligned with their spiritual way of life. Their technologies are almost entirely based on symbiotic relationship with lower forms of life. They do this by maintaining astral connection with self-morphing live crystals, microorganisms, self-organising plants, etc. As long as they can maintain this astral relationship, they have the most resilient, self-adapting technology ever known to man. In fact, each of the seven island groups of Dev Lok has their own astral engagement stations headed by a Rishi. All of them also remain connected with the central station of Devayana at Amaravati. The seven Rishis, who together led the astral management of Dev Lok are known to us as the *Sapta-Rishis*. In many ways, one can also consider these Sapta-Rishis to be like astral engineers."

"Astral engineers, Acharya? I've never heard this expression before. And if the astral engagements help cooperative co-existence with lower forms of life, it must also be feasible to maintain social harmony between humans?" Hafa asked inquisitively.

"Yes Hafa, you're spot on. Through the help of Devayana and other astrals engagement systems, the Devan citizens benefit by being able to access their own astral forms more easily. As I mentioned earlier, before the Mūrthi left, they had specifically tuned these systems to the levels of humans and other lower forms of life in Dev Lok. We're not completely sure as to how this connection happens in a scientific sense, but I'm told that it has something to do with resonance of our brainwave frequencies and aura. The pineal gland within the brain is also known to play a major role in making this connection. In fact the astral forms of all beings are always connected with the universal consciousness of Brahmn. The awareness of their astral selves provides the Devas with a unique privilege of being in constant spiritual connection with their fellow citizens and beyond. So, the sense of being 'separate' is less pronounced in their case—leading to greater degree of empathy, compassion and love for each other. It is this privilege that directly contributes to the fact that Devan society today is one of the most peaceful and progressive among all others across the world. Apart from this, they also enjoy the advantage of being in a much better condition from a karmic sense, which, of course, is one of the main reasons for their support by the Bheeshma order," Acharya Parashu explained.

"Acharya, is it that everyone within the Devas has the privilege of such higher consciousness?"

"Not everyone, Hara. The choice of uplifting themselves to a higher spiritual level is up to the humans. Being in the vicinity of Devayana definitely helps in such an effort. However, it doesn't mean that no Devas ever get deluded by ignorance. Although rare, there have been many instances of Devas who pursued the path of materialism, greed, power, aggression, domination, hatred, suffering."

The vimān now moved further, towards the remaining parts of Amaravati. Hara noticed that the entire city was made up of living crystals that could self-morph into any desirable shape. The technology of self-morphing crystals had been first introduced on Earth by the Mūrthi, primarily for construction purpose. These crystal colonies were specialised alien life-forms, brought from their home-worlds and genetically engineered to propagate on the terrestrial conditions of Earth. Many species of such self-morphing, crystalline life-forms had been used extensively by the Mūrthi, during their stay on the planet. Actually the complete city of Amaravati had been virtually 'grown' from the ground. The location of the city had been chosen carefully such that there was no dearth of terrestrial raw materials necessary to support the prolific growth of such crystals.

Extremely strong as well as flexible, the live self-morphing crystals could be influenced to grow into almost any shape or size based on a design template contained within the Devayana astral station.

The entire city was literally cultivated from the ground from scratch, using multiple living crystal species over the course of many years, each having unique characteristics. The crystals came in many colours, composition and opacity, so that together they complemented each other's benefits. Though the crystals provided the main foundation and building material, they were also bonded by metals and ceramics wherever necessary. There were also live plants that had been influenced to grow into beautiful shapes or patterns as per tasteful and aesthetic designs. In fact the complete city was a unique living ecosystem on its own, always actively attempting to provide ideal conditions for human habitation. It was also flexible enough to dynamically adapt itself as per the changing environmental conditions.

Hara was impressed with the ingenuity and simplicity of the technological advancements in Dev Lok. Yet, he had heard that the Daityan Empire was more fantastic in terms of the sheer magnitude of their engineering projects.

"Acharya, I've heard that Daityas are also known for their great scientific advancements?"

"Yes. Both Devan and Daityan nations are technologically advanced, yet they approach it differently. Daityas follow the object-based perceptive knowledge of our environment passed on by the Mūrthi and used it to further their material ambitions. They believe in understanding the physical nature of the environment and most of their science is based on such knowledge. They've learnt, experimented and developed many technologies on their own. This has enabled them to prosper and spread wide and far across the known world," Acharya Parashu answered.

Hara could not understand why Devas did not believe in such advancement and asked Acharya the same. To that, Acharya said, "It is not that they don't. In fact, both the civilisations have made tremendous advancement in understanding the nature of the objective universe. For example, both sides have even been able to harness the fundamental *shakti* encased in sub-atomic particles of physical matter. The only difference is in their approach towards the environment. Most of Devan advancements have happened along the lines of better karmic harmony with nature, whereas Daityas aim for the end results alone. The Daityan systems are generally large and powerful, yet deficient in terms of finesse. They're known to embark on huge engineering projects that clearly demonstrate human supremacy over nature. Actually, by way of large land reclamation projects, the landmass of many of their archipelago-based kingdoms has been extended well beyond their natural coastlines."

"Acharya, Devas and Daityas may be highly advanced in their own unique style, but why is it that we don't see such progress within inland nations like Bhārat?"

"This is primarily because such nations never benefited from the repository of advanced scientific knowledge from the Mūrthi—the Vigyan Vedas. Initially, very few fringe tribes used to live on the less favourable and cold terrain conditions on the mainland. Eventually, steady global warming favoured them. The receding ice-line across subtropical inland mass that they had adopted for habitation increased. King Bharat, who was originally from the Manav tribe, united many tribes into an integrated kingdom called Bhārat . Unlike Devas and Daityas, however, the civilisation of the Manavs has mostly been agrarian, with limited technological advancements. Even so, with the direct patronage from the Devas, they've been able to prosper. They proliferated to most of the river plains on their subcontinent kingdom and now constitute the most populous human civilisation on the planet."

"What about the remaining nations, Acharya?"

"Few other cultures and civilisations also came up, especially along the river basins and mountainous terrains around Bhārat. Some of these kingdoms like Gandharv, Yaksha and Kinnara have acquired much recognition and fame. These cultures are also under the general patronage of Dev Lok. Some of them have made unique advancements of their own. Unlike the Daityan pursuit of power, their culture has mostly centred on acquiring material wealth, pursuing sensual pleasures, esoteric customs, art forms, etc."

"Acharya, we know that Daityas could achieve tremendous advancements, despite the fact that their ways of life are not based on spiritual co-existence with nature. If that is the case, then where does the problem arise?" Hara asked.

"Hara, the main problem is that the technological advancement through direct material manipulation that is used by the Daityan also brings with it a number of unpleasant side effects. You've already seen the outcome of their botched genetic engineering efforts in the form of Vetals. Another problem is that because all of their technologies are essentially based on direct human intervention, they can only be sustained as such. They need enormous resources to feed their continued greed for more and more comforts, luxuries and pleasure. Having got addicted to the material luxuries, their population are unwilling to go back into a relatively frugal way of living even when the times are tough."

"The rising sea levels must surely be putting a severe strain on the availability of resources for them," Hara observed.

Acharya explained, "Yes, indeed. They've been attempting to counter the rising sea levels by raising huge stone and metal-based barriers. When advancing oceans limited the availability of resources with the passage of time, the only alternative they were left with was to encroach on the land and resources of other nations around them. This is what they have been doing for quite a few centuries now."

"I'm sure these nations must have seen this encroachment as aggression into their territory. Isn't it why they allied with Dev Lok?"

"Yes. It was only after a consortium of nations got formed under the leadership of the Bhārat King Dushyant that the Daityan aggression could be effectively checked. Indra of Dev Lok is the current head of the allied consortium known as Devarth."

"This must be another reason for the animosity between Daityan empire and Dev Lok."

"Apart from general animosity, Daityas have much to gain by defeating Devas. With Dev Lok subjugated, the balance of power would completely swing in their favour and they can then control others with impunity," Acharya Parashu clarified.

"Wouldn't the Mūrthi intervene, in case of such conflict between Devarth and Daityan empire?"

"I'm not sure they would, unless something catastrophic happens that can dramatically change the course of human evolution. Most internal skirmishes between human centres of power are likely to be seen as part of the evolutionary process."

ᛐ ᛞ ቄ

By the time they returned, it was well into the afternoon. "We need to restart soon, to be able to keep our appointment with Indra Sabha." Acharya Parashu said, as they disembarked from the vimān.

After a brief visit to their rooms, they met again and headed for the Indra Sabha. It was usually held in the main meeting hall called Pushkarni, on the top-most fifty-fourth floor of the Meru tower.

"Acharya, you'd mentioned that being in Amaravati may be part of our karmic mission on the way to Atalantpuri," Hara mentioned as they walked towards the anti-grav elevators.

"Yes, Hara. We may even need to seek some help from Dev Lok to be able to reach Atalantpuri. Devas have an effective intelligence network and they can even provide us with some contacts and information. Actually, our mission also happens to be of vital importance to them. The rejuvenation therapy and corresponding drugs for Kayakalp, under development by Daityas may have many military applications. For example, one of its direct spinoffs could be to considerably improve the fighting potential of their soldiers as well as speed-up the production of *Yantraksh*. This could, in turn, provide them with yet another military advantage over Devas."

"They've kidnapped Rishi Agastya and his wife for this purpose?" Hara asked.

"Yes. Rishi Agastya's help is vital for them to develop the critical final technique of enacting cosmic vibrations to infuse *prana*, the universal life force, during the Kayakalp therapy."

4

INDRA SABHA

The huge assembly hall, Pushkarni, was located at the top of the conical crystalline tower Meru that marked the centre of Amaravati. On reaching the base of the tower, the Bheeshma monks were escorted up through a high-speed elevator. Like many other Mūrthi technologies used in Dev Lok, the elevators were powered by anti-grav drives embedded within the tower itself. It was dusk and as the elevator ascended, Hara saw the city of Amaravati light up in its full glory. The crystalline structures of many buildings accentuated the spectacular panoramic view of the city.

Even though located at such a great height, Pushkarni was designed like an exotic garden, with full complements of indoor comforts. The central pond, which was also called Pushkarni, had large lotus flowers blooming throughout the seasons. The pond contained colourful and varied species of fish swimming around within it, creating a unique kaleidoscope of visual delight. The seats that were placed around the pond formed the usual venue for most important meetings at Amaravati. The hall itself was adorned with various genetically modified indoor trees that stayed evergreen. Many of them continued to bloom with fragrant flowers. Further ahead were comfortable seats to recline on; the dignitaries could enjoy from there the fabulous view of Amaravati and the bluish-green ocean beyond. *Somras* and other refreshments were being served regularly. The architectural design of the Meru tower was so magnificent that even those viewing it from ships sailing at the horizon were captivated by its grandeur. It was safe to say that the Mūrthi architects, who designed Amaravati and its palaces, spared no effort in enhancing the opulence of its crowning glory on top of the Meru tower.

Indra, the elected priestly King of Dev Lok, and ten of his ministers and advisors were seated around the Pushkarni. He was dressed in his characteristic white robes, a simple crown made of gold and crystal, a decorated gold band around his shoulders and wrist bands on both hands. He was a tall man with an athletic body and graceful poise. His hair was grey as expected from any eighty *ayanas* old Deva. They seemed to have been discussing a serious stately matter when Acharya Parashu and Hara walked into the hall.

Indra got up from his seat and came up to welcome them. "Welcome to Pushkarni," he said with a bow. Then turning to all those seated, he said, "Gentlemen, these are the Bheeshma monks who saved Uma from the Vetals. I'm indebted to them for their act of valour and chivalry because of which my daughter is still alive."

Among the dignitaries seated around Indra, Acharya Parashu recognised Brihaspati, the guru and chief advisor of Dev Lok. He bowed and paid obeisance, "Pranam Dev Guru". With his white flowing hair and maroon robe, Brihaspati projected an image of maturity and statesmanship. No one knew his exact age but it was estimated to be well over two hundred ayanas. Apart from being the royal advisor and guru to Indra, he was also the chief of security, as well as the primary coordinator of Devarth consortium. He was known to have been a Bheeshma monk for a brief period during his early life and still maintained close links with Brahmagiri.

"Such a pleasure to meet the legendary Bheeshma warrior monk Acharya Parashu," Brihaspati hugged Parashu and then turning to Hara said, "and this must be your shishya Hara?"

"Pranam Dev Guru," Hara folded his hand and bowed.

Indra introduced them to others in the hall, "This is Prajapati Daksh, the administrative head of Dev Lok." Daksh, who wore a red-coloured regal robe nodded at the visitors. They were then introduced to Agni Dev, Varun Dev, Yama Dev, Surya Dev, etc., who formed the core group of the ruling Devan government. Also present were two leading Generals from Maruth army— Kshetrajna and Jayanta, the eldest son of Indra.

It was Prajapati Daksh who began the serious talk, "We hear that you're on a Bheeshma mission, Acharya?"

"Yes, that was our main purpose till we met Uma at the Vetal land. Now that she is safe, we would request Indra Dev to let us continue with our mission."

"Not before you allow us to indulge you with our hospitality, Acharya. I hope you enjoyed the aerial tour of Amaravati. We're also at your disposal for any assistance for this Bheeshma mission," Indra stated exuberantly.

Acharya bowed slightly before replying, "Your Majesty, thank you very much for sparing your royal vimān for our tour today. It was certainly a fantastic experience. Much as we would love to, we can't spend more time at Amaravati. You could, however, help us by providing some information regarding the present state of tension between Dev Lok and the Daityan empire."

Indra's face turned serious when he said, "Of course, Acharya. As a matter of fact, we were discussing the same issue when you came in. The situation isn't good. It seems that unless we're able to find some diplomatic solution soon, a war is inevitable over the coming months."

"I didn't know it was already that serious. A war between Dev Lok and Daityan empire would impact everyone on the Earth and none too pleasantly. Isn't it possible to find some middle way to avoid this confrontation between two advanced nations of the known world?" Acharya Parashu asked.

"You're right, Acharya. A war is in no one's interest and I'm the last one to preach such a course. It is not that we haven't tried to reason with the Daityas. Just a few weeks ago I myself met the Daityan Emperor Tarakaksh."

"Then what is the problem, Indra Dev?"

It was Brihaspati who answered, "Acharya, as you're aware, by their very nature, Daityas need to capture and plunder natural resources to keep their industries well supplied with raw materials and enable all the material comforts for their citizens. They also need huge amounts of food to feed their burgeoning population. It seems that they've already exhausted most of the mineral and other natural wealth within the areas of their control. The rising level of sea water due to melting ice-caps is only making the situation more desperate for them. We all know that for quite a while now, they've been eyeing the fertile lands of Devarth. We've been getting reports that lately there is a massive effort on at their end to boost the military power. They're also known to have developed Anvik weapons capable of inflicting unprecedented destruction."

"Your Majesty, aren't you militarily adept to defend yourselves?" The question came from Hara.

"Yes Hara, we're more than ready to defend our nation. However, we cannot deny that any war would certainly mean death, destruction of property, loss of farmlands and extreme suffering for people on both sides. I would prefer to avoid it if that were possible," Indra replied.

"But Your Majesty, surely you must've also started preparations, to face the eventuality of a war if it is forced upon you," Hara asked insistently.

"Yes. We've also started the preparations. Unfortunately, in the past we've always been focussing on improving the lives of our population. So, even though we may be more advanced in some aspects, the harsh reality is that we're no match against Daityan empire from a numerical perspective. We may have a slight edge over them in terms of better vimāns and we've already started building war vimāns and other associated weapon systems. However, this hasn't been taken too well by the Daityan Emperor Tarakaksh. He has been actually accusing us of instigating an arms race. The heightened tension between the two nations has only been fuelling the suspicion between us," Indra Dev explained.

"Are you saying that we should definitely expect a war between Devarth and Daityan Empire soon?" Acharya Parashu asked.

"Yes, considering the criticality of their internal situation, they don't have much time. The sea water is rising too rapidly for their engineers to be able to control inundation," Indra Dev clarified.

"If they're in such a critical situation, why can't we offer some help instead? It is, after all, much better than going to war," Acharya Parashu asked Brihaspati with a sceptical look.

Brihaspati replied, "You're right, Acharya. It is definitely a better option and we've already made such an offer to them. However, I'm not sure we're in a position to follow up fully, even if they agree to accept it. The fact of the matter is that the rising sea water has impacted us too."

Agni Dev, being the head of industries, agricultural and trade of Dev Lok, told Indra, "Your Majesty, Dev Guru is right. We're also in a very critical situation. The sea water has impacted most of our coastal farmlands. Our nature-based technology is helping, but the sea water rise is too much for us to control completely. Devan citizens are yet to suffer shortage of food primarily because of two reasons. First, unlike Daityas, we have a smaller population. Second, we've been able to import food in large quantities from continental Devarth nations. Over the past few months, Bhārat kingdom has become the main food bowl supporting Dev Lok."

"Then we must perhaps share the scarcity with Daityas," Yama Dev stated. He was the head of judicial system within Dev Lok.

Agni Dev looked at him in surprise, "Why should we share food with Daityas and ask Dev Lok citizens to go hungry instead? Would the Daityas have shared depleting resources if we were in a similar situation?"

Indra looked at Yama Dev and added, "Yama Dev, let's not forget that the food supply from Bhārat is also not likely to be so stable over the coming ayansas. Global warming has affected the weather systems all over the world. Of late, we're experiencing some of the worst weather conditions. This is certainly not good for agriculture and food production has been steadily declining across all farmlands."

Yama Dev looked doubtful when he replied, "Your Majesty, are you saying that all the efforts of our scientists using the Mūrthi technology to bring rain have been unsuccessful? We all know that the farmers within Bhārat and other Devarth nations even worship you as the rain-bringing God?"

Indra smiled and answered, "We've certainly had some successes in the past, Yama Dev. However, the weather conditions these days are way beyond our control. The rivers are swelling due to excessive water melting from receding ice-lines and numerous newly-formed active glaciers. Even the courses of rivers are becoming unpredictable. There is either too much or too little rain at some of the prime food producing territories of the Bhārat kingdom. Beside the problem of rain, the rise in sea water is also affecting the coastal farms on the river deltas."

It was Brihaspati who put an end to this line of discussion, "Indra Dev, I've analysed all options to resolve this crisis and came short of meaningful solutions. We may be able to postpone the conflict for some more time by attempting to cooperate with Daityas but eventually, the continued rise in sea water would make it invalid. Anyway, our assumptions that Daityas would also try to avoid a war are unrealistic. Since they have an overwhelming military advantage over us, war would seem like a very attractive option, especially to some of their aggressive generals. They've been spoiling for an armed conflict for quite some time anyway."

Indra turned towards Varun Dev and Vayu Dev, who headed the navy and air force of Dev Lok respectively, "How is our preparation?"

Varun Dev spoke first, "Your Majesty, as you are well aware, Daityas are in a much better position with regards to their preparation for a naval warfare. Their ships are larger, more numerous and fitted with the latest weapon systems. It is well known that they've even developed some submarines capable of launching surprise attacks. Our navy stands little chance against such overwhelming superiority. As mentioned by you earlier, we may have slight edge over Daityas within the area of air force. I'll leave it for Vayu Dev to explain."

Vayu Dev addressed all those present and apprised them, "It is true that we have better and faster vimāns. But our air force certainly can't match them in terms of sheer numbers. So our overall superiority is only marginal. To negate whatever advantage we may have in this regard, Daityas have built excellent air defence systems across their empire."

"What about the support from Bhārat, Gandharv and other kingdoms?" Indra asked.

Brihaspati answered, "They're with us. Bhārat King Pareekshit has promised to provide us enough manpower to cover up any shortfall. King Kuber of Yaksha kingdom is already helping us by funding some of our weapons development and retrofitting programmes. Gandharv and Kinnara kingdoms are ready to provide any kind of assistance in terms of minerals, precious metals, medicines, etc. I fear, all of this may not amount to much when faced with an enemy as powerful as the Daityas."

The discussions then veered off to the difficulties in manufacturing larger quantities of arms and preparation of trained soldiers for the impending conflict.

Hara moved away and reached the edge of the Pushkarni hall to look at the vast expanse of ocean visible from this high platform. Brilliantly lit, Amaravati and the ocean beyond seemed calm and peaceful. He wondered what all turbulent times lay ahead for this beautiful city.

5

MAGICAL SOMVAN

The palace Vaidyas had given Haŕa the final dose of Amruth before he went off to sleep the previous night. So it was already mid-morning and quite bright when he woke up from his long, deep slumber. Once freshened up, he was raring to go and explore the fascinating city of Amaravati. Since he had been in a vimān the previous day, he decided to see it from the ground this time. He felt it better not to disturb Acharya Parashu, and quickly dressed up and left his quarters. A palace assistant from the guest section of the palace complex came up to him and asked, "May I be of any help to you, Sir?"

"No, thanks," Haŕa replied. Then on second thoughts asked, "Can you tell me how to go to the main part of your city? I would like to take a stroll."

"It is my honour to help a Bheeshma." The assistant bowed respectfully and continued, "The royal palace, where you are located now, is indeed the main part of the city." He then hesitated before saying, "Perhaps you would like to have a feel of the city outside the palace gates? If yes, I can recommend a walk through the main city arcade up to the Brahma monument. After you leave the palace gates, it is a brief walk along a straight road. Although at this hour of the day, you might find the place somewhat busy."

Haŕa thanked him and left the palace gates, walking along the sidewalk of the main pathway leading to the famous monument of Brahma. Though bright and sunny, the weather was quite pleasant and the pathway was lined with trees. There were separate pathways for vehicular traffic and pedestrians. Merchants selling various wares like perfumes, jewellery, spices, somras, etc., dotted the road meant for walking. In his flowing Bheeshma robes and long hair, Haŕa was somewhat conspicuous among the ordinary citizens of Amaravati. People were familiar with Bheeshma monks and their attire, making him a subject of fascination. Many greeted him with the characteristic Namastute as he passed by.

Haŕa was impressed to note many of the unmatched technological and architectural sophistications of the city, more apparent at close quarters than from the vimān. It was, however, fairly crowded and noisy at the busy market place. He looked around and marvelled that this was the city of Devas and was immense in its grandeur; he had heard that the Daityan city of Atalantpuri was built on a much grander scale. As part of the Bheeshma mission that they were on, Acharya Parashu and he would soon need to head for Atalantpuri. He wished to make most out of this short period of rest and rejuvenation, even hoped to meet Uma soon. Though he was unable to see as to how a Bheeshma monk could have any future with a Dev Lok princess, that didn't stop him from wishing for her company. He wondered if she also felt a similar affection for him.

It seemed the Gods had heard him. When he was about to reach the central arcade near the Brahma monument, he instinctively turned back and saw three chariots emerging from the palace. As in case of many vehicles based on Mūrthi technology still used at Amaravati, the self-powered chariots were made of a combination of crystals and metal. There were no horses to pull the vehicle and the wheels on both sides were only for ornamental purpose. The anti-grav levitation drives contained within their chassis provided enough power for them to hover over the ground at any speed.

Uma, along with a few companions, was moving towards the monument of Brahma. On seeing Hara, her eyes locked with his. A mild smile came upon her face and she whispered something to one of her companions. The chariot came to a halt and then once again sped along. Hara's eyes followed Uma and he didn't realise that the girl Uma had spoken to was standing next to him. "Sreeman Hara, I'm Rambha. Our princess has requested to meet you at the royal garden next to the Brahma monument. If you agree, I've been instructed to guide you there."

Hara was, of course, delighted to be able to meet Uma, and readily agreed. Rambha suppressed a smile and bid him to follow her. As she walked ahead, others naturally gave way to her. Hara could see that even for a low-ranking companion of the princess, the position of being part of Indra's palace gave a certain degree of respect and authority. She moved along the pathway for some time and then took a turn at the end into another walkway which was relatively less crowded. As he followed her, Hara could see the huge golden monument of Brahma in the middle of the central arcade. All around the statue, there were terraced gardens and water fountains. Rambha explained that the statue of Brahma actually stood levitated from the ground. Those who came close to the monument experienced a very pleasant, calming effect on their mind. Many people visited the gardens to enjoy the visual treat of its exquisitely designed landscape and benefit from the elevated psychic experience in the proximity of the monument.

On the sea-facing side of the monument, there was an exclusive garden and Rambha led him over there. "This is the royal garden and only the king's family, priests and other dignitaries are allowed here."

"How can I be here then?" Hara smiled at Rambha.

"Sreeman, you're a royal guest and Uma has specifically requested for your company. Besides that, you're a Bheeshma monk. By tradition, Bheeshma monks are not denied entry in any place within Dev Lok."

They reached the central spot of the garden which was tastefully decorated with blooming flowers of various shades and exotic fragrances. Never in his life had he seen any of these flowers, and assumed that they must've been nurtured by the Devas through some form of genetic hybridisation. Uma was standing in the middle of a small lawn; she rushed towards him, stopping short of touching. Rambha excused herself and left in a hurry.

"How are you feeling now, Hara? The head Vaidya told me that you had recovered completely." Hara noticed her eyes running over the snake bite on his throat. She hastily said, "Your wound seems to be healing fast. Actually the bluish tinge on the throat adds to your personality." Looking at her so close-up, Hara felt that her smile was both mysterious and irresistible.

Hara was blushing when he replied, "Thank you, Uma. This wound is nothing. How are you? Have you have recovered fully?"

"Yes," Uma replied, looking into his eyes, "but not from the pain that I feel in my heart ever since I met you."

Hara, obviously uncomfortable with such intimacy, said nothing and tried to look up at the Brahma monument, hoping that its calming effect would sooth the emotions rushing within him.

Uma continued to smile but changed the subject, "How do you like Amaravati?"

"It is the most fabulous city I have ever seen," Hara admitted and continued, "Yesterday we took an aerial tour of the city and the surrounding areas."

"Amaravati is just one of the fascinating sights at Swarga Dweep. You should see the hilly southern side of the island. It is even more incredible," Uma added.

"Southern side?" Hara asked doubtfully.

"Yes, Hara, that is where we have the magical forests of Somvan and the Souparnika River. You should see it in moonlight," she replied. Hara was mesmerised with the distant look in Uma's eyes. Then her eyes immediately brightened up and she asked him, "Would you like to see it?"

"I would love to but..."

Before he could even finish his sentence, Uma said with great enthusiasm, "Great! I'll take you there. In fact, let us go right now."

"But..."

"No more buts, Hara. Today is a perfect day to visit Somvan. Just follow me; I'll take you there myself. Let us go," she took his hand, turned around and walked forward enthusiastically.

Hara followed her, not completely sure whether this was the right decision. Uma took him straight to her chariot. She then excused the driver and her companion. "Rambha, I'm going to take Hara for a ride up to the Souparnika River within Somvan. Since it is quite far, we may need to move fast. So I'll drive the chariot myself. You can wait for me here, please."

There was an understanding smile on Rambha's face when she asked, "By when should we expect you back, princess?"

"We should be back by evening," Uma replied confidently.

The chariot hovered along well above the ground. So, once out of the built-up area within city limits, they could move cross-country without any further need to use the roads. Considering the confidence with which Uma was maneuvering the chariot, Hara hoped that she must be fairly familiar with their destination. Hara wondered whether Acharya Parashu would approve of his sudden departure. But he was also enjoying the thrill of the ride as the chariot speeded over Devan countryside.

The countryside provided a completely different impression of Dev Lok. There were buildings, but very far and few, and most of the land was under cultivation of different crops. One could clearly see that these crops were irrigated by the numerous canals that they crossed en route. It was said that Devas were able to keep the land under cultivation throughout the year because of their unique cultivation techniques and plentiful availability of water for irrigation. Like in case of the buildings at Amaravati, most of the cultivation was actually done by the lower forms of life like ants and microbes. They did everything from planting to fertilisation and final harvest. Human assistance was only necessary for maintaining the irrigation channels. There were many astral linkup stations at regular intervals, using which the Devan agricultural engineers maintained the spiritual linkup with these living organisms from time to time, to guide them through a particular farming technique. The lush green colours of the crops indicated that they were always maintained in optimum state without any chemicals, or even direct human intervention for that matter.

Soon the landscape changed from crop fields to cultivated orchards. Uma smiled at Hara as he looked around at the variety of flowering plants and fruit-bearing trees around them. It was easy to see as to why, inspite of the problems faced by the rising sea water levels, the Devas were able to maintain their lifestyle with minimum impact. Some of the trees thriving within these orchards were never found anywhere else in the world. Hara assumed that they might have been developed by crossing the native fruit-bearing trees on Earth with exotic plant genome from the Mūrthi home-worlds. Uma told him that the one of the rarest plants called *mritusanjeevani*—the primary ingredient of the medicine Amruth—was also grown here.

Within another muhurta, they were well inside the hilly jungle terrain of Somvan. Uma told him that it was so named because of the plentiful wild growth of a particular variety of extraterrestrial trees called Som. The fruits and other extracts from this tree were the main ingredients for making the famous intoxicating liquor called Somras. It was one of the major export products from Dev Lok to all parts of the world.

During their stay at Amaravati, the Mūrthi had taken great care to nurture this part of the island's natural environment. In fact, they had developed it exclusively with vegetation from their home-worlds. Somvan was known to have been one of their favourite places on the planet to relish the memories of their home environment. To the human eye, the flora and fauna of the jungle looked extraordinary and magical as they grew in all kinds of curious shapes and colours. Some trees were enormously large with huge canopies around them. It was obvious that most of the plants and the grass found in this region didn't have much dependency on direct sunlight. They were lush and lively both under shade and otherwise. Even though the trees and flowers came in all colours, the most predominant theme ranged from pure white to bright red. In fact, the whole jungle was a kaleidoscope of different colours with exotic fragrances to complement it. Similar theme extended even to the small animals and other living creatures scurrying around the woods. Their extra terrestrial origin was clear in the manner they seemed to blend and thrive within the vegetation all around them.

Uma explained how Somvan was considered to be highly sacred, because of which very few Devas visited it frequently to maintain its sanctity. Many believed that these woods still held the spirits of the Mūrthi from bygone era. Hara wondered as to why Uma herself didn't seem much influenced by such beliefs. Considering the confidence with which she was moving around, it was clear that she was a regular visitor to these woods. They soon reached the small Souparnika river.

Uma halted the chariot near a tree and beckoned Hara to follow her along a narrow trail on the river bank. Hara followed her, continuing to enjoy the sights unfolding around them. Multi-coloured butterflies flew around the flowers of various perpetually-blooming trees and plants. The sweet chirping of exotic birds blended with the regular sounds of leaves rustling in the gentle wind and water cascading down small tributary streams into the river, creating a symphony of natural music. Within another half muhurta or so, they reached their destination. Perched on a small hillock across the river was a crystal gazebo. It seemed that from its height, the place must provide a fantastic panoramic view of the complete Somvan with the river Souparnika meandering through its woods and valleys. There was a small rowboat tied to a pier near the bank. Uma went up to the boat and asked him to get on board. Hara was quite hesitant at first, for the boat seemed somewhat frail to withstand any strong currents. He did, however, agree when Uma reassured that she had crossed the river using such boats many times. He assured himself that this was Dev Lok and she must be familiar with her homeland. He was continuously surprising himself from the manner he was unable to resist any suggestions, howsoever foolish, as long as they came from Uma.

When they started rowing, it soon became apparent that they had taken the decision too hastily. Like in case of most parts of the world, global warming had made the rate of flow within even small rivers unpredictable. Souparnika had also become rough, especially around the middle. As the currents started getting too strong, they found it difficult to control the boat. Soon they were struggling to even keep it afloat. He could now see the signs of uncertainty and fear in Uma's eyes. On signal from Hara, they started rowing furiously to try and reach the nearest bank. The flow of the river was too strong for them to fight, and they were already hundreds of dhanus away from the nearest pier. The river was dragging them deep into the Somvan forest.

It must have been just another half muhurta when the boat capsized. They were now swimming desperately, holding on to the overturned boat for support. With one hand holding the boat, Hara swam against the current with all the energy he could summon within his body. Even so, he had to struggle for another half muhurta before they could get the capsized boat up to the nearest bank of the river. Fortunately, they had reached a bend within the river and the fury of the river had ebbed.

"I'm sorry, Hara. I never knew the river would be so rough. It seemed so calm from the banks..." Uma said, still panting to regain her breath.

"Too late to worry about that now." Hara replied and then looking at her intently, a broad smile started materialising on his face when he asked playfully, "But tell me, are you also one of the exotic creatures that inhabit these magical forests? You certainly look like one." With soaking clothes sticking to her skin, she looked almost like a mermaid.

Uma tried to smile back, but she was already shivering with cold. The hilly region surrounding them was cold, being totally drenched only made their situation worse. Hara knew that it would become even colder when it turns dark in another two or three muhurtas and realised that it was definitely a rash decision on his part to have followed Uma to this remote area, with hardly any help around. Even if they started walking now, it would be well into the night before they could reach the chariot. Once it gets dark, however, it was doubtful that they would be able to trek at all through the rough and unfamiliar terrain. It may be quite a while before their delayed return makes Uma's companion Rambha alert the royal guards. Uma told him that even if Indra came to know about this, it was doubtful that he would send a search party till next morning. Somvan was revered as the mystical realm of the Mūrthi and most Devas considered it inauspicious to disturb it during night time, especially during a full moon night when it was said that the holy spirits of the gods roamed around these woods.

Hara's first priority was to find a decent shelter for the two of them. They settled for the canopy of a nearby tree located at an elevated point near the river bank. Its wide leaves would provide some temporary protection. Fortunately, the sky was clear and the full moon was already rising over the horizon. Hara started building a friction fire using dry twigs around the tree.

"Let me scout around to see where we are stranded," Hara said as he got up after adding few big logs into the fire. Apart from wanting to give some privacy to Uma to dry out her clothes, he was also keen to know the terrain around them.

He managed to climb up a steep hill nearby from where the complete landscape of the southern part of Swarga Dweep could be seen. From this vantage point, the colourful vegetation of the Somvan gave an impression of an exotic carpet. It was already twilight; at some distance down the river, he could see the twinkling lights of a small town. Hara estimated that it may take them at least four muhurtas to reach the lights. He made a mental note that the town seemed very close to the banks of the river near one of its bends. Since the terrain was undulating and there was no clear trail, it seemed safest that they spend the night at this location itself and start off in the early hours of the morning. It was getting dark, so he turned around and headed back. On his way back, he collected some succulent looking fruits to share with Uma.

By the time Hara returned, Uma had dried her clothes and was standing near the fire, enjoying its warmth. She saw him approaching and asked, "What did you find?"

"Nothing much! I noticed a town somewhere down the river, but it will take some time to walk and it may not be safe at this hour. The terrain is rough and it would soon get dark, especially under the thick foliage and trees. We may need to spend the night here itself," Hara said. From the smile on her face, it was clear that Uma was not particularly displeased with the situation.

Uma told him that the fruits he had picked were from the Som trees, commonly found in this region. They were known to be delicious and mildly intoxicating. From the slightly elevated place where they had camped, one could get a fairly good panoramic view of the woods around them. As it turned dark, the complete jungle took a surreal appearance and being a full moon night, the trees reflected their full glory of colours. Apart from this, their leaves themselves seemed to give out a faint phosphorescent glow, complementing the moonlight even further. Some parts of the forest were covered by low hanging mist. "No wonder they called this a magical forest" – Hara thought. He looked at Uma who was sitting next to him. They had been in similar situation in the past at the Brashtaranya forests too. But here there was no worry of any Vetals chasing them or the apprehension as to what would happen the next day. It was as if they had the complete Somvan at their own disposal.

"I guess it was very irrational of us to make such a spur-of-the-moment decision to visit Somvan today," Hara stated reflectively.

"Are you sure, Hara? I have nothing to complain about. This trip has given me an opportunity to be with you again." She gave a beaming smile while taking his hand into hers. It was obvious that the Som fruits were having their effect on her.

"Is everyone in Amaravati so direct in their expression?"

"Not all. But I don't wait for too long to express myself. Who knows when we're going to meet again?" Uma replied smiling.

Hara's emotions were tumultuous and he was trying hard to keep them under control. He thought it best to change the subject and asked, "Why do they consider Somvan to be magical? I know that it is beautiful and all but..."

"This forest was created by the Mūrthi when they lived in Amaravati many eons ago. By tradition, young couples used to come here for their honeymoon, away from others. People believe that their spirits still reside in these trees and come out to revive their passions during every full moon night."

"Oh! Today is a full moon night. Does it mean...?" Hara asked doubtfully.

"If you believe in the Dev Lok fairy tales, then yes! You never know, we may already be in company of the spirits of Mūrthi lovers," Uma giggled loudly.

They remained awake, talking for a long time, late into the night. The moon had moved past the zenith and the fire had become embers. Hafa got up to feed some more logs into the fire. Once it was bright, they settled down to get some sleep. He noticed that Uma had crept near him and they were leaning on each other, unconsciously huddled together for mutual warmth. She held his hand within hers as they continued to observe the slowly changing fine hues of the forest and shifting patterns of the mist hovering over it. In such close proximity, Hafa had to really control the urge to take her into his arms. But some part of his heart couldn't help wondering if she would like that. It was a relief that they were so tired and sleep was already creeping in. Hafa thought what would the spirits of Mūrthi lovers be thinking, looking down upon them in this condition as he drifted off to sleep.

♈ ♍ ♀

They got up early next morning. After refreshing themselves, they started walking along the banks of the river and soon hit a small trail. The track was a tough one with many obstacles on the way. Hafa was not sure whether it was deliberate of Uma to ask for his help to negotiate even the simplest of obstacles, but he didn't mind. He knew that their overnight escapade would remain etched in his memory forever and he wanted to relish it as much as possible.

After walking for another three muhurtas, they soon reached the township that Hafa had seen from the hillock the previous night. Not long after their arrival, a search party chariot from Amaravati picked them up.

"Would your father be annoyed that you had to spend a night alone with me at the Somvan?" Hafa asked with concern.

"Maybe yes; maybe not. Anyway, you shouldn't worry about that, I'll convince him," she seemed confident.

"Like you convinced me to come along?" Hara smiled.

"Do you need convincing to be with me Hara?" Hara looked up and noticed Uma's serious expression and her eyes locked on him, unblinking.

"Frankly, no. I would like nothing better for the rest of my life." He replied without hesitation.

"Then please stay for some more time at Amaravati, Hara. There are many more places for us to visit...and maybe...get lost?" Uma asked mischievously.

Hara's heart was thumping. He managed to say, "I would love that..." Then he stopped mid-sentence and continued, "Uma, you must know how different we are. You're a royal princess of Dev Lok and I'm a Bheeshma monk avowed to a hard life full of risks and rigours. Our being together is not likely to be accepted by the society."

"Then we will make them accept it. There is no law against it within Dev Lok," she said matter of factly.

"It's not that," Hara hesitated.

"Is it that you don't like me? Or you don't want to spend your life with me, because you find the life of a warrior monk to be more exciting, adventurous and fulfilling? Or is it that there is already someone in your life?" Uma asked, visibly hurt.

Hara looked at her intently and said, "No, Uma. There's nothing in this world that I wouldn't give up to be with you. To spend this life with you would be the ultimate gift."

"Then why are you so resistive, Hara? Is it something to do with your past life?" Uma asked anxiously.

"Acharya Parashu and I are on a Bheeshma mission. We're expected to soon infiltrate deep into the Daityan Empire and will surely face extreme perils on the way. There is no certainty that I would be able to return alive. I don't want you to be in pain if…"

Hara wanted to tell her more but he knew that could jeopardise their mission.

"You leave that to me, Hara. I'll wait for you even if it takes many births." Uma was almost in tears by now.

"So would I, Uma. I was only making clear the difficulties ahead of us before we can be together forever," Hara said softly.

Uma smiled back, "Okay, Hara. I'll do whatever you ask of me."

"Uma, the mission that I'm likely to embark on is most confidential. Even sharing it with your father may not be a good idea. So, our feelings for each other must remain our secret till I return from the mission. Once I leave Amaravati, it may take a few weeks, or even months, before I can contact you again." He then took out the bracelet tied to his right arm and gave it to Uma. "This was given to me by the Bheeshma Maha Guru Vashist, as a symbol of Bheeshmatv—my spiritual identity. I leave it with you to keep till my return from this mission."

Uma took the bracelet, held it close to her heart and said, "This will give me the strength to wait for your return. I'll pray to Lord Vishnu to keep you safe and sound till then."

6

DAITYAN DILEMMA

Daityan Emperor Tarakaksh stood at the parapet of the highest citadel of Tripura. The three impregnable citadels that formed the royal fortress called Tripura were perched on a lofty mountain cliff, right in the middle of Atalantpuri – the capital city of Daityan Empire. It was built by Adi-Maya, the legendary Daityan chief architect and scientist many centuries ago.

Daityan Empire comprised many archipelago-based kingdoms like Atala, Patala, Vitala, Sutala, Talatala, Mahatala, Rasatala, etc. Apart from his role as the Emperor of Daityan Empire, Tarakaksh was also the direct ruler of Atala archipelago with Sweta Dweep being the most prominent island within it. Tarakaksh had appointed his two younger brothers as the governors of Atala: Kamalaksh was responsible for Sweta Dweep and all other islands of Atala, while the mega capital city of Daityan Empire named Atalantpuri was governed by Vidyunmali. They ruled from the citadels of Tripura, with top-most one belonging to Emperor Tarakaksh, the one below it to Kamalaksh and the third one, right above Atalantpuri, to Vidyunmali. The three brothers were the dynastic descendents of the famous Daityan Emperor Vritra who was killed during a fierce war between Daityan Empire and Devarth many generations ago.

Tarakaksh was a middle-aged tall man with a powerful built, a characteristic unique to all aristocratic Rakshas clan men. His face had an intense look, with lines of worry etched deep around his eyebrows as he surveyed the vast expanse of the city of Atalantpuri below. The city he had seen so often, surrounded by ocean on all three sides with a few ships docked at the nearest port and many others scattered around, moving in and out of the lagoons within the three tiered artificial reefs surrounding the harbour city.

"Pranam, Your Majesty." Tarakaksh turned around to see Mahisha walking towards him, "Ah, Mahishasur! It has been a while since we met. What brings you to Tripura?" *Asur* was the customary title used to honour anyone from Daityan royalty; Mahisha was the King of Patala archipelago, the second major island nation of the Daityan Empire. He was also the chief of security of the Empire itself. Unlike Tarakaksh, Mahisha was a second generation mixed breed between Rakshas and Danav clans, the two main ethnic groups of the Empire. He was of medium height, with a somewhat bulging girth around the waist. Even though his coarse face and muscular body structure reminded one of a powerful buffalo, his eyes were alive and shifty, clearly reflecting a cunning and crafty brain behind them.

"Your Majesty must already know of the desperate times we're going through in Patala." Mahisha looked at the Emperor with a grave expression on his face.

Tarakaksh was well aware, but such was the nature of these times. He had spent enough time wondering why this cursed phase of global warming had to happen now, when it was time to enjoy the fruit of many years of labour and development of the Empire.

"Has there been another wave of floods in Patala?" Tarakaksh knew that Patala was one of the most low-lying archipelagos and therefore particularly vulnerable to inundation. Although the climate around the planet had been warming steadily for many centuries, the high waves had started only recently. Tarakaksh had sent reconnaissance vimāns towards the southern ice-shelves to check its cause. It was learnt that huge blocks, the size of small islands were slipping into the sea regularly from those frozen legacies of ice age, triggering small tsunamis across the world. There were also reports of increased tectonic and volcanic activity, and many parts of the Empire experienced regular tremors. Apart from the incidents of inundation from sea, lately the weather patterns had also turned nasty with regular heavy rainfalls, thunderstorms and cyclones.

"Yes, Your Majesty. This time the waves have wiped out twenty per cent of the arable landmass within Patala."

"Hmm. What is the progress of elevating the embankments to defend the shorelines? Aren't Maya's men doing their job properly?" Maya was the present chief architect and scientist of the Daityan Empire.

"Maya's teams are hard at work, Your Majesty. In fact, many of them bore the brunt of the small tsunami that hit our southern shores yesterday. The death toll is already well above 2,000." Mahisha replied sombrely.

This was bad news. Such reports of land loss and catastrophic deaths had been coming from many parts of the Empire. The Kings who administered various provinces of the vast Daityan Empire looked up to the capital Atalantpuri to offer a solution. Tarakaksh knew that unless he was able to control the situation, the Empire was in real danger of slipping into a vicious internal strife. Each nation within the Empire had a huge population that needed to be fed and loss of every inch of fertile land would only make it more difficult.

Tarakaksh sighed and looked at Mahisha, "These are bad times for the Daityan Empire. All the strengths that we've acquired over many ayanas with the efforts of so many seem ineffective when faced with nature's temperaments."

"Your Majesty, our misery is also because Devarth is unfairly holding on to most of the fertile land within the known world.

Even with far lesser population, they have more cultivable land than the entire Daityan Empire put together." Mahisha was quick to place the problem squarely on the shoulders of Devarth.

Tarakaksh looked back at Mahisha, "That is also because we've been increasing our population at such a fast rate over the last few decades, whereas their numbers have remained more or less steady. We can hardly blame them for that."

Mahisha bowed when he replied, "Your Majesty, pardon my impudence but when our own population is near starvation, this is hardly the time to discuss our past mistakes. We have a situation that needs resolution. If the complete cultivable landmass on known parts of the world were to be put to industrial farming like we do on our Talas, there would be more than sufficient food for everyone. The main reason for the global shortage of food is the low-yielding farming techniques used by the inland nations of Devarth. Their insistence that cultivation needs to be in harmony with nature is fine for words but impracticable when faced with a starving population."

Tarakaksh sighed. This was the kind of convoluted argument that majority of his councillors also had. He knew the problem, the solution that these people were hinting at and its consequences. It was, however, difficult even for an Emperor to go against the opinions of the heads of nations. "You've stated similar views before as well, Mahisha, and so have the others. You do realize that this means war? Even though we may have numerical superiority, Devarth nations are formidable opponents. Devas also have the advantage of closer links with the Mūrthi. War would mean substantial redirection of our resources presently involved in combating the fury of nature from sea."

"Your Majesty, benefits of war far outweighs all the other alternatives. Also, it needn't even be a full-fledged war. If we can intimidate them enough to come to the negotiation table for sharing their farmlands, that would be victory enough."

"And how do you suggest we intimidate them?"

"Your Majesty, Devarth would be amenable to negotiate with us if we can create a situation that compels them to do so. This is also the view of our informer within the Indra Sabha." Mahisha smiled slyly.

"Force, intimidation and terror are not always the solutions for all problems, Mahisha. Outcome of such endeavours is invariably unpredictable. We also need to worry about the Mūrthi."

Mahisha chose his words carefully, "Your Highness, we Daityas have struggled and worked hard to achieve what we have. It is only befitting to reap its rewards now. Besides, it is not even a matter of rewards here; we are compelled to do whatever possible for securing our own survival. We all know that the Mūrthi wouldn't interfere at this juncture; all such human conflicts are likely to be seen as evolutionary processes in terms survival of the fittest. Moreover, there are severe limits beyond which the Mūrthi can't influence human affairs."

"Hmm. By the way, what is the progress on our Kayakalp project?"

"It is in final stages now. We are, however, having difficulty with the astral technology that is needed to develop it properly. Unfortunately we have lost the knowhow of such advanced Mūrthi science with time. In fact, access to such technologies must also be one of our negotiation terms with Devarth."

"Okay, let me think over your suggestions. This will also need to be discussed in the Asur Sabha," Tarakaksh stated in a sardonic tone. He knew that the turn of events were not moving in line with right Karma, but then again, these were desperate times.

"There is one more thing, Your Majesty. We have information that Devas might make a clandestine attempt to rescue Agastya and his wife."

Tarakaksh took a deep breath. He had been totally against the idea of forcefully holding Rishi Agastya and his wife captive in the first place. However, it was also true that their hope of being able to develop the Kayakalp process had improved substantially since their arrival.

"Do what you need to do to prevent it," Tarakaksh said, waving his hand carelessly.

7

AN EMPIRE IN CRISIS

Emperor Tarakaksh sat at the head of Asur Sabha with his brothers beside him. All the kings of various archipelago kingdoms of Daityan Empire were present there. As usual, the Asur Sabha was held on the highest citadel of Tripura. The hall where it was held was known to be a technological marvel. The members of the Sabha were seated around a three dimensional model of the Empire, Dev Lok and other nations. By clever use of the Mūrthi technologies, all participants could actually see the visual presentation of any event as they were discussed. The three crystalline walls surrounding the hall could morph into display units when required, especially for demonstrating military operations. The fourth side was covered with a transparent layer of photo-chromatic crystal, hugging the circular contours of the citadel. This provided a commanding view of the Atalantpuri city and the ocean surrounding it for hundreds of miles around.

The Asur Sabha had been called by the Emperor to discuss the repercussion of repeated natural disasters being reported from all around the Empire. Tarakaksh had also invited the Maya, the architect of all the mega engineering projects around the Empire and the primary advisor to the government on all scientific matters. The position of Maya was held by a member elected by the Asur Sabha on the basis of his merits and achievements. The current Maya was from the Rakshas clan and over the course of his past 150 ayanas of life, he had been the scientific advisor to two Daityan Emperors. He was highly respected by most within the ruling class for his achievements. However, he stayed away from politics and focused all attention on his field of responsibility with zest and commitment. Known to be a spiritual man and an ardent worshipper of the Mūrthi Lord Rudra, his personality reflected a calm and composed demeanour.

Tarakaksh looked at Maya and asked, "Asur Maya, are we in control to defend this threat from Mother Nature?"

Maya looked around at the Asur Sabha and replied, "Your Majesty, to be honest, I'm afraid we are steadily losing this battle."

"Are you saying that with all the technologies and resources at our disposal, we're unable to counter this crisis?"

"Your Majesty, it is not that we haven't applied our resources and technology. Any other nation in our place would've already collapsed under the impact of nature's fury of this magnitude. The trouble is that rising sea water is going to be a continuous phenomenon for many decades and perhaps even centuries in future."

The effect of global warming was most severe on the tropical island nations of the Empire. Over the past many centuries, Daityas had substantially extended the natural landmass of their archipelagos by reclaiming land from the surrounding reefs and lagoons. Such artificially-created terrain called *tala* provided the main landmass for farming all across the Empire. The low-laying nature of these farmlands also meant that they were generally more prone to inundation by rising levels of the sea. When faced with such problem, they had gone about controlling the situation in a classic manner—by direct intervention through mega engineering projects. Daityan architect and scientist Maya's team had been busy with multiple projects like building stone and metal embankments, walls and canals to keep the land cultivable and safe for human habitation. However, steadily but surely, nature seemed to be winning the battle.

"Have we been able to find any solution to resolve the declining production of food?"

Maya was quiet for a while, apparently considering his response before giving words to it, "Your Majesty, as you are aware, most of our food comes from the lush grain fields on the Talas within and around our tropical islands. The oceans have also been providing us with abundant sea food. Apart from this, animals reared in farms and hunted from the forests have also supplemented the diet of Daityan citizens. Not just one, but all these reliable sources of food have been impacted due to global warming."

"Why should the availability of sea food be impacted? With the rising sea level, surely the size of the oceans is only increasing?" Tarakaksh was curious.

"That may be so. However, strangely the rise of sea water seems to have affected the ocean currents which are the lifeline for fish. The changes in the temperature have also modified the type of fish population around the world. Anyway, the fact is that we are noticing substantial reduction in the catch of sea food. Our fishing boats have to go farther and farther into the ocean to catch enough quantity of fish. The turbulent ocean condition and the frequent storms are not helping either. Ironically, the rising sea water levels have increased our dependency on grain and other land-based food," Maya replied.

"What about animal-rearing and wildlife?"

"Your Majesty, Daityan weakness for the taste of meat is actually a problem rather than a solution. Large portions of our grain are actually used up as feedstock for animals being reared for their meat. We've tried to control this but it is also a sociological issue. Daityans love their meat to such an extent that they're prepared to fight for it even under situations of extreme scarcity. The rich and wealthy want to ensure that their dinner table is never without fresh meat. So the grain that could've fed large populations is proving to be insufficient. As regards wild life, which is a priced delicacy for most, we've more or less hunted them to extinction from our island jungles. Same is the case with the mainland forests under our control."

"So what is the solution?"

"The obvious solution is to acquire farmlands that are not likely to get impacted by the rise of sea levels. This means that we may need to eventually migrate to mainland terrain," Maya replied carefully.

"Are you saying we need to abandon the entire infrastructure that we've built here over centuries, and move like refugees to restart life in the land of *pishachas* and barbarians?"

"It wouldn't be all that bad, Your Majesty. We have enough knowhow and resources to be able to make such a migration as smooth as possible. I've identified many river basins within mainland forests under our control that are suitable for rebuilding our way of life. The ice-cover on the surface of the planet is receding fast. This means that more and more land is getting exposed to sunlight and getting warmed up. Over the next few decades, there should be more than sufficient landmass at our disposal. Wildlife would naturally propagate, improving our meat supply. We're also attempting to start agricultural activity in places suitable for it on the mainland," Maya explained.

In fact, to compensate for the loss of island landmass, Maya's men had already started creating farmlands on some of the wild continental landmass under Daityan control. However, it would take them quite a while to clear jungles, fertilise the soil, make irrigation arrangement, control pests and wild animals, etc., before steady supply of food could be expected. This may take years of effort. So, inspite of all the resources at their disposal, the rate at which new farmlands could be created was substantially lesser than the rate at which it was being lost. Redeployment of resources for creation of new habitation centres also meant lesser attention towards controlling the urgent problem of inundation. Eventually, the net outcome was that they were losing cultivable fertile land at a steady rate. They had even attempted to increase the production within the remaining available land by way of industrialised farming processes. But when the environmental conditions changed at such a rapid rate, it was extremely difficult to keep pace.

"Is it going to be sufficient to feed the Daityan population?" Tarakaksh asked.

"My calculations say that we can create farmlands to cultivate just about sufficient food on mainland before the inundations starts affecting our supply from the islands and the oceans Seriously. This is, of course, assuming that we don't continue to use the grain as feedstock for meat production," Maya replied, addressing all within Asur Sabha.

Mahisha, the king of Patala and Daityan chief of security intervened, "We have serious doubts about your calculations, Asur Maya. I've also got some estimates made in my kingdom which say that the new farmlands are not likely to be available on time. Besides this, there are many variables that are still unknown. How can we be sure this arrangement would work?"

"I wouldn't deny that Mahishasur. You're right that there are many factors which are not likely to be in our control. That makes an accurate estimate impossible," Maya admitted.

"In other words, if your estimates prove to be incorrect, which they might under the given circumstances, many Daityan citizens would starve. That would be catastrophic, not to speak of the instability it can create within the Empire," Mahisha retorted.

"Is Mahisha's concern legitimate, Asur Maya?" the Emperor asked.

"Your Majesty, we don't have enough data on how future events of global warming are going to unfold, so I can't deny his concerns. Incidentally, Patala being a low-land nation and most of its land having been reclaimed from sea over the course of the past century, it is going to be impacted the first and the worst. In fact, that is not the only problem. We've already noticed high levels of seismic activity throughout the Empire. If this gets accelerated, it is safe to assume that some of our island nations that were built around tectonic faultlines of the Earth's crust, may even suffer catastrophic consequences of earthquakes and volcanic eruptions."

There was a high murmur around the Asur Sabha as the kings of many affected island nations started asking questions.

"Quiet," the Emperor gestured with his right hand. The Asur Sabha soon became silent. Then he once again turned to Maya and asked, "How many nations are likely to be impacted by this new threat?"

"It is very difficult to predict accurately, but roughly fifty per cent of the islands within the Empire may get impacted."

"Your Majesty, I will not allow my kingdom to be reduced to destitution and food handouts if there is an alternative solution," an agitated Mahisha declared loudly.

"What is your suggested alternative solution, Mahisha?" the Emperor asked, even though he knew very well what the answer was likely to be.

"Your Majesty, the solution is clear and simple in front of us. We can easily tide over this crisis if Bhārat and other nations of Devarth were to share even half of their cultivable land with us," Mahisha replied.

"Do you think Devarth would simply hand over their land to us, thereby putting their own population under stress? We must not forget that they've also been affected by global warming. Even though the impact may be somewhat less, their situation is certainly not good enough to be able to willingly share their land with us, whatever offer we may make to compensate for it," the Emperor stated doubtfully.

"I didn't mean that we merely request them, Your Majesty. Today, Daityan armed forces are the strongest in the world. We don't need to go to anyone with a begging bowl," Mahisha responded without hesitation.

"That would mean war with not only Bhārat, but also Dev Lok and other kingdoms," Maya reminded.

"Yes, indeed, Asur Maya. Even you would compute that given the circumstance, the chances of victory and survival through war provides much better odds than continuing to combat sea and seeking refuge elsewhere," Mahisha stated sarcastically and then turned to look at the Emperor for his implicit concurrence.

"Go on," Tarakaksh encouraged.

"Let's also not forget the sociological impact. Widespread food scarcity would certainly cause a civil war within the Empire. This may lead to internal strife and fragmentation of our nation which may in any case be exploited by Devas, who're just waiting for an opportunity to subjugate us. On the other hand, war could actually unite our people as it would give them a common goal and enemy," Mahisha stated emphatically.

The Emperor rose from his seat, cleared his throat and addressed the Sabha in general, "Your point of views have merit, Mahishasur and Maya. However, the decision to go to war with Devarth is not an easy one. I need to examine all the options thoroughly. I would also like to give some more time to Maya to come up with an alternative solution that doesn't involve bloodshed. We will soon meet to discuss this again. By the way, is there any news of a supposed Bheeshma mission to rescue Rishi Agastya? Have we arrested these monks who dare to confront the Daityan security in our own backyard?"

"We have news that they are likely to arrive at Atalantpuri soon. I've arranged to get them taken into custody as soon as they land," replied Vidyunmali confidently.

Tarakaksh turned towards his youngest brother and said, "Good, Vidyun! The responsibility to ensure that they don't succeed is yours."

8

BHEESHMA MISSION

It was late at night and Hara was fast asleep when Acharya Parashu woke him up. "Hara, Dev Guru Brihaspati has requested for our company in his chamber."

The young official who'd been sent by Brihaspati seemed nervous and requested them to be as quiet as possible. Acharya Parashu was worried about this strange request, but coming as it was from Brihaspati, he surmised that it must be matter of extreme importance.

Hara dressed up quickly and followed the two through secondary gates at the periphery of the palace compound. It was quite dark with the moon having set at least a muhurta ago. Strangely, the artificial lights of this area in the city were also switched off. Was it deliberate? Even though it was almost pitch dark, there was some starlight and they could somehow manage to see the way ahead, even if barely so. The official took them to the outer walls of the palace towards the rear side of the Meru tower. Then they moved around the tower itself and reached the sea-facing side of the structure. Looking up, Hara noticed the imposing conical edifice of the tower. Soon, they reached a narrow pathway with regular steps that seemed to loop around the tower. Since there was no supportive railing, the official signalled them to keep close to the walls to avoid a fall.

After climbing up this path for a while, the official leading the way stopped suddenly. As Hara bent slightly forward to look down, he realised they had come up a few floors. The official kept his palm fully stretched against the tower fortification, closed his eyes and focused. Suddenly the wall caved inwards to reveal a much wider platform. At the far end of this platform was a door, faintly illuminated by the blue light emanating from the crystal interiors of the walls. The official walked in through the door without hesitation and asked Acharya Parashu and Hara to follow. It led them into a long tunnel. After some distance, there were steps leading down. The eerie blue light coming from within the crystal walls helped them find the way through the steps. Then one final door and suddenly they were inside a large and comfortable room. Hara assumed that they must now be somewhere deep inside the Meru tower structure.

Brihaspati was peering into some documents projected on the holographic crystal displays when they walked in. Hara immediately recognised the ancient Brahmic language. This lingual system was rarely used these days. The more popular language under use within Dev Lok was Sanskrit.

"Pranam, Dev Guru," Acharya Parashu bowed towards Brihaspati and Hara followed suit.

"Come, come, Acharya Parashu and Hara," he looked up at the two and greeted them. He looked at the young official who had brought them here. He took the signal, bowed and went outside the door. An unseen crystal block slid in and the door was closed.

"You must've surmised that the reason of summoning you here at the dead of the night is to discuss something extremely critical. What I'm going to say must never reach anyone other than you two. Do I have your Bheeshma word of assurance on this?"

"Yes, Dev Guru. You have my word," Acharya Parashu replied.

"Mine too," Hara added.

Brihaspati stroked his beard and said. "Thank you. As you might've already realised, the Devan way of life is in extreme danger. The downfall of Devas, if it were to happen, would have repercussions across the world." He looked into the eyes of Acharya Parashu and continued, "At the very least it can lead to complete domination of the Daityan way of life and this world may descent to become a perpetual zone of conflict between warring nations."

"Dev Guru, you know that we're on a secret Bheeshma mission. Is what you're telling us in any way related to this mission?" Acharya Parashu asked, worried as to what connection they had in this conflict between Devas and Daityas.

"You must know, Acharya, that everything in this universe is interconnected. The fabric of Karma is interwoven in so many ways. Your mission is extremely critical to the sequence of events that may unfold in the coming days."

Since Acharya Parashu remained silent, Brihaspati continued. "Acharya, as you are already aware, I've been a Bheeshma monk myself in the early years of my life. It has, however, been quite a while since I surrendered my Bheeshmatv. Now my karmic path is more in line with politics rather than direct action. I do keep close interaction with Maharishi Vashist, though. Your mission of rescuing Rishi Agastya and his wife is an extremely important one. In fact, the karmic chain of events that it can initiate may indeed be the only hope for Devarth and most of humanity. As we know for some time, a war seems inevitable. The rising sea water is not expected to abate anytime soon since we're at the end of the epoch of ice. This planet is going into a warm phase which means that soon many of the Daityan islands are likely to be inundated and their population driven towards starvation or immigration. The only way Tarakaksh can retain the integrity of his Empire is by capturing the farmlands of Dev Lok and other inland kingdoms. Their old enmity and mistrust against Devas would only hasten this event."

"Dev Guru, I'm sure Dev Lok wouldn't let itself be pushed over so simply? Surely they, along with other inland nations, have the capacity to face any threat from the Daityas?" Hara asked.

Brihaspati sighed and replied, "Hara, your confidence is characteristic of a Bheeshma monk and I uphold a similar belief. However, as a statesman, I also know the situation in more detail from a political perspective. As mentioned by Indra Dev at the Sabha, Devan civilisation is mainly based on constructive aspects of life. Most of the systems that we've built so far are not exactly designed to be used for aggression. Some of them can be used for warfare with additional modification—as in the past—but at their sub-optimal capacity. Devas have always managed to win wars by clever usage of their military, diplomatic as well as spiritual resources in outwitting the enemy. This was fine when our opponents were at best an equal match from military perspective. This time, however, the situation is very different. Daityas have achieved unprecedented technological superiority over the course of past few decades. In line with their aggressive nature, they also manufacture specialised weapon systems designed for warfare. If all these factors were not enough, the Daityan army today completely outnumber the Devarth defence forces by a numerical superiority of nearly ten to one. Daityas have comprehensive industrial infrastructure across their Empire that can sustain their war efforts almost indefinitely. Having a much larger population actually puts the balance of power for sustained war in their favour. In short, the situation is such that they may gain much more by going to war than by avoiding it. The Daityan Emperor Tarakaksh and his advisors are well aware of this. I feel that they're just waiting for an excuse."

Acharya Parashu said, "Dev Guru, we do understand the criticality of the situation. What can we do to help? As you know, we're soon scheduled to embark for the Daityan capital city of Atalantpuri to rescue Agastya Rishi and his wife."

Brihaspati looked at Acharya Parashu and smiled, "You're a man of action, Acharya. The help that I'm going to seek from you is more subtle. In return, I would provide you with all the necessary resources to succeed in this mission."

Acharya Parashu bowed gently and said, "It would be our honour to be of any assistance to your cause, Dev Guru. There is nothing hidden from you, and we would definitely need your support for this mission." Then after pausing for a while he continued with a question. "I'm also assuming that there is another matter associated with this mission, which is why you've summoned us in this manner?"

"Acharya, I have complete confidence in your capability and sincerity. For some time, I've been having a doubt that there is a mole within Indra Sabha. In fact, of late, I've been observing that Emperor Tarakaksh outmanoeuvres us on too many occasions for it to be a matter of coincidence alone. However, it is still not clear as to who is feeding him with all the sensitive information from Dev Lok."

Hara thought about Uma. Is she in some sort of danger because of all this internal turmoil within Dev Lok? Being the daughter of Indra should hopefully provide her with enough security? He then asked Brihaspati, "Dev Guru, do you doubt anyone?"

"I've been trying to find out, but in vain. This person has been extremely clever to guard his identity. So far he has successfully thwarted all my attempts to uncover his identity and intentions."

"Dev Guru, please pardon my ignorance but could you please enlighten me regarding the structure of Dev Lok government?" Hara asked. He was not sure whether it would be of any use, but if their mission to Atalantpuri has got something to do with Dev Lok, one might as well know about the parties involved in more detail.

"Of course, Hara. Dev Lok is a group of seven large islands namely Swarga Lok, Bhuvar Lok, Svar Lok, Mahar Lok, Jana Lok, Tapa Lok and Satya Lok. The population comprises primarily two ethnic groups called Vasus and Adityas. The main island is called the Swarga Dweep, within which the Devan capital city of Amaravati is located. The ruling system is based on a government that is elected once in around 100 ayanas and appointed by the Sapta-Rishis. If someone dies during this period, there is a process to replace him. All those holding positions can also be removed anytime by the Sapta-Rishis, provided there is plausible reason to do so."

Brihaspati stopped for some time to look into a display screen in front of him before continuing, "The Indra Sabha, which is the seat of Devan government, comprises mostly priestly ruling class. As you might know, all the titles like Indra, Brihaspati, Prajapati, Agni, Varun, Yama, Surya, etc., are actually appointed positions within the Sabha. There is no permanent individual with that name, although many hold these titles for their lifetime. Our individual personal names are insignificant and all are generally known by the position he/she holds. Indra is the head of the state of Dev Lok and also the supreme commander of the elite military force called the Maruth. The title Indra continues, even though the person holding it may change once in about a 100 ayanas. Brihaspati heads the advisory and diplomatic role; Prajapati is the administrative head of Dev Lok; Yama Dev is the head of our judicial system; Agni Dev heads the energy, industries, agriculture and trade; Varun Dev heads the navy and merchant shipping; and Vayu Dev the air force. Vishwakarma is the chief architect, engineer and scientist responsible for all building and manufacturing works. He heads all major engineering projects ranging from the civil works at Amaravati, combating sea erosion, etc., to building and retrofitting of vimāns and ships for warfare."

"Guru Dev, I assume you have no cause to suspect any one of them?"

"To the best of my understanding, all the members of Indra Sabha have impeccable integrity and have no reason to betray Dev Lok. Yet, it is a fact that state secrets that can only be privy to them, seem to be reaching Tripura."

"I'm sure you must've explored other means of acquiring information," Acharya Parashu asked.

"You mean technological or meditative ways? I've already employed all such means and found nothing. What I'm telling you now is not even known to Indra; he will be informed once I'm completely sure. Till then, even he remains part of my list of suspects," Brihaspati said with grave intensity clearly reflected in his words.

Acharya Parashu changed the subject and asked "Dev Guru, we're grateful for the trust that you've placed in us. Please enlighten us on what we must do to be of help."

"Of course, Acharya, I was coming to that. The full karmic purpose of your mission to Atalantpuri is still not completely clear to me. But I do feel that the answer to my worry may actually be available at the Daityan capital Atalantpuri. You must be alert to such information if it comes your way. It may also be an opportunity for you to understand the defence systems of Atalantpuri and its impregnable three-tiered fortress of Tripura."

"Dev Guru, your wish is our command. Please rest assured that we'll try our best to obtain whatever information we can gather to help you," Acharya Parashu assured.

"Thank you, Acharya. I have no doubt that your contribution will be remembered for a long time to come."

"When do you advise us to start?"

"You must leave tomorrow itself, as your prolonged stay at Amaravati can arouse suspicions. You must not share with anyone the destination that you are headed towards. Once you are there, you may contact Prahalad; he lives in the western part of the city. He is a Daityan citizen and son of Hiranyakashipu, who is one of the Generals within the inner circle of the Emperor's counsellors."

Acharya Parashu smiled when he said, "Dev Guru, it seems you too have some important informants within the Daityan Empire."

"It is my duty to keep an eye on all Daityan affairs. Prahalad is the worshipper of the Mūrthi Lord Vishnu, and he has assured me that he'll help you. He is aware that Agastya Rishi and his wife have been held captive by Tarakaksh and doesn't approve of it. However, he is not likely to betray his countrymen. Moreover, I am not sure how much information even his father Hiranyakashipu would have about Daityan plans."

"We will keep that in mind, Dev Guru. How do you suggest we travel?" Acharya Parashu asked.

Brihaspati thought for a moment before replying, "I've arranged for you to travel disguised as Gandharv merchants by a Devan ship that is sailing out of Amaravati tomorrow morning. The ship will take you to the Gandharv port of Kambhoj. There, you should find Amatya; he is the Captain of a trade ship headed for Atalantpuri. You should hopefully be able to reach Atalantpuri unnoticed within another week or so." He paused again and asked with finality, "Is there anything else you need from me?"

Acharya Parashu shook his head, but Hara said with slight hesitation, "Dev Guru, if it is not too much trouble, would you kindly inform Uma that I had to leave suddenly?"

Brihaspati looked at Hara for a while. He had been informed of the escapades of the young Bheeshma monk and Uma at Somvan. "Yes Hara. I'll inform her."

With these words, Brihaspati signalled with his hand and the young official who had courted them to the place returned to the chamber. He bowed at the old man and placed his palm on a different part of the wall around the crystal room. As he focused on it for a while, the crystal wall suddenly retreated to reveal another door. Acharya Parashu and Hara bid farewell to Brihaspati and followed the young official to reach a niche within the palace courtyard.

Back in the dimly-lit chamber, Brihaspati wondered whether he should further meditate on the new turn of events. Surely the fond relationship that had developed between Hara and Uma may have an important connection to the flow of Karma?.

༒ ༴ ༶

Hara was standing on the bow of the Devan merchant ship, enjoying the steady cool breeze from the sea. Acharya Parashu was on the bridge with the Captain of the ship. They had left Amaravati three days back. Hara's long hair had been tied in a ponytail to avoid recognition and he also sported a rather expensive looking turban and some jewellery. Brihaspati had also provided sufficient gold coins and some gemstones to help them in their mission. There are times when money can prove far more effective than skills and strength.

Hara was unhappy at not having been able to bid farewell to Uma. But he also knew that meeting her would have been against the interests of their mission. Their arrival at Amaravati had been conspicuous enough and there was no point is rousing additional suspicions from anyone. He hoped Uma would get his message and understand the reason for his hasty departure.

The ship in which they were sailing wasn't too big. It was mainly used to trade artefacts, documents, jewellery and medicine between Dev Lok and other Devarth kingdoms. As in case of most Devan technology, the hull of the ship was constructed out of live self-morphing crystals, bonded and encased at places by metal. The external structure was also covered with carved wood for enhancing the visual appeal. Like all transportation systems, the ship's main source of energy came from engines based on the Mūrthi technology. Some ships also used additional sources of energy like magnetic drive, solar power, wind power etc—all optimised to suite the environmental conditions. Few ships even had crystalline Anvik drives that could harness the energy of atoms to generate huge quantity of power when needed. However, such ships were mostly found with the navy. Similar to most Devan systems, micro-organisms had been co-opted to maintain the general integrity of ship, both above and below the water. Devan marine engineers were even known to employ dolphins and other fish species for various operations within the seas.

Hara turned around to see Acharya Parashu walk up to him, "Excellent view, isn't it?"

"Yes, Acharya," Hara agreed.

Acharya Parashu looked at Hara closely and said, "Hara, I'm aware of your feelings towards Uma. You'd need to take a decision on it once this mission is over. I just want you to know that I will support your decision, irrespective of what it is."

Hara looked up at Acharya and smiled before he replied, "Thank you, Acharya. But the truth is, I'm myself not sure what I must do. I dearly wish for the company of Uma. Yet first and foremost, I am a sworn Bheeshma."

"Sometimes it's better to follow our heart, Hara. You will know about your Karma when the right time comes."

"How do we know what is our Karma, Acharya? Even if we do, isn't it within our power to alter it?" Hara asked.

"By knowing our own nature, Hara; our Karma is a reflection of that very nature. Our nature is nothing but the habits, beliefs and tendencies that we've built-up within us, based on past experiences," Acharya Parashu explained.

Hara looked intrigued and wondered, "If we've ourselves been responsible for this nature and if it is this nature that defines our Karma, then we should be in a position to control it, too."

"The difficulty is often not that we don't know we are responsible for our Karma. It is that we get so involved in it that our reaction on what should be done about a particular situation is coloured by our nature. So our perspective of the Karma itself could be flawed."

"If we're unable to have the correct perspective of Karma, how can we ever hope to correct it?" Hara asked doubtfully.

"That is the fundamental problem of life for most humans. In order to get the correct perspective of everything, including our Karma, we need to be able to look at ourselves from a witness's perspective. This is easier said than done. We're like machines, programmed to follow our inner urges which are nothing but our innate nature. To understand this programme, we need to try and stop being like a machine. This is what we attempt to do through meditation."

"Yes, Acharya. It must be somewhat like the manner we Bheeshma monks evoke Jwalaprabha," Hara said.

"Our Jwalaprabha is a manifestation of the connection with our primary self or consciousness. With sufficient training, we're able to establish a direct link with our kundalini channel—the route towards the source of all manifested energy within the universal consciousness—and then channelise it into action. However, you must remember that this action is also defined by our Karma."

"But Acharya, you just mentioned that we can conceptualise the nature of our Karma by being a witness to our own self?"

Acharya Parashu looked at the lone, low cloud hovering over the horizon and wondered if it would rain again. Ever since global warming had changed ocean currents, precipitation and rain was very frequent around the tropics. "Indeed, Hara. But conceptualise is perhaps the wrong word. Conceptualisation happens within the realm of thought, which in turn are themselves based on our nature. So it is an incorrect tool to examine ourselves. We need to take one step back and transcend into a thoughtless, yet aware state. Remember, not to get confused between awareness and thoughts. For most people, the act of thinking defines the evidence of consciousness. This is a fundamental flaw. Thinking is the action of the consciousness based on the nature of the thinker. It may be the proof of existent consciousness, but being a product, it can never examine its origin. At best we can analyse the nature of the thinker; but such deductions could also be flawed and inaccurate."

"But then how does one get out of this cycle?"

"It is possible by focusing on pure awareness alone, in a state of total thoughtlessness. When the Maharishis reach this state, they can observe themselves through awareness, unaided by thoughts or conceptualisation."

"Are you saying that we would innately know our Karma when it is needed?"

"Yes, Hara. But you have to remember that it must come from your true consciousness, not corrupted by reasoning, conceptualisation, thinking, etc. A yogi who lives in the *now*, the present moment alone, is not disturbed by concepts of past or future. After all, past and future are nothing but conceptualisation within the mind-sphere and are virtually built, based on the template of our memories. If we don't conceptualise, there would be no thoughts of the fruit or fears of our actions to influence our actions in the present. Our action would then be pure and for universal benefit, not corrupted by the habits, tendencies and resultant aspirations of our personal ego." It had started drizzling so they decided to get back into the cabin of the ship.

9

FRONTIER TOWN OF KAMBHOJ

The port town of Kambhoj on the Gandharv coast was a busy place. Being located at a geographically central spot between major sea-faring nations, it was ideal for trade. The favourable tax regime and general atmosphere of free trade prevalent in Gandharv kingdom also made it an attractive point of business for multiple shipping companies. Even though Gandharv was part of the Devarth group of nations, the town encouraged active business with both Devan and Daityan sides, which was one of the reasons for its prosperity.

Apart from a small farming and fishing community living adjacent to it, the town was mostly sustained by the shipping trade. Like any frontier port town, it was a cauldron of multiple cultures. The street was abuzz with people from various racial lineages and traditions, and one could hear many languages being spoken at the same time. The cuisines served in the restaurants also reflected the blend of various tastes. Since the growth of the town had never been properly planned, the overall infrastructure was pretty rustic, with no particular design or pattern to boast of. The streets were narrow and the buildings mostly made of stone and wood. The only large buildings were the warehouses used by various shipping companies to conduct trade between multiple nations.

It was already well into the afternoon when Acharya Parashu and Hara disembarked from the Devan merchant ship at the Kambhoj port. The captain bid them farewell and left them on their own. They needed to look for Captain Amatya, but making a direct beeline towards him would be a mistake. They were, after all, impersonating jewel merchants and first needed to conduct some trade. Acharya Parashu had been to this town before. He led the way to a jewel trader to sell some of the gems that they had carried from Amaravati.

The trader was a short, rotund man with a pudgy nose and a huge turban covering his balding pate. His overzealous attitude made it obvious that he was making unreasonable profits from two naïve merchants. Acharya Parashu ignored it as it gave him an opportunity to ask for his payment in Daityan currency.

"I hope to travel to Atalantpuri on another trading trip. Having Daityan currency with me would be most useful. I heard the Daityan toys are in great demand these days within the inland nations?" Acharya Parashu asked, as if answering the inquisitive eyes of the trader.

The trader smiled back, "Yes, Shreeman. Not just that, people these days are crazy about anything produced in Atalantpuri. It seems there are even Yantraksh out there who can manufacture products round the clock. I'm told these artificially made men don't need to sleep and can work continuously. Of late, however, there has been some scarcity of these goods." He stopped abruptly and looked around to ensure no one was listening, and continued in a low volume, "People say that the complete manufacturing industry within Atalantpuri is now focused on producing military ware."

Acharya Parashu feigned surprise and asked him with concern in his voice, "Are they preparing for some war?"

"Don't you know that there is an impending war between Daityas and Devas?" the trader said with great pride, mocking the ignorance of these two naïve traders.

"I heard about it, too, Sreeman! But couldn't believe my ears. And if the war does happen, who do you think is going to win? You know, we traders prefer to be on the winning side," Acharya Parashu asked in the characteristic tone of a merchant.

"Daityas, without doubt." The trader seemed totally convinced. "The Empire is far stronger than Dev Lok and all other kingdoms put together. Their army is many times bigger. Daityas are also technologically much superior. They are certain to win."

"In that case, we better be on their side when war breaks out," Acharya Parashu said smiling, before getting up and adding, "We need to find some place to sleep. Can you recommend any?"

"You'll find a *nidragrah* at around two kroshas from here down the street towards the west," the trader stretched his hand in the direction of the place. Just as Acharya Parashu and Haŕa got up to leave, he warned them in a low voice, "Be careful on the road; there are *pisachas* on the way, ready to rob men anytime."

Acharya Parashu had heard about the thieves and dacoits called pisachas who would waylay any prosperous-looking merchant, given an opportunity. This was a menace in many frontier towns where local law was slack at best. Most merchants, therefore, moved around with their own personal security guards.

As the sun had already set and the daylight was fading fast, Acharya Parashu and Haŕa decided to walk directly towards the nidragrah. Less than half a krosha along the narrow lane, they saw few tough looking armed men approaching from the front. The way their looks were focused on the Bheeshma duo, it was clear that they were the targets. Haŕa turned around to notice another similar party coming from behind them. It did not take him long to make out that these were the pisachas that the trader had warned them about and they were laying a trap against the two merchants, foolish enough to move around without bodyguards. Haŕa's hand automatically moved to the hilt of his Spatishūl but Acharya Parashu stopped him, "No Haŕa! we're in disguise; we'll need to get out of this situation like any other ordinary merchant. No one must know that we are Bheeshma."

The pisachas stopped in front of the monks. An ugly looking guy with a huge frame, who seemed to be leader, walked up to them and said, "Traders, we have you surrounded with at least nine men. There is no way to escape. We'll let you go, provided you hand over all your possessions."

Acharya Parashu looked at the eyes of the pisacha leader and said calmly, "We are merchants from Atalantpuri and our bodyguards are following us. They carry pulse-ray weapons. I suggest you let us pass unless you don't value your lives."

The pisacha leader sneered, "You think I would fall far that? We know you're not from Atalantpuri or Gandharv. Your accent gives you away clearly. We've also made sure to check that you don't have any bodyguards. I'll not give you another warning. If you delay any further, be sure to lose your lives as well as property."

Life was too cheap in these lawless towns and it really made no difference to these pisachas if they were to kill a couple of hapless merchants. Acharya Parashu and Haŕa braced themselves to defend against an imminent attack. Acharya Parashu hoped that if he could bring down the leader, others would perhaps hesitate.

"Leave these traders alone pisacha; unless you wish this to be your last day," the booming yet commanding voice came from the balcony of the building on their right side.

The leader looked shaken; he turned towards the sound just in time to see a huge man in a ship Captain's attire walking down the stairs. He was followed by at least 15 fully armed sailors.

The tone of the pisacha leader changed completely when he said, "Captain Amatya Rakshas? We didn't know these traders were your friends. We would've never dared harass them if we knew."

"You better scoot fast along with your pack, before I make you shove that blunt thing in your hand up your—you know where," Captain Amatya warned, with obvious mirth.

The *pisacha* leader got the message loud and clear. He signalled his companions and they slowly retreated into the gathering shadows on the street.

"Welcome to Kambhoj, traders. I can see that you've already started liking this town," he laughed as he folded his hands to greet them with a Namastute.

Acharya Parashu noted that Amatya had not addressed them as Bheeshma, which either meant that he didn't know about them or was pretending. Acharya Parashu thought it best to continue with their cover. "It is a relief to meet to you, Captain Amatya, and more so for your coming in at the right time. We're grateful to you for saving us from this tight spot," he gestured at the fast-retreating pisacha gang.

"These pisacha vermin have spoiled the town. Someone needs to send them packing back to the tribes where they've come from," Amatya cursed with apparent distaste and continued, "Good thing we could meet up, though. I've been expecting your arrival for quite a while. Now that we've met, your safety is my concern. The ship is scheduled to set sail tomorrow morning and so we'll spend the night within its quarters. Then turning to one of his sailors, he ordered, "Go tell that incompetent cook of ours that unless our guests appreciate what he prepares, I'll have him thrown out into the sea."

⊤ Ш ⚲

The ship that they were sailing now was very different from the one that got them from Amaravati to Kambhoj. This was an old, rustic and large merchant liner made at the shipyards of Patala, the industrial island complex of the Daityan Empire. It was a conventional ship and most of the energy needed for the power plant came from burning coal and wood. Because of this, chimneys above the ships spewed hot smoke into the sky continuously. The structure of the ship itself was big and grand. Its hull was mostly made of metals. As in case of almost all Daityan-made ships, although a lot of systems were automated, they needed continuous maintenance resulting in many crew members on board. This ship also contained a huge holding space for storage of minerals and other goods.

In fact, such ships were in common use for the prolific trade that happened between various nations. Works of art, minerals and medicinal products were one of the main exports from Gandharv to Daityan Empire. The Yaksha and Kinnara kingdoms also had their unique niche and traded extensively with Devas and Daityas. Yakshas were especially known for their gold, diamonds and other precious gems, making their kingdom one of the richest within Devarth. On the other hand, Bhārat kingdom's main export was mostly grain and other farm products. In return, Daityan Empire exported heavy duty manufactured items ranging from mechanical transport, ships, vimāns and armaments to building materials, toys and household appliances. Daityan-manufactured items were relatively inexpensive and easy to operate, making them highly popular.

Devas also exported items that they specialised in, like high-tech visual and audio communication technology products, entertainment systems, special medicines and aphrodisiacs, hallucinogen drugs and, above all, the most popular intoxicating beverage—somras. In fact, somras was in such great demand across the civilised nations that it had become one of the major exports from Dev Lok. Devas also had virtual monopoly in the fields of education and spirituality. Free trade existed between most nations for almost all goods except the ones that related to Mūrthi technologies, which were under direct supervision of the ruling regimes and elite priests. Recently, however, food-grains had also become a highly restricted commodity and were controlled directly by the governments.

The ship was expected to take a week or so to reach the famed city of Atalantpuri. It had been raining for the past two days and the sea was very rough throughout the journey, making the navigation difficult. The crew members were fully engaged in keeping the course and speed of the ship. Meanwhile, the Bheeshma duo attempted to interact with the crew and learn as much as possible about the city they were visiting for the very first time. They spent their evenings in the company of Captain Amatya.

"This infernal weather! It has never been so bad. Ocean journeys are getting rougher by the day. They say global warming is the main reason," Captain Amatya swore at his bad luck.

With consistently turbulent conditions in the seas, life was getting increasingly difficult for all those involved in shipping business and Amatya didn't seem too pleased with the turn of events. Even though nearing middle age, he was quite agile and active. The intelligent, piercing eyes under his bushy brows, and the slightly greying beard covering a strong jaw-line, accentuated a sense of implicit authority. Like other men from the Rakshas clan, he was tall, with a muscular and strong body structure. Even though some found it somewhat intimidating to be in his overwhelming presence, most of his crew adored his honest and straight-forward, yet affectionate nature. He had an easy sense of humour and those who came to know him closely found it quite pleasant to be in his jovial company. Apart from being able to actively participate in discussions on almost any subject, he was also considered to be a quite a connoisseur of art and beauty.

"What do you think is the reason behind global warming, Captain?" Hara asked, initiating a conversation.

"Oh, I'm not sure. A few scientists claim that this is part of a cyclical process. For a long period of time, we've had major portions of the Earth covered with ice. The tropics had the most salubrious climatic conditions and best cultivable land. I suppose that is one of the reasons why the Devan and Daityan civilisations developed on the major island groups at the tropics. Now all that is set to change."

"So, global warming may be bad news for both Devas and Daityas who occupy the tropical islands. It may, however, be good for those who occupy areas with less pleasant climatic conditions like Bhārat and other continental nations," Hafa said, wanting to know more from the Captain.

"It seems so. But it would be a long time before they get the full benefits of the warmer climate. You see, fertile farmlands are required for sizable human habitation. The receding ice-line may expose more and more soil, but it might not be cultivable straight away. Such raw soil needs to go through few generations of wild growth before they have enough organic materials necessary to support cultivation. Over the course of next hundred ayanas or so, we may actually have more farmlands at these regions that are currently too cold to support plants and grasslands. Unfortunately, by then the tropical islands that we depend on now may get completely inundated and submerged under the rising sea. The changes are happening too rapidly for most humans to adapt to them. So, the net outcome is still unpredictable." Amatya explained.

"Does this mean that Devan and Daityan nations based on tropical islands are going to steadily lose land, whereas the nations on mainland are going to gain?" Hafa asked, admiring the scientific perception and knowledge of the Captain.

"Yes, looks like that. To compound the trouble, there may also be some tectonic activity leading to earthquakes and volcanic eruptions. Such reports have already come in from various regions on earth."

After a pause, he continued, "This is bad news, particularly for the Daityan Empire. You see, Daityas have actually built many cities along the subterranean fault-lines that must have encouraged the very formation of their tropical islands eons ago. In fact, their engineers have even been able to exploit the geothermal activities on these islands to their benefit. Today, many of the cities around the Empire draw thermal power from the geothermal vents below the islands where they are located. Patala industrial complex is a case in point."

"So, Daityas seem to be affected the most under the impact of global warming," Hara stated.

"Yes. That is why there are fears of an armed conflict between nations. After such a long period of stability, now we have a situation of unprecedented scarcity and strife. In such times, it is natural for powerful nations to start eyeing the bounty of their neighbours."

They had moved into the Captain's private quarters now. Amatya smiled, "My dear Bheeshma monks, when you're with me alone, you can stop pretending to be merchants."

Acharya Parashu's doubts were confirmed that the ship Captain knew their real identity all along. Anyway, this was to be expected since Brihaspati himself had recommended him. What he was not able to fathom was the reason why a member of Rakshas clan was helping Devas?

"Please accept our apologies, Amatya. I'm Parashu and this is Hara. We were not sure whether you knew about our true identity. As you are aware, we are Bheeshma monks and have a mission to take care of at Atalantpuri," Acharya Parashu said, hoping that he would continue to get cooperation from the Captain.

Amatya looked at them and smiled, "I know all about your mission, Sir, and it would be my pleasure to help you undertake it. I am sure you must be wondering as to why a Rakshas is helping what is essentially a mission against his own country?"

"You're frank and straight-forward, Amatya! I like that in a man and we would also prefer to deal with you similarly. To be honest, the thought did cross my mind," Acharya Parashu replied.

Amatya took a deep breath before saying, "I'm a true Rakshas and I love my country. Unfortunately, Daityan Empire is not what it used to be. Those in power now are only interested in self-aggrandising themselves with pursuit of material wealth and pleasure. The condition of the citizens has been steadily declining. During my younger days, I used to take pride in the fact that we had an ideal combination of spiritually and material progression. Daityan Empire had both wealth as well as knowledge, our Maharishis possessing direct astral blessings from the Mūrthi Lords. Most of our past Emperors were worshippers of the great Mūrthi Lord Rudra. It is also during that glorious period that Tripura was constructed as the crowning glory of Atalantpuri." He looked down and continued with gravity in his voice, "Now however, the ruling class of the Empire are only intersted in pursuit of power and material pleasures."

"It is indeed sad to hear about the deterioration of a glorious civilisation. What do you think is the cause for this change?" Acharya Parashu asked.

"Acharya, I admire your sense of empathy for Daityas, but it is not easy for me to answer that question. The deterioration has happened slowly, over a period of time. The current Emperor Tarakaksh has come under the bad influence of power worshippers. One of his chief aides is a wily character called Mahisha, who is the worst of them. Tarakaksh's brothers—Kamalaksh and Vidyunmali—have also been steadily becoming power hungry and morally corrupt. They've all moved away from the spiritual foundation on which this Empire grew and prospered."

"What about their recent scientific achievements? I've heard the current Maya is a skilful scientist and architect?" asked Hara.

"Yes, Hara. The current Maya is still active within his domain. I'm told he is a spiritual man and also an ardent worshipper of the Mūrthi Lord Rudra. However, he does not hold much influence over the affairs of the state anymore."

"Just to confirm, is Maya also involved in the project of developing Kayakalp process?"

"Indeed, he is. I'm told they have already completed construction of the Kayakalp rejuvenation and treatment centre within Tripura where even severely deteriorated bodies can be brought back to life. But the final process is still under development."

"Much has been said and heard about the fortress of Tripura and the layers of its defences. Was it constructed using Mūrthi technology?" Hara asked.

Amatya looked at Hara intently and said, "Not entirely. Adi-Maya, who built the citadels, actually improved upon it with many indigenous innovations of his own. However, he built it with direct astral blessings from the Mūrthi Lord Brahma. In many ways, Tripura is similar to the Dev Lok; its foundation is crystalline and reinforced with metal. The structure was built using such materials that no weapon system known to man can destroy it with ease. When necessary, all three citadels can project separate powerful defensive force-field shields around themselves. Tripura marks the centre of gravity of Daityan military might."

"Amatya, I am amazed at your knowledge and insights. They are far superior to what can be expected from any average goods ship Captain," Acharya Parashu stated admiringly.

Amatya's expression was sombre as he said, "I've not always been a goods ship Captain. Not too long ago, I used to be one of the most honourable Admirals of the Daityan navy." Acharya Parashu could feel the pain in Amatya's words as he continued, "But then there was one time when I was given direct orders by Mahisha himself to massacre the inhabitants of an entire Rakshas island who had dared to protest against the blatant industrialisation of their homeland. I could gather that the islanders were not at fault but Mahisha wanted to teach all rebellious island groups a lesson. Since I did not see much good in this violent action, instead of exterminating them, I got them moved to another friendly island. This infuriated Mahisha, who advised the Emperor to strip me of all my titles, wealth and family honour. My elder son was sent to work in one of the dangerous industrial operations, while I was imprisoned for three years. While in custody, I learnt of the accident in which my son was killed." Tears welled up in Amatya's eyes when he narrated his painful past.

Acharya Parashu came up and put his hand over Amatya's shoulders, "I can feel the pain you suffer, my friend."

Amatya wiped his moist eyes and touched Acharya's hand, "Even though I know well that Mahisha was directly responsible for my fate, the orders came from the royal house of Tarak. After this incident, I could not bear to live in Atalantpuri and left with my wife and younger son to settle at the Gandharv city of Lonar. There, I took up this new profession as a merchant ship captain. I am sure this also clarifies your doubt as to why I'm supporting a Bheeshma rescue mission. I was unable to save my son but if I can help save another family, it would take a little burden off my chest."

"Amatya, I know that your pain is inconsolable. But we hope that your karmic path eventually leads you to happiness and peace." Acharya Parashu tried to assuage him as best as he could. Then changing the subject, he said, "You said Daityas used to be a spiritually advanced nation. Then how did this change come about?"

"I have spent a long time trying to figure out the complete cause, Acharya. I do, however, feel that this has a lot to do with a new religious practice that seems to have caught the attention of Daityan citizens in general, and the royalty in particular. It is being propagated by a new sect headed by a self-proclaimed prophet called Moyisur. He is said to know many dark skills of sorcery and can perform visible miracles, the most notable being that of reviving the dead. He propagates a virulent and fundamentalist form of religion that rejects all association with the Mūrthi or spirituality in general. This religion actually promotes selfish accumulation of material wealth and pursuit of pleasure during life the prospects of similar gains after death. Death, intolerance and aggression to inflict pain and suffering on fellow humans are glorified while compassion and love are looked down upon as weaknesses. They expect complete faith and loyalty of the followers towards their cause and even encourage them to commit acts of terror to propitiate their imaginary god. At the same time, they are also propagating ideas of a society based on narrow-minded perspectives, draconian rules, hatred, intolerance, whimsical retributions, acts of cruelty, slavery, subjugation of the weaker sex, etc."

Acharya Parashu was perplexed at this revelation, "But I don't get it, Amatya. If this new religion brings so much suffering, why are people following it?"

"That is one question for which I have no answer too, Acharya. The motivations of true human nature are still a mystery to me. I surmise that the answer has got to do with the present turbulent times. When people face extreme difficulties in all aspects of their life, some tend to seek shortcuts—even if it is seems immoral. The factors that define the morality of an idea can change, to be replaced with convenient self-possessive ones. In general, I feel people are less interested in the difficult path of spirituality to seek distant results. They've become more and more short-sighted and measure their happiness in terms of instant pleasure, material gratification, etc. This only makes things worse as they get entangled in the web of karmic cause and effect which keeps feeding on itself. Very soon, greed, hate and desire will supersede the feelings of love and compassion, which only makes things worse."

"It doesn't seem like a pretty situation within the Daityan Empire," Haŕa remarked.

"That is true, Haŕa. I can't say I'm very proud of being a Rakshas anymore. But not everything is as bad as I've stated. There are still many decent, fair, honest, hard working and spiritually enlightened people in the Daityan society. All hope, I guess, is not lost."

10

CITADELS OF TRIPURA

The most prominent feature of the Daityan Empire that could be seen by all travellers as they approached Atalantpuri was the fortress of Tripura with its three 'revolving' citadels. The illusion of perpetual revolution, created by light reflecting from the force-field shields around individual citadels, was complete. Almost inevitably, anyone approaching Atalantpuri from the sea or air were mesmerised by the captivating sight of Tripura. Acharya Parashu and Hara were no exception. They were standing near the bow of the ship as it approached the city harbour. The rains had stopped over the last two days and it was bright and sunny with clear skies.

Amatya had explained to them the overall structure of the capital city of Daityan Empire the previous evening. The archipelago of Atala was one of the major land masses within the mainstream Daityan nations and 'Atala-ant-puri' literally meant the 'city at the end of Atala'. The main island within this archipelago was called 'sweta dweep', or the 'white island' due to the characteristic white colour of limestone-based mountains, marble constructions and beaches surrounding it. The multiple reefs that surrounded the harbour city broke up the waves, the frothy reefs also famously known as the 'milky seas', further reinforcing the image of the 'white island'. The harbour city jutted out of the island like a tongue, with rocky outcroppings projecting to the ocean. The main harbour had been virtually carved out on all the three sides of this limestone based outcropping. In fact the architects who built Atalantpuri had also worked on the reefs such that they were now in the form of roughly three concentric circles, around the city. The reefs protected the main harbour from the rough, direct waves of the ocean. The unique structure of these reefs not only created an ideal lagoon around the main harbour but also contributed to its water being flushed out regularly by the ocean currents and tides. It was a recent concern that the rising sea water would soon submerge these reefs and endanger the safety of the harbour. One of the major projects of Maya, the chief architect of the Empire, was to prevent this.

A huge rocky mountain, almost 900 dhanus high, jutted upwards, right from the middle of the city of Atalantpuri. The dense, limestone-based mountain was nearly rounded on every side and had a pillar-like shape with a cross section of nearly half krosha. With clouds hovering around the top almost throughout the year, it was very difficult to see its summit from the city of Atalantpuri at its foot. Adi-Maya had built Tripura citadels on this very mountain because of which the whole feature was sometimes called the Tripura. Many Atalantians had come to call it 'the pillar of heaven', 'Atlas' etc. Being the royal palace, military command centre and administrative headquarters, Tripura was indeed the centre of power within the whole Empire and adorned it like a crown. The three citadels together made such a commanding presence that Tripura looked like the very crown of the Daityan Empire.

For anyone looking at them from ground, sea or air, the reflection of light from the three independent force-field shields around Tripura seemed to shimmer in concentric patterns. This was the reason for the strange illusion that the three circular citadels seemed to be in perpetual motion in relation to each other. In fact, the invisible outer force-field shields of each citadel were powered separately, such that even if one, shield breaks down, others could compensate till the damaged one is restored. The fortress was designed in such a way that it would be impossible to destroy the citadels unless a single weapon could break through all the three force-field shields simultaneously.

The three circular citadels, stacked one on top of the other, demonstrated the very best in Daityan technological advancements. Adi-Maya had built the fortress to last for ages, making liberal use of both Mūrthi technologies and indigenous innovations. The citadels were powered by multiple Anvik generators housed deep within the mountain. Each citadel was designed as a completely independent military platform with full array of projectile as well as radiation weapons to defend it. All three citadels also had several decks of combat vimāns on standby to fly out at short notice. Long range missile launchers plus projectile and pulse-ray guns were positioned around all the three citadels. These missiles and guns could easily destroy any approaching vimān or ship within minutes of it being detected. During the past wars between the Empire and Dev Lok, Daityas had used Tripura as an effective and impregnable command and control centre. All the attempts by Dev Lok to destroy Tripura had failed miserably.

Tripura was completely self-contained. There were nine high speed anti-grav levitation based elevator systems that linked the citadels with each other as well as the city of Atalantpuri far below. All necessary supplies were either brought up from the base station located at the bottom of the mountain complex or directly flown in through vimāns. Even so, with sufficient provision to stock water and food, the fortress was designed to last on its own for several months.

As they got down from the ship, it became obvious to Acharya Parashu and Hařa that Atalantpuri was unlike any other place in the world. Some of the buildings were architectural wonders within the known world. It was obvious to any visitor that the city was ages ahead in terms of sophistication of infrastructure and technology. To Hara, the city seemed like a total opposite to the kind of chaos they had experienced at the Gandharv port of Kambhoj. The complete harbour had been organised to sustain high levels of commercial shipping traffic. As soon as the ship sailed in, the custom officials from the harbour inspected their goods, checked credentials of the ship and passed on responsibility to the operations team. The ship's goods were then moved off to a warehouse nearby and the Captain was given a bronze token to identify them. Unique use of technology could be seen in all aspects of operations. The officials used audio and video systems that seemed like magic to outsiders. No wonder many newcomers ascribed such high grade technology as sorcery of the Rakshas, the aristocratic clan of the Daityan Empire.

Most of the heavy duty work was done by machines and was supervised by men. What caught Acharya Parashu's and Hara's attention were the famous artificially created men of Atalantpuri — Yantraksh. The size and characteristics of these genetically engineered creatures depended on their application. They were used in all aspects of life, ranging from construction to warfare. It is said that the original process for creating Yantraksh was invented by the Adi-Maya. Later generations gradually increased its sophistication and variations. One of the main advantages of Yantraksh was that they didn't need to sleep at all and could work almost continuously. In general, one Yantraksh was considered equivalent to at least ten humans in terms of productivity.

The crew were still taking in the fantastic view of the city and the Tripura citadels towering over it when Amatya came up to them with strange urgency and said, "It is time for us to leave the harbour." He then turned to Acharya Parashu and Hara and whispered, "There is heightened level of security across all Atalantian harbours and ports. It seems they have royal orders to arrest anyone suspicious."

Hara was tense as they moved up to the harbour check point set up by the royal guards. He could feel the Jwalaprabha welling up inside him as it usually does before an impending danger.

This time, however, he focused on it to maintain the meditative stillness of mind. He remembered Acharya Parashu's words, "A yogi must have control over his mind. Great powers are made available to only those who have the capability to control them. If a Bheeshma warrior can use the explosive energy at his disposal in the form of Jwalaprabha, he must also be able to get into a state of *Stithapragya* to remain extremely calm."

There were two Rakshas priests at the royal check post who examined or questioned each visitor to the city. They also had a few assistants who entered the data and maintained records. There were many soldiers scattered around, including two that seemed like the Yantraksh guards.

"Where are you from, Shreeman Tamvuru?" The senior Rakshas priest asked, looking at Acharya Parashu. Tamvuru and Ativahu were the Gandharvan proxy names of Parashu and Hara recorded on Amatya's ship logs.

"Sir, we are humble merchants from Gandharv. We've brought with us some unique gems which we hope to trade for the popular toys manufactured in Atalantpuri," Acharya Parashu replied with a polite smile.

"You don't look like merchants. Please step aside so that we can check your records in detail," the Rakshas priest said eyeing Acharya suspiciously.

The experienced priest had good reasons to be suspicious. Even though dressed like merchants, the gait and athletic body structure of the Bheeshma monks hardly fitted the profile of any merchant that he had seen.

"These merchants are with me, sir," Amatya added from behind.

The official bent to his side and looked at Amatya for a while, and said, "We are only doing our job, Captain Amatya Rakshas. You know we couldn't be more careful in these troubled times."

"You're right! But Tamvuru is an old friend from my navy days. Like me, he is also a retired sailor. Ativahu is his son. This is their first visit to Atalantpuri. Apart from business, I was hoping to give them a memorable tour around the city and show them the hospitality of my Rakshas friends," Amatya smiled while continuing to look straight into the eyes of the priest.

The Rakshas priest relaxed and smiled back, "Of course, by all means. Anyway, if they're with you, I've nothing else to ask. You are free to go. Have a pleasant stay at Atalantpuri."

It was clear that Amatya wielded a fair amount of influence within the harbour. Even though he was officially no different from any other merchants, everyone knew of his past as an Atalantian hero of the elite navy corps of Daityan Empire – The Navatakavachas.

"Be careful not to speak too much to these officials. They're trained on accents and various other means to identify suspicious people," Amatya warned them as they walked further from the port check points.

"We will remember that, Amatya, and we are indebted to you," Acharya Parashu said gratefully.

The surface transport system at Atalantpuri was unlike anything Hara had seen. In many ways, they were much more sophisticated than those at Amaravati. The anti-grav levitation drive, based on Mūrthi technology, was the main source of power for many of the sophisticated public transportation systems within the city. Daityan engineers had also developed a host of innovative features to enhance their comfort and utility. The primary high-speed transport systems moved along railed pathways, well-coordinated and controlled by a central management system.

Along with these, the inhabitants of the city also used more mundane horse-drawn carriages and chariots for personal transportation. These conventional vehicles plied on separate roads meant for them. Outsiders were amazed at how such high-tech and traditional systems seemed to coexist and even complement each other. The transportation based on the Mūrthi technology was expensive and, thus, used by the elite class;

most of the citizens used indigenous systems. Irrespective of variations in modes, the roads, pedestrian pathways, supportive infrastructure like bridges and underground drainage systems, etc., had been maintained very well, thanks to the care of officials and the vision of early architects who built the city.

After instructing the crew to take care of his ship, Amatya led Acharya Parashu and Hafa to a nearby public transportation terminal. They embarked on a rail-based vehicle which took them past the central city, then turned around mount Tripura, towards the military and residential areas at the western outskirts of Atalantpuri. The view all along this brief journey was simply fabulous. As more parts of the city were revealed, it became clear that the Daityan civilisation was truly a reflection of Mūrthi systems perfectly coexisting with indigenous human ones. Most of the high-rise structures were made of the locally-available limestone or marble. The roofing comprised clay tiles encased in carved wood or metal seams. The streets were mostly straight and well planned. On both sides of the street, the well planned drainage systems were cleverly concealed under neatly placed stone slabs.

Atalantpuri had one on the most advanced water delivery systems created anywhere in the world. Main supply of water came in from a distant dam on the main Sweta Dweep. Liberal tropical monsoon rains ensured that the dam remained in optimal capacity throughout the year. In fact, there were several other dams supplying water for irrigation, direct consumption and recreation. Atalantpuri, being the single largest city on the island as well as the capital of the Empire, had a dam supplying water exclusively to it. Elaborate, well-maintained gardens interspersed around the city provided idyllic locations for the citizens to stroll and socialise. Even the walkways were dotted with gazebos where citizens could rest and enjoy the spectacular panorama of the city and surrounding seas.

11

EQUATION OF KARMA

Acharya Parashu, Hara and Amatya disembarked at a stop near the residential township on the western side of the harbour city. Amatya looked around and said, "Prahalad's bungalow is just a krosha away. It is best that we walk."

Acharya Parashu and Hara readily agreed. The temperature was pleasant and even though the sky was cloudy, there was no rain. From the tree-lined elevated pathway on which they walked, one could see the complete western part of Atalantpuri and the ocean that surrounded it.

"It is surprising to believe that even in such an advanced city that caters to perhaps every need of man, there are extremes of pain and despair of the kind you mentioned earlier," Hara addressed Amatya as he continued to relish the fabulous view of the great city.

"Is it not the dilemma of all humans, Hara? We look for the means to make us happy and struggle to achieve it. Eventually, with a lot of perseverance, when we actually reach our goal, happiness still eludes us and seems no closer from when we begun," Amatya stated reflectively.

Acharya Parashu finally answered, after being engrossed in observing and admiring the architectural perfection of the imposing structure of Tripura looming above the city. "Yes, Amatya. It is indeed a tragedy, not because goals shift, but also because it is useless to look for happiness in material advancements. While we are in this conceptual world, one must definitely seek to be comfortable, healthy and progressive, but that's not enough."

"Are you saying that we don't do enough to achieve happiness, Acharya?" Amatya asked.

"We usually do what our intellect tells us to do—the bare minimum needed to achieve the sensual or materialistic indulgences, which includes the gratifications of our mind. But unfortunately, our mind is almost entirely structured on our sensory perceptions, memories and thoughts that happened in the past. In many ways, the source of information it uses to come to a conclusion is unreliable," Acharya Parashu continued.

"But is there a more reliable source for deductions than our own mind?" Amatya asked doubtfully.

"Yes. Instead of believing in the unreliable deduction of our limited mind, if we merely use it as a tool to trace our true love, it will definitely lead to happiness. For reasons mentioned earlier, this tracing must happen without any support whatsoever from memories, past conclusions, knowledge, thoughts, habits, intellect etc. In this manner, if we honesty pursue our true love without any prejudice whatsoever, it will invariably and inevitably point towards our own self. After all, isn't it the honest truth that anything or anyone we love outside of our self is only because we've associated our perceived self with it or him/her in the first place? Our absolute love for our self in whatever form is a clear indication that the happiness must reside within our self. In fact, the source of true love, happiness, absolute truth and God are one and the same. Looking for them within the conceptual world of our ego is pointless. We'll find them only where they actually exist – within ourselves."

"Acharya, I understand that by suggesting the inward path, you're perhaps meaning that meditation is the only path to true, long-lasting happiness. This is fine for a monk but common people find it difficult to understand it. Most of the people believe that actions of correct moral standards would lead them towards happiness. Why is it that even those who live by such standards find it difficult to achieve happiness?"

"This is a question that baffles many people. When they're unable to experience happiness by following their best judgements, they start mistrusting it. And in the process, instead of looking at their inner self, they search for external agencies to provide them with an answer."

"Is that wrong Acharya? After all, most of the concepts we learn are gleaned from either our own experiences or the knowledge gained by others within this world itself?" Amatya's expression changed and Acharya could read apprehension on his face, so he smiled and added, "There's nothing wrong with it, Amatya. Initially we adapt new ideas because it appeals to our own mind's rational and moral sensibility. Later, however, the mind identifies itself with such concepts and then onwards, it is not about rationality, but love for our own ego."

"Acharya, are you saying that there is nothing which can be stated as a universally correct moral way of living in this world?"

"It is always difficult to perceive a correct way of living that is defined by our personal moral concepts of good and bad. In fact, one's idea of morality is rooted in perceptions alone. A lofty mountain like the one over there on which Tripura citadels are perched may look perfect, grand and stately from one side. Yet from a different perspective, it may look ugly and evil. Even though it is the same mountain, it could be perceived differently depending on the point of view. If the same person can have such radically varied views, think about the perceptions different people might have. Different people with different minds, diverse memories and dissimilar beliefs are bound to think of the same thing differently."

"Acharya, is that not what all religions try to achieve—provide a common moral concept which appeals to all?"

"Yes Amatya, prophets who formed the religions have attempted to find simple rules which tend to apply to most situations and, therefore, appeal to a majority of the people. Even so, some of these rules couldn't have appealed to few who may lose a certain advantage in society for themselves because of the same. So, it became necessary to reinforce these rules with vague concepts like God. In many cases, such rules are also defended by ideas of fear and reward like pain or pleasure, hell or heaven, etc."

"So what is wrong with that Acharya, if such religious ideas provide some degree of stability and happiness?"

"Nothing is wrong; religious ideas do help many to follow a common path towards happiness. However, trouble starts brewing when a religion, instead of being a guide to lead us towards happiness, becomes an end in itself. When the followers start identifying their own self with that religion, their ego takes over all sense of rationality and morality. Soon the real purpose of a religion to seek happiness is lost and that marks the beginning of suffering."

"I agree to that, Acharya. But, for most people their religion is closely associated with the concept of God. They even justify suffering in the name of God."

"Unfortunately, yes. They justify suffering for themselves as well as others in the name of God. They're unable to realise that the very idea of God as they perceive him/her is yet another external concept created by their own mind. Have you seen anyone who is absolutely happy by merely following the concepts of a God?" Acharya asked.

"No Acharya. But I've never been able to understand why." Amatya admitted.

"And have you considered that it might be because what religions preach needn't be the entire truth about God?"

"But didn't followers find a particular religion appealing because it was closer to the truth in the first place?" Amatya expressed his bafflement.

"Yes, Amatya, but people's perception of religion also keeps changing. The change may happen to an individual within his lifetime itself. Religious concepts and rituals that were relevant earlier may start seeming incorrect with the passage of time. Apart from this, over the course of time, religious ideas which seem to have a powerful influence over people's lives may end up being tools in hands of a few who conceive opportunities to exploit the masses through them. Sometimes, the concept of God itself gets used as a means to exploit rather than lead people towards happiness." "You mean to say people are not able to see through that this is happening?" Amatya asked.

"It is very difficult to see through something that you've identified with your own ego. Besides, most find it hard to question their personal concept of God. In fact the idea of God is used to reinforce the motives of their ego regarding fulfilment of some desire in future. Such state of mind is an ideal breeding ground for suffering."

"Acharya, you seem to suggest that as long as these desires are there, they would block one's happiness?.."

"Yes, Amatya. You've hit the nail on the head. Even though we inherently seek happiness, our very desire for it can be a folly."

"Our common experience is that we desire for something and when we achieve it, we get happiness. Now you're saying that to desire is by itself incorrect. Is it not like stating that it is incorrect to move towards happiness?"

"No, Amatya. Happiness is indeed our primary goal in life. The problem arises with the path we take to reach this happiness. Seeking happiness through external desire is a total folly. Even when we achieve such happiness, it is short-lived. It is like the example of a man carrying a heavy burden getting relief when he unloads it for sometime before lifting it once again. For most humans, happiness is a fleeting feeling often associated with success or a sense of achieving something; in short, fulfilling or relieving a desire. We all carry many burdens of attachment with desires within us. These attachments or desires motivate and drive our day-to-day actions. But as one desire gets fulfilled, another hastily replaces it and keeps us going. Then like the man bearing the load, the story repeats itself."

"But why do we pick up another desire at all, especially when we are in a state of happiness?"

"That is the problem with the human condition, Amatya. We get attached to another desire because we're unable to believe that we can be happy without them. We pick up desires because we feel a sense of incompleteness within ourselves. Having lived all along with a belief that attachment to desires would bring us happiness and completeness, it is difficult to shake off these habits. Our past experiences and tendencies also prompt us to pick another desire. So we keep moving from desire to desire and with so many attachments hooked on to us and pulling us in all directions, true happiness keeps eluding us."

"Acharya, for most people, desires are the motivators for action and a state without desires is invariably understood as an inert state without action," Amatya mentioned doubtfully.

"You have raised a very pertinent point, Amatya. This is indeed something most people find difficult to understand, especially when viewed through the prism of their prejudices and innate tendencies. Firstly, it needs to be made clear that there is nothing called 'inert state without action'. It is certainly not 'inaction'. In a karmic sense, 'inaction' is merely another form of 'action' as much as 'fear' is another form of 'desire'. You're right that most of us tend to associate any type of action with desire. Since actions are an inevitable necessity to exist within the conceptual world we live in, desires are seen as the engines driving them and, therefore, necessary. However, desires and continued sense of incompleteness can never provide us with lasting happiness. If we want to retain happiness – which can only happen when one is complete and desireless – then the only course left is to seek another source to motivate our actions. Once we achieve this desireless state, it will inevitably lead to self-content, love and happiness. Furthermore, the tendency to expand such a state to encompass everything we perceive is inevitable. It is almost like light, which wipes out darkness, even though it is complete in itself. It is only such a tendency that can drive us towards correct karmic action."

"Acharya, aren't the actions that are motivated by the concept of God essentially correct?"

"Such actions can be correct, if we don't corrupt the very concept of God with desires motivated by our ego. Unfortunately, the problem for most is that their idea of God is tied up with their limited personal beliefs, prejudices, religious concepts, traditions, rituals, etc., which are nothing but some of the facets of their ego."

"Acharya, if I understand it correctly, the flaw is only in having desires promoted by our limited virtual self or ego. Motivation for action driven by our correct identity should lead us towards happiness," Amatya seemed unsure as he put forth his perception.

"Yes. Incorrect identity, with a limited virtual self, is indeed one of our basic problems. The limited virtual self or ego being incomplete by itself generates desires. Such desires lead to incorrect karmic actions and, therefore, unhappiness. So the key is to resolve our true identity following which, everything else tends to fall in place on its own."

"We also find many who choose 'inaction' willingly when they have no desires to motivate their action," Amatya stated his perplexity.

Acharya Parashu smiled, "Karmic action is implicit in both cases – action or inaction. So we're always compelled to 'act' either way. As long as we are in this conceptual world, there is no escape from the equation of Karma. The best option, therefore, is to choose the correct action that wouldn't leave any karmic residue."

"Acharya, most people believe that all actions need a specific purpose in the form of results, which is also the basis of our desires as there is always a desired goal. You seem to imply that actions don't need a specific purpose and can be driven by a general inner motivation alone. Without a goal within the conceptual sense, how can we have a plan? And without a plan, how can we achieve anything?" Amatya's confusion was apparent.

"I gather that you intend to say that there is a purpose behind our desires, even if it does not necessarily lead us towards happiness. Well the truth is that there is, as there is purpose for everything that happens around us, howsoever insignificant, there is purpose in progress, as much there is purpose in decline; there is purpose in creation as much as in destruction; there is purpose in efficiency as much as in apathy; and there is purpose in goodness as much as in evil. Understanding the purpose of the body is not within the intellectual capacity of the cells that constitute it. It requires a level of perception beyond our limited mind or intellectual capacity."

"Acharya, if we conclude that we can't truly understand the purpose because of our intellectual limitations, then to establish a direct link between our actions and goals is also meaningless. It means that the goals or destiny are totally out of our control in terms of action. But this is not how we see the world around us. Invariably, our destiny seems to be influenced by our actions?"

"Our destiny is surely influenced by our action, especially since we are a part of the cosmic plan or purpose. You see, the problem is not with the plan, purpose, destiny or action, but in our unwise attempt to limit them within the confines of our intellectual deductions and assumption that they are in our direct control. As long as the plan seems to proceed as per our beliefs, we accept it in the form of direct cause and effect and take credit for its favourable outcome. When it doesn't, we're lost, stressed and suffer pain."

"So you're saying that the destined event as per the ultimate cosmic plan, would definitely happen or not happen, notwithstanding whatever we may do to influence it?"

"Indeed so, Amatya. Contrary to popular belief, we have very little control over the cosmic plan. If we have any desire or fear that motivates an action, that action is also ultimately part of the cosmic plan itself. This plan will take its own course, with or without our help. The only thing that we can possibly do consciously is to align ourselves with it in order to seek happiness and minimise suffering. Instead of attempting to forcefully change the world around us towards our limited and self-obsessed idea of what is necessary for peace and happiness, the attempt should be to seek internal change within us to such a state where we find ourselves at peace with the world as it is. Once we find peace and happiness within, the world around us will follow suit automatically. This is because first, this world around us is really a conscious projection of our own mind and second because our actions in such a state would be in tune with the universal plan and not in conflict with it."

"What about our responsibility towards the cosmic plan? How do we align ourselves with the cosmic plan if we can't even understand it?"

"It is not as difficult as it sounds. It can be done by keeping away from the influence of desires or fears promoted by our limited virtual self or ego. In other words, one can do it by remaining centred on our real self, love and happiness. That is the natural course which will inevitably align you with the cosmic plan and also motivate you towards correct action or responsibility."

"Now I understand your point, Acharya. So, all the burdens of responsibility and stress we usually carry to fulfil our desires are meaningless?"

"Not only meaningless, Amatya, they may actually be counterproductive if they work against the cosmic plan. This can also wrap us within the cause and effect cycle of Karma."

"If our worries are so meaningless, why do we keep carrying them throughout our lives, Acharya?"

"We carry them only as long as we remain ignorant of ourselves, or delude ourselves to be in control. It is like a man standing on a ship, trying to push it and deluding himself that he is in control of its movement. He continues to reinforce his belief of control and congratulates himself as long as the ship's course and his whims match. When it doesn't, he cries!"

"I see your point, Acharya. It seems that the only recourse anyone has is to rid oneself of ignorance. As you've said earlier, this is only feasible through the reliable source of wisdom – which is our true selves, without any influence whatsoever from mind, intellect, memories, knowledge, senses which are linked to things external to us."

"Yes, Amatya, the only recourse is to gain gyan through the truly reliable means—inward meditation."

"Acharya, I'm now able to understand the purpose of meditation with more clarity. However, isn't it true that man's salvation is also possible by true surrender to God?"

"That's right. Complete surrender to God is indeed a potent means to get enlightened. But remember that *true* and *complete* surrender is a necessity – which again inevitably leads to a meditative state."

"Acharya, how can true surrender to God be equivalent to meditation?" Amatya was doubtful.

"To explain that we'll need to first explore the meaning of God. To most of us, God is a product of our religious beliefs. Unfortunately, even while ascribing the status of omnipotence to God, most people attempt to confine him within the bounds of some religious beliefs, customs, language, rules or rituals. In short, they attempt to bind God to the concepts of their mind, memories, intellect, knowledge, prejudices and senses – the very aspects that define their ego. Obviously 'complete surrender' to someone whom you're also trying to 'bind' within the concepts of your own mind is simply absurd."

"What is it within us that attempts to bind the concept of God?"

"That is obviously all of those unreliable faculties within us like our mind, memories, intellect, knowledge, etc., the gist of which is nothing but our ego or the very unique personality that many of us are so proud of. So it wouldn't be wrong to say that it is our ego that attempts to 'confine or limit' the concept of God."

"And how can we stop this?"

"By *completely* surrendering our ego to God. And this means surrendering everything, even the concepts of our pet religion which proposed the idea of a particular God in the first place. This is one of the greatest barriers for most people. They tend to chase the idea of 'surrender to God's will' without relinquishing the one thing that would bear some real results in that pursuit — surrendering their own ego and the religious beliefs that are supported by it."

"Acharya, so whether through pursuit of true wisdom by understanding one's real self or by complete surrender to God, the key seems to be that of losing our ego."

"That's right. By ego, we mean almost all the concepts within the realm of our limited intellect or mind, e.g. memories, senses, knowledge, concepts, ideas, and desires—almost everything that gives sense to our objective, wakeful world. In the first method of seeking inner wisdom, the ego gets ignored by not making use of it. In the second method of complete surrender to God, we actually surrender our ego itself. Either way the ego sheds off because of disuse."

"The ego sheds off due to disuse? Is it really possible?" Amatya was curious.

"It is, my dear Amatya. In reality, the ego is nothing real. It is like a mirage or reflection or a virtual entity. It can only sustain by depending on other relative aspects like memories, tendencies, past deductions, prejudices, etc. The framework of world that we build around ourselves depends on the intellect or mind. Similarly, the mind depends on memories to make sense of the sensory inputs from the world. Ego sustains because of the self-delusion of its own existence for which continuous interplay between the aspects that create it in the first place is necessary. Once you ignore ego or surrender it completely and, in a way, put it to disuse, you deprive it of the very facets that nourish it. Without sustenance, and being as such only illusionary, it simply withers away."

"But what are we without ego or our unique personalities? Wouldn't we then be like mindless zombies?" Amatya asked in obvious confusion.

"That is an interesting question, Amatya. But I'm sure that while asking that question, you have assumed ourselves to be nothing but our egos. That isn't correct. In fact, ego is the barrier which stops us from understanding our true selves. It is our identification with our ego that has always been the flaw. In the absence of ego, we would identify ourselves with what we truly are – universal beings and part of the concept of God itself. Being a part of God can also be surmised as *being* God oneself. With such an identity, our perception needn't be confined within the limits of our ego as it did before. The perception then becomes universal, all-encompassing and truly impersonal. In such a state, we continue to retain all our limited faculties like intellect, sensory perceptions, physical capability for action, etc. The only difference is that the mind then gets well within our control, rather than controlling us. The mental framework needed to make sense of sensory perceptions, and the actions that follow it are also in our firm control. Since such actions are *motivated* by our true universal self, they are well-aligned with the universal cosmic plan. In this manner, we end up working with the original plan and not in contradiction to it; we don't get wrapped up within the cycle of Karma because we don't create any cause for it. This further helps us remain on the correct universal course of *action*, the course of God."

"Acharya, you mentioned that the framework of this world for most is created by their mind, based on the reference points of their ego. With our ego replaced with universal wisdom, these reference points change, thereby rebuilding the mental framework of the world in the correct format. Then Karma is no more applicable. Why is it so?"

"This is so because Karma is indeed one of the universal laws of nature based on which a mental frame is built in the first place. It is similar to the force of gravity that defines one of the physical laws of nature while building any framework of space and time. Our egos may provide the reference points and architectural structure but the framework that gets built must still obey the laws of Karma." Acharya explained patiently.

"Acharya, you stated that our mind is a tool. So I can understand that anything that gets built through this tool must obey the laws of Karma. This must mean that the laws of Karma are ingrained within the nature of the mind?"

"That's correct. Our mind is a manifested extension of our own universal self or God. It is a tool that works within the confines of the universal law of Karma. Our mind works perfectly well as it must, till the point it is not corrupted by the delusion of ego. If corrupted, the framework of this objective world that is created by our mind tends to become skewed and flawed. The universal laws of Karma, which are intrinsically aligned to achieve the original plan, attempts to automatically correct this flaw. These attempts create a pattern of cause and effect. Karma as we understand, it is nothing but this pattern and its impact on our ego."

"Acharya, I've understood that Karma is the pattern of cause and effect generated out of wrong actions motivated by our limited ego. Yet we, that is our ego, has always thought that our mind is completely within its control. Why is that?"

"Think about it this way, Amatya. How can the mind—which is a manifested extension of our universal cosmic self—be under total control of our ego? Yes, it can indeed be corrupted by our egos as long as we're deluded to believe that our ego is ourselves. Yet, even in its corrupted state, mind must intrinsically obey the laws of Karma. So the mind is never entirely in control of our ego. The outcomes of our action or destiny are never in complete control of the ego even within the distorted framework that it creates as per its convenience in the first place. This is indeed one of the main causes of all suffering."

"Acharya, it is understood that to alleviate ourselves from suffering, we must trace out our original identity. This can't be done using a corrupted mind. It can neither be done by action decided by the same corrupted or deluded mind. Action through deluded mind can only attract Karma. Pure action can only happen through pure mind. To access our pure mind, we must attain our correct identity. Isn't all this very confusing?"

"Not at all, Amatya. If we accept that our mind may be corrupted by our ego, such a mind is useless to us in our effort to attain our true identity. So this effort must first happen without the aid of mind. This is indeed possible since our true identity is certainly not part of the mental framework of the mind. Our true identity or awareness is the originator of the mind, not its conceptual product and can, therefore, exist independent of the mind. Everything is mental conceptualisation except the awareness of our true self. Such continuous self-awareness without the pull towards external mental conceptualisation, must inevitably lead us straight into the core of our true self. This process of inward shift of identity is the true purpose of meditation. Once we've attained the true identity of our true self, ego which is a pseudo-identity will dissolve away just like darkness gets dissolved away by light. Without the corruptive influence of the ego, our mind is pure and can be directly used by our true universal self to create the correct mental framework. *Action* that happens in this framework is well-aligned with and *motivated* by the universal cosmic plan. Therefore, such action doesn't attract Karma. Without the vagaries of false identity with the pseudo-self or ego and the cause-and-effect pattern of Karma, there is no conflict within us and thus, no suffering. Without suffering, our intrinsic nature of total happiness or bliss shines forth continuously and inexhaustibly."

Amatya smiled after a while and said, "Acharya, I think I understand it now. My profound thanks to you for this insightful discussion on Karma."

Acharya Parashu turned his face toward the citadels of Tripura and said, "We must actually thank the Mūrthi who passed on such knowledge to humanity in the form of Vedas so many eons ago."

12

DAITYAN SOCIETY

"It is an honour to have you as guests at my humble abode," Prahalad said as he welcomed them to his bungalow. It was located within the residential colony built on the gentle slopes between Tripura and Atalantpuri city. Prahalad came from an aristocratic lineage of priestly Rakshas clan with distant links to the royal house of Tarak. Even though Prahalad was a tall, well-built Rakshas and somewhat intimidating because of fierce looks, his overall demeanour in terms of conduct was gentle, courteous and polite. His neatly combed black hair and flawlessly fair, taut skin also indicated that he was much younger in terms of age.

Few hours later, Hara stood at the terrace of the bungalow, enjoying the excellent view of the western side of the city and surrounding sea. It was evening time and sun would be setting in another muhurta or so. It was a pleasant day with a cool breeze blowing from the sea. Hara was lost in thoughts about his impending mission. "Would Prahalad help them? Is he on their side in the first place? Would they walk into a trap being prepared for them? Would he ever be able to meet Uma again?" His mind shifted from one thought to the other. This, for him, was one of the most dangerous Bheeshma missions. Acharya Parashu and he had entered into the direct domain and the power centre of the Daityan Empire. It was a daring rescue operation with hardly any clear plan in place.

"It should all be over in another two days, Hara" Acharya Parashu said, almost as if he could read Hara's mind. Hara hadn't noticed Acharya Parashu walking up to him on the terrace.

"Yes, Acharya. Do you think we could trust Amatya and Prahalad? After all, they are Rakshas themselves."

"We'll know soon enough, Hara. I've meditated on this for a while now and don't see any karmic conflict so far. As Bheeshma monks, we should be prepared to face anything that Karma has in store for us."

"Yes, Acharya. You are right. That is not..." Hara said in a low tone.

"I know what is occupying your mind, Hara. Don't worry, you'll surely meet Uma in near future," Acharya Parashu assured him with a smile.

"Acharya, I'm trying to control my emotions but don't know why her thoughts keep coming back to me so often," Hara admitted, almost apologetically.

"Nothing unnatural about it, Hara. This is bound to happen when you love someone. Right now, however, you need to remain focused on the mission." Then looking over Hara's shoulder, he said, "I believe Prahalad is requesting us to join him for dinner."

Prahalad and Amatya were engrossed in a serious conversation when Acharya Parashu and Hara entered the dining hall. On seeing them enter, Prahalad got up warmly and said, "Welcome Acharya Parashu and Hara. We have an assortment of Atalantian delicacies for you; hope you enjoy them."

When they sat together after finishing a sumptuous dinner, Acharya Parashu said, "Prahalad, I must admit that I have never tasted such delicious food. I didn't know that Atalantpuri had such good cooks."

Prahalad's smile was warm when he said, "It is our pleasure to serve you, Acharya. And yes, Atalantpuri is well-known for its culinary specialities. In fact, this harbour city has been a melting pot of so many cultures for a long period of time; the flavours and smells from all over the world have converged, giving rise to unique culinary styles. The variety of food available within the city markets is simply mind-boggling."

"From what I've seen so far, Atalantpuri is indeed a unique city, with its own special character," Acharya Parashu agreed and then asked, "Being one of the most prominent cities of the world, I assume it must have migrant population from multiple ethnic backgrounds?"

"Yes, Acharya. It is the migrants from all over the world who've given the city its distinctive character. The main native ethnic groups are the Rakshasas and Danavs. The business community mostly comprises of Yakshas, while the Gandharv community dominates the medical and cosmetic trade. We also have a large number of migrant Manavs from Bhārat kingdom, who are the main source of labour. There are some Devas living here too, practising esoteric healing techniques and trading the popular liquor Somras. In many ways, it wouldn't be wrong to call it a global city."

"The technological advancement that I've seen in this city today is far ahead of any other place in the world," Acharya Parashu agreed.

"Acharya, you should've seen this city in its days of glory, about 75 ayanas ago. Notwithstanding all the glamour still around, the fact is that the city has been in a state of decline for some time," Amatya said in a nostalgic tone.

"I couldn't agree more. Usually the visitors to the city only notice the glitz, glamour and technological prowess of the city. Unfortunately, it has a nasty underside, too. It is almost like an infection which has been spreading for quite some time now," Prahalad said, concurring Amatya's views.

"What is the reason for this change, Prahalad?" Hara asked.

"To my mind, there are many reasons. First and foremost is corruption that comes with power. This is especially applicable to the ruling class. Such corruption in terms of morality tends to spread among the administration and judicial system that hold the society together. It manifests in the form of injustice perpetrated on common citizens. Injustice brings in suffering, which further vitiates the environment. Second, there is a great deal of disparity in the standard of living. In the early days, there were corrective mechanisms to contain such disparity within morally acceptable limits. Now, however, corruption has rendered all such mechanisms ineffective. The rich are getting richer every day and the poor continue to slip into hopeless poverty. The food shortage that has started hitting us due to rising sea levels has only made things worse," Prahalad replied with a tone of sadness and loss.

"Who are the main ruling class within Atalantpuri?" Hara asked.

"In this regard, Atalantpuri is a reflection of the Daityan Empire in general. The elite ruling class and aristocracy come from Rakshas clan. Danavs comprise the majority population and are considered a step lower in social strata, forming the working class. That said, we do have few Danavs who're rich and even hold senior government positions. But it is relatively rare compared to Rakshas. There is always a simmering tension between the two clans."

"Are there any racial differences between them?" Acharya Parashu asked.

"Yes, Acharya. For thousands of years, Rakshas clans used to inhabit the fertile and cooler hilly regions of the Daityan island groups whereas Danavs have always lived in warm and humid coastal plains. Based on the geographical disparity that the two sections have inhabited over the years, Rakshas, in general, have tall, strong and powerful body structures. Danavs, on the other hand, are of medium height, with slighter and agile bodies. Till recently, intermarriage between both communities was totally prohibited. Now, however, they are not as strict as they used to be; one can easily find people of mixed lineage, clans and castes within Atalantpuri."

"I've heard that Rakshas have also been traditionally the custodians of the Mūrthi knowledge?" Acharya Parashu asked Prahalad.

"Even before the formation of the Daityan Empire, Rakshas have been technologically much more superior to Danavs. Being more educated and relatively more spiritually advanced as compared to Danavs and other clans, they had the privilege of direct interaction with the Mūrthi and were able to carry forward the knowledge obtained from them in a consistent manner. This is also the main reason why they came to dominate the Daityan society with the passage of time. After all, it was the Rakshas kings who integrated the Empire over the course of many generations around 500 ayanas ago, into the form we know it today," Prahalad replied.

"Is it true that Rakshas also live much longer than the others?" Hara asked.

"Probably yes. Apart from having a relatively longer lifespan, they also get access to better nutrition and expensive medication. As in all societies, many of the rich and powerful within Rakshas clan continue to seek better opportunities to enhance their physical prowess even further. One of the latest fads of our royalty is the Kayakalp project. The official purpose of developing Kayakalp therapy is that it is expected to give new lease of life to many who are ailing due to age or diseases. It is also rumoured that it may also lead to development of drugs that could considerably enhance the fighting potential of the soldiers in battlefield."

"We have had some news of the Kayakalp project and assume that Agastya Rishi and his wife have been held captive for the same purpose," Hara put forth with some hesitation.

"Yes, Hara. As far as my knowledge of it goes, I'm told Rishi Agastya's contribution is critical to the research efforts of developing the Kayakalp rejuvenation process. As it is directly promoted by the royalty, this is one of the most important ongoing projects under Maya's stewardship. Actually, the Rishi had come here voluntarily on request from Shukracharya. It was only later when he suspected that his efforts may get misused for military purpose that Agastya turned against the project. By then, it was too late since he and his wife were already at Atalantpuri. He has since then been extending unwilling cooperation. And I know this is why you're here." Prahalad addressed Acharya Parashu and Hara as he spoke.

"Why is Rishi Agastya's cooperation so important for this project?" Hara wanted to know Prahalad's point of view on it.

"You see, the final process of Kayakalp needs invoking the universal life force of Prana at an astral level. I'm told there are only a handful of Rishis who have the meditative skills necessary for such astral invocations."

"Making a spiritual person like the Rishi work under coercive threat and duress is bad Karma," Hara stated contemptuously.

"I agree. But I'm assuming that your attempt to rescue the Rishi and his wife has also got some other karmic purpose. We all know that the coming days are not going to be pleasant at Atalantpuri. The rising sea level due to global warming and melting ice caps is not going to stop anytime soon. With more than 30 percent of farmland already inundated, sizeable population of the Empire may soon need to migrate to more conducive locations," Prahalad said.

"Or grab cultivable land by force from other countries," Hara mused aloud.

"Yes Hara, such a possibility must already be under consideration if I understand the current rulers of the Empire correctly. That would mean war with Devarth. If this is not enough, the corruptive influence of a new religious order is making life difficult for most people in Atalantpuri. None of the possible future scenarios seems promising in any way. As they eventually unfold, it would certainly be calamitous for Atalantpuri and the people living here. It may look quite stable for now but we are actually sitting on a tinderbox. Before a spark hits it, I would prefer that my family is away from this place. And that also answers why I'm helping you on this mission," Prahalad admitted.

"Pardon my asking, but is that the only reason, Prahalad?" Hara asked, and then glanced at Acharya Parashu.

"You have every right to doubt my actions. Why, inspite of being an aristocratic Rakshas, I am attempting to help you? I'm fully aware that apart from the unpatriotic aspect, it is also extremely dangerous for me and my family. If the Emperor or his security chief Mahisha were to know of my role in supporting your mission, death is a certainty. This might sound odd to you but I'm an ardent worshipper of the Mūrthi Lord Vishnu. It is the Lord who has guided me all through my life. It is enough to say that whatever I'm doing is part of my Karma and this direction came to me from the Lord himself. I don't know how the future is going to evolve but the Lord must know the benefit of what I'm doing."

"Prahalad, in order to follow correct Karma, one must always trust one's inner self more than anyone else. Anyway, are there many who still worship the Mūrthi Lords within the Empire?" Acharya Parashu asked.

"All of the ruling class and most of the Daityan citizens have always been ardent worshippers of the Mūrthi Lords Rudra and Vishnu. It is indeed through their blessings and support that this civilisation has reached such pinnacle of success. Now, it must definitely be a sign of the end that a new draconian religious order is gaining popularity. The Emperor, his brothers and most of the ruling class have started following this new religion which appeals to their corrupted state of mind and justifies all their wrong actions. Deviation from the karmic path by so many would surely attract the ire of the Mūrthi Lords. I foresee that the disintegration of the Empire is not far."

Acharya Parashu sensed that the discussion was deviating into another realm and tried to change the subject. Looking at Amatya he asked, "As someone with experience in Daityan military, what do you think the outcome would be if there were to be a war?"

Amatya considered the question carefully for a while before answering, "Outcomes of wars are always unpredictable, Acharya. All I can say is that the odds seem to be overwhelmingly in favour of the Daityan Empire."

"Dev Lok constitutes no less an opponent, Amatya. It would be incorrect to underestimate them," Acharya Parashu reminded.

"You are right, Acharya. Devas have always been able to bring up some form of extraordinary advantage during the past wars with Daityas. It may be possible this time as well. However, the advantages that the Daityas enjoy under present circumstances are unprecedented."

"Amatya, I'm sorry if I sound over-inquisitive but can you give us some idea about the military strength of the Daityan Empire?" Hara asked.

"I can understand your concern, Hara. It is no secret that the Empire has the strongest military forces ever organised by any nation in the past. Two of the primary wings of Daityan military are known as the Navatakavacha and Kalakeya. Both military wings have their own navy, land army and air force formations and are completely independent. The less numerous but elite Navatakavachas comprise the Rakshas clan whereas the much larger Kalakeyas comprise mostly Danavs. Their combined strength may exceed well over a million soldiers. That is not the only advantage. Daityan armed forces have formidable weapons, armaments, transportation systems, warships, armed vimāns, with technological superiorly unseen in any past wars. There is no country which comes even close to match the military might of the Empire today."

"If Empire is in trouble, it might be a very tempting solution for them to wield their military might. Prahalad, you're right to worry about the future. War is indeed a strong possibility. Anyway, let's focus on our immediate mission. Do you have information on where Rishi Agastya and his wife are held captive?" Acharya Parashu asked.

"I've been following up on it for some time, Acharya. As of now, they're stationed within a separate bungalow around two kroshas from the Kayakalp complex. This bungalow is almost like a mini fortress with armed soldiers guarding it round the clock," Prahalad answered.

"How many soldiers? Do they have a pattern of duty shifts? Are there any alarm systems?" Hara wanted to know.

"I'm not completely sure, Hara. I've planned for us to do some reconnaissance tomorrow. You may want to familiarise yourself with the plan, timings, route of entry, exit, etc. We may also need to use some additional disguise to be able to roam around these locations without arousing too much suspicion," Prahalad replied.

13

CONFRONTATION

Acharya Parashu and Prahalad looked at the entrance to the bungalow. Hara and Amatya had taken another route to look at the rear of the building and the passage leading up to a nearby beach. All of them were disguised as proponents of the new religious order, based on Prahalad's advice that any suspicious activity from such lot may look usual to passersby. The bungalow was actually perched on an overhang from the main mountain of Tripura. The spot had been chosen well. It was impossible for anyone to approach the bungalow from anywhere except the front. The entry opened up to the main road. They could see at least 15 soldiers on guard at the entrance. On careful observation, Acharya Parashu noted that a few of them were actually like the Vetals that he and Hara had confronted at the Brashtaranya.

By the time they met again at the residence of Prahalad, it was already late afternoon. Amatya had gone to meet some friends and was the last to join. After taking refreshments, Acharya Parashu laid out the basic plan.

"Before we begin this operation, I've some important information to share," Amatya announced.

All the eyes looked at him enquiringly.

"I've just met an old friend who attends the Asur Sabha. Mahisha, the chief of Daityan security, seems to have come to know that a rescue attempt is likely to be made soon. He is not sure who, how and when, but has anyway asked for upgrading the security at the bungalow. Emperor Tarakaksh has also directed his youngest brother Vidyunmali to personally ensure that the rescue attempt doesn't succeed."

"In that case, we may need to launch this operation immediately. It is quite possible that they may decide to move Rishi Agastya and wife to another, more secure location for a few days," Acharya Parashu said.

"Are you sure you want to undertake this operation now, Acharya? With the heightened level of security, it may be difficult if not impossible, for anyone to even get near the bungalow, let alone rescue the two," Amatya was full of doubts as he looked at Acharya Parashu.

Hara, who had been observing the beautiful view of the setting sun as seen beyond the terrace, replied, "Leave that to us, Amatya. We can handle the 15 or so guards. Even after knowing about this mission, the Daityan rulers seem to have grossly underestimated the Bheeshma."

"Maybe you're right, Hara. But you must be prepared to face stiff resistance. The Rakshas soldiers guarding the bungalow are the best from the elite corps of Navatakavachas. They're well trained in use of all weapons as well as unarmed close combat."

"I'm sure they are, Amatya, and am not doubting or underestimating their potential. What about the artificial creatures that we found among the soldiers today?"

"They are the Yantraksh fighters, who are feared even by the best Navatakavacha soldiers. These creatures were built using genome from multiple species using genetic engineering technology inherited from the Mūrthi. They've also been selectively bred for many generations to enhance their fighting skills. The imperfect ones get dumped off in Vetal land. The finally perfected and controllable Yantraksh fighters are then commissioned as royal guards. They're not only inherently powerful but have lightning fast reflexes and even faster minds to match," Amatya said.

Acharya Parashu had been listening to the dialogue and finally intervened, "Amatya, you're right that it is going to be extremely difficult and dangerous. It is also possible that we may perish while attempting this mission. But there is one thing you can be sure of: we will not get captured and put you or Prahalad in danger."

On hearing this, Prahalad pitched in, "There is more to this world than material capabilities alone. If this is the course that Lord Vishnu wants me to take, I'm sure it is the right Karma. I trust this to be the case for Acharya Parashu and Hara as well. If we are indeed on the path of right Karma, all our perceived barriers will fall apart."

"Wish I could have your confidence, Prahalad," Amatya said smilingly and then thought for a while before adding, "One last thing. You must expect Vidyunmali to be there at the bungalow, too. Vidyunmali is the best among the Rakshas clan in close combat skills. Apart from having the exceptional ability to wield swords with both hands, he is also known to be very shrewd. Expect the unexpected when dealing with him."

"We'll keep that in mind, Amatya and are grateful for the valuable information. The only advantage on our side may be the fact that we can choose the time to attack. Surprise is the one factor—even if a small one—which may give us an edge to catch them unprepared. Let's plan to attempt the rescue at precisely one muhurta before sunrise tomorrow morning. Prahalad, I trust you would be able to convey to Rishi Agastya to remain prepared?"

Parahalad nodded in agreement and Acharya continued, "Amatya, as discussed earlier, it would be best that you keep a boat near our rendezvous point on the beach closest to the bungalow. You may also want to keep your ship started up and ready to sail off as soon as we get on board. If everything goes well, we should be able to be on your ship along with Rishi Agastya and his wife by sunrise."

As everyone nodded and understood the plan, Acharya broke the gathering, "Let's all get some rest. Tomorrow will be a hard day."

𐤕 Ш ϙ

Acharya Parashu and Hara surveyed the entrance gate to the bungalow. Both were dressed in their characteristic monk's attire. As part of the Bheeshma ritual of preparation for combat, they had woken about three muhurtas before sunrise. After a refreshing bath, they had spent one complete muhurta in deep meditation to align their internal Jwalaprabha with universal kundalini shakti. By the end of their meditation, they we fully charged.

It was still dark but there was sufficient starlight to be able to clearly see three Yantraksh soldiers pacing the road in front of the entrance. Since these genetically engineered creatures required no sleep and remained primed and ready for action anytime, they were often deployed as the first line of defence. Acharya Parashu silently signalled Hara to take the left route and approach them from the opposite side, well camouflaged through the nearby vegetation. Hara understood the pincer movement of attack that Acharya had in mind. If surprised from both sides simultaneously, the defender's attention might get split, thereby giving them the slight advantage they needed. Acharya Parashu then took out his Spatishūl and silently approached the entrance from the right.

As expected, the Yantraksh soldiers were taken totally by surprise as Acharya Parashu and Hara simultaneously emerged from opposite sides. Even before the Yantraksh could gather what had happened, the extremely sharp crystal weapons thrown by the two Bheeshmas had struck them. The Yantraksh closer to Acharya Parashu went down and was dead well before hitting the ground, the Spatishūl having pierced its throat and broken the spine. The second Yantraksh had Hara's Spatishūl stuck into its chest up to the hilt, but surprisingly, it turned towards him as if nothing had happened. As Hara approached him, the Yantraksh leapt forward and struck out its right foot with incredible speed. Hara could hardly realise its intention before the foot hit him in the midriff. He was thrown five clear dhanus away and fell sprawling on the ground. Had it not been for the Jwalaprabha coursing through his body that partly absorbed the blow, he would have died from internal haemorrhage. As such, he could barely recover when he saw the Yantraksh pounce at him with its sword in hand. Hara knew that he was looking at death. Lying on the ground in a totally bruised, helpless state, he could hardly manoeuvre or even roll over.

As he approached him, the creature raised its sword arm for the final blow, but hesitated a bit, probably due to the discomfort of the Bheeshma weapon stuck into its chest cavity. The opportunity was enough for Hara. Within a blink of the eye, he lifted himself up to his knees and from that position took hold of the handle of the Spatishūl. Using all the strength that could be mustered into his arm, he withdrew the sharp weapon, while carving up the internal organs of the creature's body. The beady eyes of the creature went wide and then blinked shut as it slowly dropped sideways onto the ground.

The third Yantraksh had already surged into action at a speed impossible for any human to achieve. Within a split second, he had taken out a broad sword and launched himself at the now unarmed Acharya Parashu. The Bheeshma veteran saw the line of attack aimed at his chest and feigned to block it with his left arm. However, as the Yantraksh swung in with the strike, he stepped aside to raise his right hand and project his Jwalaprabha towards the weak spot on the throat of the creature. The humanoid stopped suddenly as if his throat had been struck by an invisible hammer. Taking advantage of his brief respite, Acharya Parashu looked at and focussed on his Spatishūl which was still held stuck in the throat of the fallen Yantraksh, two dhanus away from him. Immediately, the telekinetic link made connection and the weapon dislodged itself and flew into his hand. Turning around, he swung low, aiming at the softer exposed part of the humanoid's midriff. The sharp Bheeshma weapon sliced the lower belly of the creature, disembowelling it in the process. Before it could attempt to get up, the next blow of the Spatishūl had cut off its head.

The sound from the third Yantraksh must have warned other guards and within no time, they had all of the Navatakavacha Rakshas soldiers to deal with. Four of them attacked Hara, who had just got up from ground. The soldiers were good fighters and with numbers on their side, it was very tough to engage or fight with all of them at the same time. Fully conscious of the odds against him, Hara willed his Jwalabrabha into the Spatishūl. The self-morphing crystalline weapon emitted an iridescent blue glow as Hara swept it at the two swords striking at him simultaneously. The look on the face of the Navatakavacha soldiers was of bewilderment when they saw the sparkling weapon sheer off the hardened steel blades of their swords clean, as if they were made of softwood. Exploiting their surprise, Hara suddenly crouched low and swept his sabre arm in a continuous arc at the ankles of the other two soldiers. They screamed as the Bheeshma weapon cut off their legs below them and their bodies stumbled backwards.

Three Navatakavacha soldiers circled around Acharya Parashu. They struck at him from all sides together. This was a situation against which almost all Bheeshma warriors were trained to perfection. As the swords struck, he bent low to slip through a gap while sinking his elbow straight into one soldier's lower stomach. The soldier went down wincing, only to be decapitated within the next instance. By the time the swords of remaining two soldiers struck empty ground, the Acharya had already dispatched another by chopping off his spine. The third had no chance against the experienced warrior monk; all he could see in the final moments of his life as he looked up was a flash of the crystalline edge of the Spatishūl nearing his neck.

It was all over in another few seconds. The Yantraksh and Navatakavacha soldiers lay dead or wounded around the Bheeshma monks. Acharya Parashu looked at Haŕa and together they moved into the courtyard of the bungalow.

"So you're the famous Bheeshma warrior monks of the Bhārat kingdom?" said the young Rakshas standing in the courtyard and taunting them with a pulse-ray weapon of Mūrthi legacy in his hand. He was Vidyunmali.

"It is indeed a daring thing to come to the Daityan capital and attempt to rescue Agastya from right under the nose of the Emperor. After I've dispatched you both, he may even give out posthumous awards for such bravery," he continued to sneer with mock admiration.

As Haŕa advanced towards him, Vidyunmali shot an energy pulse at the sky, "Don't come any closer, monk. One single deadly pulse of this Mūrthi weapon can kill you many times over. No, I'm not particular about how I kill you, even though it may be preferable to capture you both alive. Our scientists might be delighted to get a chance to dissect your bodies and examine what is so special about Bheeshma monks," he laughed aloud. Acharya Parashu signalled Haŕa to stop and moved in front of him, "Don't fall for his taunts, Haŕa. Get behind me immediately. This is my *Guruvachan*."

Haŕa hesitated for a moment and eventually got behind Acharya Parashu. This was the first time that Acharya Parashu had ever evoked Guruvachan – the bond of oath between a Bheeshma guru and shishya.

Vidyunmali laughed, "Okay! So you want to be dispatched by seniority? No problem at all. Let it be the old one who is the first to meet his maker."

By then Acharya Parashu was already in a state of deep Stithapragya, with his Jwalaprabha aligned straight with the source of kundalini shakti. He could feel the cosmic energy of Brahmn course through his soul and body. The clarity of his spiritual vision was complete, and not just at the physical level of time and space. Every movement around him came to a standstill as if time itself had stopped. In slow motion, he saw the hand of Vidyunmali squeeze the initiator of the pulse-ray gun and a bright pulse of high energy radiation emerge from the weapon directed towards him. Even as the focused pulse of the ray weapon approached him, Acharya Parashu had already positioned both his hands in the characteristic yogic posture of *Mārak Mudra*. The high intense radiation pulse warped the time-space fabric of the force-shield in front of the elder monk and was deflected off to the right.

There was a stunned look on the face of Vidyunmali as he saw the powerful pulse get deflected off the body of the elder Bheeshma. This was the first time he had witnessed the pulse ray fail and he could not believe his eyes. Being a quick thinker, he moved the controls of the weapon to the extreme peak and launched a volley of deadly pulses at the senior monk. All the pulses reached the invisible kundalini force-shield in front of the Bheeshma veteran and were deflected sideways to create explosions wherever they hit.

On seeing the pulse-ray gun being ineffective, Vidyunmali threw it away and quickly drew out his own crystalline sword. Acharya Parashu stood still, calm and composed, with his grey hair and beard waving in the morning breeze. The Spatishūl in his right hand sparkled with an iridescent blue, characteristic of the Jwalabrabha coursing through it.

"There is no time to lose, Hara. Go and get the Agastya family while I deal with this Rakshas," Acharya Parashu told Hara without looking at him.

As Hara moved into the bungalow to get Rishi Agastya and his wife, Acharya Parashu and Vidyunmali faced each other.

The young Rakshas was the first one to launch an attack with his sword but it was immediately blocked by Acharya Parashu. Their crystal weapons collided, creating explosive sparks around them. It was clear that Vidyunmali was well-trained in most of the close-combat techniques as had been pointed out by Amatya. He was athletic and powerful and sidestepped many classical moves from the Bheeshma monk. To an observer, the combat sequence would've looked like a well-rehearsed ballet. Each movement was precise and instinctively measured. Even during the course of the high speed combat sequence, each of them looked for weak spots in the opponent.

The combat continued for more than a kala. Vidyunmali seemed to have adopted a strategy to tire out his older opponent. It was only because of the enhanced Jwalabrabha coursing through his body that Acharya Parashu was able to cope up with the intensity of such unrelenting physical exertion. In fact, his body and limbs merely followed his astral form, which was now in complete sync with his inner soul. Vidyunmali seemed to instinctively sense that he couldn't allow the Bheeshma to evoke his extraordinary telekinetic powers of kundalini and, therefore, continued to attack him without any respite.

It was only the flicker in the eye of the younger Rakshas that gave away the surprise he had in store for Acharya Parashu. Even while blocking a strike from the Bheeshma monk, his left hand dipped inside his tunic and came out with a projectile weapon. His left hand coordination in this dynamic state of motion of the combat sequence was surprisingly steady when he pulled the trigger to release a deadly dart towards his adversary. Acharya Parashu could see the dart coming towards him in such close quarters only because he was expecting it. Even so, it was too late to completely avoid it. The dart struck his right shoulder and he staggered back from the impact. This unexpected movement tripped off his step and he started falling towards his left. His right arm came down as if paralysed and the Spatishūl fell off from his grip.

A broad smile materialised on Vidyunmali's face as he moved in for the kill. He jumped up and dived in for the final blow. As he landed, his crystal sword impacted against Hara's Spatishūl who had moved in to intercept the blow. When he emerged from the bungalow, Hara had seen Acharya Parashu starting to fall and had leapt in to intervene. While Acharya attempted to recover, Hara and Vidyunmali faced each other.

Hara was aware that his beloved guru had been wounded and knowing the power that Vidyunmali's weapons could unleash, he was not sure whether he would survive. The expression on his face was of pure fury when he took up the Tāndav position of combat. Without slightest thought of his own safety, Hara launched himself against his adversary like a wounded lion. The motion of the Spatishūl in accordance with the Tāndav mudras was unbelievably swift – almost like lightning strikes in close quarters. Vidyunmali, who opposed him, had never seen anything like this before. He struggled to keep pace but Hara was unstoppable. He was now totally one with the universal shakti that coursed through his entire being. With eyes wide with mad rage and almost in a state of trance, Hara had absolutely no control over himself. He was like a cosmic machine of destruction, bent on consuming anything in its path and it seemed that nothing could stand up against such terrible wrath. Within just another krastha, Vidyunmali stood still, waiting for the inevitable. His sword had been blown away and he was completely defenceless. Hara raised his Spatishūl for the final blow that would cleave off his opponent into vertical halves, from skull to groin.

"No Hara! Don't kill him," Acharya Parashu shouted at the last moment. The sound of his guru brought Hara back from the trance of his rage, "Why Acharya? He deserves to die."

"That may be so Hara. But right now, he is unarmed and helpless. Bheeshma monks don't strike those who are defenceless," Acharya Parashu reminded.

Vidyunmali couldn't believe his luck when Hara slowly lowered his Spatishūl and walked back to his guru. The dart that had struck the Bheeshma veteran was still embedded in his shoulder. Even though excruciatingly painful, fortunately it had not pierced any vital organ. Taking Hara's hand, he slowly got back on his feet. Still exhausted by the fierce combat sequence earlier, he was doing deep pranayam breathing to regain his physical strength. Then, looking at Rishi Agastya and his wife, who were watching the scene with gaping eyes, he said, "There is no time to lose. We must move quickly and reach Amatya's ship before any Daityan reinforcements catch up."

𐤀 Ш ϙ

Emperor Tarakaksh was in his private chamber when he heard Mahisha seeking urgent audience with him.

"What is it Mahisha?" he asked.

"Your Majesty, I have come with bad news. As expected, there has been an attack at the bungalow housing Rishi Agastya. The attackers have managed to successfully rescue the Rishi."

"What? The enemy has entered our high security zone and conducted a successful attack right under our nose? How many attackers were there?"

"It was the two Bheeshma monks that we had been informed about earlier," Mahisha said with his head lowered.

"So you're saying that inspite of having been forewarned, just two monks could negate the complete Daityan security?"

"Your Majesty, we had beefed up the security at the bungalow. There were at least fifteen soldiers guarding the place, including three Yantraksh. I was also planning to relocate the Rishi today itself but the monks surprised us by launching a stealth attack during early hours of the morning. They have escaped by a ship belonging to Rakshas Amatya. I believe another young Rakshas named Prahalad was also involved. Our vimāns are still trying to track their ship on the high seas, but the weather conditions are very bad today...."

"I still can't believe that two monks could neutralise fifteen soldiers. Now you are saying two Daityas from Rakshas clan were also party to this?" Tarakaksh asked in a surprised tone.

"Amatya is no more a Daityan citizen after he was dishonoured a few years ago. Prahalad is the son of one of our illustrious Generals – Hiranyakashipu. I believe they expected us to track them down and, therefore, have moved out along with their families." Mahisha replied and then hesitated before continuing, "Your Majesty, there is another very bad news. Vidyunmali..."

"What happened to my brother?" Emperor asked anxiously.

"Based on your directions, Vidyunmali had taken personal change of the guards at the bungalow. He was also killed in the attack."

"What?" The expression on the face Tarakaksh changed from surprise to that of deep remorse, "My younger brother . . . is dead?"

"From the evidence on the site, it is clear that he fought valiantly, but was mercilessly chopped down by the Bheeshma monks."

"Please leave me alone," the Emperor said, tears already welling in his eyes. Mahisha made a hasty retreat, even as he struggled to suppress the sly smile slowly materialising upon his lips.

14

SOJOURN AT GANDHARV

It took them over 15 days to reach Lonar, the second largest city of Gandharv kingdom. This is where Amatya's family was located after he had migrated to Gandharv. Acharya Parashu had agreed that it might be a good place for all of them to rest and recuperate before deciding further plans. Amatya had deliberately navigated his ship along a circuitous sea route to mislead any potential pursuers. Fortunately, the journey was relatively uneventful except for the inclement weather on the way. The bad weather might have also actually helped shake off any attempts by Daityan vimāns to intercept them on high seas. While in the ship, Acharya Parashu's wound on the shoulder had been attended to by Agastya Rishi himself. They had disembarked from Amatya's ship at a discrete beach near the port town of Kambhoj before continuing on a four-day journey on land in Lonar. Amatya's contacts within the town had helped them purchase a few horses to speed up their travel along the trade route.

The daring rescue of Agastya from Atalantpuri by two Bheeshma monks was rejoiced throughout Devarth. Special words of appreciation were sent by Indra. From Devan perspective, it was definitely a strategic advantage that Rishi

Agastya would no longer be available to help their enemy continue the development of Kayakalp rejuvenation system and its possible misuse for military applications. Brihaspati had himself come up to Lonar in a Devan vimān to meet them. He had a detailed discussion with Agastya regarding the state of progress made by Daityas in various scientific endeavours. He was also somewhat disappointed about their inability to gather any tangible information regarding the suspected mole within Devan leadership. The Gandharv King Dwapar had reassured Amatya and Prahalad that they would be given all assistance to start any business of their choice. Prahalad had got his family along and hoped to start a new life within Gandharv itself.

At last Hara could get to be with Brihaspati alone for a moment. The Dev Guru actually pre-empted what was in Hara's mind ever since his return from Atalantpuri, "I'd met Uma few weeks back and she was exceedingly anxious about you. I had suggested that to keep her mind steady, it may be best that she continued her dance lessons at the Apsara Academy of Lonar."

"Are you saying Uma is here at Lonar?" Hara asked with obvious elation.

"Yes Hara, she came two days after you embarked on this mission from Amaravati. She may not be able to contact you on her own, without creating a scandal. However, if you wish to visit the Apsara Academy, that shouldn't be a problem," Brihaspati smiled back and then continued, "They may even let you join one of their dance training programmes. It would be most interesting to see a Bheeshma monk dancing, instead of fighting." Brihaspati laughed aloud while patting Hara's back.

༏ Ш ༞

A few days later, Amatya came to visit Acharya Parashu and Hara. The Gandharv King had requested the Bheeshma veteran to stay at the royal palace itself as he still needed medical attention of the royal Vaidyas. With the aid of regular dosage of Amruth, he was recovering fast but it needed a few more weeks of healing for him to move around freely.

Hara and Amatya decided to take a walk up to the city centre of Lonar. Though fairly small in size, Lonar was indeed a beautiful city with artistic architectural features almost wherever one looked. Unlike Amaravati or Atalantpuri, however, mechanical transport or any kind of high-tech systems were rare and only available to the extremely rich who could afford imported luxuries. The most common mode of transport was based on horse-drawn chariots. The town planners had taken this into consideration and there were excellent walkways all over the town. It was obvious that Amatya, who had migrated with his family here few years earlier, was quite familiar with the city. He led Hara into one of the grand walkways.

"This town seems quite foreigner-friendly, Amatya. I can see people from all races and cultures," Hara said.

Amatya who was looking over some local business interactions happening nearby said, "This is a city built for trade to flourish, Hara. Gandharv owes much of its prosperity to its business-friendly culture. Due to their trader-friendly policies, many Gandharvan ports and towns have become some of the most favoured trade hubs across the world. Businessmen from all over the world prefer the friendly, free, and open-minded environment that they can experience here. The tax being extremely low also helps them."

"If the tax is low, how does it benefit the Gandharv nation?"

"Low tax is more than compensated by the sheer volume of trade. Besides, Gandharv kingdom also benefits from being able to trade its own unique produce with ease. As you might know, Gandharv is renowned for its medicines, herbs, exotic beauty-enhancing cosmetics and above all, the exquisite jewellery that gets exported to all corners of the known world. The general environment of tolerance and free mixing of culture, races, ideas, and art from across the world has helped them develop a society that is peaceful yet progressive in all aspects of life."

"Amatya, I've heard Gandharv being referred to as the land of music, dancing and Apsaras. Is that true?" Hara asked, trying to hide the excitement in his voice.

"Indeed, it is. Gandharvans have keen interest in art, sculpture, music and dance. Women, in general, enjoy far more freedom here than anywhere in the world. In fact many of their customs actually favour the fairer gender. Apsaras of Gandharv are famous for their exquisite beauty and dancing skills." Amatya smiled and continued "Maybe we should visit the renowned Apsara Academy? It is not very far from here."

"Yes, that would be great," Hara smiled.

𐤀 𐤔 𐤊

The evening dance performance was just about to begin at the Apsara School of Dance Arts. Hara and Amatya had managed to get a front seat. Amatya had also brought his wife Tilotama along. As the curtain was raised, the audience gasped, totally mesmerised by the fantastic and elaborate settings on the stage, which created an immediate illusion that they were in some other world. Then the dancers emerged one by one, performing perfect dance sequences. As per the tradition with all Apsara dance sequences, majority of the dancers were of the fairer sex.

Each of them were dressed differently but within the overall theme of classical Apsara style. The dresses were simple and elegant but they still managed to somehow enhance the implicit sensuality of the dancer's curves. The exquisitely crafted jewellery adorning their bodies complemented the effect even more. Much to Amatya's and Tilotama's surprise, Hara almost stood up involuntarily as Uma made her entry. The diamond jewellery used to secure the brilliant white dress to her delicate body enhanced its radiance under the stage lights. It was clear that her divine form hardly needed any more adornments. Yet the small white and yellow flowers freshly woven on a golden headband seemed to accentuate her goddess-like grace even further. On noticing Hara sitting right in front of her eyes, she missed the beat and tripped over one step in surprise. Her eyes opened wide but then she controlled herself and continued to perform.

Soon, the dancers were performing the celestial ballet that completely absorbed the attention of the audience. Hara's eyes were focused on Uma, and hers on his. It seemed that a wild surge of intoxicating energy had risen up within her and it overflowed into the fluid yet precise rhythms of her body movements. Hara could actually hear his heart thumping as the intensity of Uma's sensual and passionate dance sequence reverberated on his soul. Even from a distance he found his astral self being drawn towards Uma's persona.

The crowd went wild with applause watching the graceful and exquisite performance by the Apsara dancers. No one except Amatya's wife Tilotama seemed to have noticed the invisible connection between Uma and Hara. She was smiling as she looked sideways at the mesmerised, totally smitten look on Hara's face.

After the performance, Hara met Uma behind the stage. "How are you?" they asked together so neither could understand the other.

"You look beautiful," Hara stated.

"Is that all you have to say after so many weeks?" Uma asked in mock complaint.

"You were and are always on my mind, Uma. So time has no meaning," Hara replied with a smile.

"After you left, I couldn't stay at Amaravati anymore. So I came here to continue the dance lessons." She was silent for a moment and then continued softly, "Dev Guru Brihaspati told me that your mission was a very dangerous one. I learnt only recently that you'd been to the Daityan capital of Atalantpuri."

"Yes, the mission was a risky one. And to tell you the truth, it is only because of Acharya Parashu that I'm still alive. He has himself been injured and is now recovering at the Gandharv royal palace."

"Oh," Uma exclaimed and continued, "I must visit him immediately. Is there anything I can do?"

"You can visit him tomorrow. He is out of danger and is recovering fast," Hara reassured her.

None said a word for a while as they silently looked at each other. Uma broke the silence by asking, "Hara, now that your mission is over, I hope you're free to spend some time at Lonar?"

"I would like nothing better, Uma. If your dance academy allows admission of new male students, maybe I could join some classes too? Perhaps I could even have the privilege of your instruction sometimes," Hara said light-heartedly.

Uma's eyes went wide with excitement, "I'll ensure that you are admitted."

"Frankly, I don't know how long I would get to stay at Lonar. But as long as I'm here, I don't want to miss a moment being with you," Hara said softly.

Over the course of next few months, Acharya Parashu had recovered from his injuries. Inspite of requests from the Gandharv King Dwapar to continue to stay at the royal palace, he preferred to shift into more frugal environments and had established a small Ashram at the periphery of Lonar. Amatya and Prahalad had partnered to start a new trading business and were already doing very well. Prahalad migrated to the port town of Kambhoj with his family whereas Amatya and his family stayed at Lonar.

Hara would later recall these few months that he spent at Lonar to be the best ones of his life. The environment was pleasing and he liked the free and tolerant culture of the Gandharvan society in general. He did join the Apsara School and learn to dance. Amatya and Hara became close friends while Tilotama was particularly fond of Uma. She was also often delighted to play cupid between the couple in love.

𐤀 Ш ϙ

"I suppose there is no particular rule against it. But I don't recall having heard of any 'Dancing Monks of Bheeshma'," Hara confessed in mock exasperation to Chitrasena, the chief patron of the Gandharv Academy of Dance Arts. They were at the royal palace on invitation from the Gandharv King Dwapar for discussing the plan for Vasantotsav celebrations due in a few weeks. Vasantotsav was the most popular festival in the whole of Gandharv kingdom.

"Hara, there is always a first time for anything. Why can't a Bheeshma monk be a good dancer as well? You're a naturally gifted dancer with your own unique style. With a few months of training, you've already become the most popular dancer in the academy. I have overheard other members refer to you as Natarāj, the cosmic dancer," Chitrasena replied.

"I was simply attempting to modulate my instinctive combat movements into a dance sequence. Sometimes we Bheeshma monks develop unique styles of combat to suit our own strengths and natural advantages," Hara answered modestly.

"Oh! I can see that your distinctive style of dancing might've definitely come from combat practice. Actually dancing is really not all that different from close combat. You've such perfect control over your movements even while performing complex sequences. I've never seen such wild yet synchronised movements from any male dancer so far. The intensity and the sense of rhythm are simply outstanding. In Gandharv, we encourage the artists to follow their natural instincts by choreographing such exclusive styles to perfection. Do you have any particular name for this style?"

"Within the Bheeshma circles, my style of close combat is known as the Tāndav."

"Tāndav, indeed! We'll call your style of dance also by that name. Would you be willing to give a performance during the dance festival of Nrityotsav that we plan to organise next month?"

"Nrityotsav?" Hara asked.

"Yes, Hara. It is part of the celebrations of Vasantotsav."

"I'll give a performance if Uma joins me."

"That's not going to be too difficult to arrange," Chitrasena said with a broad smile on her face.

Tilotama was listening to the conversation and said, "Hara, why don't you consider following a dance career at Gandharv? I know Uma would be delighted if you did."

"Tilotama, first and foremost, I'm a Bheeshma monk," Hara replied sternly.

Tilotama smiled while replying, "Not for long if you're planning to marry Uma!" Hara kept quite so Tilotama continued, "Please do consider it, Hara. I don't think your Bheeshma guru will object."

"Tilotama, my guru would always encourage me to pursue my Karma."

Amatya also happened to hear this bit of their conversation and asked, "So, what is your Karma, Hara?"

"I am not sure, Amatya. We Bheeshma monks are trained to instinctively feel out our correct karmic path. Ever since I have come to Lonar, it has been somewhat confusing."

"No wonder," Amatya laughed, "That they say love has enough potential to carve its own karmic path for nothing." He then continued on a more serious note, "Hara, not everyone in this life gets a chance to follow the path of love. It is not easy but the outcome is definitely worth it. Go for it even if you have to veer away from the path of your Karma," Amatya advised.

'You're probably right..." Hara mused doubtfully.

"To be uncertain of our future is perhaps a good thing. By the way, when are you planning to ask for Uma's hand from her father?" Tilotama was insistent on keeping the discussion firmly focused around the subject of marriage.

"It is not that..." Hara looked at her.

"Do you love her, Hara?"

"Very much. You know that," Hara replied.

"And I know she worships you, Hara," Tilotama said, "So then what is the problem? Are you worried that her father might say no?"

Amatya cut in, "I don't think Indra is going to object. If I'm not wrong, he must already know about you both. Anyway, Bheeshma monks are held in such a high esteem within all of Devarth that a marriage like this would only enhance his own stature. Besides that, now you're such a popular dance artist of Gandharv, too," he laughed with gusto while patting Hara's back.

"It is not Indra's objection that I am worried about; it is the timing," Hara said, looking down.

"What is wrong with the timing, Hara? I know Uma would like nothing better," Tilotama asked.

Hara was silent for a while before answering, "I instinctively feel it best to prolong the present moments as long as possible. Before leading a grihastya way of life, I would need to surrender my Bheeshmatv. I'm okay with that but it is not just that. Once married, we may be encouraged to move to Amaravati and get involved in the turbulent circumstances of these times. Acharya Parashu tells me that even if nobody would admit it openly, preparations for a war have already begun at Amaravati."

Amatya agreed, with a somewhat serious tone, "I've heard of these rumours, too. The merchants seem quite jittery about it, but so far it has been excellent for business. There is a lot of demand for raw materials and medicines both from Daityan Empire and

Dev Lok. Not sure how long the good times are going to last though. Here at Lonar, people are living oblivious of the trouble brewing around them. We can hope that its status as a trading haven may continue to keep Gandharv a neutral territory for some more time. This is not likely to be the case at Dev Lok though."

Tilotama interrupted in mock anger, "You men are always reluctant when it comes to getting into commitments and look for one excuse or the other. There is never going to be a perfect time for marriage. So why wait? If you want, you could avoid all the pomp associated with royal weddings and get married here at Lonar itself. Just give me your consent and I'll arrange it all myself."

"How?" Hara was curious.

"Hara, Gandharv is a free society. I feel the citizens here are freer than any other place in the world, and their traditions match such freedom. One of their customs is the solemnisation of marriage with mutual consent of the couples alone. They call it Gandharv Vihah. I'm told many couples around the world travel to Gandharv to marry, especially when social situations in their own countries don't permit it."

Amatya smiled and looked at his wife in admiration, "That is a great idea, Tilotama. I never knew I had such an intelligent wife."

"Yes, you men are too chauvinistic to recognise a woman's intelligence, right?" Tilotama replied, mocking anger.

Amatya laughed and looked at Hara, "On a serious note, it may be a great idea for you and Uma to go for a Gandharv Vivah. It may not be politically incorrect either considering these times, if I may say so. Devraj Indra may find it difficult to conduct a royal wedding at Amaravati, in the backdrop of all the fear and anxiety associated with the preparations for war. It would certainly suit him better if Uma gets married in Gandharv tradition, especially if he consents to the same. Actually Devas recognize Gandharv marriage more than any other society. I'm told the maximum foreign couple who solemnise their marriage by coming over to Gandharv are from Dev Lok."

"Thank you, Amatya and Tilotama. First and foremost, Uma should like the idea. If she does, I would need to take Acharya Parashu's blessings and then take Indra's consent," Hara stated enthusiastically.

15

ASHRAM OF PARASHU

The Ashram was only a collection of few hutments. It was barely outside the periphery of Lonar town, yet well away from its hustle and bustle. Even though everyone knew full well that Acharya Parashu was capable of defending himself, the Gandharv King Dwapar had requested that the Ashram be located within the proximity of the royal guard's outpost. His name was now famous across the world and there was fear that Daityas may seek some sort of revenge against him. Though reluctant in the beginning, Acharya Parashu had accepted the king's suggestion. There were already a few shishyas who had joined the Ashram, wishing to be in close company of the renowned Bheeshma veteran. Over the course of time, if some of them were able to activate the Jwalaprabha within, they may even get to become future warrior monks of the Bheeshma order.

There were looks of admiration in the eyes of the shishyas when they led Hara to Acharya's hut.

"Come in, Hara," Acharya Parashu had just finished his morning meditation when Hara reached his hut.

"Pranam, Acharya. I hope you're completely recovered now?" Hara asked, referring to the injury that the Acharya had suffered during their adventure to Atalantpuri.

Acharya Parashu waved acknowledgement and replied, "Yes, Haŕa. It has healed and I'm fine. Please sit down and tell me how are Amatya, Prahalad and others?"

"They're well, Acharya," Haŕa said and then continued hesitantly, "Acharya, I was told by the messenger that you wanted to meet me to discuss an important matter?"

"That can wait, Haŕa. First tell me how are your dance lessons proceeding? I've heard that you've become quite a popular dance artist within Gandharv? People have even started addressing you by the name Natarāj," Acharya Parashu smiled while asking.

Haŕa smiled back, "The dance training has been useful Acharya. It just so happened that with a few choreographic modifications, my combat style has been appreciated here as a unique dance form."

"That is good, Haŕa. Is it only dance that is keeping you at Lonar?"

"Well, I have friends like Amatya. And then you're also close by…" Haŕa replied hesitantly.

"You don't have to be shy with me, Haŕa," Acharya laughed and then continued, "How's Uma?"

"She's also a great dancer, Acharya. In fact we're practicing together to perform a duet during the Nrityotsav at the Vasantotsav festivities at Lonar. I hope you would attend…"

"I would indeed, Haŕa. I'm glad that you're happy. It is not in the Karma of everyone to get love; what you have is very precious. Secure it at all cost. I'm sure the idea of marriage and grihastya must have occurred to you. Dancing is a good career, too," Acharya smiled while asking.

"Yes, Acharya. Amatya and his wife Tilotama have been behind me to tie the knot with Uma as soon as possible. They have even suggested a Gandharv Vivah to avoid the complications of a royal wedding."

"And what does Uma feel?"

"Uma is ecstatic but would like her parents' blessings," Hara said.

"I would also recommend a Gandharv Vivah given the current situation at Dev Lok. Brihaspati hinted of it when he was here a few weeks back. I'm sure he would recommend the same to Indra Dev when the time comes."

"Thank you, Acharya. Your blessings are most important to me."

"My blessings are always with you, Hara. However, you would need to decide this path by yourself based on your karmic insight. It would also mean giving up your Bheeshmatv, but that is not that big a problem. Even Maharshi Vashist took up grihastya for many years before re-joining the order. Though officially not part of the order, you would always remain a Bheeshma as long as your Jwalaprabha is bright and insight to Karma steady."

Hara wanted to tell Acharya Parashu that his insight had been somewhat confusing for the past few months but decided not to. He thought it'd be wise to tell him later and asked instead, "Acharya, you were to tell me about an important matter?"

"Oh, yes! Maharishi Vashist feels that the Bheeshma might be of help in attempting to resolve this crisis of war looming over the world. He has advised that we help Devas in whatever way we can."

"And is this the view of complete Bheeshma order also?"

Acharya Parashu paused a while before answering, "A world level war that may soon happen between Devarth and Daityan Empire, followed with the inevitable turmoil of global warming is likely to be catastrophic to humanity as a whole. There is a danger that all we've achieved as a civilisation since the Mūrthi ascended from their physical form eons ago might get completely wiped out. It is important that even if there is a war, Daityas don't win it. If Daityas were to get control of the world, we're likely to lose all of our spiritual heritage and plunge into a prolonged

Dark Age or even extinction as a species. I'm sure the Mūrthi don't want that to happen. This is also the perception of the Sapta-Rishis who maintain regular astral contact with them."

"Acharya, if Mūrthi didn't want Daityan domination, why did they let them acquire such power over others on the world?"

"It is not that simple, Hara. Daityas are no different from other humans; there are good and bad among them, as is the case with Devas, Manavas, Gandharvas and Yakshas. There are even a few great spiritually-advanced Maharishis of Rakshas lineage and they maintain astral interactions with the Mūrthi. Their main guru, Acharya Shukra, regularly interacts with Sapta-Rishis at Dev Lok. Lately, however, as we came to know from Amatya and Prahalad, a majority of them have been moving away from spiritual advancements and indulging in singular pursuit of material wealth, power and pleasure. While this in itself is not bad, its karmic impact is that of decline for the human species. Every pursuit of gathering material wealth by someone means poverty for someone else. After all, wealth and power have any meaning only against a backdrop of poverty and weakness. Similarly every attempt to pursue sensual pleasure creates a karmic opposite in the form of pain; every form of material satisfaction or comfort creates a counter-effect within the mind leading to further dissatisfactions either at the physical level or the mental level. This is like a disease and it is only incidental that Daityas happen to suffer from it more than others."

"But Acharya, what about all the scientific progresses that they've made? You've seen the splendour of their achievements at Atalantpuri. Even if we discount their lust for wealth and pleasure, surely their technological advancements have benefitted mankind. They've been able to control diseases, improve agriculture, and build industries providing employment to all the citizens. Their technologies even help them counter the effects of rising sea water," Hara was sceptical about taking Daityas as completely depleted.

"You're right, Haŕa. Their achievements are certainly worthy of appreciation. However, a civilisation is not to be judged by its wealth, comforts and technological or medical advancements alone. It is also important to understand its mental advancements – especially at a spiritual level – which is the precursor for real happiness."

"Are you saying that Daityas are deliberately moving away from spiritual advancement and, therefore, towards unhappiness?" Haŕa asked.

"It is impossible to judge the level of happiness based on one's material pursuits. Everything that Daityas have achieved neither adds nor reduces their levels of happiness. Just like in the physical world, for every action there is a reaction; action in pursuit of material aspirations invariably creates a karmic imbalance which would tend to correct in future. So their state of ephemeral happiness keeps vacillating."

"Acharya, is this not the way most humans live their lives?"

"Yes that is true enough. In the spiritual sense, however, this is a stagnant state. Consistent movement away from our spiritual nature towards material aspiration leads to eventual decline of human spirit. Within the nature of evolution of intelligent species, this can manifest in the form of either over-consumption of resources or self-destruction. The ultimate impact is a steady decline and eventual extinction of the species. Along with themselves, they also drag down other species within their sphere of influence. Till recently, the material pursuits of Daityan Empire were probably offset by some degree of spiritual growth as well. Unfortunately, this has changed over the past few decades."

"Oh, so you mean to say that the order of Bheeshma also feels that if it becomes necessary to take sides in this war, it is to be with the Devarth?"

"Yes, Haŕa. It is safe to say that the future of humanity depends on ensuring that Daityas don't get to dominate the world. Since war may be unavoidable, this is only feasible if Daityas don't win. The Bheeshma would continue to be in support of the Devas."

"Are we to go on another Bheeshma mission, Acharya?" Hara asked reluctantly, thinking that this may mean separation from Uma for some time.

"Brihaspati has requested for our help on a specific task. I told him that I would arrange to have other Bheeshma monks assigned for this task but he trusts only you," Acharya Parashu paused for a while before continuing. "This should be more of an internal mission within Amaravati itself and you may not need to be separated from Uma for too long," he finished with a smile.

"Oh, does that mean we are to go to Amaravati, Acharya?" Hara asked.

"Not we, Hara; I won't be coming. It is not there in my karmic path. This is to be undertaken by you alone. Dev Guru Brihaspati would be there to help you."

Hara was a bit taken aback and exclaimed, "I've never undertaken a mission alone, Acharya. You've always been there to guide me."

"It is now time for you to be independent, Hara. You've actually been more than ready for quite some time. This is a path we all need to take at some point in life. I'll always be there to guide you at the astral level," Acharya said softly.

"Thank you, Acharya. You also mentioned that this is to be an internal mission?"

"You remember Brihaspati telling us while we were at Amaravati that he has been aware of a serious security breach within Dev Lok. He has still not been able to identify the source but it is obvious that someone at a very senior level has been cooperating with Daityas and passing on essential information."

"I remember that Dev Guru Brihaspati had also mentioned the possibility of a mole within Indra Sabha itself?"

"Yes, Hara. But now it is emerging that he or she may not only just be a mole. This person may also have his or her own personal agenda. Apart from passing on secret information, he may also endanger the stability of Dev Lok, especially at these critical times."

"So they want Bheeshma to play detective?"

Acharya Parashu smiled, "Hara, as you know they can only request a Bheeshma. We shall always remain committed to our code of Karma alone. As I've said before, it is for you to sense whether a mission is to be your karmic path. Yes, this mission may involve some bit of deductive skills but more importantly, it is also a protective one. There is reason to believe that the life of Devraj Indra may be in mortal danger."

"Oh," Hara exclaimed, his immediate thoughts going to Uma. She would definitely prefer Hara to be protecting her father.

"Now you understand the gravity of the situation." He cleared his throat and added, "This may also be an opportunity for you to get close to Uma's father," Acharya Parashu continued smilingly "and who knows, maybe even ask her hand in marriage?"

Later after Hara had a simple meal with Acharya he finally came to bid farewell and take his leave.

"I'll need your blessings to be successful in this mission, Acharya," he said and touched Acharya's feet.

"*Vijayi bhavah*, may you be victorious. My blessing will always be with you, Hara," Acharya Parashu said, keeping his hand on Hara head. He looked towards the hills some distance away from the Ashram and continued, "Life is an illusionary karmic path, Hara. You'll always be right as long as you follow it with firm conviction and strength that you can access from your own true self. Even the end of this physical life is no end at all, but a mere change of scene along this path"

When Hara was about to leave, Acharya asked him to wait for a while and whispered something to one of the disciples.

He went out and returned in a few minutes, accompanied by a young monk. He looked somewhat oversized for a monk with a strong, muscular body and a swingy gait to match it. Acharya Parashu smiled as he approached them and said, "Hafa, let me introduce you to your new Bheeshma apprentice on this mission. His name is Nandi."

16

DAITYAN COUNCIL

The Daityan Emperor Tarakaksh had called for a private conference with his close aides. In attendance were Kamalaksh, Acharya Shukra, Maya, Mahisha and Narakaksh, the chief of Daityan armed forces. They were at his royal chamber, right at the edge of the topmost citadel of Tripura. The royal chamber overlooked the western part of the island.

The Emperor looked around at his aides and stated, "Gentlemen, you all are well aware that the Empire is in a state of crisis due to the continued inundation of our farmlands. For past many months, we've been patiently exploring all the alternatives to a war with Devarth. Inspite of our best efforts, an armed conflict seems inevitable. Before we venture any further in that direction, I would like to clearly understand the fundamental strengths and weaknesses of the Empire against Devarth's. Let me first request Maya to brief us about the current situation from his techno-strategic perspective."

Maya got up from his seat and said, "Thank you, Your Majesty." Then, turning towards all present he continued, "I'll first explain the high grade Mūrthi technologies available to both Daityan and Devarth nations. As you all know, the scientific knowledge of Vigyan Vedas handed down by the Mūrthi is accessible to very few. To understand the knowledge contained in these scriptures, one requires very special skills and advanced training. Within Daityan Empire, it is only known to a select few Rakshas scientists. On the Devan side, this knowledge is kept preserved by a small section of the priestly community called Vasus. It is also true that humans are yet to completely assimilate this knowledge to put it into full technological applications. Build-up of any such technology still requires some form of astral linkage with the Mūrthi lords. Till now, at best we've only been able to maintain such systems built in the past. The two major centres of Mūrthi technology on both sides are Tripura and Amaravati."

"Are they both of similar grade from a military standpoint?" Mahisha was curious.

"That is difficult to say since the application of the knowledge by both sides has been fundamentally different. You see, Tripura was built as a fortress with full military defence capabilities, by using regular as well as Mūrthi technologies. Even though mostly automated, it still requires fairly high maintenance by a team of highly qualified Rakshas."

"What about Amaravati?"

"The Dev Lok capital Amaravati was built by the Mūrthi when they used to inhabit Earth. It was built based on completely unconventional methods of astral link up with natural living systems—a specialised spiritual technique developed by the Mūrthi during the later years of their stay on Earth. Being mostly based on natural systems, it gives them an edge in the form of resiliency and efficiency. For example, they're able to maintain the complete city of Amaravati with far lesser human resources as compared to Tripura. Since the structure is based on live self-morphing crystal technology, it is able to adapt better in response to rising sea water by simply growing upwards. From a military perspective, however, the city of Amaravati has only defensive force-field shields."

"These shields based on the Mūrthi technology must surely need enormous power to sustain? It is also known that almost all of our power requirements for conventional technologies are provided by the Mūrthi power plants. I've always wondered how it is possible for these power plants to produce so much energy without any input in the form of raw materials," Kamalaksh asked curiously.

Maya sighed and answered after a brief pause, "Asur Kamalaksh, to answer your question, we need to understand the structure of this universe. It was realised by the Mūrthi many eons ago that our universe in all its vastness is a mere anomaly within the infinite Brahmn. This infinite Brahmn can be understood as perpetual and silent potentiality which also means inexhaustible energy or unfathomable void at the same time. Though it is difficult to perceive the Brahmn in a conceptual sense, let us understand that out of this potentiality, manifestation of an infinite variety of conceptual or physical realities are feasible. Our universe can be seen as one such reality. It may be sufficient for me to say that the Mūrthi found a way to tap into this infinite source of energy in a limited manner. The energy extracted in this manner must, however, be limited to just what is necessary for use. Uncontrolled extraction can disrupt the space-time fabric of the universe and that would be catastrophic. So the technique that they used has an equation which inhibits energy intake beyond a limit. This is why we need multiple power plants to sustain high energy systems. Even though our scientists have been able to duplicate this technique, they're still not completely clear as to how it actually works. So, any improvement or modification of the power plant technology is only feasible through the support and direct astral link-up with the Mūrthi Lords."

"Thank you for the information, Maya. Honestly, most of such esoteric Mūrthi science is beyond my understanding. We leave it for you and the scientists to deal with it. Anyway, coming back to discussions about our strengths, what about transportation technology?" Kamalaksh asked.

"In terms of vimān and land-based vehicles, we need to consider both the Mūrthi and indigenous technology. There are very few purely Mūrthi technology-based vimāns or land transport on both sides. We have a few such vimāns within Tripura fortress itself and a land transport at Atalantpuri and other cities, while Devas have some at Amaravati. The Mūrthi vimāns and land transport can move at very high speeds and have almost indefinite range. They use a combination of techniques like anti-gravity, magnetic levitation, etc. Most of the vimāns also use wings to acquire additional lift and range. Due to the limited numbers available, both sides have so far been using them for transporting the royal house or for specialised operations alone. They can, however, be retro-fitted with weapon systems when needed."

"Are these the only Mūrthi technologies in use outside Tripura and Amaravati?"

"Not really. The Mūrthi technologies are used for a variety of civilian and military applications. For example, both sides have a few original pulse-ray hand weapons of Mūrthi legacy. Being relatively rare and highly-prized possessions, these are usually available only for protection of the royal household."

"It is known that Mūrthi had allowed duplication of some power plant systems by humans?"

"Yes. The Mūrthi made an exception in case of power plants alone. This was the only technology that humans were allowed to duplicate on their own without direct help from Mūrthi Lords. So, even though we've developed large number of indigenous systems, the power plants driving them are still based mostly on the Mūrthi technology. Devas have a slight advantage in this case because their power plants have much higher power to weight ratio. This helps them build better vimāns. So, while most of the conventional vimāns on both sides are based on regular wings, theirs are faster and have a longer range compared to ours. In case of land transport systems, we make up for lower power by using multiple units on heavier vehicles. As regards ships, which in any case require multiple power plants, we are evenly matched."

"What about our armed forces? Don't we enjoy technological superiority?" Emperor Tarakaksh asked.

"Your Majesty, our armed forces are better but not necessarily because of the Mūrthi technologies. We have made a lot of advancements in perfecting conventional indigenous technologies. It is by application of such engineering techniques that our ancestors were able to build magnificent cities like Atalantpuri. Except for the power plant, most other components of our ships, transportation systems and vimāns are built indigenously. Our projectile weapons and other military hardware are considered to be deadliest across the known world. They are indeed one of our main exports. Sturdy transport vehicles developed by us are used across the Empire as well as the world. Almost all aspects of Daityan way of life has been touched by our thriving industrial base. Altogether, they directly contribute to the unrivalled superiority of our armed forces."

"How do Devarth fare in this regard?"

"Well, the technological developments at Devarth have mostly been limited to what has been achieved by the Devas. As I mentioned before, most of their developments have been based around tweaking natural systems for civilian use. For example, we know that one of their unique skills is to be able to control weather and initiate rain. The scientists working directly under Indra have fine-tuned these skills and it is regularly used to help irrigate the farmlands throughout Devarth. Not much is known about it but I'm told that the technique involves seeding the clouds using microorganisms that tend to actively condense latent moisture into water drops. Indra's scientists have also been able to harness this technology into military applications when needed. They have developed a unique weapon using which the lightning bolts from the clouds can be directed at specific targets. Known as Vajra, Indra has used it in many past wars with the

Empire. As far as my knowledge goes, they have only one such weapon system and, therefore, the scope of its application in a large-scale war is limited. Its use for warfare is also dependent on the availability of heavy cloud formations above the battlefield. Devas are also good at using the astral link with microorganism to improve farming, thereby increasing food productivity even under poor soil conditions. They have even developed some dual use esoteric technologies like astral projection, but we're not clear whether it has any particular military advantage as such. As I stated earlier, they do have an edge when it comes to vimāns though. Our scientists are still working on improving our aviation systems."

"So you're saying that except in aviation sector, we have a clear technological superiority over them?" the Emperor asked.

"Your Majesty, it is difficult to define technological superiority when both follow different methodologies. Apart from their unconventional techniques of astral engagements, Devas do use conventional science as well, especially for building intricate machineries like transport systems, ships, vimāns, etc. They are equally good if not better than us in terms of overall sophistication. However, our main superiority has been in the manner we could industrialise the process of manufacturing. So, in sheer numbers, power and robustness, we're in a much better position. Incidentally, I totally forgot to mention our progress in tweaking the genetic engineering and breeding techniques handed over by the Mūrthi for military applications. Due credit for that must go to our Rakshas scientists. Experiments in this area have helped us develop a brigade of the fearsome Yantraksh. There is no one who can match their ferocity in battle," Maya said.

"What about the progress of our Kayakalp project?" Kamalaksh asked.

"The project is progressing well. We are now in the final stages of developing the process of infusing Prana. This requires enactment of some unique astral techniques of resonance with cosmic vibrations. After Rishi Agastya was rescued a few months back, it has been tough. But we are making good progress," Maya replied.

"Hmm," Kamalaksh mused, "It seems Devas are far more advanced than us in such matters."

Acharya Shukra looked at Tarakaksh and said, "This is one of the reasons why I've been recommending that even in case of a war, we must never destroy Amaravati. The capital city of Dev Lok holds too many secrets of Mūrthi technologies."

"Good point, Asur Guru. We'll certainly keep that in mind when we develop the primary strategy of war," Tarakaksh said.

༒ Ш ☿

After a brief intermission, they reassembled. Emperor Tarakaksh looked at Narakaksh and asked, "Narakasur, what is the equation of military power between Daityan Empire and Devarth. I know that we have clear superiority but it would be good to hear it from you."

"Yes, Your Majesty," Narakaksh got up from his seat, went up to the nearest wall and pressed on it lightly. The whole wall lit up into a holographic map, clearly highlighting the landscape of Daityan and Devan nations. The position of the various land, naval and air force based military formations on both sides were clearly indicated. He then continued, "First let me briefly explain the state of conventional military forces at the disposal of both sides." Narakaksh paused for a while to articulate his thoughts before continuing, "As regards navy, we have two major formations of Navatakavachas and Kalakeyas which include the marine forces. Navatakavacha formations comprise predominantly of Rakshas and Kalakeya formation of Danav clans. Between both formations we have around sixteen thousand battle ships, frigates, and smaller crafts. Compared to the 9,000-

odd ships at the disposal of Dev Lok, we enjoy overwhelming numerical advantage in naval warfare. I'm still working out the detailed strategy but as per the overall plan, we should attain naval supremacy over the oceans within a month or so after launching the offensive."

"That seems like a clear advantage. I'm assuming that the naval strength should give us control over all the important sea trade routes during war. What about the air and land force?"

Narakaksh touched a pressure point on the screen which displayed various numbers on the screen. He then looked over all and said, "In terms of air power, neither side hold any particular advantage. Though the Devan vimāns are faster and have more range of flight, we have higher numbers. As regards land forces, we have a well-equipped regular army of more the 800,000 comprising both Rakshas and Danav soldiers. The only forces that can match them from Devan side in terms of battle prowess are the Maruths numbering around 170,000. They are the elite corps of soldiers at the disposal of Indra. Devas may also be able to marshal a strength of around 200,000 regular and irregular soldiers from all of the Devarth nations. Even then we would have clear numerical superiority."

"So where are you planning to conduct the main battle?" the Emperor asked.

Narakaksh took a while to carefully think before speaking, "Your Majesty, our strategy would be to first weaken the enemy's morale. This will affect their capacity to take right decisions and make the subsequent battles easier for us. There are some proposals on how to achieve it but I'll come to that later. Right now, let me only focus on the main strategy of the war. Since we have overwhelming superiority in naval power, we would first exploit that strength by cutting off their sea trade lines. This would starve Dev Lok of vital resources from their mainland allies. We know that a significant part of their food supplies come from Bhārat. The next part of the plan would be to lay siege on their ports, thereby effectively isolating their islands from each other. Even if they may continue to use vimāns, it is hardly going to be of much use for moving their troops around or for securing sufficient quantity of vital resources to sustain the war. Soon thereafter, we will land our army at the southern shore part of Bhārat kingdom. Without direct support from Dev Lok, Bhārat will have no choice but to either fight us themselves or surrender their land. Once Bhārat capitulates to our demands, it is only a matter of time before other nations follow. We would ask them to either hand over half of their cultivable land or get into a more favourable and exclusive arrangement of trade. For example, we'll insist on being the sole recipient of food exports at rates fixed by us. The surrender terms would also include free immigration and special status for all Daityas who want to settle down in their nations. We'll establish a strong garrison of our army near their major cities and cultivation centres. By then, starved of resources, Dev Lok should have no choice but to accept our terms of surrender, and that would seal our complete victory over Devarth. One of the important terms of surrender by Dev Lok would be that they hand over the secrets of some of their unique technologies."

"This is simply brilliant, Narakasur" Tarakaksh exclaimed. "If your strategy works, we might be able to secure complete victory." Then he got up and addressed all present, "I'm now convinced that we have more than enough strength to wage and win an armed conflict with Devarth. Considering the dire situation that we are in, there seems little choice but to flex our military might. Even so, if it is feasible, I would like to avoid a war that may result in enormous loss of life and property." He then turned towards Mahisha and said, "Please prepare a document of ultimatum addressed to Indra and explain the crisis that we face within Daityan Empire. Tell him that even though we have the military capability to occupy all nations of Devarth, we are still seeking an amicable solution. If a common understanding can be reached that they either lease half of Bhārat farmlands, or agree to our terms of trade and immigration, there would be no need for a war. Do clarify that even if we take control of their farmlands, we would only use it till we're able to find an alternative solution to our crisis. After that, the land would be returned to Bhārat. Their farmers and other citizens living in that part can also stay and assist us in cultivation. Failure to accept either of our proposals would give us no choice but to unleash an all out war."

"Of course, Your Majesty. I'll have it prepared and despatched today itself," Mahisha reassured him.

Tarakaksh turned towards Narakaksh and said, "Meanwhile, you must continue with your battle plans, preparations and force manoeuvres. In case our efforts of diplomacy fail, we will need to launch a swift and comprehensive military operation on all fronts. I want a decisive victory in least time and with minimum efforts or bloodshel."

"Yes, Your Majesty. We will be ready," Narakaksh assured him.

17

THE ULTIMATUM

"Dev Guru Brihaspati, do you suspect someone in particular?" Hara asked.

They were inside Brihaspati's secure chamber at Amaravati. Hara and Nandi had reached Amaravati the day before by a special Devan vimān. Uma had been extremely reluctant to stay back at Lonar and wanted to return to Amaravati. However, upon Indra's insistence that she stays away from the conflict zone that Dev Lok was developing into, she reluctantly gave in. Hara had reassured her that his mission to Amaravati shouldn't take long to complete and as soon as he was able to identify and thwart the risk to Devraj Indra, he would return. She was somewhat appeased when Hara mentioned that he would also take this opportunity to get to know her father better and ask for her hand.

"Not really, Hara. All we know is that the source is at a very senior level within the Devan government—probably a member of the Indra Sabha itself. You are aware how the information about your mission to Atalantpuri had reached Tripura before you."

"Yes, of course. Acharya Parashu was nearly killed during the mission because of that breach," Hara agreed.

"Very few members within the Indra Sabha were aware of the Bheeshma mission to Atalantpuri. It is a sure indication that this person must be very close to the Sabha itself. Since the threat is so close to the Dev Lok leadership, it only compounds the risk. Based on my suspicion, I've been discretely monitoring the activities of all the members of Indra Sabha, without rousing their suspicions. I work relentlessly on the hope that the traitor remains confident of his hidden identity and makes some mistake so that his identity is revealed," Brihaspati said.

"Does that mean you're sure that the traitor is a member of the Indra Sabha?" Hara asked.

"It would be reasonable to assume so, Hara. However, I don't have any proof to point a finger at anyone," Brihaspati replied with some disappointment in his voice.

"Dev Guru, how do you suggest that I help you?" Hara asked.

"I'm going to announce your inclusion into the Indra Sabha as a Bheeshma advisor. This will help justify your presence in all the meetings. From that point onwards, we may need to simply follow our instincts. I'll keep you updated of all the information I receive from my sources. I have a strong feeling that something is going to happen soon enough; you must be on the guard."

༈ ༄ ༅

The Indra Sabha was seated around Pushkarni with Indra at the head on his crystal throne. Apart from the usual members of the Indra Sabha, the Kings and chief advisors of Bhārat, Gandharv, Kinnara and Yaksha kingdoms were also present. As suggested by Brihaspati, the announcement of Hara's inclusion had been made and he was also part of the gathering. Nandi had stayed back with the Maruth soldiers stationed outside the hall.

Indra looked at all and stated, "Gentlemen, the reason we've gathered today is to examine the ultimatum that has been conveyed by Daityan Emperor Tarakaksh." He then opened the official scroll brought in by an assistant and read out its contents.

"In short, they've asked that we either lease them half of the land within Bhārat kingdom or allow trade and immigration as per their terms. Refusal to agree on either would mean war."

There was uproar in the Sabha as members began talking among themselves, some trying to raise their voice to be heard. Brihaspati rose and signalled everyone to be quite, "I request you all to be patient and allow everyone present here to give their views. Since the ultimatum concerns the Bhārat kingdom directly, I think we should first hear what Bharat King Pareekshit has to say."

King Pareekshit got up and announced vehemently, "The kingdom of Bhārat shall never hand over its land, nor surrender its sovereignty, even if we have to fight with our bare hands."

Sensing the feelings of the king, Indra expressed with fervid concurrence, "We are completely with you, Pareekshit. If the Daityas want war, we will give them that."

Prajapati Daksh looked at Indra and asked, "Your Majesty, should we not at least examine the proposal of Daityas? I earnestly feel that leasing land or allowing softer trading terms are much better alternatives when compared to destruction."

"Prajapati, first this decision is for Bhārat King Pareekshit to take. He has already put forth his views, and I respect it. One of the founding rules of Devarth is that we support each other and put up a joint front when any particular kingdom faces external military threat. In any case, this ultimatum seems more like an excuse to create internal conflict within Devarth. They know very well that either of their proposals would lead to eventual subjugation of Devarth and, therefore, never be acceptable to us. Daityas have been looking for a confrontation any way."

"But Your Majesty, your prime responsibility is towards the citizens of Dev Lok," Daksh insisted.

"Enough!" Indra raised his hand, "I know what my responsibility is and it doesn't include abandoning our close allies in times of crisis in it. Dev Lok will stand besides Bhārat if there is to be a war."

Pareekshit bowed to Indra when he said, "My sincere appreciation, Devraj, for your commitment to stand by us during this time of crisis."

"You're welcome, Pareekshit. This is a time of crisis not for you alone, but the entire Devarth, and we all need to stand up and face it together. Now that we know a war is inevitable, let us focus on our plan of action."

Kuber, the king of Yaksha nation had been quiet so far. He now asked, "Indra Dev, we all know that Dev Lok is the most advanced nation within Devarth. You have the direct benefit of Mūrthi technology, most of which we don't even understand. As in case of past skirmishes with the Daityan Empire, it is our hope that Dev Lok would rise up to the occasion this time as well. You'll have the support of the complete Yaksha kingdom at your disposal."

"Thank you, Kuber. Dev Lok would use its full resources to thwart any military misadventure against Devarth. However, unlike previous times, the bitter reality is that Daityas have amassed huge military hardware and resources over the course of past few decades. They also have clear numerical superiority over us. So, even if some of our forces may be better, they can easily overwhelm us with sheer number of resources at their disposal."

Hara had been listening intently all this while and finally asked, "Your Majesty, are you suggesting that in case of a full-fledged war, Devarth would definitely fall? Is there nothing that we could do to cripple the Daityan Empire? Do they really have no weak spots?"

Prajapati Daksh intervened, "It would indeed be a miracle if we can cripple the Daityan Empire." Then turning to Indra, he continued, "Your Majesty, instead of desperately looking for miracles, we should perhaps examine the option of reconciliation with Atalantpuri. Maybe we could negotiate with them to reach some amicable understanding?"

Indra replied sombrely, "I appreciate your concern, Prajapati. It is well-known and accepted that Daityas have military superiority over us. Nonetheless, let us not forget that our predecessors have beaten them in almost all wars in the past. They did so inspite of the Daityan numerical superiority by skilfully engaging their own unique advantages in the form of force-multipliers. As in case of the past, we can also seek some advice from the Mūrthi Lord Vishnu. With his insightful advice, I'm confident that we can find some way to resist Daityas even against such overwhelming odds that confront us now. Hara is perhaps right. While we continue to enhance our defences, let us also attempt to focus on any weak spots in Daityan defences, to enable us to apply our limited force against that."

It was Brihaspati who answered, "Daityas do have some structural weaknesses within themselves. For example, unlike us, theirs is a single Empire, directly under the control of one Emperor. Their kings are not allowed to take independent decisions, especially on military matters. The complete Empire is controlled from Atalantpuri—more specifically from the Tripura citadels."

"Are you suggesting that we destroy Tripura towers?" It was Daksh who asked, with sarcasm evident in his words.

"Not really, but let us not discount that either." Brihaspati replied before continuing, "I know that Tripura has the strongest defences and most of it is built using Mūrthi technology with the help of Lord Brahma. None of our weapon systems come even close to be able to breach its defences. Yet, if ever we find a way to do so, that would definitely put an end to the war."

"Thank you, Guru Dev. We should also perhaps seek advice from the Mūrthi Lord Vishnu himself. Could we prepare for astral link-up with him through Devayana please?" Indra asked and continued while looking at others, "Meanwhile, we still need to find ways to defend our nations against aggression from the Daityan Empire. I understand Agni Dev has already planned out our strategy for defending Swarga Dweep and other islands of Dev Lok. Varun Dev and Vayu Dev are also pulling together a viable plan of action to counter Daityan offensive from sea and air. Today we hope to study the plan for defending other nations of Devarth."

18

VICIOUS PROPOSAL

"Has Indra responded to our ultimatum?" Emperor Tarakaksh asked Mahisha. They had just returned after surveying some of the flood-effected archipelagos and were seated in the Asur Sabha at Tripura. Also seated with them were the Emperor's brother Kamalaksh, Maya and Narakaksh, the chief of Daityan armed forces.

"The reply came today morning, your Majesty. They've offered us some assistance but it is like pittance when compared to what is needed to address our crisis. Their answer for both our proposals is a clear no. It is also stated that they are prepared to meet us on the battleground but would not part with a single inch of land without a fight," Mahisha replied.

"So they give us no option but war. If that is what they want, so be it. We will rout out the Devarth from the face of this Earth," an angry Tarakaksh roared.

"Yes indeed, Your Majesty. We will end the chapter of Devarth forever from the history of this world. They still seem to be under the illusion that Dev Lok can somehow check mate the Daityan Empire," Mahisha stated, articulating his words carefully.

Tarakaksh then asked Narakaksh once again to brief him regarding his preparation and plan of launching the armed offensive on Devarth. The discussions were then directed towards the strategy of war.

Towards the end of their discussion, Tarakaksh asked Narakasur, "Before I declare war, I have a final question for you. As the chief of Daityan armed forces, are you completely confident of winning this war?"

"Your Majesty, we have war-gamed our plan extensively under various scenarios and are more than confident of its victorious outcome. However, it does depend on some critical assumption. The first one being that the enemy shouldn't have too many Maruths stationed on the mainland when we launch the offensive. Second, they don't have any strength other that what we're already aware of. Third, that Mūrthi wouldn't be able to intervene actively. Our bitter experience in the past has been that Devas come up with something totally unexpected when they're driven into a corner."

"You can never trust Devas on what they come up with. Do we have any information on what they are planning?" Kamalaksh asked, looking at Mahisha.

"Yes, indeed. The fools seem to think that they can strike a blow on Daityan Empire by destroying Tripura. They've even brought in a Bheeshma monk as advisor to the Indra Sabha. Maybe they're looking forward to his spiritual advice regarding warfare," Mahisha laughed.

"This seems to me like either a desperate idea or a diversionary tactic. We all know that it is impossible for them to even come close to Tripura, let alone breach its force-field shields or destroy it," Narakasur said mockingly.

"Okay, let us still examine the feasibility of this idea. What would it take to destroy Tripura?" Tarakaksh asked in a serious tone.

Narakasur smiled before answering, "Your Majesty, they need to be either totally mad or foolish even to think of destroying Tripura. We all know that Tripura is the only structure in the whole world that was developed specifically as a formidable military platform using the Mūrthi technology. To begin with, our navy will not allow any Devan ships to come anywhere close to the citadels. Even if they somehow manage to do that, the big guns on Tripura will blow them to smithereens. If they attempt to launch an aerial attack, either our combat vimāns stationed at Atalantpuri or the Mūrthi vimāns within Tripura itself can be launched to shoot them down. Even if some vimāns manage to slip by, I am sure our missiles and air defence guns in Tripura will make short story out of them."

"I agree that this is extremely unlikely but just for the sake of argument, let us assume that they do manage to get past your naval armada, guns, vimāns, etc?"

"Sure, Your Majesty, let us consider it through to the end. We suppose that one or two of their ships or vimāns manage to slip past all our defences and get close enough to put Tripura within their gun range. The invisible force-shields of Tripura are so strong that even the most powerful weapon systems made by Mūrthi technology can't breach it. It is a multi-layered shield that no projectile or pulse-ray weapons can ever hope to penetrate. Even Anvik projectiles would barely scratch the multi-layered shields. If this were not enough, the shields of each of the three citadels are powered independently. In the unlikely event that one gets breached, others take over seamlessly till it is restored. The only way to expose the citadels is by breeching all the three shields simultaneously. We can't even conceive in our mind the kind of enormous power that is needed to breach all three together," Narakaksh explained.

"Thank you, Narakasur. This is very reassuring," Tarakaksh said. Then he got up, and said, "Please carry on with your final preparations. I'll decide about the day to launch the offensive and let you know. Our first attack would also be an implicit declaration of war."

As all others rose up, he looked at Mahisha and said, "We can now have that meeting you've been requesting for. Please meet me at my royal chambers conference room. Do get along Asur Guru Shukracharya and my brother Kamalaksh."

As the Daitya Sabha dispersed, Acharya Shukra, Kamalaksh and Mahisha followed the Emperor to his chambers.

When others had settled down, Emperor Tarakaksh asked Mahisha, "I hope this is important, Mahishasur; we all have plenty of work to do in preparation for the war."

"Yes, Your Majesty, it is," Mahisha replied. Addressing everyone, he said, "We know that the situation of rising sea water is critical. All of our islands have been more or less impacted. Only Atalantpuri is safe for the time being because of the barrier reefs as well as the high ground that it was built on. Once the war starts, our complete national resources are going to be diverted to that end. This also means that our effort to control the sea water is going to be severely curtailed."

"Yes, indeed. But that is the nature of all wars. Resources need to get diverted to ensure that we win the war decisively," Kamalaksh said.

"Yes, Kamalaksh, I do understand that. However, let's also not forget the implication of uncontrolled inundation of our islands. Even now, most of our farmlands on the Talas are below the sea level and are only sustained by constant pumping out of water and continuous maintenance of the securing embankments. If there is a single breech, it would be catastrophic for that island," Mahisha said in a grave tone.

"This is a concern for me too, Mahisha," Emperor Tarakaksh said looking at him, "I can also understand your worry that the kingdom on the Patala is impacted the most. However, this is not the time to discuss problems of individual nations. We're going to this war together and all kingdoms need to share its outcome – both in terms of suffering and victory. As a special consideration, your kingdom of Patala will be the first to get rehabilitated after the war. So you must consider this war to be a win-or-perish situation."

"Thank you for your concerns, Your Majesty, but I was not referring to Patala alone. You see, based on the plan put forth by Narakasur earlier, it is going to take many months of trade route blockade, naval siege, land battle campaigns and negotiations before we may have some semblance of victory. Only then may we be able to either migrate our citizens or supplement their food supply. Unfortunately, we don't have the luxury of so much time. What if while we lay siege on Dev Lok, our own islands start getting inundated? Food supply may immediately get restricted since we are already running on extremely low reserves. Once hunger starts, clashes between communities would spark off. The age-old tension between Rakshas and Danavs may come to surface and can even explode into a full-scale internal conflict. The fact that most of our military garrisons would be vacant and stationed at some distant land for war would only worsen the situation. There would be no one to control any untoward internal strife when it actually happens. Insufficient troops to enforce law and order may encourage some people to raid the military war reserves for food and other supplies. Without sufficient supply of food and other war logistics, our soldiers would immediately feel the pinch. If this happens, you may need to divert a substantial portion of the armed forces to control the internal situation at home. A weakened force structure in the frontlines may get exploited by the Devas to launch a counter-offensive. The consequence could be totally catastrophic for the Empire. We may lose the war even before it starts. In fact, our offensive can open up so many fault lines within our structure that we could simply crumble against the slightest kick in the form of an effective counter-offensive by the combined forces of all Devarth nations."

Emperor Tarakaksh looked at Mahisha with wide eyes as he understood the gravity of what was being implied. For a while there was pin drop silence within the chamber. After a few moments, the Emperor spoke, "I can see that there is merit in your point, Mahisha. Thank you for highlighting the possible adverse impact of what we're going to undertake." Then he looked at others and asked, "What do you have to say to this?"

Kamalaksh was the first one to speak, "We seem to be running out of options. If inundation of islands is inevitable, what choice do we have? Mahisha is probably right about the possibility of unpleasant scenarios in case we were to launch prolonged war operations against Devarth. However, if we don't take this action now, there may never be another opportunity again. We may get so wrapped up in internal problems that it would be impossible to consider it again. That would also mean a steady decline of the Empire as we keep running from pillar to post to support our refugee population."

The silence that followed was deafening. At last, Mahisha spoke, "There is a possible solution, even though it may not be something everyone would approve of."

All eyes were focused on Mahisha when he continued, "Your Majesty, I feel that we are already in a very desperate situation. It is now a question of the complete fragmentation of Daityan Empire unless we take some drastic action soon."

"Go on, I'd like to hear what you wish to suggest," the Emperor encouraged him.

"What we need to do now is subject Devarth to a shock treatment of such proportions that it forces them to submission as early as feasible, without having to go through a prolonged war."

"How is that possible? What do you have in mind?"

"Your Majesty, you know that over the course of last few years, our scientists have perfected the weaponisation of Anvik technology. They've already built many such devices and we had even tested one of them in a desolate island a few years ago," Mahisha said.

"Yes, of course. I'm told our scientists still have few devises with them. So what are you suggesting we do?"

Mahishasur looked at all intently before proposing, "I am suggesting that we drop such a device on one of Devarth cities using a long range Mūrthi vimān."

All faces in the room bore looks of confusion. Finally, the emperor asked, "Are you suggesting that we kill hundreds of thousand innocent civilians in one single explosion?"

"This is preposterous and completely against *YuddhaDharma*," Acharya Shukra interjected.

"It is not so preposterous, Your Majesty. If we stick to ideals like Yuddha Dharma, our end as an Empire is certain. This is the time to ruthlessly look after our own interest. There are always civilian casualties in almost any war. By the time the war we are preparing to launch anyway is over, many times more civilians are likely to end up dead. All I'm suggesting is that we limit it to one single event. The shock wave it would send across Devarth is likely to paralyse them completely. Surrender would follow if we threaten to launch another device."

Emperor Tarakaksh considered his own response carefully before answering, "It is said that everything is fair in war if there is a solid purpose behind it and if it leads to overall benefit. There may be a point in what Mahisha is suggesting. If we can win this war without too many casualties, what is wrong in considering that option?"

"Daitya Raj Tarakaksh, don't tell me you are considering this crazy idea? This is madness," Acharya Shukra said with controlled anger.

"Asur Guru, with due respect, I don't find this idea to be such a crazy one. Mahisha is right that this may actually mean saving millions of lives. We can end this war in our favour even before starting it in full swing," Emperor Tarakaksh said.

"Daitya Raj, let us not forget that the Mūrthi still have some influence over Earth. They would never allow us to go too far in this manner."

"Asur Guru, I'm aware that you have only the welfare of Daityas in mind when you say this. But I really don't see as to what Mūrthi can do about it. Are they likely to do anything to help humans when the rising sea water destroys half of our farmlands? Are they even concerned? They willingly left this planet for humans to rule. You have yourself told me that they believe in natural evolution of the human species. We are perhaps now at such an evolutionary cusp. Maybe it is time for Daityas to take charge of all the civilised nations and bring order, such that all are put on the correct path towards growth and prosperity."

Shukracharya was about to answer when Kamalaksh asked, "Which city do you have in mind, Mahisha? Is it Amaravati?"

"No, I'm well aware that we need to take over Amaravati completely intact," Mahisha said.

"Then which city are you proposing that we destroy?" Emperor Tarakaksh asked.

"I'm still thinking it over, Your Majesty. It wouldn't really matter too much as to which city it is; it must not be too insignificant. At the same time, it should also not be a very large city, the destruction of which would completely destroy that nation. After all, we want to keep their administrative systems intact when we move in. That is the best way to control their population when we occupy them. We'll even continue to allow their own kings to rule as long as they pay their tributes to us."

"What if Devas also decide to do the same? We know that they also have the capability to launch Anvik weapons on our islands?" Kamalaksh asked.

Mahisha was smiling when he answered, "I've considered that possibility as well. We all know that Devas would never take such a reckless step without consulting the Mūrthi Lords. Second, their spiritual way of life wouldn't allow such a ruthless act of revenge. Besides that, even if we were to consider it as a possibility, what I'm going to suggest next may take care of that problem as well."

Once again, all eyes were on Mahisha as he continued, "All of you are aware that Prajapati Daksh of Dev Lok has been sympathetic to us. We have been indulging him with promises of power, wealth and pleasure, in return for close cooperation. He has also been our chief informer from Amaravati."

"So what do you have in your devious mind, Mahisha?" the Emperor asked.

"I know that Daksh has been nurturing the idea of becoming the next Indra. He believes that by helping us, he could force Devas to surrender and if that happens, we would instate him as the new Indra. In fact, we have been actively encouraging this line of thought to get his utter devotion towards our cause."

"Frankly, I may even consider it seriously after we subjugate the Devas," Tarakaksh said with a smile.

"Your Majesty, all I'm suggesting is that we direct him to hasten his quest by assassinating the current Indra."

"Assassinate Indra? What would we achieve by that?" Emperor asked.

"In this case, timing is the key, Your Majesty. Assassination of Indra and Anvik destruction of one of Devarth cities should happen almost simultaneously. We know that Devarth would be stunned when one of their cities gets ruthlessly destroyed by us with a single weapon. The only person who can either order retaliation or rally the Devarth nations against us is Indra. If Indra is also killed simultaneously, it would be like a double sting. With Amaravati in internal turmoil to select a new leader, they're not likely to be able to put up any viable resistance. In this state, all we need to do is to send out a warning that a second Devarth city would be destroyed unless the inland nations surrender unconditionally."

Emperor Tarakaksh smiled and said, "Mahisha, even though what you suggest is absolutely immoral, I see its ruthless simplicity. If this is what takes to save the Empire, so be it."

Daksh, the Prajapati of Dev Lok, was peering into the holographic visual screen of the Daityan communication device from his bungalow at the western end of Amaravati. The device had been smuggled in from Atalantpuri many years ago. He could clearly see the live image of Mahisha as they discussed the plan of action.

"Mahisha, what you're asking me to do is too risky," Daksh said.

"My dear Daksh, you know that this is a risk well worth the benefits," Mahisha said with a sly smile on his face.

"That is easy for you to say. Even if I'm able to kill Indra, how is it going to benefit me? Dev Lok is not going to fall by the death of its Indra alone."

"We know that, Daksh. That is why we have a simultaneous plan to drop an Anvik Astra on one of the Devarth cities."

"How is that going to help? It may only infuriate the Kings of Devarth."

"It will not infuriate them, Daksh, just terrorise them. Destruction of one city would only be the beginning. Thereafter, we are going to declare that any nation that resists us will attract an Anvik attack on its capital city itself."

"Okay, so you may get away with overpowering their will to resist. But you've still not told me as to how that is going to help me. If I were to kill Indra, I'll be declared a traitor for sure," Daksh asked doubtfully.

"If you were to kill Indra, the Dev Lok is likely to get into an internal crisis. This crisis, when combined with the threat of total annihilation from an Anvik attack, would completely demoralise the government of Dev Lok. That would be the ideal opportunity for you to take charge of the situation. No one is likely to have the propensity to resist, when you present them with a solution to resolve that crisis."

"What solution are you talking about, Mahisha?"

"It is natural that when threatened with either annihilation or surrender, a more amicable third alternative from your end would definitely get wide acceptability."

"What do you mean by third alternative?" Daksh asked suspiciously.

"My dear Daksh, you must know that unless absolutely necessary, Daityan Empire has no intention of physically occupying Dev Lok or any other Devarth nations. We are only seeking better trading and immigration terms that are favourable to us. In return, we would offer the proposition that the Devarth can save substantial cost to their nation by dismantling their military. Where is the need for them to have an army when the Daityan armed forces would commit to provide all the protection they need?"

"Your mind does work in a devious manner, Mahisha," Daksh said admiringly before continuing, "But no matter how you sugar coat it, many would clearly see such a proposition as nothing but abject subjugation."

"Not necessarily, Daksh. In fact, that is where you come in. You can offer to negotiate better terms with the Daityan Empire since you have such a good relationship with us. When you do that on behalf of Dev Lok government, we would naturally oblige with most of your terms. People would look at you as a saviour of Dev Lok from the crisis looming over their head. You may also be seen as the most deserved person to replace Indra. We will ensure that your being Indra is indeed one of our terms during the negotiations," Mahisha said, his cunning disposition well evident even through the holographic visual screen.

Daksh thought over it for a while. Then he looked up and said, "How do you expect me to kill Indra? You must know that he is one of the most well-protected persons on Dev Lok."

"We are aware of this difficulty, Daksh. That is why you must kill him when he is in a most vulnerable situation. Being a Prajapati, you are a member of the Indra Sabha. It may be best that you kill him during a meeting of the Indra Sabha members."

"You mean in clear view of others? I would immediately get killed or arrested by the Maruth soldiers," Daksh said emphatically.

"That is not very likely to happen, Daksh. Once Indra is dead, there would be a vacuum of power. We know that Maruths are accountable to Indra alone and no one else. So, as soon as you kill Indra, you must declare yourself to be the new Indra. You must state that you killed Indra purposefully to preserve the interests of Dev Lok itself. You must say that you were left with no other option but to terminate Indra in order to avoid dragging the people of Dev Lok into a messy and pointless war with the Empire. You must drive home that it is futile to go for a war, the outcome of which is predictable. There are already many sceptics within Devarth who think that their kingdoms stand no chance at all against the ten to one overwhelming military superiority of Daityan Empire and that the war would only prolong the inevitable."

"Hmm, you may be right. Being the administrative head of Dev Lok, once Indra is dead, I would automatically become the next head of state. If I can put that across as the new Indra, I would resolve the crisis without any further bloodshed or humiliation, many of them may be tempted to offer their approval," Daksh stated and then thought for a while before continuing doubtfully, "But I know that Dev Guru Brihaspati wouldn't stand for it. I'm sure he would find a way to outwit me."

"I am aware of the fact that Brihaspati is already suspicious. Even after Indra is killed, he might come up with some surprise. That is why I suggest that you kill him right after Indra is dead," Mahisha stated without hesitation.

Daksh smiled and said, "That should be easy. I have no respect or regard for him anyway. With his exalted status as the Dev Guru, he has been a pain in my neck for far too long." Daksh sneered, "Nevertheless, if I were to agree to your suggestion right away, there still remains one fundamental question – how do I kill Indra?"

Mahisha had a wicked smile on his face when he said, "Daksh, it is good that you agree with our plan; I can assure you that you won't regret. I've already had a discussion with the Emperor and he has assured full support for your claim to the Dev Lok throne. We would publically endorse our support to you. But before you kill Indra and Brihaspati yourself, please attempt another alternative."

"What? You have a better alternative?"

"Yes indeed, my dear Daksh. I needed to know your willingness to go far enough, before I could tell you about this. You see, as such the Emperor is under severe pressure to declare war. He also believes that an Anvik attack on one of the Devarth city is the quickest way to victory. When he learnt that the two Bheeshma monks who killed his brother Vidyunmali are located at the Gandharv city of Lonar, he wants that city to be the first target. This Anvik attack is to be conducted next week itself. Now, I have intelligence reports that Indra's daughter is also studying dance at the Academy of Apsaras in the same city. Her presence at Lonar offers a window of opportunity for you to persuade Indra or Brihaspati to visit there. It would be perfect, if they are also located at Lonar when we launch the Anvik attack. Kill two birds with one stone, so to speak."

"Okay! I can attempt to encourage either or both of them to visit Lonar. But you must know that given the critical situation at Dev Lok, they are not likely to agree."

"No harm in attempting it, Daksh. If they agree, it would save you a lot of trouble. But you must remember that you have only another week for this; the window of opportunity is very small. The date for launch of Anvik attack has already been fixed by the Emperor and even I can't change it. If by any chance you can't persuade either Indra or Brihaspati to visit Lonar on the night when Anvik attack is launched there, you must then kill them before that event itself."

"What difference does it make whether I kill them before or after this Anvik attack?"

"Isn't it obvious, Daksh? Once the Anvik attack is launched, there would be panic all across Devarth, which is indeed our intention. Soon thereafter, we are going to make a declaration that there would be only two options for the kingdoms of Devarth—either surrender or suffer another Anvik attack on one of their capital cities. If at all anyone can marshal any resistance, it is Indra. With his influence among the Devarth kings, he might manage to persuade them to stand up against us. The security within Indra Sabha may also increase, making it difficult to take any weapon inside when you make your move. So, in case you can't persuade Indra or Brihaspati to be at Lonar on the day of the Anvik attack, then you must eliminate them from the scene at the earliest opportunity before that event itself."

"I can see your logic, Mahisha. This brings us back to my earlier question. How do I kill them? You know that I'm no soldier?"

"That shouldn't be a problem. All you need to do is point the pulse-ray handgun at Indra and pull the trigger. At point blank range within Indra Sabha, you can hardly miss," Mahisha said.

"Pulse-ray gun? I have no such weapon with me," Daksh stated in utter confusion.

"Why do you worry so much? You will soon have it; it is being smuggled to Dev Lok even as we speak. These are weapons of Mūrthi legacy that are very compact, yet fatally effective."

By the time they ended the conversation, Daksh was already in a state of excitement. He knew that the plan was sound. It now seemed certain that his dream of becoming the ruler of Dev Lok would be a reality very soon.

19

DEVIOUS DECEIT AT PATALA

Mahisha, the chief of security of the Daityan Empire and King of Patala was located deep within the subterranean mines of his kingdom. Even though the gold deposits of these mines had exhausted many generations ago, they were still known as Patala mines complex. The mines were well-protected from the elements with huge retaining walls all around it. During the past, when gold used to be extracted from these mines, it had one of the best military grade security systems. Mahisha had enhanced it further and converted the place into the most advanced genetic research and development lab within the Empire. Since these underground labs were built within his own kingdom under his direct control, the location of this facility or even its very existence was a secret known to almost none, including the Emperor. Actually Mahisha had a sinister and clandestine reason to keep it a closed secret from all.

The lab's purpose was singular—develop the fiercest Yantraksh who would be directly loyal to the kingdom of Patala alone. Due to the proximity of these mines to underground geothermal vents, there was abundant energy available for ready use and so the labs could operate with least external support. The research facility was manned by the most prominent scientists from various parts of the known world that Mahisha could motivate, cajole, bribe, coerce or threaten for cooperation. Many of them had been kidnapped and were now permanent prisoners within this underground facility for years. His influence within the Empire had ensured that the labs contained the most advanced infrastructure necessary for its operations.

Mahisha was now standing on the mezzanine floor, overlooking the huge subterranean hall where the Yantraksh were grown in man-sized transparent crystal compartments —also called the 'artificial wombs'. The artificially engineered Yantraksh bodies floated within the dense fluid inside the artificial wombs, in various stages of development. A single umbilical cord provided the extraordinarily fast growing bodies with all necessary nutrients and hormones. The brains of the Yantraksh bodies were yet to gain consciousness but their programming as per controlled instructions to define the structure of future behaviour patterns had already started.

Mahisha asked Moyisur, "How do you like the progress we've made since you visited last time?" Moyisur was the prophet of the new religious order that had gained such popularity all across the Empire. His broad shoulders and strong body indicated his Rakshas lineage. He wore a bright red robe and some complementary jewellery of black beads. His head was completely bald and the eyes above a large crooked nose were fierce and penetrating, almost giving the impression of a vulture peering over its prey. It was well-known that he had tens of thousands of followers who were prepared to do anything for him, including sacrificing their lives in the name of paradise and other material pleasures he promised them after their death. They revelled in the over-simplistic interpretations, esoteric dark rituals, violent retributions, abject faith, and other draconian religious ideas propounded by him. Most of those who followed his religious faith worshipped him as God and those who didn't, feared his merciless retributions. Even the Emperor was wary of the extent of religious control that he had been able to establish over the population within all parts of the Empire. What the Emperor didn't know was that Moyisur was also the illegitimate son of his father Tarak. This relationship was known to none other than Moyisur himself and his mother who died when he was a child—a low cast Danav woman who had once attracted the lustful fascination of Tarak during his youth. He was also aware that the relationship would never be recognised even if he declared it to the present Emperor. He would have to snatch the crown that he felt he deserved—after all, he was the firstborn of Tarak. Now, the day was not far when the control of the complete Empire would be in his hands. The only person who knew about his ambition for power was Mahisha, his longstanding childhood friend and ardent follower of the new religion that he had nurtured.

"Excellent, Mahisha. It seems that you are well-poised to initiate the process of creating a Yantraksh army?"

"Yes. We are nearly there. All we need now is the technique of infusing Prana into these Yantraksh soldiers."

"Why do you need that? Aren't the Yantraksh created without such infusion also as effective in battle?" Moyisur asked.

"They are. But there are many difficulties. First, they can't breed so we need to create each one of them and the cost is immense. Second, they are not controllable because of which too many of our products get wasted away as Vetals. Third, their skills are still limited to the extent of their synaptic brain alone. Fourth, they never had what we all call an astral soul, the inner resource of consciousness. Lastly, their life spans were very limited so we have to replace them frequently. Now with the new techniques of genetic engineering combined with pranic infusion, we hope to create an upgraded generation of Yantraksh who are far more superior and powerful as compared to the current breed. They would also be completely loyal to Patala alone," Mahisha said.

"I believe the Kayakalp project at Atalantpuri also involves similar process for infusion of Prana?"

Mahisha displayed one of his characteristic sly smiles while replying, "Yes. The Kayakalp project has always been a false front. Actually it was initiated based on my advice, to develop a rejuvenation spa for royalty and maybe some complementary drugs for enhancing the fighting prowess of Daityan soldiers in battle. However, its real purpose has always been to develop the crucial processes necessary for the Yantraksh upgrade programme here at Patala. With almost unlimited financial support of the Empire, we could conduct most of the expensive research and developments in the garb of the Kayakalp project. We have been successful in camouflaging it; so much so that Maya, who is heading it, doesn't know that the results of their development efforts get passed on directly to Patala."

"That is brilliant, Mahisha. So you're the real benefactor even as Asur Sabha remains deluded regarding the prospects of a Kayakalp rejuvenator. You have cleverly kept them eagerly waiting for its completion, by hanging a carrot in the form of possibilities of perpetual youth in front of them. But what about the sudden rescue of Rishi Agastya? Has it not affected your plan?"

"Unfortunately, it has. Rishi Agastya had nearly completed the development. His untimely rescue has definitely delayed the programme. Since then, Shukracharya has taken the lead and he's assured to complete the remaining part soon. Anyway, such slight glitch or delay should hardly impact my long-term plans," Mahisha replied.

"I can see that you're already planning far ahead," Moyisur grinned.

Mahisha was all smiles while replying, "It is easy to predict the future, my friend. The Emperor has already decided to go ahead with a war with Devarth. It is certain that we are going to win the war. So over the course of next few months, Daityan

Empire would have supremacy over almost the entire known world. By then, due to prolonged war, the elite formations of Daityan army would have also got weakened considerably. Fatigue would have set in and they would be in no mood to face another conflict anytime soon. That would be the time to unleash my Yantraksh and Vetal army."

"Did you say Vetal, the marauders living in Brashtaranya?"

"Of course, Moyisur. Over the course of last few decades, we have dumped far too many Vetals into that area. Their strength is now substantial enough to form one or two army formations. I'm already in secret talks with their leader. It is well-known that even though Vetals are somewhat uncontrollable, due to their wild nature, they are far fiercer in combat, compared to our regular Yantraksh. Besides that, the new breed of Yantraksh that we hope to create would also be able to establish some form of direct link with all the existing Yantraksh formations of the Empire. As per their psychological conditioning, the existing Yantraksh and Vetals would find themselves compelled to obey their new superior generation. Virtually overnight, I would have more than enough Yantraksh and Vetal soldiers under my direct command."

"You have an interesting plan, Mahisha. However, we all know that the present Daityan regime would never allow it. The Emperor would himself declare you a traitor."

"I'm expecting that. As such, Patala is one of the strongest kingdoms within the Empire. Once I have the Yantraksh and Vetals on my side, I would have more military strength under my command than the Emperor. Then what he declares is immaterial. I'm confident that by the time the war between the Empire and Devarth is over, none within his administration or army would be keen to wage another nasty civil war with Patala. They will definitely come to the negotiation table."

"So what do you hope to achieve by that?" Moyisur asked.

"Is it not obvious, Moyisur? I will ask for complete autonomy of Patala along with rights for half the booty of the war with Devarth. I would definitely insist on Dev Lok being put directly under Patala control, too."

"Fantastic! I must tell you that you do have a wily mind, Mahisha. You hope to be able to exploit the Mūrthi technologies available with Dev Lok to reinforce your control still further," Moyisur looked at Mahisha in admiration.

"That will enable me to not only extend my powers, but also make Patala the most powerful kingdom within the Empire in the years to come, far surpassing the strengths of Atala, including the Tripura. That is when I would challenge the Tarak house to abdicate and declare me the new Emperor."

"And what do you plan to do if they refuse?"

"That is going to be very difficult for Tarakaksh. By then, he is likely to have very little support within Asur Sabha with most kings of the Empire already aligned with me. If he resists any further, I'll stage a swift coup d'état. Being the chief of security of the Empire, I know all the loopholes of Tripura. Even before he realises it, Tarakaksh would be either dead or in my custody as a prisoner," Mahisha laughed aloud.

"Your plan seems sound. But have you thought what you'd do if the people of Atalantpuri object to your rule? They are not likely to accept you as their new Emperor. Even if you control them by force, it may lead to large scale internal strife and social unrest," Moyisur said.

"That is where you come in, my friend. You would have by then declared your religious affiliation with me. With your religious support, no one in the public would dare to object my rule," Mahisha said.

"Excellent! You would definitely have my support. But what do I get in return?" Moyisur asked shrewdly.

"Anything, my friend. I would replace Shukracharya and appoint you as the new Asur Guru. Your religion would be the state religion and you would have complete freedom to convert anyone, either through motivation or by force. And if you come to think of it, you'd be just as powerful as the Emperor – that is me," Mahisha said in an assuring tone.

"Perfect planning! I must grant it to you Mahisha; I've never heard such a crafty, yet well-planned and far-sighted strategy from anyone. Yes, we will rule the complete known world together. But I have just another doubt."

"Yes, Moyisur? Ask me anything," Mahisha was in an exuberant mood.

"How did Vidyunmali die? I've heard some rumours from my sources that he was alive when the Bheeshma monks left, after rescuing Rishi Agastya?" Moyisur asked with evident glee.

"So you know, eh? Yes, the young punk was alive when I reached the bungalow, soon after the Bheeshma left the place. In fact, he had himself called for my help."

"And?"

"Well, I found him in an injured state on the ground, bleeding but alive. He could have easily recovered with some medical help. But I didn't think his survival would do me as much good as his death would."

Moyisur looked puzzled, , "Why do you say that?"

"Isn't it obvious, my friend? Vidyunmali's death is one of the main reasons why the Emperor has agreed for this war so readily, especially the part of Anvik attack. He has been in an emotionally charged state for many months now and feels psychologically compelled to seek some form of revenge. That is exactly what I was counting on anyway," Mahisha stated with a furtive smile pasted on his face.

"So you killed Vidyunmali?"

"Yes. I had arrived at the bungalow before anyone else. There were dead and injured soldiers lying all around. Vidyunmali was also lying injured, in a totally helpless state. His crystal sword had fallen next to him. I took it up pretending to examine it, and then with a single swift swoop decapitated his head. Thereafter, it was only a matter of dispatching all the injured soldiers lying around so that they don't speak. By the time I called in the reinforcements, all were dead and permanently silenced," Mahisha's loud laughter reverberated around the underground hall.

20

ATTEMPT AT ASSASSINATION

"We can at best hold them for a week or so before they lay siege to our islands. As far as blockade of our trade lines is concerned, there is little that can be done," Varun Dev stated. The small group of advisors and aides were seated in Indra's chamber.

Indra said, "Thank you, Varun Dev." Then looking at Agni Dev, he tried to confirm, "I understand that we have sufficient stock of provisions on all the Dev Lok islands."

"Yes, Your Majesty. We have sufficient reserves of food and other basic necessities to last us for many months. However, if there is to be indefinite naval blockade of our harbours and ports, it would certainly impact our life in many ways," Agni Dev replied.

"Prajapati Daksh, you've already told me that arrangements are afoot to create a regulated distribution of food and daily necessities to Dev Lok citizens?"

"Yes, Your Majesty. We've already activated the war time administrative procedures. Apart from food, we have sufficient reserves of water for daily usage and agriculture. The distribution would need to be controlled so as to maintain the minimum requirement levels for emergent condition. We should be able to sustain for few months without any external support," Daksh replied.

"How is the war time recruitment progressing?"

"It is progressing well. But I have noticed some reluctance among many to go to faraway lands to wage a war, the purpose of which is still not clear to them."

"That is to be expected. Our population has been getting soft for too long. What is the state of our food production?" Indra asked.

"The rising sea water has impacted us, but not as much as it has affected the Daityan islands. Our agricultural techniques, with extensive support from microorganisms, need less water and so cultivation happens even at the hilly regions and brackish soil conditions. The overall impact has been somewhat subdued and people are yet to feel the pinch. Many feel that the government is over-reacting," Daksh replied.

"I had expected this sort of reaction because there is still a false impression of security among some people. They don't realise that the food security that we've been enjoying so far is also partly because of extensive imports from Bhārat and other Devarth nations. Anyway, we would need to keep up the pressure on recruitments. New recruits would have to be imparted with some minimum military training before induction into the army. Let's not forget that if there were to be a naval siege, it would then become impossible to get our troops across to the mainland nations," Indra stated emphatically.

Daksh was silent for sometime before saying, "Indra Dev, people are asking as to why we are so keen to send troops to foreign nations when our primary responsibility is to protect Dev Lok islands?"

It was Brihaspati who answered, "Prajapati, our islands are fairly well-protected with strong coastal defence systems. We also need to see the situation from the enemy's perspective. They're not going to achieve much by capturing our relatively small island groups. Their main target is likely to be the food bowl of Devarth. So if there is to be a land battle, it would be within the mainland territories."

"That may be so, Dev Guru. It is still difficult to convince the Dev Lok population that they need to send their sons and husbands to battlefield to protect another nation's territory," Daksh retorted.

"That's enough Prajapati," Indra said, "This is the kind of convoluted selfish arguments that can open us for exploitation by Daityas. Devarth drives its power from cooperation and mutual assistance in times of crisis. Without support from our allies or if indeed they come under the control of Daityas, our nation would fade into insignificance. It would weaken us further and put us under threat of subjugation; it will dramatically change our way of life. At times of crisis like this, we cannot afford to waste time on building a consensus. If need be, I'm prepared to evoke my special powers of martial law and bring the administration under the direct control of Maruth forces."

Daksh was silenced instantly. He realised that if Indra did this, his own role as Prajapati would become meaningless.

Indra Dev continued and asked, "In case of naval blockade of Dev Lok, it may not be feasible to mobilise any of our forces. So all the troops assigned for support of other Devarth kingdoms must be despatched before that. We also need to consider that our troops deployed on the mainland kingdoms may need continuous support from Dev Lok. Do you have any idea on how we can go about it?"

Brihaspati turned to face him and answered, "This is indeed something to worry about. Once the blockade is in place, vimāns may be the only means for maintaining some form of minimum supply lines. I'm hoping that this going to be possible."

"We would definitely try to maintain our airways clear, Guru Dev," Vayu Dev said before continuing, "Fortunately, we still have a slight edge over Daityas in this regard."

The discussions then took a direction towards where should they strategically position the Maruth Army so that they are able to react to Daityan aggression most effectively.

༼ Ⅲ ♀

Hara wouldn't have realised it, had it not been for his unique perceptions as a trained Bheeshma monk. Even as all others in the gathering were immersed in discussions on the strategies and war plans, he felt his Jwalaprabha welling up within him. From past experience, he knew that this sixth sense could only mean two things—either imminent danger or the arousal of his inner consciousness. Either of it meant that there had to be a purpose for it within the equation of Karma. He was also sensing danger from within the Devan leadership group sitting around him. He directed his Jwalaprabha to his sensory perception of human aura. He could see the people sitting in front with enhanced clarity, with their auras defining their mental state. There was no doubt that the only one who had a vacillating aura in front of him at this point was Prajapati Daksh. Looking at his face, Hara also realised that his eyes were shifting slightly and had assumed a vacant expression. So the danger is definitely from Daksh. Hara could see that unlike others, the right hand of Daksh was under his robe. What is he up to?

Within moments, the situation unfolded into an ugly one as Prajapati Daksh got up from his seat, his hand was holding a device Hara had seen recently—the Mūrthi pulse-ray handgun similar to that used by Vidyunmali against them at Atalantpuri. Even as all others present in the room were struck with surprise, Hara noted that the eerie glow on the weapon head meant that it was fully charged to discharge a fatal pulse. The weapon was pointed at Indra Dev. At this point blank range, there would be no chance of a miss. All present were spell bound and too shocked to even move.

"What are you doing, Daksh?" Brihaspati was the first to react.

"Can't you see what I'm doing? I'm going to put an end to this nonsense. A king who cannot lead his people in the correct direction has no right to live."

"This is treachery," Indra Dev managed to say, still in shock to see Daksh pointing the business end of a Mūrthi pulse-ray handgun at him.

"What do you mean the Indra can't lead?" Brihaspati asked, attempting to distract Daksh into talks and buy some time to think of an alternative.

"You know very well what I mean. I have been saying it for a long time already. Leading the nation into a war situation simply to self-aggrandise his personal agenda is not what is expected of a king. We all know that a war with Daityan Empire would only mean total ruin for Dev Lok."

"But Daksh, what are you going to achieve by murdering Indra?" Brihaspati asked.

"Murdering? This is no murder. It is a summary execution. Being the Prajapati and, therefore, the second-in-command of the Dev Lok government, it is my duty to intervene when the incumbent Indra takes a decision with an unsound state of mind," Daksh seemed like a man possessed.

"Don't you accuse me of unsound mind, Daksh. It is you..." Indra responded vehemently.

"Say whatever you want, Indra. Very soon you would be meeting your maker anyway. I'm going to take charge of the Dev Lok," Daksh stated confidently.

"Daksh, please think over what you're going to do again. Even if you declare yourself to be the new Indra, it will make no difference unless the Sapta-Rishis approve it. You must know that they would never endorse anything in duress. Even the Mūrthi..." Brihaspati tried to pacify Daksh.

"Who needs endorsement of the Sapta-Rishis or the Mūrthi?

We should now be seeking endorsements from Tripura. Whether you all consider me as the new Indra or not makes no difference. Either way, we all are soon going to be under the direct rule of the Daityan Emperor."

"So you are the traitor who has been spying for Daityas?" Brihaspati accused him. He was desperately trying to taunt Daksh so that he remains engaged in conversation.

Hara's Bheeshma instincts had kicked in the moment he understood Daksh's intent. His Spatishūl had already leapt into his right hand from the holster and he was waiting for the right moment to take the next action. The timing had to be perfect, such that Daksh wouldn't realise his move and attempt evasive action. The opportunity happened when Daksh was somewhat distracted by Brihaspati's accusation. His attention wavered, and he turned slightly towards the Dev Guru.

Hara was waiting for such an opening. He leaned forward, simultaneously turning on the ball of this left foot. As he rose from his seat, his body was already turning fast, with right hand picking up angular momentum. All this happened even as Daksh, realising a threat from the Bheeshma monk, attempted to redirect the pulse-ray handgun towards him. Hara's Spatishūl was partially self-morphed even as it was in motion through the air, propelled by a final flick with his hand. Time seemed to stand still as multiple simultaneous actions happened around those present—so fast that by the time anyone's mind could comprehend it, everything was over.

Even as Daksh brought the pulse-ray handgun in line with Hara's head, and the sinews of his hand started contracting upon the finger to pull the trigger, the semi-morphed Bheeshma Spatishūl had penetrated his throat and sliced off the jugular vein. He staggered back, totally shocked while the pulse-ray handgun in his hand slipped and fell down on the ground. His hands went up to his throat as blood started spewing from the wound as well as his mouth. He gasped for breath and slowly fell back on the ground. Another few moments of writhing and it was over. Prajapati Daksh of Dev Lok lay very dead, with steady flow of blood from his throat surrounding his lifeless body.

Once again, the first to get out of the stupor was Brihaspati. He walked up to kick away the pulse-ray handgun, hoping that it wouldn't explode on them and called out to the guards waiting outside. Maruth guards rushed in immediately and Nandi came in with them. They quickly formed a barrier around Indra. On direction from the leader of the guard, one of them quickly picked up the handgun and whisked it out of the chamber.

Indra Dev was too shocked to say anything, and could barely muster to whisper, "Thank you, Hara!"

21

TRAGEDY OF LONAR

It was past midnight when Hara woke up with a start. He had been sleeping in his guest room at the royal palace of Amaravati. Instinctively, he went up to the window and looked out. It was a dark night with the outline of Amaravati city visible below the star-specked sky. Strangely, his Jwalaprabha was again in a roused state. There seemed to be no apparent danger since everything was calm and quiet. The room itself was well secure and the window was covered with a thick crystal, so there was no scope of an uninvited entry. He looked within the room at the Spatishūl kept on a low table just a little distance away. He knew that he could grasp it in case of need with an instant telekinetic projection of Jwalaprabha. If everything seems so peaceful, what could have woken him up with his Jwalaprabha in full form? – He wondered. He sat down and attempted to meditate, but couldn't. His astral self seemed to be very tense and disturbed. He tried to calm himself down by hoping that it might be due to the residue of the earlier high-adrenaline action sequence at Indra's chamber. Maybe it was because he was still jumpy, considering the extremely narrow margin by which he'd been able to save Indra.

The meeting had come to an abrupt end after the gruesome death of Daksh. Indra had dismissed all. Hara could make out that Indra was actually very annoyed with himself. Maybe he was annoyed that he'd ignored consistent warnings from Brihaspati, not to trust his close aides the way he did. Maybe he was annoyed that he couldn't see it coming. Maybe he was annoyed as to why the Sapta-Rishis and all other spiritual people within Dev Lok couldn't see this coming? Maybe he had a doubt as to whether they actually cared? Maybe he was annoyed that the destiny of Dev Lok passed through the hands of a young Bheeshma monk? Maybe this would get him to see Hara more favourably when he asks for Uma's hand? Maybe... Hara continued to jump from thought to thought as he drifted back to sleep.

After an hour or so, he woke up again. But this time it was because of the consistent knock on his door. He opened the door to see Nandi standing in a fully dressed state.

"What happened, Nandi? Why are you dressed up at this late hour? Is everything alright?"

"No, Hara. The Devan communicators have received a message from Gandharv that there has been an incident at Lonar," Nandi said breathlessly.

"What sort of incident, Nandi?"

"Not sure, Hara. Gandharv troops who're apparently stationed around 60 kroshas away heard huge explosions from Lonar about two muhurtas back. Some reported to have seen extremely bright lighting-like flashes from the same direction. They themselves also experienced a minor earthquake at the same time. Now they're unable to establish any communication with Lonar and so have dispatched a ground team to investigate. Dev Guru Brihaspati has talked to Gandharv King Dwapar on a *doordhwaniyantra* that enables communication across a large distance and has been assured that he would get the latest information as soon as possible," Nandi said hurriedly.

Hara's immediate thought was of Uma, and he pleaded within himself that she be safe. To Nandi, he said, "Thank you, Nandi. Give me a few seconds and I'll come with you to meet Brihaspati."

When they met Brihaspati, Hara could see the clear signs of worry on his face. "The news is not good Hara," Dev Guru said as soon as he set eyes on Hara and then continued, "There is still no communication from Lonar. Some unconfirmed reports talk about a huge crater in the middle of the city and total devastation all around. The reports are based on hearsay and I am not sure whether they are totally reliable or exaggeration."

Hara's face was grave with worry. He silenced his heart and tried not to jump to conclusions and said, "Dev Guru, what do you propose we do? Uma…"

Just then a messenger came with the latest message from Gandharv. As he read through it, Brihaspati's face fell further. "What is it Dev Guru? Tell me the truth, please," Hara asked with concern mounting in his voice.

"I can't lie to you, Hara," he looked up and continued. "This news has come from Gandharv King Dwapar after he did an aerial reconnaissance himself. Lonar city has been completely demolished by some powerful explosion. In the wordings of Dwapar, "there is nothing but a smouldering crater and broken buildings in place where once was Lonar." Clear evidence indicates that every single living being within and around the city limits has perished."

"Have you checked the whereabouts of Uma and Acharya Parashu?" Hara asked, desperately hoping that they had somehow been spared.

"Yes, Hara. King Dwapar says he has tried to verify it from various sources. Uma and Acharya Parashu were within the city limits when this happened," Brihaspati's voice faltered.

As he returned to his chamber, Hara was still in a state of shock. After the initial disbelief, the gravity of what had happened was only slowly sinking in now. "What had it come to?" - He thought. It seemed that everyone dear to him had perished from his world in one single incident—his beloved Uma, revered guru Acharya Parashu, his friends Amatya and Tilotama.."How could he bear this trauma?" Now nothing mattered. All his Jwalaprabha, meditation, combat skills, and knowledge came to nothing. Life had no purpose left now. Death would be sweet…

For Hara, the next few days just passed by like a horrifying dream. Brihaspati knew Hara's terrible state of mind and wisely left him alone. This bitter pain had to be endured by him alone and no amount of consoling would help. Nandi was the only one who stayed with him, all the time, caring for his guru. He brought food but Hara refused it every single time. He didn't even take water unless Nandi forced him to. He was practically surviving on Somras that the palace staff had been kind enough to provide, in order to help subdue the pain. On the third day, Nandi had just left and Hara was slowly drifting back into yet another yoga-nidra.

"How are you, Hara?" It was Acharya Parashu smiling down at him.

"Acharya, are you really alive? They told me…" Hara got up and asked, 'Is… is Uma also well?"

"What is the meaning of life, Hara?" Acharya Parashu asked.

"Life is what I have lived so long Acharya, and much of it in your good company."

"Then we both must be alive since I am sitting here, right in front of you. Can't you see me as vividly as before?"

"Yes, but…"

"You're worried because this conflicts with the recent memory when you got the news that I'm dead?" Acharya Parashu asked.

"Yes, Acharya, and I'm also not clear as to how we reached here at Brahmagiri? As per my last memory I was at Amaravati…"

"Hara, in your wakeful conceptual state which you call reality, you are indeed at Amaravati. The only thing that has changed for me is that I'm not sharing that state with you anymore."

"So you're dead, and I'm dreaming about you. Is that it?" Hara asked, with bitter disappointment evident within his words.

"Is it so difficult to understand? I'm dead if you believe your wakeful state to be the only reality of existence."

"Acharya, are you saying that you're actually alive in all states except my wakeful one?"

"That is one way to understand it, Hara."

"Acharya, all I know is that the pain that I experience is real. What am I, without you or Uma?"

"You've always been, are and always will be what you are Hara. You've always been alone within your own conceptual world that you call reality. No one could ever enter it or leave it. No one could ever think your thoughts. No one could feel your emotions, pleasures or pains. Your fondness for Uma was also your own feeling alone."

"I can understand that, Acharya. But it still doesn't reduce my anguish or suffering."

"All our sufferings are due to continued attachments with the objects of our thoughts in a conceptual state which we consider to be the only reality. I'm not suggesting that you stop your feelings. After all, the suffering that you're undergoing now is part of your own Karma. If it helps you, please understand that I'm not suffering anymore. I'm in my original state now, and would stay so till any residual Karma paves my path ahead. As regards Uma, who knows you may even meet her in the future sometimes within your current wakeful reality itself when your respective karmic paths converge."

"So what is my Karma, Acharya?"

"Your Karma is what you're experiencing now in your wakeful state. There is much that you need to do in the days ahead. Don't fall back into inaction, paralysed by the pains caused due to your past attachments. Follow your course of correct Karma the way I've taught you. Remember that Uma, I and all who are dear to you will always be with you…"

Hara woke and found Nandi shaking him vigorously. Concern was writ large on Nandi's face as he said, "Hara, I thought we'd lost you. I've been trying to wake you up for the past half muhurta…"

"I'm fine, Nandi," Hara managed to say and got up. "I need to freshen up, and then do some meditation."

"Hara, Dev Guru Brihaspati had called. He said that you're welcome to join the war command and control centre."

"Is Devarth already in a state of war?"

"Yes, Hara. Ever since Daityas launched the Anvik Astra at Lonar…"

Hara one again felt emotions welling up within him. This time, however, it was that of pure anger.

22

ADVICE FROM THE MŪRTHI

Over the past few days, Brihaspati had been in a state of continuous action. He had no choice when he saw Indra and his wife Sachi break down in front of him on being told about the Lonar incident. Brihaspati shared Indra's pain but kept a sombre expression himself. He had already got the message that it was a Daityan Anvik attack and knew that this was clearly a declaration of war with a purpose of sending shock-waves across Devarth. More attacks may follow, maybe even on Amaravati itself. Within hours, the force-field shields around the city had been raised and Maruth formations put on high alert. The overall atmosphere at Dev Lok was extremely tense. Air force had also got into a heightened state of readiness, to take off and shoot down any perceived aerial threat.

Brihaspati met Hara on the way to the Devarth war command and control centre. On seeing Hara dressed in the original Bheeshma attire, he smiled and remarked, "Hara, it's good to see you. Much as I share your personal tragedy, the Lonar incident has also triggered a world war between Devarth and Daityan Empire."

"Yes, Dev Guru. Nandi briefed me about the situation after I came to my senses. Please pardon me for withdrawing myself into a shell for all these days."

"Your pain and anguish are understandable, Hara. Only time can subdue its impact, and we all are compelled to follow our Karma."

"Dev Guru, is it confirmed that the Anvik Astra that obliterated Lonar was launched by Daityan Empire?"

"Yes, Hara. Within hours of that incident they threatened to launch another attack on Hasthinapur, the capital of Bhārat kingdom. We now know that their plan was to terrorise Dev Lok and other nations of Devarth into submission. The assassination attempt of Indra Dev was also part of the same plan to disorganise Devarth leadership. Thanks to you, the Indra is alive and all of Devarth now clearly see the deviousness of Daityan rulers. It took me some convincing but we were able to rally the Devarth nations together for joint resistance of the Daityan plan."

"So what stopped Daityas from launching another Anvik Astra at Hasthinapur?"

"Within hours of their ultimatum, Indra sent a counter threat that our Anvik Astra is also ready to be launched at Patala archipelago. This seems to have put their Anvik misadventure under control for the time being. They've instead launched a conventional offensive. Naval battles are raging in seas on multiple fronts even now. Our navy is still resisting them as best as possible but it is only a matter of time before the Daityans have control over all the seas routes."

"How much time do you have?"

"It is difficult to say. Based on the current rate of attrition, I would say that Daityan ships may occupy our seas within two weeks or so. I guess their plan is to lay siege to all of the Dev Lok harbours and ports to arrest us from extending any support to the inland nations. Their main land attack might happen there."

"Dev Guru, I thought that their main enmity was with Dev Lok?"

"That is true, Hara. But they achieve nothing by attacking us directly. We have a string of powerful defence systems across our borders and Amaravati has a strong force-field shield around it. It is much more economic for them to spend their strength against other Devarth nations. With no support from Dev Lok, Bhārat and other nations will capitulate to the mainland attack from Daityan army within a matter of weeks. Once they have control over inland nations, they can then focus on tackling us island at a time."

They had reached the war command and control centre. Brihaspati requested that Hara also join them. Hara went along in the hope that diverting attention to the progress of war might help him forget some of his personal pain.

The Devarth war command and control centre was abuzz with activities. Varun Dev and Agni Dev were taking briefings from their Admirals and Generals regarding the update on various fronts. Hara settled down on a seat to hear the ongoing briefing about the naval battles raging around the main trade routes between Dev Lok and other inland nations. Within just another half ghati, Brihaspati came up to him and said, "Hara, Indra Dev has requested that it would honour him if you could attend today's Indra Sabha. There have been some new developments and few of the Sapta-Rishis are also likely to join us."

⟲ Ш ⚶

The general ambiance within Indra Sabha was very different compared to the ones Hara had attended in the past. The expression on everyone's face was that of grave concern. Indra tried to put up a brave front to keep the motivation levels high, but Hara could see that deep down, even he was fighting against a profound sense of anguish.

Besides the usual team, this time they also had the Sapta-Rishis. Once everyone settled down, Indra Dev said, "Gentlemen, you all know the critical nature of the situation that we face. Devarth is engaged in a losing war against Daityan Empire. Considering their unprecedented and overwhelming numerical superiority, it is only a matter of time before we face defeat. I don't have to tell what such defeat would mean to our way of life. The only recourse we had was to seek support from the Mūrthi Lords and that is what we've attempted. With help from Sapta-Rishis, we were able to establish an astral link with the Mūrthi Lord Vishnu who has always been benevolent to us in the past during times of crisis. The great lord was most sympathetic to our plight but stated that he is unable to intervene directly. He did advise us on what needs to be done if we are to stand any chance to get out of this difficult situation. I'll leave it for Dev Rishi Narad, who represents the Sapta-Rishis, to tell us the gist of what was advised by Lord Vishnu."

"Thank you, Indra Dev," Dev Rishi Narad said as he got up from his seat and stood facing all within Indra Sabha. "Today morning we were able to link up with the Mūrthi Lord's home-worlds using the Devayana astral chamber. As a result of our collective meditation, we were able to get our astral forms into Vaikunth – the home-world of the Mūrthi Lord Vishnu. Before I get to the advice from the Lord, let me also tell you what an extraordinary experience it was. The milky ocean of Vaikunth was pristine and the brilliantly blue Mūrthi Lord lying on the thousand-headed serpent was indeed a divine sight to behold. Our astral forms seemed to just float over the milky ocean till we were face-to-face with the Lord."

"Dev Rishi Narad, with due respect, many of us have had similar experience when we made astral link with the Mūrthi worlds through Devayana chamber. It is perhaps the absolutely surreal and unusual setting of those worlds that makes us awestruck whenever we visit them. It would, however, be really great if you could kindly focus on the subject matter of our discussion," Brihaspati attempted to interrupt Narad without wanting to offend him.

"Of course, Dev Guru. Pardon me for getting distracted but the experience was simply awesome. I'll now stick to the advice from the Lord. After much deliberation between us on various aspects of the current situation, Lord Vishnu is of the opinion that it is only the complete destruction of Tripura that can put an end to this conflict and avoid total defeat for Dev Lok."

Agni Dev who was listening intently till now intervened, "Dev Rishi Narad, this is something we've already examined earlier. We know that nothing within our disposal including the most powerful Anvik Astras can destroy Tripura and Atalantpuri. Daityan fortress of Tripura was constructed by direct application of Mūrthi technology and its defensive capability is unlike any other in this world. Even Amaravati, the city built by the Mūrthi themselves, can't match the three-layered force-field-based defensive systems of Tripura."

"Agni Dev, Lord Vishnu was also aware of all that, which is why he has advised us to take another course of action. None of us knew this but it seems that when Amaravati was constructed by the Mūrthi Lord Brahma, he had also attempted to build a special aerial ship to defend it. Its build-up was not completed before the Mūrthi left Earth so there was no mention of it. He didn't specify the purpose for which they tried to build it in the first place, but advised that its construction could be completed by us even now, with due help from Lord Brahma."

"Dev Rishi Narad, you mentioned it to be an aerial ship. Does it mean that it can fly like a vimān?" Brihaspati asked.

"Yes, Dev Guru. That is what Lord Vishnu said. This ship named Pinaka has no wings, yet it can fly faster and farther than any vimān. It has its own invisible force-field shield. It has a main weapon system which is based on projecting the innate potential energy of the cosmos into the physical world. If it can be powered up to link up with the universal shakti of Brahmn, the destructive energy emanating from this weapon would be more than sufficient to demolish even the fortress of Tripura."

"We thank Lord Vishnu for showing us the way. If this is true, we can surely win this war against the Daityas," Indra Dev stated, now somewhat excited.

Dev Rishi Narad quickly added, "Indra Dev, this might look like a solution but it is not as easy as it seems. Lord Vishnu said that firstly we would need Lord Brahma's help to identify its secret location within Amaravati. Even if we can find it, the ship is not likely to be in a state to fly. Its build-up needs to be completed with further help from Lord Brahma."

"I'm sure this can be taken care of. Our chief architect Vishwakarma is an expert of Mūrthi-based technologies and with astral support from Lord Brahma, he can surely bring it up to standards. Lord Brahma would definitely help us, since this has been advised by Lord Vishnu himself," Indra said confidently.

Dev Rishi Narad paused for a while before clarifying, "Yes Indra Dev, Lord Vishnu did say that we can expect help from Lord Brahma and also that the ship can be made ready within a few weeks. The main problem is not that. This ship was made for use by the Mūrthi alone and its main weapon system needs to be linked to the universal potential shakti within the Brahmn itself. No one except Mūrthi Lord Rudra is at a level of spiritual advancement to be able to make such a link."

"How is that possible, Dev Rishi Narad? We all know that it is extremely difficult to even get audience with the perpetually meditative Lord Rudra. He is certainly not accessible through the Devayana astrals chamber. Great Maharishis spend years in deep penance before they can rouse him from deep meditation. Even if he accepts to help us, the Mūrthi Lord can't be here in his physical body," Brihaspati was worried and doubtful.

"Dev Guru, Lord Vishnu was aware of this difficulty as well. But he did say that there is a solution if someone had the courage to undertake it," Narad said hesitatingly.

"Go on, please."

"Lord Vishnu said that while he was on Earth, the Lord Rudra had a special device that he used to engage with for enhancing his astral meditative perceptions. This device is still located somewhere on this planet. If sincere attempt is made by a spiritually advanced human to engage with this device, he may be able to gain quick access to Lord Rudra. However, this is something that has never been attempted before."

"Thank you, Dev Rishi. I take it that if we're able to find this astral enhancement device of Lord Rudra, it may be possible to gain access to him. But even if someone can do that, how is it going to help? You yourself said a while ago that only Lord Rudra himself can activate the primary weapon system of this ship called Pinaka?" Brihaspati asked with evident uncertainty.

"Yes, Dev Guru, that is what Lord Vishnu said. The primary weapon system of Pinaka can only be set off by directly channelizing the potential shakti of the cosmos. Even among the Mūrthi Lords, only Rudra has the ability to channelise such massive amounts of pure energy through his inner kundalini channel. Metaphorically, Lord Rudra is known to have access to the universal shakti of Brahmn through the 'inner eye' of his tantric kundalini channel. This has been done on many occasions in the past and the enormous destructive energy that emanates into the physical world is called Rudraksh."

"Dev Rishi Narad, it is understood that only Lord Rudra can open his tantric 'inner eye' that channelises the universal potential shakti of Brahmn into the physical reality. But still, you've not answered as to how this can help us if Mūrthi Lord can't be present in his physical form to do it here on the Earth?" The question was from Indra Dev.

Dev Rishi Narad looked at Indra and said, "Yes, Indra Dev, we have a problem in this regard but Lord Vishnu did offer a solution for that too. He said that if a human is sufficiently trained and spiritually advanced to be able to perfectly align his kundalini channel with that of Rudra, the Mūrthi Lord can then project the Rudraksh through this individual into the physical world for a few seconds."

"Do we know of anyone who has the capacity to do this?" Indra Dev asked in bewilderment.

Dev Rishi Narad waited for someone to answer. When no one spoke, he continued, "I should also mention here that according to Lord Vishnu, even if someone where capable of doing this, it might be the last thing he ever does. No human has ever been able to channelise the kind of tantric energy that we are talking about. Even if there is slightest deviation from extreme meditative focus by such an individual, the enormous kundalini shakti can get short circuited into his own physical body. This would of course mean instant death. In short, there is highest probability that anyone who attempts it wouldn't survive."

There was deadly silence within the Indra Sabha. At last Rishi Atri, one of the Sapta-Rishis said, "As we interacted with Lord Vishnu, we also requested him to tell whether anyone from Sapta-Rishis could do this. Unfortunately, he said that Sapta-Rishis may be spiritually advanced but don't have the physical skills necessary for such a task. This requires high degree of mental as well as physical coordination. Only someone who has high degree of experience in accessing certain amounts of kundalini shakti in the past can do this. Lord Vishnu also said that in all probability, this individual needs to be prepared to perish in this attempt…"

"I'll do it," Haŕa stated summarily. Everyone turned towards him in surprise.

"But Haŕa, you're a young Bheeshma monk with hardly any experience of astral link-up with the Mūrthi Lords," Rishi Atri objected.

"That may be so, Dev Rishi. But all the qualifications spelt out by Dev Rishi Narad indicate towards the capabilities of Bheeshma monks anyway. Some of you may already know that we Bheeshma have the benefit of Jwalaprabha—the tantric perception we're born with—to access and store very limited amounts of kundalini shakti within our astral aura. As regards my survival in this endeavour, that is matter of Karma anyway. If it is my Karma to perish in the process, so be it."

"But Hara..." Brihaspati hesitated.

"Hara is right, Dev Guru," Dev Rishi Narad said. "Most of what was mentioned by Lord Vishnu about individuals who qualify for this task fits in well for the Bheeshma. They have the ideal profile of being able to match spirituality with physical action. Advanced Bheeshma monks are well-known to be able to access the kundalini shakti to project superhuman telekinetic power into the physical world during combat. I don't know about Hara, but a Bheeshma monk would indeed be the ideal person to undertake this task."

Hara got up to address everyone present, "I'm Hara, the disciple of the legendary Bheeshma monk Acharya Parashu, who was killed at Lonar a few days back. It must be a matter of Karma that has got me involved in this war. I'm more than willing to do whatever is necessary to engage with Mūrthi Lord Rudra. I will leave the final decision up to you."

Indra Dev looked at all others and said, "Gentlemen, we are in the midst of a war. There is very little time for deliberations and whatever needs to be done, must happen quickly. Advice from Lord Vishnu has given us renewed hope. The Mūrthi aerial ship must be readied fast. I direct Vishwakarma to start this effort immediately. All necessary support shall be extended to him." He paused and then looked at Hara before continuing, "On behalf of Dev Lok, let me firstly extend my sincere thanks to the Bheeshma monk Hara for preventing the assassination attempt within Indra Sabha. I'm aware that it is he who has suffered the most from this war so far. But even under such tremendous emotional pain, if there is anyone I know who can pull off the extraordinary feat of embodying Lord Rudra's powers to stop the Daityan aggression, it is Hara. Unless anyone has any objection, I accept his request to undertake the quest for gaining access to Lord Rudra. Dev Lok will do everything within its power to help him."

There was silence within the Indra Sabha for quite some time. Then Brihaspati spoke, "As directed by Indra Dev, we shall immediately direct our efforts to follow the advice from Lord Vishnu. Success depends on Hara's ability to gain access to Lord Rudra." He then looked at Dev Rishi Narad and asked, "Do we know the location of the astral enhancer using which Hara may access Lord Rudra?"

"Dev Guru, we do not know the exact location. Lord Vishnu did say that this astral enhancer called Rudrapeeth is somewhere in the vicinity of Mount Kailash, north of Yaksha kingdom. Only the Naga tribes who live in that region know of its exact location," Narad replied.

Brihaspati thought for a while before addressing the others, "Nagas are the elusive tribes who consciously stay away from contact outside their own community. Not much is known about them, except that they are ardent worshippers of serpents. This has given birth to so many superstitions and myths about them. Some say they possess magical powers and have links with the underworld. It is, however, known that the Mūrthi Lord Rudra and his followers used to live in the vicinity of Mount Kailash. In fact, Lord Rudra had given refuge to all kinds of living forms, especially serpents, during an age when early humans attempted to exterminate them from their domains. This is also why he is popularly known within the legends as Pashupati."

"If that is the case, I would like to go there at once. Dev Guru, do we have any kind of contacts with Nagas?" Hara asked.

"Unfortunately, that is a problem Hara. We could send in vimāns to find them but it is likely to be of no use. The vimāns are also known to develop strange engine trouble and crash if they venture into that region. I believe it has something to do with the defence systems that the Nagas inherited from their Mūrthi masters. Even the inhabitants of Yaksha kingdom, which is adjacent to this area, have rarely seen them. The land of Nagas is called the Sarparanya and is considered totally forbidden for outsiders. Nagas are known to live in subterranean caverns which provide them protection from the harsh weather conditions in that region. Some say there are geothermal vents and hot water springs in some areas, providing pockets of warmth to these underground caverns. Even when ice sheets covered everything within that latitude around the world, this particular area remained barren, probably due to the extremely dry conditions prevalent there. It is also high altitude and extremely cold."

"What about Mount Kailash and the nearby lake called Manasarovar? That place is well-known as it has been a human pilgrimage centre for many centuries?" Indra Dev asked.

"Yes, Indra Dev. Ever since the departure of the Mūrthi Lord Rudra, Mount Kailash and Manasarovar Lake have been revered as holy spots. When surrounding areas are extremely cold and freezing, the water of Manasarovar remains in liquid state throughout the year. Legend says that this is again due to some strange Mūrthi technology. It is also known to be an excellent place for meditative advancement. The area surrounding the lake has been the favourite spot for many seeking astral connections with their inner self. Actually, as far as I know, there is only one mountain trail from Yaksha kingdom that leads to Manasarovar and it passes through Sarparanya. The Nagas mostly leave alone the travellers passing through this trail during the pilgrimage season, unless they veer off into surrounding areas or attempt to go towards Mount Kailash itself. Sarparanya is also believed to be infested with a ferocious alien serpent species from the Mūrthi worlds called Takshak. Many who either got lost or attempted to explore around this region, have never been seen again," Brihaspati replied.

"So what would you suggest for me to do, Dev Guru? If the secret location of Lord Rudra's astral enhancer is only known to Nagas, I would need to make contact with them," Hara said.

"I cannot be of much help in this regard, Hara. All I can do is suggest that you may take the trail up to Manasarovar and from there, attempt to go towards Mount Kailash. You would definitely face the Nagas that way. From that point, it is only your Karma that may lead you."

23

SARPARANYA

Hara and Nandi had been on the Manasarovar trail for the past two days, riding on yaks, the popular beasts of burden in that region. A vimān from Amaravati had taken them straight to the Yaksha capital Alakapuri. They had met the Yaksha King Kuber who helped them get all necessary provisions to start along the trail up the mountains towards Manasarovar. Not being the pilgrimage season, it was unlikely that they would meet anyone on the way. Even though not sure as to where and when they may meet any Naga, Hara had decided it best to trek the way up to Manasarovar and beyond.

The landscape along this high altitude trail was totally barren. So it was strange that region was known as Sarparanya, literally, the forest of snakes. They could see some bushes here and there, but nothing resembling a tree could be seen anywhere. A few small birds could be seen pecking the seeds on some shrubs. Apart from this, there was no sign of life. The weather was completely unpredictable. On the first day, during the morning it was bright and sunny and they were exposed to the intense highaltitude radiation from the sun. Even the rocks around the region seemed to be totally tanned, having been exposed to extreme elements for eons. By evening, however, it was totally overcast and windy. During night, a small cave along the trail provided some refuge from high-speed cold winds. Within the cave they found a small stock of firewood left by past travellers. Nandi lit up a fire and they soon dozed off, totally tired from the exertion of the climb. They started off again as soon as it was morning. The next day was downcast, misty and very cold and as they gained altitude, the temperature continued to plummet. Hara and Nandi had to put on an extra layer of clothing to stay warm. By the time they reached the Manasarovar Lake, it was already late evening.

The landscape around the lake was absolutely surreal. The weather had cleared and the full moon was in its full glory on a cloudless sky. The pristine waters of Manasarovar reflected some distant hills as well as the imposing and mesmerising view of Mount Kailash. No wonder the lake and its surrounding were known to enhance the spiritual aura of those who came here to experience it. Was it just because of such fantastic venue or was it due to what many believed—some subterranean psychic enhancement systems left behind by the Mūrthi, who used to live in this region eons ago? No one knew for sure. Anyway, according to legends, this was known to have been one of the favourite places of meditation by the Mūrthi Lord Rudra while he was on Earth.

The temperature of the lake water was certainly not as cold as it ought to be, given its location at such a high altitude. Because of this, the shores of the lake were lined with green grass, shrubs and flowering plants. Surprisingly, there was even a small flock of majestic looking white swan, swimming around the shores. There were no prominent features around the lake but a few extraordinarily huge bael trees close to the shores provided some shelter from the elements. These trees were known to have been a particular favourite of Lord Rudra as it reminded him of similar ones in his own home-world. They decided to build a fire and huddled together to get some sleep.

Hara looked at Nandi as he built the fire using some deadwood lying around. His presence was reassuring. Inspite of Hara's repeated reminders regarding the dangers, Nandi was adamant to accompany him. Though reluctant in the beginning, Hara had ultimately given in. Now when they were in the midst of nowhere, Hara felt glad that he had the company of his Bheeshma apprentice. It reminded him of Acharya Parashu with whom he had shared so many adventures in the past. The memory of his revered guru also brought with it the emotions of pain and despair. He had to make a conscious effort to withdraw his mind from the past and keep it focused on the present.

Hara knew that this was an extremely risky trip. Even if he did get to Rudrapeeth, the astral enhancer of Lord Rudra, there was no guarantee that he would succeed. No human is known to have used this Mūrthi machine that could instantly direct the mind inwards, right into a state similar to the astral self of Lord Rudra himself. If the human mind was not capable of taking such stress, it would get decimated and the person would be dead even before realising it. The energy that would get generated in the process would vaporise his physical body. But death was something that Hara would welcome, if it helps terminate the tragic memories of that fateful night. In any case, what was left in his life after that single stroke of destiny when he had lost almost everyone near and dear to him. Memories of Uma and the joyful days spent with her at Lonar kept coming back to his mind. Those days would never return but he must move along, on the path of his own Karma. This trip had given some purpose to live on for now.

Next day, after taking a refreshing dip in the clear waters of the lake, they started off on foot. The yaks were left to graze on the grassland surrounding the lake. Hereafter, there was no clear path to be taken or trail to be followed, except their instinct. As Brihaspati had suggested, Hara decided to trek towards the imposing monolith of Mount Kailash. Nandi followed, carrying whatever provisions he could, on his strong shoulders. After they left the area surrounding the lake, the landscape once again started becoming rugged and barren. At places, the climb was steep and they had to support each other to negotiate. There were some faint foot trails but not clear enough to follow, so they were moving only with the general direction of Mount Kailash to guide them.

They had reached a small plateau interspersed with huge boulders, when Hara felt the sense of danger. His Jwalaprabha was pulsating, clearly indicating that some action was imminent. He looked at Nandi and knew that he was having similar premonitory sense experienced by all Bheeshma warrior monks. There was nothing out of ordinary to sense any danger, but it seemed very close. Hara was just about to take out his Spatishūl when a shower of fine needles struck them from all around. Immediately turning around, Hara attempted to identify the source of the attack, but it was too late. The poison tipped needles had already initiated their effect within his body.

𐤕 Ш ৡ

When he woke up, Hara realised that he was inside what seemed like a huge cavern. Even though there was no sunlight, many strange twinkling points of the light placed all around the cavern provided sufficient illumination. His hands and legs were bound together but otherwise he seemed fine. Nandi was lying next to him in similar bondage, still unconscious. The temperature inside was fairly comfortable and Hara wondered whether they were still in the area with freezing weather conditions.

"So you're awake, stranger?" someone spoke in the ancient Mūrthi language of Brahmi. Hara turned around to see a tall man donning a strange costume; he had a trimmed grey beard and matted hair flowing well below the shoulders. Even more unusual was the live snake casually draped around his shoulders.

The one who spoke also had a self-illuminating gem secured on the middle of his forehead, by use of a headband. Altogether, he portrayed a fierce profile.

"You are the Naga," Hara said, remembering his lessons in Brahmi.

"And you? This is a forbidden land for outsiders."

Hara could see Nandi waking up. He looked around as Hara replied, "I'm Hara, the Bheeshma monk."

"We're aware that you are Bheeshma, which is why you are still alive. Why are you here? Even Bheeshma have no business to come to Sarparanya," the Naga spoke. As he spoke, two of his companions joined him. They whispered something to him and he looked at Hara, "You both have been summoned by the Naga King Vasuki." He looked at his companions and nodded. They untied the legs of the prisoners but kept their hands bound in shackles. When Hara and Nandi got up, they were asked to follow the group. Two more Naga soldiers holding strange trident-like weapons joined them. The Naga took them to the nearest wall and pressed an iridescent point of light on a doorway. A pathway opened up and they followed the Naga.

The Naga leading them seemed to be the leader, because Hara noticed the doorkeeping soldiers bow down as he passed. He said, "I've already told you my name. May I know yours too?"

"I'm Shankh," he seemed to be a man of few words. All of the Naga seemed to wear similar unusual dressing that clung to their skin. In fact, the dress complemented the colour of live snake draped around everyone's neck or shoulders. After passing through two more doorways and another corridor, they soon reached what seemed like an enormous cavern. This was decorated with extraordinary stone sculptures and lit brilliantly with thousands of the same iridescent points of light. Seated across the cavern on a stone throne, highly decorated with serpentine patterns, was an old man with a long, white beard. The long matted white hair on his head was partly tied into a bun on top and partly fell up to his hips. When Hara and Nandi were close to him, Shankh raised his hand indicating them to stop. Then he bowed and moved back.

The Naga King Vasuki got up from his throne and walked down towards them, "I'm told that both of you are Bheeshma monks. Is that correct?"

"Yes. I'm Hara and this is my apprentice Nandi."

It was only when Vasuki came close to him that Hara could see the piercing eyes of the Naga monarch. He was taller than Hara and even at the apparently advanced age, had a very graceful gait. The light emitting gem on his forehead—similar to the one worn by Shankh—was secured by a thin yet intricately carved gold band. Like other Naga, he also had a fearsome snake draped around his neck with its head erect and hood fully distended. The eyes of the snake seemed to follow its master's wherever he looked.

King Vasuki looked over at both of them, first Hara and then Nandi. Then he came back to Hara and examined him once more, "You're indeed Bheeshma. I can sense the aura of Jwalaprabha coiled up within you." Then he came close and examined the blue colour on Hara's throat.

"This blue colour around your throat, what is this? How did you get it?" Vasuki asked.

"I was bitten by a Karkotakan snake when we had to pass through the Vetal land."

"You're still alive after a bite on the neck by Karkotakan?" he seemed surprised.

"Apparently so," Hara replied in a somewhat annoyed tone.

"Don't mind my curiosity, Bheeshma. We Naga know a thing or two about snakes," King Vasuki smiled before continuing, "I'm yet to see a human who has taken a Karkotakan's bite and yet lived to talk about it. You must have some extraordinary inner constitution to be able to resist the trauma of such a deadly snake bite. No wonder my troops told me that they had to jab you with multiple poison darts to make you unconscious."

"The healing process was assisted by my guru. I am sure the treatment by consuming Amruth must've also helped reverse the effects of the bite," Hara replied, attempting to sound polite and pleasant.

"Yes, of course. By the way, who is your guru?"

"My guru was Acharya Parashu," Hara replied, trying to remain calm and control the welling emotions as he said his guru's name.

"Acharya Parashu? You are Parashu's shishya?" Vasuki asked in surprised tone.

"Yes, I was ... Your Majesty. You seem to be familiar with the Acharya…"

"There is much about us Naga that many don't know. Yes I've had the privilege of Acharya Parashu's company from time to time during my trips outside Sarparanya." Then he called over a soldier and asked him to release their hands.

He looked back and said, "Hara, the disciple of the legendary Bheeshma Acharya Parashu is most welcome to the land of the Naga. I consider your guru to be my friend and he has helped me get out of some tight spots in the past. I extend similar friendship to you, too." Then he asked doubtfully, "Did I hear you say he was your guru? Does this mean you've parted ways?"

Hara couldn't hide his emotion when he replied, "Acharya Parashu was killed in the Daityan Anvik attack on Lonar."

"Oh! I heard about the attack on Lonar but never knew…"

༶ ɰ ၃

"I'll be most happy to help you, my friend. But what you ask for is nothing but a death wish. I can't allow you to waste way your life like this," Vasuki said as he heard Hara's request. They were sitting in a small chamber within one of the royal caverns. The room was fairly well lit, with the similar iridescent gemstones they found everywhere.

"Does this mean you know the location of Rudrapeeth?"

"Yes. It is one of the legacies of our tribe's association with the Mūrthi Lord Rudra many ages ago."

"Then you must help me reach it, Your Majesty. This is the only way to maintain the correct karmic course of humanity. It is the opinion of Lord Vishnu, too," Hara requested.

"Hara, Lord Vishnu must know the dangers of abrupt engagement with Lord Rudra through the Rudrapeeth. It has been attempted many times in the past. All of them where fairly advanced in spiritual terms. Most were Yogis, few were Naga and one was definitely a Bheeshma. All of them perished the moment the device got activated. So you see, being a Bheeshma is no guarantee that your case would be any different," Vasuki said.

"Your Majesty, if so many had perished while attempting to use Rudrapeeth, why is it that no one has heard about it?"

"Because we Nagas try to keep it that way. No one has ever been allowed to confirm even the existence of this device. All attempts to use it were made many years ago. Since there has never been a success and those who got to try it didn't live to talk about it, even the knowledge of its very existence probably faded away." Vasuki said.

"I understand that this device was used by Lord Rudra himself when he used to live near Kailash, before leaving Earth to take up his present astral form?" Hara asked.

"Yes, that's right. As you might've heard, Lord Rudra is the most spiritually inclined among the Mūrthi Lords. Even when physically living on Earth eons ago, he used to remain in deep meditation for most of the time. The device that you know as the Rudrapeeth is actually a simple platform. It has energy set in such a manner that it can link up with the mind of any intelligent being who sits upon it. The device is tuned up to the level sustainable by Lord Rudra. Human minds are too feeble to engage at such levels," Vasuki explained.

"Do you know what happens when a human attempts to sit on this device?"

"I've not experienced it myself but we have its description recorded from the days when my Naga ancestors used to serve Lord Rudra and other Mūrthi living near Kailash. It is understood that only the purest mind, which is totally devoid of any thoughts, can engage properly with the resident tantric power of Rudrapeeth. Even an iota of thought about the mortal world would be dangerous. So, just like it enhances the spiritual state of engagement with one's universal self, it also enhances any stray thoughts a thousand times. Such thoughts could either be positive or negative like sadness, sorrow, fears, doubts, anger, etc. Now, you must know that thoughts always happen in terms of duality. This means that one could never have pleasant thoughts without there being no seed of unpleasant ones. In fact, the term pleasant by itself holds a meaning when seen within a backdrop of unpleasantness. Similarly, all of the so-called positive thoughts have an automatic opposite pair that remains within them in the resident seed form. Human mind, by habit, attempts to deal with the unpleasant thoughts by trying to eliminate them even while holding on to the pleasant ones. Our memory provides enough fuel to propagate such thoughts which keeps vacillating from pleasant to unpleasant. Very few fortunate ones are able to keep the positive thoughts in dominance most of the time. Even for them, however, self-defeating, new thoughts within the field of perceived reality keep surfacing. Emotions which are the residue of such thoughts also follow them like a shadow. Trouble happens when even a speck of emotion gets multiplied within the Rudrapeeth and immediately catch the attention of our thoughts. This creates an avalanche of thoughts and emotions which is simply beyond the capacity of our mind to control. When overwhelmed with such a deluge of thoughts and emotions, it just simply shuts down," Vasuki explained.

Haŕa was quiet for some time. Then he said, "Your Majesty, I've already decided to face my Karma which seems to point me towards the Rudrapeeth. Acharya Parashu used to tell me that a world dominated by Daityan way of life would only lead to decline and possible extinction of human species. There is an opportunity for me to do something about it now. If attempting it leads to my death, so be it."

Vasuki sighed and said, "I can see that you've made up your mind, my friend. Since you are the shishya of Parashu, I'm duty bound to help you achieve success in this endeavour. So yes, we will take you to the astral enhancer of Lord Rudra. However, there are two more problems. First, as per our tradition, entry to the chamber of Rudrapeeth can only be allowed to someone who becomes a Naga prince."

"Does this mean you wouldn't allow me to go there? I thought you said..." Haŕa asked hesitatingly.

"I can only allow you to enter there if you acquire the status of a Naga prince. For that to happen, you must harvest your own *Nāg Mani* from Takshak serpents."

"Takshak serpents, Your Majesty?"

"When the Mūrthi used to live in this region during the early periods of their stay on Earth, they had conducted many genetic experiments. Takshaks are a species of serpents created by them during this period. These creatures have most of their genetic materials from an alien serpent species from Mūrthi home-worlds. They are huge, fierce and highly intelligent. They've adapted themselves to the environmental conditions prevalent in this high altitude terrain."

"You said something about harvesting a Mani?"

"Yes, Haŕa. Manis are the gem-like shining objects you find all around our caverns. It provides us with the much-needed visibility."

"Your Majesty, is it a Mani that adorns your forehead? I have seen it with Shankh and a few other Nagas."

"Yes, indeed. To be a Naga prince, you have to obtain your own Mani, pried out from a live Takshak serpent. It is an extremely dangerous mission that a Naga must undertake to become part of our ruling class."

"Are you saying that only the one who has obtained a Mani can be allowed entry into the Mūrthi cavern housing Rudrapeeth?"

"Yes, Hara. If you need to go to the chamber where the Rudrapeeth is placed, you must first become a Naga prince, for which you must obtain your own Mani. This means that you need to be prepared to subdue a Takshak serpent on your own and take out its Mani."

Hara thought for a while and asked, "You had mentioned there being two problems; what is the other one?" Hara asked.

"The second problem is that even if you're able to obtain a Mani and become a Naga prince, you may still need to wait till the specific full moon day two months later."

"That may be too late, Your Majesty. By then, the war may already be over."

"There is nothing you or I can do about that, Hara. Rudrapeeth becomes active only on special occasions, as it is tuned in line with the Mūrthi calendar. You can only pray that the war is not over before you're able to make this attempt to engage with Lord Rudra. This is a matter of karmic providence and it is best to leave it to that."

Hara knew that there was no point in arguing with Vasuki on this matter. He hoped that Devarth defence forces would be able to resist Daityan invasion for at least two months. It is best to focus on what he must do in the short term and leave the outcome to Karma. "Your Majesty, where can I find a Takshak serpent? Will you help me?"

"Before you agree, you must know that as per our past records, only one out of ten who venture out on such a daring task ever succeed; the remaining end up in the belly of these ferocious serpent predators."

"If this is what I must do to get access to the Rudrapeeth, so be it. Will you help me get to a Takshak?"

"If you're willing to take the risk, we will. Anyway I don't see as to how this is going to be any more risky if you're doing so to gain access to Rudrapeeth," King Vasuki smiled.

"I'm willing to take my chances, if that is indeed my Karma."

"So be it! Shankh and a few of our trackers will help you approach a Takshak tomorrow itself. However, they're forbidden to intervene when you face the serpent. If you do somehow subdue a Takshak and harvest its Mani, I promise to take you up to Rudrapeeth. I don't know your karmic path, so can't predict your future. Even though you're not a Naga, your skills as a Bheeshma may help somewhat when you face off against a Takshak."

"Just one more query, Your Majesty. How does this Mani glow in the dark? I've seen that it is far brighter on your or other's forehead compared to the ones placed around your caverns."

"The Naga way of life exists due to many gifts from our past masters, the Mūrthi. We still use many of their know-how handed over to us many eons ago. The use of Mani is just one of them. The Mani that is found on the forehead of the Takshak serpents is a sort of astral organ. They use it to link up with their higher astral self as well as get better awareness of their environment. As part of their evolutionary adaptation on Earth, they've also been able to use the Mani to convert some of their internal life force into physical radiations in the form of light. Like the Mūrthi led by Lord Rudra used to do, we Nagas take out the Mani from the serpents and use it much the same way. When it is on our forehead, we're able to convert part of our life force into light as and when we wish to. As in case of Takshak, once engaged with human Prana, it also provides us with extra-sensory perceptions. That is why we sometimes call these Manis secured on our foreheads as our 'third eye'. The Manis you find placed around the caverns mostly belong to our dead ancestors.

Even when placed on the cavern walls, these Manis manage to link up with the energy inherent within all objects in contact with them and give out a dim glow. So the illumination that you see on them is effectively the latent pranic energy extracted from Earth itself. Even though dim in terms of luminance, sufficient numbers of them provide us with enough light and visibility within these underground caverns. Duly supplemented with sunlight entering through various vents during day time, these caverns are bright enough for us to inhabit them indefinitely," Vasuki explained and then looking at Hara continued, "I suggest that you take a good night's rest. You'll need all your skills and energies tomorrow."

"Your Majesty, I'm thankful for all your help," Hara smiled back.

King Vasuki nodded and then directed Shankh to take Hara and Nandi to the guest chambers.

24

TAKSHAK

Under normal circumstances, no Naga ever dared to venture into this part of Sarparanya—the abode of the mighty serpents called Takshak. It was late afternoon by the time they reached the small re-entrant valley. Throughout the day, Hara, Shankh, Nandi and three Naga scouts had scoured this particular region of Sarparanya, well-known to be frequented by the serpents. Even the expert Naga scouts found it extremely difficult to track down these elusive and intelligent creatures. Takshaks were highly perceptive to their environment and their sense of smell was extremely acute. They usually ambushed their potential prey as it got close to where they lay in absolute stillness. Nagas had a famous saying that, "If you see a Takshak, be assured it is the last sighting of your life." Even when close, the only way to detect the presence of a Takshak is to offer it some form of bait.

Shankh and the Naga scouts stopped as they reached the entrance to a small valley and turned to Hara, "A Takshak has definitely passed through this place not too long ago. I would advise you to get into the valley and attempt to subdue the serpent as soon as possible. Once it gets dark, the odds against you would be too high."

Hara nodded and said, "Thank you, Shankh. Can you just tell me as to how do I get to see this serpent?"

"That shouldn't be too difficult. In fact, the Takshak will find you on its own as you move into the valley. You will yourself become the bait to attract it towards you."

"Wonderful," Hara smiled and then asked, "How long will you wait for me?"

"It is a small valley ahead and you're likely to encounter the Takshak within another half a muhurta. In any case, everything will be over within the next muhurta. We'll wait for another two muhurtas and then leave. It is not safe to hang around this spot once it turns dark." Shankh paused and looking intently at Hara asked, "Bheeshma, I hope you're well aware of the risk to your life? This is the last opportunity for you to turn back. Once you get into that valley, you would have to either subdue the serpent or become its meal for the day."

"Thank you Shankh. You've explained this to me before as well and I'm grateful for that. Anyway, this is my Karma and I must face it, irrespective of what the outcome may be."

"Then we wish you good luck," Shankh said.

Hara turned towards the valley and started walking to the entrance; he heard Shankh call out to him, "One more thing, Bheeshma. The only way to outguess a Takshak is to be able to see its astral aura and based on it, predict its next move. So, if you have such a perception, be sure to use it fully."

Hara waved acknowledgement and moved on. The valley that he got into was a small one with a single opening outwards. The rear side was blocked by some landslide that must've happened years ago. As such it was devoid of any major vegetation, probably due the extremely arid condition of the land. This could also have been because no humans or animals ever entered this place. If anyone did, he usually never returned back. Apart from this, it seemed somewhat strange that the place was almost absolutely quiet. Not that there was much sound at this highaltitude terrain conditions anyway; but it was never this quiet. There was always the sound of wind blowing or some small animals or birds scurrying around the bushes or grass. Here, though, it seemed unnaturally quiet. If there was a serpent in this valley, it had chosen to remain well hidden. Hara could already feel the Jwalaprabha welling up within his body indicating the impending danger and need for karmic action. He willed it to course through his mind to enhance its astral perceptions. Then he sensed it, rather than seeing.

The serpent seemed to come out of nowhere and even with his heightened astral perceptions, Hara would've missed it, had it not been for a faint shadow from the fading sunlight. The serpent had silently crept up behind him. As he turned around, Hara stepped sideways to avoid the direct bite from the enormous hood of the snake hovering over him. The serpent reared back, somewhat surprised that its initial attack had failed.

The size of the snake was enormous. Around twenty-five dhanus long, its body was coiled into a bundle of muscle, ready to pounce anytime. The scales that extended throughout its body seemed to shine and almost shimmer in the evening twilight. The patters of colours changed rhythmically throughout the scales and the enormous body seemed to just blend into the environment around. No wonder no one can see a Takshak even while close to it. It had an almost perfect camouflage system like a chameleon, dynamically adapted to change as per environmental visual patterns. The hood stood nearly three dhanus from the ground and towered over Hara's body. It was extended fully and the eyes that stared at him directly seemed almost human. Looking at them Hara felt transfixed, almost mesmerised.

Hara had to will himself to come out of the magnetic influence of the snake's eyes and look for any weaknesses. There seemed none. The only thing that gave away its extra terrestrial origins was the odd-looking fangs and the Mani embedded within its forehead. It was not unlike the ones he had seen adorned by

Vasuki and Shankh, but on a real Takshak's head, it looked almost like a beacon. The fangs were too short for the size of such an enormous snake but he knew that this was more than compensated by the potency of the venom that the serpent could inject through them.

The serpent seemed to be sizing him up. Perhaps, like Hara, it could feel the astral aura emanating from his adversary. Perhaps it was perturbed by the Jwalaprabha that it could sense within this human. Hara had himself seen the astral aura of the snake. It was too bright for a terrestrial reptilian species; the aura of Takshak was almost as bright as that of an average human. As he continued to look at the snake, Hara involuntarily drew out his Spatishūl. Even as he did so, he missed the movement within the body of the Takshak as it had uncoiled at high speed and the tail lashed at him from behind. It hit him unexpectedly with such a force that he was thrown five clear dhanush away and fell down on the dusty ground. His Spatishūl was thrown far out to the side opposite of where he lay. To get it back into his hand, all he needed to do was focus on it for an instant and make a telekinetic link. However, with the serpent watching him this closely, it would be too risky. He knew that the Takshak was waiting for any opportunity for him to be distracted enough to launch its final strike against him. One bite or even a scratch by those fangs containing deadly poison would be enough to kill him many times over. Maintaining eye contact with the serpent, he got up to his feet slowly. In his totally unarmed state, he must have looked defenceless, so the snake seemed to be savouring its final moments of victory. Hara could see the mouth of the snake open to expose its terrifying fangs.

Hara wouldn't have understood the intension of the snake had it not been for the change in its aura and a slight twinkle within the Mani on its forehead. The serpent's tail moved behind Hara's body to distract him to expect another attack from behind, while simultaneously its hood came down to make the final killing strike. As Hara had expected this, he had already withdrawn himself into his inner self to concentrate on channelisation of his complete Jwalaprabha into one single telekinetic force-field and project it outward using the yogic technique taught by Acharya Parashu—the Mārak Mudra. Unlike his guru, however, this was the first time Hara was using this tantric skill in a combat situation. He was not completely sure of how to calibrate the kundalini force behind it. He would have to trust his karmic instincts.

The serpent was surprised to see its prey hold ground even as it moved in for the final strike. In fact the aura of this human seemed to remain steady and even brighten up somewhat—not from fear but from anticipation for action. The snake's instincts indicated that something was not right. Instead of veering back in terror on seeing the approaching fangs as most of its victims did, this human seemed too calm. Before he realised that he needed to change his tactics of attack, it was too late.

The snake's hood was just one dhanus away from the final strike on Hara's body when he felt his Jwalaprabha course through the Mārak Mudra. It started slowly but within an instant became a torrent. The universal shakti that was flowing in through his kundalini channel manifested itself into a powerful force-field within the space-time continuum, and exploded outward. The striking hood of the alien snake had no chance against it. At such close quarters, the force-field smashed against it with tremendous energy. Its fangs broke from the impact and the hood, along with its heavy body was thrown outwards before collapsing to the ground. The serpent's body writhed involuntarily for few more seconds before becoming quiet. The Mani on the serpent's forehead was already losing its sheen when Hara called out to Shankh to help him.

When Shankh reached him, Hara was already attempting to pry out the Mani from the forehead of the snake. Shankh looked at Hara in surprise, as he'd never expected this Bheeshma monk to emerge alive from this encounter. "You need to gently move around the Mani to loosen it free. Let me help you," Shankh said and helped Hara pull out the Mani embedded within the serpent's forehead.

"You have to connect with the Mani immediately before it loses its life-force," Shankh removed his own headband, replaced his Mari with the new one and handed it over to Hara. "Please put this on and spend some time to focus on it. The Mani needs to get readjusted to your Prana life-force," Shankh instructed.

Hara lifted the headband with the new Mani secured upon it and tied it over his head. He could immediately perceive its presence as the astral aura of the Mani connected up with his own life-force. The Mani slowly started getting bright and soon it was aglow.

"I've never seen anyone's Mani shine so brightly. It must've really made a strong connection with your life-force," Shankh commented in a surprised tone.

"The bright shine is because of the Jwalaprabha coursing through it," Hara replied. Then he continued as Shankh and others looked on in wonder, "Jwalaprabha is the tantric kundalini force that supplements the life force of a Bheeshma monk."

"No wonder you were able to subdue the Takshak is such a short time," Shankh said in admiration.

Hara looked at the fallen serpent and said, "I do feel sorry for this serpent. After all, I've just killed it for my own selfish reason."

"This Takshak is not dead, Bheeshma. It is only unconscious and will wake up soon. As regards its Mani and fangs, they will grow back soon."

"Oh…I didn't know that," Hara looked at Shankh in surprise.

Shankh smiled back at him and said, "Takshaks are extremely difficult to kill. They have incredible recuperative capability and live for hundreds of years. We've had cases where the Mani has been harvested from the same serpent many times."

"Harvested many times? Do you mean you take out Mani on a regular basis? It seems like a cruel practice to me."

"Not so regularly, Bheeshma. As per Naga custom, the Mani can only be taken by a single individual. So if someone wants to have a new Mani, he needs to risk his life alone. Generally only one out of ten hunts ever succeed. So majority of the time, anyone who attempts it, ends up in the serpent's belly," Shankh said. Then he looked at the sky and continued, "We must start back immediately. It's going to get dark very soon.

25

PINAKA

"Your Majesty, this aerial ship is a unique expression of the Mūrthi technology on Earth. It is far more advanced than we initially imagined. The ship's earlier logs show that it was called the Pinaka. I believe the Mūrthi built it as a mobile platform to defend Amaravati. By the time it was almost ready, they had decided to move on to their astral levels and leave the Earth for advancement of human species. When they realised that they couldn't trust humans with such a powerful weapon, they stopped building it further. The aerial ship was decommissioned and put into indefinite storage within this underground hangar at Amaravati," Vishwakarma, the chief architect and scientist of Dev Lok, told Indra as they stood on a viewing platform overlooking the huge hangar where the build-up of the Mūrthi aerial ship was in progress. The vimān and its hangar had actually become the centre of hope for Devan leadership. Indra had requested that the next war briefing be held on the viewing platform at the hanger itself.

"If this hangar was here all this while, why didn't we know about it?" Indra asked.

"Devraj, we still don't know many secrets about the city of Amaravati, which was one of the main habitation centres of

Mūrthi during their stay on Earth. While they handed it over to us before leaving the planet, all operational details were given to the first Vishwakarma. It is possible that Mūrthi kept the whereabouts of this ship a secret, fearing its misuse. Even now, we were able to locate it only with explicit guidance from Lord Brahma, after he agreed to help us complete its build-up. As you can see, this hangar is just below the main courtyard of the Devayana astral station of the city," Vishwakarma replied.

"Is the aerial ship completely ready for operation?" Indra asked.

"It may take a few weeks before it is completely ready," Vishwakarma replied before continuing, "Actually, we would've never been able to access its controls without direct help from Lord Brahma. After first establishing a direct astral connection with the ship himself, Lord Brahma has been helping us commission its various systems."

"Thank you, Vishwakarma. We're grateful for all the support the Mūrthi Lords are offering us during this critical time. Are we likely to be in a position to pilot this aerial ship soon and use it in the war?"

Vishwakarma replied, "Pinaka operates at an entirely new level of technology that we are not familiar with at all. Its internal systems are controlled by an artificial mind with a distinctive consciousness of its own. It is as if the complete aerial ship is a living entity. It has to be piloted by mental commands alone. An invisible astral umbilical cord gets established between the ship and its commander as well as the base station."

"Are the weapon systems also controlled by mind commands?" Indra asked.

"The ship is capable of defending itself. It has a powerful force-shield all around the hull which can negate any projectile or pulse ray attack. The ship's own weapon systems are capable of firing all around it to destroy any enemy targets within its range. However, the main weapon system can only be activated by the commander. As you know, activation by itself is not enough. The energy torpedo from this weapon is designed to hold enormous destructive power which can only be marshalled by the Mūrthi Lord Rudra himself."

"I'm aware of that," Indra Dev said and looked at Brihaspati, "Guru Dev, do we have any news from Haŕa? He is our only hope if we are to ever wield this aerial ship against Tripura."

"Not yet, Devraj. All we can do is hope that he has been able to meet the Naga and would somehow gain access to Rudrapeeth."

"I hope Haŕa is able to succeed in his mission before Devarth capitulates against the Daityan onslaught," Indra said and then looking over at Varun Dev asked, "What is the progress of war on the seas, Varun Dev?"

"Your Majesty, our navy has been putting up stiff resistance against the Daityan onslaught, and in spite of their overwhelming numerical superiority, we have been able to retard their progress on many fronts."

"How long can you check the enemy's advance?" Indra was getting anxious after not having heard from Haŕa till now.

"We'll try to sustain the consistent pressure from Daityan navy for another two weeks or so. After that, I'm afraid it would be all over. We may still continue to offer some pockets of resistance here and there but Daityas would by then be able to lay siege to all of our important ports and harbours. We have information that their elite naval formations called Navatakavachas have already left Atalantpuri and are heading towards our islands."

"Thank you for the information, Varun Dev. Let's hope the efforts of our brave navy are going to give us enough time to organise and launch a counter-offensive very soon," Indra Dev said. Then he looked at Brihaspati and asked, "Dev Guru, how are our allies faring?"

"Devraj, as you are well aware, our allies within Devarth don't have any navy of their own. They've always relied on our support to help protect their merchant ships and sea trade lines. They do have a sizeable land army and it is ready for battle. Between all of the Devarth nations, the total strength of our troops is around 300,000. Based on our intelligence reports, Daityans have despatched a naval armada containing well over 500,000 ground troops for attack on the peninsular Bhārat. They are likely to land on the shores of Kanchi, towards the southern part of the subcontinent. Another 300,000 ground troops are held as reserves and primed for mobilisation on short notice from their island garrisons. So there is a big disparity in numerical numbers. Daityan soldiers are well equipped and they have huge numbers of mechanical transport. Many of them are armoured and designed specifically for application in battle. They're also carrying significant number of long range projectile guns."

"What about our Maruth army?"

"Out of our nearly 170,000 Maruth troops, around 60,000 are deployed to defend Amaravati and other Dev Lok island groups. Remaining formations comprising a total strength of 110,000 have been deployed at critical positions of the Bhārat subcontinent. They are the only forces who have the capability to resist Kalakeya mechanical formations and Yantraksh battalions of Daityan army."

Indra Dev was silent for some time as he went over the information in his mind once more and weighed his words before speaking, "Gentlemen, considering the overwhelming superiority of Daityan army and navy, I can see that it may not be possible for us to put up a resistance for too long. Our only hope is the air force which has better vimāns in comparison to Daityas. If we can apply this superiority intelligently, it could perhaps provide a force-multiplier effect," he addressed Vayu Dev to know his opinion.

Vayu Dev got up and addressed everyone present, "We're indeed using our superiority in the air by supporting the ongoing naval operations. Once the main land battles start, we'll provide our troops all necessary support from the air. This should even out any advantage the enemy may have in terms of long range projectile guns. We have also deployed our air force in air-to-air combat against the Daityan air force formations. Altogether, considering the number of simultaneous battle fronts that have opened up, our aerial support can only be very limited. There is another point that we must keep in mind: the vimāns of both Devan and Daityan sides were not specifically designed for war. We've retrofitted them with projectile and pulse-ray guns but their accuracy and effectiveness has never been proven in any past wars."

"Vayu Dev, please do remember that you need to keep some reserve of vimāns to provide aerial support for Pinaka," Indra Dev reminded him.

"Of course, Your Majesty. I'm well aware that at this point our main hope is to launch an air-based counter-offensive lead by Pinaka. We will use all of our reserve air power to create a safe corridor for 'Pinaka' to reach up to the Tripuran airspace. However, once our vimāns are within the firing range of Tripuran guns, they might get shot out of the sky like flies near a fire. So from then onwards, Pinaka would be on its own."

༈ Ⱳ ⚥

The Daityan Emperor Tarakaksh was standing near the green lawns of his royal garden, waiting for Acharya Shukra. The huge garden which was perched over the top-most citadel of Tripura had its own mini lake. The lake also served as one of the water reservoirs for the citadels. Cleverly concealed special pumps located at Atalantpuri continuously replenished the water which cascaded into the lake through artistically landscaped waterfalls. Tarakaksh walked up to his favourite viewing point on the edge of these gardens from where he could survey the oceans on all three sides of Sweta Dweep. He noted that the oceans were surprisingly calm today. In contrast to the deep blue waters all around, the reefs surrounding the island shimmered white and frothy as waves passed over them. Many battleships could be seen moving in and out of the naval base of Atalantpuri. He turned around to see Acharya Shukra approaching through the lawns.

"Welcome, Shukracharya. You wanted to see me?"

"Yes, Daitya Raj. You know these are testing times for the Empire. All the progress that we've made over the course of so many centuries seems to have brought us to this point. This war would determine the future of Daityan way of life, or indeed that of humanity as a whole."

"Are you still worried about our having dropped the Anvik Astra on Lonar?"

"Yes. The logic behind that action was that it would be the fastest way to end this war and secure a clear victory for the Empire. Now, however, it has already been many weeks and we're still engaged in a conventional war, without any indication towards its ending."

"War plans never remain the same, Acharya. Our victory may be delayed but it is a certainty. I'm informed that our navy has secured victory on most fronts. The admiralty of Navatakavacha is already in the process of blockading Devan ports and harbours. Our land army formations, supported by a naval armada, are ready to make a beach-head at the southern peninsula of Bhārat. It should now only be a matter of weeks before they threaten the nations of Bhārat and Gandharv. Victory is well within our grasp."

"Daitya Raj, we may be in a position of superiority for now. This, however, does not guarantee success. We all need to eventually face our Karma. Using Anvik weapons in war was against the basic principles of the tenets of war; the Karmic consequences of such an act will definitely catch up with Daityan destiny," concern was evident in Shukracharya'a voice as he spoke.

"Acharya, our fate is defined by our actions and, therefore, it is under our own control. This makes us directly responsible for it. Wars are won by military strengths and strategy. If it means compromising on ethics sometimes, so be it. Anything is considered fair in war, and history clearly shows that it is always the victor who determines the future course of destiny."

"Daitya Raj, please don't make the mistake of underestimating the Devas. They must have stationed many formations of their Maruth army on sensitive sites within the Bhārat subcontinent. Maruths are famous for their valour and tenacity. Even with numerical superiority on our side, it is not going to be an easy run for us on land. Let's also not forget that Devas still hold control over the skies. I've also received intelligence reports that seem to indicate that Devas are building some sort of special vimān to attack Tripura itself?"

"Yes, Acharya, I've seen that report, too. It must be one of their desperate efforts in a war they are, so clearly, losing. We all know that Tripuran shields can't be breached using any weapon system at the disposal of Devas. Maya once told me that as per Brahma, no one on this Earth has the capability of destroying Tripura. Even among the Mūrthi, it is only Rudra who may have a chance of denting it. And as we all know, Rudra is no more on this planet."

"The Mūrthi may not be on this planet but they still maintain astral connections with many humans," Acharya Shukra reminded.

"Acharya, astral connections may be useful in spirituality but not on the battleground." Tarakaksh laughed before continuing, "Anyway, if it helps alleviate your concerns, I've already ordered Tripuran defence systems to be uplifted to the highest grade. Even if Devas are able to get their vimāns close to us, there is nothing that they can do except entertain us."

26

INVASION OF BHĀRAT

"Where are the Daityas likely to land their army?" King Pareekshit of the Bhārat kingdom asked General Jayadrath, the commander of his armed forces. They were seated within the operations hall at Hasthinapur, the capital city of Bhārat, along with General Kshetrajna, the Commander of the Maruth army of Dev Lok, and Brigadier Nilambar, the second son of Indra. Three Maruth divisions under Kshetrajna had been stationed near Hasthinapur in support of the Bhārat kingdom.

It was Kshetrajna who replied, "Your Majesty, as per Devan intelligence reports, the Daityan army comprising at least 17 divisions of Kalakeyas are likely to land near the beaches of Kanchi."

"Hmm. Seventeen divisions are too much for us to handle. Is there any way we could resist their advance?"

Jayadrath got up and moved near the huge map of Bhārat displayed on the wall of the operations hall. Then pointing towards the location of Kanchi on the eastern coast of the subcontinent, he stated, "Based on our analysis, it can be deduced that the Daityan army is likely to head for Hasthinapur and Chitrarath.

We plan to send one division of our army to attempt and inflict maximum damage to the Daityan forces during their landing, a time when they are likely to be most vulnerable. Thereafter, it would be multiple battles of attrition at strategic bottlenecks of their advance. If they are able to defeat all our attempts to stop them, then we will take the final line of defence near Madhura along the river Yamuna. I understand that the Gandharv army is also planning a similar strategy."

King Pareekshit turned towards Kshetrajna and asked, "We're extremely thankful to Dev Lok for sparing us the precious military resources of Maruth army. I'm sure your support would go a long way in our ability to put up a viable resistance to Daityan attack on Bhārat kingdom."

"You're most welcome, Your Majesty. I'll do my best to advise as well as contribute towards all your efforts to resist this Daityan offensive. We know that Dev Lok is safe for the time being as the Daityan focus is likely to be on subjugating Bhārat and Gandharv kingdoms first."

"General Kshetrajna, could you please explain briefly the strength of the Daityan Army?"

"Yes, of course, Your Majesty. The Daityan armed forces comprise two wings called Navatakavacha and Kalakeya. Both these wings have their own divisions of army, navy and air force with a mixture of Rakshas and Danav soldiers. Navatakavachas have higher proportion of Rakshas in comparison with Kalakeyas. From an overall perspective, however, Danav soldiers are more numerous in proportion to the general population of their Empire. They comprise mostly of infantry, the foot soldiers of Daityan armies. They use conventional low-tech weapons like swords, shields, lances, arrows, etc. The Danav soldiers are generally used to hold the ground within defensive positions after an offensive campaign; while the Rakshas soldiers use high-tech weapon systems like projectile launchers, artillery guns, armoured vehicle based brigades and, of course, the navy and the vimān based air force. Very few pulse-ray handguns of Mūrthi legacy are used by important generals of the army. In order to balance out and optimise the capability of both resources, all the military units have both types of troops. They also have some elite, purely Rakshas formations for specialised operations."

"So the troops likely to be deployed for offensive against Bhārat are mostly Danavs?"

"Yes. I'm given to understand that they are likely to send Kalakeya formations that mostly have Danav troops. These formations may also have some Rakshas troops to man the high-tech specialised weapon systems. Most of the battle may be based on conventional weapons complemented by some specialised high-tech ones. They are also likely to employ one or two battalions of Yantraksh."

"Jayadrath, do we have information as to when they are likely to land at Kanchi?"

"Yes, Your Majesty. As per our intelligence, the landing may happen within a week. We've already despatched a division of our soldiers under the leadership of General Pradhyumn. He should reach the landing site and set up defensive positions on the beaches within another day or so," Jayadrath replied.

ϒ Ш ♀

The Chief Commander of the Daityan army Narakaksh looked out toward the ocean from the bridge. Narakaksh was part of the royal house of Tarak at Tripura and he had been specifically appointed by Emperor Tarakaksh as the task force commander, in-charge of the land offensive on the Devarth inland countries. The land army commander of the task force, General Mareech, was in discussions with Admiral Sambara, the commander of the Daityan naval armada. They were on the main flagship of the armada containing around 6,000 ships of various size and purpose.

"By when are we likely to reach the landing site?" Narakaksh asked.

Mareech turned towards him and looking out to the sea, saying, "Your Highness, as you know, the sea has been rough all through our journey. So we may be delayed by a day or two. Most likely, based on current estimate, we should reach near the landing site at Kanchi by tomorrow evening."

"We must expect Devas to have understood our intention. They might have warned Bhārat to set up some beach-based defences around the landing site location," Narakaksh warned.

"Yes, Your Highness. Our mechanised landing crafts are ready to launch the offensive by the early morning day after tomorrow. Our ships have enough naval projectile guns to provide us covering fire before the landing. Even if the Bhāratans have managed to set up some defences, they are not likely to be able to stand up to our onslaught."

"Good. In that case, can we review your plan for advance thereafter?" Narakaksh asked.

"Sure, Your Highness. Would you like to accompany me and Admiral Sambara to the battle operations room? I'll brief you regarding our strategy on the virtual model itself."

They moved along the starboard side of the ship and entered the battle operations room. The operations room had been built to purpose with large maps of various parts of the Devarth and Daityan Empire on display. General Mareech reached up to the three-dimensional model that showed the landscape of the Bhārat subcontinent laid out in the centre of the room. Within this model, the military formations of Bhārat and Gandharv kingdoms were clearly marked as per their current locations. Similarly, the Daityan plan of advance and the military formations to be deployed for the same were also displayed.

General Mareech turned towards Narakaksh and started the briefing: "We've around 500,000 troops at our disposal. Most of them are infantry formations of Danav soldiers. Once we're able to establish a beach-head at Kanchi, we would launch our armoured mechanical transport-based brigades towards Hasthinapur and Chitrarath. These formations are likely to come under some form of attrition from the Maruth units of Dev Lok but we're confident to bypass most of them. The armies of Bhārat and Gandharv have no mechanical transport-based formations to be able to match our speed of manoeuvre across the subcontinent. We may also have an edge based on the high-tech systems at our disposal, which are well manned by trained Rakshas soldiers. Considering the predictable rate of advance, these formations should reach their destinations within three weeks or so. Once they manage to reach the capitals of Bhārat and Gandharv kingdoms, they'll block all main supply lines and roads, thereby effectively isolating these cities from external support. We may not be able to contain them completely but that shouldn't matter. Part of the mechanical transport would double back to pick up additional troops and weapon systems from the main infantry formations and over one or two round trips, they would be able to build up enough strength to contain the cites with infantry alone. This would relieve the mechanised troops to outmanoeuvre any resistance from Maruths."

"What about the state of mobility of the Maruth formations?"

"It is only the Maruths from Dev Lok who have some form of mechanical transport. But that is not much. By our estimate, their total transportation capability cannot provide for more than 70,000 troops, even though there may be around 100,000 of their ground troops deployed around Bhārat and Gandharv kingdoms. Comparing this with our strong mechanical formations with transportation capacity for 150,000 troops, there is not much they can do to resist us. At best they may be able to delay our infantry by a week or so, but within the larger scheme of events, that shouldn't matter at all."

"Okay. And what about the infantry formations that follow?" Narakaksh asked.

"Your Highness, the main body of our Kalakeya infantry formations advancing on foot and horses are likely to take around two months to join the holding forces deployed earlier, around the enemy's capital cities. I don't think Bhāratan army will be able to offer any viable resistance till then. They may, however, set up defences at the critical bottlenecks like bridges, valleys, etc. We've already anticipated such an eventuality. We would simply contain them with one or two battalions and continue the advance with remaining formations. We can always mop them up later once they are cut off from their logistic supply routes. All of these battles are likely to be based on conventional low-tech weapons on both sides."

"I guess it is also likely that they would demolish most of the bridges and river-crossing points?"

"Yes, Your Highness. Our forces are well prepared to take care of that. Most of our mechanical vehicles have amphibious capability. So they can simply wade through the water at any suitable location. As you can see on this model, our vimāns have already reconnoitred and marked many such suitable crossing points along all the rivers and other obstacles enroute. As regards the infantry formations, each of them have their self-contained engineering units that are capable of deploying transportable metallic bridges. This will help transport all the heavy artillery equipments as well."

"Are we planning to conduct the main battles near their capital cities?"

"Yes, Your Highness. That will be to our best advantage since we would have the support of the troops sent earlier, who would already be in well-invested positions around these cities."

"How long do you think it will be before we've softened them enough to offer our surrender terms?" Narakaksh asked.

"As per my estimate, once the final battle is over towards the end of next two months, there will be no cause for resistance from the Bhārat or Gandharv side. By then, we would be directly threatening their capital cities. The Kings of both nations may then have only two options – either surrender or run away."

"Yes! But I would prefer them to surrender. We would like them to continue the administration of the nation even as we look after the interests of Daityan Empire."

ༀ Ⴎ ♀

The commander of the southern division of the Bhāratan army, General Pradhyumn, found it extremely difficult to even come out of his bunker to visually assess the situation. The continuous pounding by the naval artillery projectile guns of enemy flotilla was simply too intense.

Based on Devan intelligence sources, the Bhāratan division had reached the coastal areas of Kanchi two days before the expected landing. With just enough time to construct few underground bunkers, he knew that many of his soldiers were at risk of being exposed to the relentless gunfire from the Daityan ships. Inspite of personal risks, he ordered his aides to accompany him to the rocky overhang adjoining the beaches.

The site that greeted him was something he would never forget in his life. As far as his eyes could see, all along the coastline, the sea was full of ships from the Daityan armada. There were at least 5,000 ships in the flotilla. The smaller ships carrying soldiers were towards the front, closer to the beach, and the heavier large ships behind them were anchored for giving the cover of artillery fire. Even as he saw, the mechanical landing crafts were moving up to the beach to launch the first wave of attack.

The artillery fire ceased as soon as the Kalakeya soldiers landed on the beach. They quickly regrouped into multiple battle formations and started off towards the Bhāratan defensive positions. The first battle for the subcontinent of Bhārat had started.

27

RUDRAPEETH

Whenever he put on the headband with the Takshak Nāg-Mani on his forehead, Hara was able to experience the unique extra-sensory perceptions around him. His innate Jwalaprabha enhanced the effect even further. He realised why the Nagas called the Mani their third-eye. On return after his encounter with the Takshak serpent, Vasuki had himself received him and said, "Hara, please remember that by our tradition, anyone acquiring his own Mani automatically becomes a Naga prince. I'm not sure if you will succeed is engaging with the Rudrapeeth, but if you do, and thereafter return back to your world, you will always be welcome to our land anytime."

The next few weeks of stay with the Nagas were generally uneventful. Guided by Vasuki or Shankh, Hara and Nandi had the opportunity to explore many of their wonderful caverns spread across Sarparanya. They were captivated to see the various exotic ways of Naga life. They learnt that most of the caverns were natural formations which, over many generations, had been linked up with each other into a huge labyrinth of an underground world. Many of the caverns were actually situated over subterranean thermal vents found in the region which provided them with sufficient warmth throughout the living quarters. The lower reaches of some of these mountainous caverns opened into lush open valleys with thick vegetation and farmlands that were well irrigated with water from the warm springs.

Since Mūrthi Lord Rudra and his followers living near Mount Kailash were served by the Nagas, the latter had been privy to some very unique technologies. Like the Mūrthi, they could astrally link up with lower life-forms; it enabled them to generate a steady supply of food from the farmlands and forests.

Like their earlier masters, the Mūrthi, Nagas were particularly fond of serpents, and most grown male members invariably carried a snake draped around their bodies at all times. Bonding with a serpent was indeed one of their initiation rituals before youth. These snakes, which were specially reared to adapt to a life on the body of a Naga, were bonded with their masters at the astral level and helped enhance his natural sensory perceptions. It was even said that the serpents helped facilitate direct astral link-up with lower forms of life. In this regard, the Naga princes also had the additional benefit of the Nāg-Mani on their forehead.

They also used some Mūrthi power plants to sustain the life support systems like air and water supply conduits within the caverns. The perpetual dim light from the Nāg-Manis illuminated the caves. Inspite of having all the Mūrthi technologies that helped them survive in this inhospitable terrain, Nagas lived a relatively tribal and spiritual way of life, completely in tune with their natural environment. Except for occasional visits outside by a few members, they vehemently resisted interaction with external, surface-dwelling civilisations.

☥ Ⱉ ⚥

On the 49 night after their arrival to the land of Nagas, they stared the trek towards the entrance of the secret cavern housing Rudrapeeth. It was a full moon night and King Vasuki led the way, followed by Shankh, Hara, Nandi and a few Naga soldiers. The location of the entrance was known only to very few Nagas to discourage overzealous adventurers. They started towards south, but the winding and almost untraceable track eventually turned and twisted towards the general direction of Mount Kailash. As they moved closer to Kailash, Hara could see the panoramic view of the terrain changing all around them. The harsh climatic conditions of this high altitude terrain created a unique, barren landscape which had its own pristine beauty. Even when they had started getting breathless due to the rarefied oxygen levels, it was difficult to tear one's eyes away from the breathtaking sights unfolding around them on all sides.

By afternoon, the weather conditions started worsening. Vasuki cautioned that a storm was likely to be on the way and requested everyone to hurry. The storms in these cold, dry places were somewhat similar to desert storms with dust and sand blowing at high speed, rendering visibility to almost zero. Fortunately, they were already quite close to their destination. Vasuki, walking ahead, took a sudden turn around the corner of a rock face and they followed. The sight beyond this point was nothing but celestial and mesmerising. Right in front of them and almost at eye level was the full glory of Mount Kailash. Hara wanted to stop for a while but the wind had started picking up speed. Vasuki warned that the dust storm would be upon them any moment and sped up. Everyone was aware how difficult a dust storm could make their trek at this hour, and they followed Vasuki without question.

Few more steps and Vasuki disappeared into what seemed like a dark niche between two cliff faces. Hara hesitated to follow but was soon relieved to see that this cavern was also dimly lit by some Nāg-Manis placed inside it. As their eyes got adjusted to the dim ambient light, the darkness slowly melted away to be replaced by a spectacular view of intricate stone carvings all around the huge cavern. Everyone gave out exclamations of wonder as they looked around. On the walls, he could see many inscriptions in ancient Brahmi. There were stone and metal statues of various humanoid forms placed all around. Some seemed to be representing various stages of human development, but most were unfamiliar. Even though the eyes of these life-size statues reflected a serene expression, their sheer size made them imposing and somewhat intimidating. Looking at these statues, Hara realised that the Mūrthi were at least twice as tall as an average human. Farther along the cave, there were statues of the three primary Mūrthi Lords – Brahma, Vishnu and Rudra. Lord Brahma was shown in a sitting position with four heads and flowing beard, Lord Vishnu was shown lying on a multi-headed serpent and Lord Rudra in a yogic meditative posture. Hara looked at the statue of Lord Rudra closely. He was seated on what seemed like a crystalline block in the yogic posture of *padmasan*, with eyes closed. The face looked intense as well as serene at the same time. Does he look the same now after so many centuries? Does he not age while in his meditative astral form? Hara wondered.

Hara was lost in thoughts when Vasuki came near and said, "Hara, the Rudrapeeth is located in a room at the end of this cavern. From this point onwards, only those having their own Nāg-Mani can proceed forward."

"As you say, Your Majesty." Hara said and looked around. Nandi and the Naga soldiers were still absorbed in looking at the wondrous carvings and sculptures positioned all around the cavern. Only Vasuki and Shankh seemed familiar with the place and Hara followed them as they moved forward through the cavern. Few paces further along, they stopped in front of what seemed like an intricately carved metal wall. Vasuki took out his Nāg-Mani from the band on his forehead and briefly touched it against a spot at the centre of the wall. The white wall transformed from its metallic texture into a transparent crystalline one. A few moments later, the crystalline texture changed into a liquid suspended in the air. Within another moment, even this dissolved into nothingness and they were looking into the room beyond.

There was a faint red glow from within the room so they could peer inside it even without the aid of external light. Actually it was difficult to call it a room because it didn't really seem to have any particular dimension or shape as such. All around was nothing but just an infinite void. The object in the middle, that seemed to remain suspended without any support whatsoever, was a simple solid and roughly rectangular crystal block which was also the source of the iridescent glow. The glow was not continuous but pulsated with a rhythm, much like someone's heartbeat.

"This is it, Hara! What you see in front is indeed the Rudrapeeth. Now it is entirely up to you. I've already explained to you the dangers of what you are planning to attempt. We can't accompany you any further. In the physical sense, all you have to do is move forward and sit down on the crystal block ahead. In the mental sense, however, you would be stepping into an altogether different dimension. If you're able to hold on to your pure self, it may lead you up to the astral form of Lord Rudra. If not, your body would get so hot that within moments it would get vaporised into nothing," Vasuki explained.

"Thank you, Lord Vasuki. This is what I've come all the way here for. Just one more question. That platform is obviously quite a pace away and seems to be suspended in mid-air. Without any ground to walk on, how do I reach there?"

"Hara, beyond this point the laws of the physical world don't apply any more. You have to rely on the solidity of your mind alone. Have faith in your Karma and move on. You have my best wishes."

Hara had a last look at Vasuki, Shankh and Nandi standing farther on. Then he turned and faced the platform once again. Taking a deep breath, he turned his whole attention inwards. Focusing on the Jwalaprabha, he let it slowly uncoil into its full glory. Maintaining his attention inwards, he directed the complete force of the stored kundalini tantric energy towards blocking his memories and outward attentions. Time seemed to slow down as he stepped forward into what looked like a void ahead of him. It seemed as though he had stepped on solid ground, though he couldn't be sure whether this was the physical reality or a mere projection of his mind. His eyes were firmly focused on the crystal platform as he walked towards it. At one moment, the platform seemed far away and the next he was standing next to it. He understood that time and space had no meaning within this region. He placed his hands on the platform. It seemed soft, warm and almost alive. Turning around, he sat on the Rudrapeeth in a characteristic meditative sitting posture of padmasan. He then folded the palms of his hands together in the linga mudra. Keeping his spine erect, eyes closed, summoning all the Bheeshma meditative skills, he turned inwards and plunged in.

Hara was now in a realm where the fabric of time or space didn't exist. There was nothing like past or future. It was as if complete existence was totally and firmly in the present moment alone. There was no sensation in his body or even the mind. At this point, he had no perception of even his own personality or ego as an individual. There was nothing except pure awareness of bare and simple existence. His identity with the one and only cosmic consciousness started slowly and very soon it grew into overwhelming proportions. It was as if he knew nothing and everything at the same time. The spiritual energy of the Rudrapeeth was now fused with his own. Very soon there was nothing but pure joy.

Then suddenly, he was pulled backwards, but not into his familiar physical form. The sensation was still serene but the sheer ecstasy that he felt a moment ago was no more there. His skills, as a Bheeshma was of no use in this state. Without the help of Jwalaprabha to hold them, the memories and emotions rushed in. Unlike earlier, however, they were now in his control and could be checked at will. Is this what people experience when they die? He wondered. Even as he was settling to experience the sensation or the lack of it without any physical body or sensory organs, he found himself looking into a face that seemed faintly familiar. It was a face with eyes closed in meditative silence that he had seen earlier within the cavern. The matted locks of hair cascading down the face seemed to have a life of their own. The body was strong, yet regal and as in case of Nagas, draped around the neck was a fearsome snake with its hood fully erect and distended. The legs were folded in the characteristic padmasan and hands were on both knees, fingers forming a perfect yogic posture of *dhyan mudra*. He felt, rather than recognised, that he was face-to-face with none other than the astral form of the Mūrthi Lord Rudra. Even as he recognised it, the face seemed to come alive and suddenly both the eyes opened. Hara felt the piercing stare of the Lord of destruction penetrate his persona.

"Hara, you have reached," Lord Rudra said. There was no movement on the lips to formulate any words. It was simply projected to Hara's persona.

"Lord Rudra, I bow before the glory of your divine self," Hara said.

"There is no one else to bow before, Hara. You are indeed my reflection itself," Lord Rudra's lips were still closed, but within Hara's mind he could sense the Lord smiling.

"Almighty, did you say I am your reflection?"

"Yes Hara, that is true. The physical life that you perceive is nothing but one of my dreams. So you and I are the same."

"I understand, my Lord, that all the physical beings are just manifestations of your supreme self."

"True! But you must not mistake the astral form you see now to be that of the supreme self; that is just another of its manifestations."

"My Lord, I may get to learn what you say over the course of my life. Right now, however, I've come to seek your help in doing what lies ahead within the path of my Karma."

"Yes, Indeed," Lord Rudra seemed to smile again before continuing, "You do have an incredible karmic path ahead of you, Hara."

"Lord Almighty, if you know my Karma, you must also know that I need your help to follow it through," Hara said.

"Of course, Hara. You have come to seek my help in destroying Tripura," Lord Rudra simply stated.

"Destruction of Tripura is the only way for the war raging on Earth to come to an end. This is the only course open for there to be any hope for future growth of humanity," Hara tried to justify.

"The destruction of Tripura would lead to deaths of hundreds of thousands of humans. Yet you're right that it seems to be the karmic path for human civilisation as a whole on planet Earth."

"My Lord, please tell me – what is it that I must do?" Hara asked.

"You've already done all the right things, Hara. Just follow your Karma. From this point onwards, it is my Karma, too."

Hara was quiet for a while and then asked, "Lord Almighty, as per Lord Vishnu, Tripura can only be destroyed by launching the main energy torpedo from the Mūrthi aerial ship Pinaka that is being readied now at Amaravati. This energy torpedo needs to be powered by the universal shakti accessed through the kundalini channel of your divine grace alone."

"Lord Vishnu is correct. Now that you've come to me, we will return to Earth together."

"My Lord, are you saying that you would take a physical from to accompany me to the Earth?"

"No, Hara. Your and my astral forms will merge into one entity till our karmic actions together get exhausted."

"Is that possible, my Lord?"

"Yes, Hara. Did I not say that both of us are mere dreams of the same single self? As per the karmic plan, these two dreams must merge together for some period of time. Once the purpose of that action is over, we will separate once again. But even after we separate, we will have a strong astral bond with each other. In many ways, Hara and Rudra will mean the same for all living entities on Earth."

"Lord Rudra, it would be my honour to have your company within my own self."

"That is our Karma. Are you now ready for the merger? And do understand that this is not without dangers? Your physical body and brain are not familiar with my Mūrthi perceptions and mind. They will struggle to retain our merged personality. We would, therefore, need to limit it to the level of human capacity alone. Even so, it will be put on extreme stress when the inner eye of my kundalini channel is opened to let in Rudraksh, the universal shakti of Brahmn. I'm hoping that the training and austerities you've undergone as a Bheeshma warrior monk would help sustain such a stress."

"My Lord, I'm prepared to face my Karma, irrespective of the consequences," Hara was firm.

Lord Rudra seemed to smile one again and silence followed. Then it happened. Hara sensed his astral form expanding with new levels of consciousness which he had never experienced before. Within that expansion of awareness, he could also feel the pulsation of his persona building upon a new vibration—the vibration of the primordial sound *OM*. The expansion reached a crescendo and then his whole being just exploded. What followed was a sensation of deep calm and peace like he had never known before.

28

DEVARTH'S FINAL HOPE

Hara looked down at the passing panorama of Bhārat subcontinent below the vimān. He and Nandi were on the way towards Amaravati. King Kuber had himself sent them off in his own royal luxury vimān Pushpak. In comparison with the vimāns usually in service around the world, this was a fairly large and powerful one with many luxurious amenities on board. Handed over to Devas by the Mūrthi lord Brahma, the Pushpak had been in service with Dev Lok till it was gifted by the tenth Indra to the then Yaksha King a few centuries back. The vimān was very steady in the air and totally comfortable to fly in.

The last few days had been like a dream for Hara. Ever since Lord Rudra linked his persona with Hara's, he could sense the astral umbilical cord between them. It was as if the Lord Rudra was deep within himself. He could even understand the thoughts and feelings of the Mūrthi Lord as much as possible through his limited human mind. The perspectives of the world around him had also changed dramatically. Gone were the regrets of past or apprehension towards future. The feeling was as if the river of his life had found its ocean – a state of perfect Stithapragya.

The change within his personality had been apparent to

all. Naga King Vasuki had knelt down in front of him when he returned from his meditation on Rudrapeeth.

"Welcome back to the Earth, Lord Rudra," he had said. Hara had neither objected nor encouraged him. If it helped someone to believe that he was a medium of communication with Lord Rudra, why not?

They had returned to the Naga caverns by early hours of the morning. Nandi told him that he had remained on the Rudrapeeth for only half a muhurta or so and from his perspective, it was nothing extraordinary. Vasuki and Shankh knew otherwise, having witnessed a few getting vaporized on the same pedestal in the past. Based on Hara's request, Vasuki had contacted the Yaksha King Kuber, who arranged to have them picked up by the Pushpak vimān near the Manasarovar Lake.

༾ Ⅲ ༾

By the time they landed at Amaravati, it was already late evening. Indra Dev, Brihaspati and all other Devas of Indra Sabha were present to receive him. Sapta-Rishis came up and bowed to him.

On request from Brihaspati, they went straight to Indra Sabha. Indra Dev addressed everyone thus: "Gentlemen, Hara has returned after successfully meeting Lord Rudra through the astral enhancement platform of Rudrapeeth. Dev Guru Brihaspati tells me that this is the first time in our history that a human has been able to sit on Rudrapeeth and continue to live. Anyone who's not qualified to engage with Lord Rudra would've simply got vaporised. Return of Hara is proof that we finally have the blessing of Lord Rudra."

There was a standing ovation from all present, reflecting a great sense of awe and euphoria. Then Brihaspati said, "I have no doubt that it is indeed Lord Rudra that we have among us today in the physical form of Hara. With the Lord on our side, we shall definitely win in preventing the catastrophe of Daityan domination."

"You're too early in jumping to conclusions, Dev Guru. If you are to be delivered by Lord Rudra, it is only because of your past Karma. It would be better if we focus on the current situation within the battlefield," Hara attempted to remind him smilingly.

Brihaspati got up and said, "Yes, Hara. Much has changed since your, I mean Hara's departure for this mission. We are now directly looking at complete annihilation or subjugation by the Daityan Empire."

"Have you lost all the battles?"

"Not all of them. We've won some, but lost many. Our brave soldiers have put up valiant resistance even against overwhelming odds of battlefield superiority of the Daityan army. Our Maruth formations did as best as they could. We attempted to use almost all of the weapon systems at our disposal. Even Indra Dev fought many of the battles. However, the onslaught of the Daityas was simply too strong. Many of the towns and cities of our allies have been laid waste. More than half of the Bhārat kingdom is already under the control of Daityan army. I wouldn't want to mention the casualties suffered by us so far; it would suffice to say that almost 40 per cent of the combined Devarth armed forces have been killed, wounded or taken prisoners."

"What about Dev Lok itself?" Hara asked, worried that it might already be too late to reverse the Daityan onslaught.

"Most of our navy has been decimated. The Daityan naval formations of Navatakavachas are already surrounding our island and laying siege to any shipping movements. We're completely arrested on these islands now. They've already captured some of our islands and we're soon expecting a land attack from their ships on Amaravati itself. There are reports that fresh landing force formations have been despatched from Atalantpuri. The only slight advantage we have is in air power. It has helped us keep the airways clear and enabled some movement. It is, however, insufficient to move any number of troops. We've just about sufficient strength of vimāns to launch a single attack on a specific target." Brihaspati paused for few moments before continuing, "I'll be honest with you, Hara. Our only hope is the Mūrthi aerial ship Pinaka. As it is only Lord Rudra who can launch its main energy torpedo, we've been earnestly waiting for your return."

Hara meditated on his astral link with Lord Rudra for a while, looked around and said, "Indra Dev, please go ahead and prepare the Pinaka for battle. Lord Rudra will energise the weapon when necessary."

"Thank you, Hara. If it is agreeable to you, we'll launch the vimān based counter-attack on Tripura tomorrow morning. Vishwakarma and the Sapta-Rishis have kept the Pinaka in a fully operational state. I'll escort you to the aerial ship at around two muhurtas before dawn."

29

BATTLE OF ATALANTPURI

As the Mūrthi aerial ship Pinaka rose above Amaravati, its crystal hull caught rays of the rising sun and shimmered like a brilliant gem in the early-morning sky. The citizens of Amaravati looked up at it in utter amazement. They had never seen such an amazing and awe-inspiring sight before. The wingless structure made it look more like a ship than any vimān they had ever seen. Yet, the majestic aerial ship was more graceful than any vimān could ever be!

The two forward-pointing weapon platforms on both sides gave it an interesting shape that vaguely looked like a celestial trishul head. The streamlined aerodynamic structure of the ship's hull was sleek, but its immense size and surging power projected the impression of a predatory bird unleashed from its cage. Even though the huge, yet magnificent ship seemed to be able to manoeuvre in the air with fluid ease, there was no sound of engine or for that matter any direct sign indicating its source of power. The only hint was the slight iridescent glow of the anti-grav drives towards the rear and the thunderous sonic boom created when the mighty ship slipped through the air to cross its own pressure waves. Once it reached a certain height, the ship simply turned westward and accelerated forward. The Devan escort vimāns that followed it, struggling to keep up.

Inside Pinaka, Hara sat on a platform not unlike Rudrapeeth. Pinaka was not just an aerial ship; it was a living entity with a mind and consciousness of its own. Even before its flight sequences began in the morning, its commander had to set up an astral link with the ship's mind. Much to the chagrin of Indra and others gathered at the hangar in the morning, first two attempts by Hara to link up with the ship had failed. Then Hara had smiled, realizing his obvious folly. There was nothing to try. It was the effort itself that distracted his attempt to seek within. All he needed to do was to keep his mind devoid of conceptual thoughts to let the presence of Lord Rudra emerge from within. In the very next instant, the link was established and the ship's systems came to life. Then it was a matter of feeling the complete ship and its subsystems to be an extension of his own material body.

Hara had never piloted a vimān before and so experienced the awe and thrill of being in control of the horizons for the first time. Like all first time pilots, he tried to put the machine through its paces. The mind controlled Pinaka responded like a dream. It was, however, somewhat disorienting to see the sudden acceleration of the ship through the screen but feel only a mild subdued impact inside the gravity controlled cabin.

"Can you hear me, Hara?" He was roused back to reality of the task at hand by the voice of Brihaspati. The sound was loud and clear as if he was hearing his own voice within the mind.

"Yes, Dev Guru. I can hear you loud and clear," Hara replied without speaking, as if in telepathic interaction.

"Hara, could you kindly slow down? Our escort vimāns are having a tough time following you. In fact, you also need to correct your course towards Tripura."

"Sure, Dev Guru. I'm sorry but it was irresistible to test Pinaka's response mechanisms." Within a few seconds he had steadied the aerial ship and slowed it down to match the speeds of other Devan escort vimāns. There were not many of them, even though Indra had deployed almost all of the Mūrthi vimāns at his disposal to ensure maximum support for Pinaka. That was the only way they could offer some semblance of support to the aerial ship when it reached Daityan airspace.

"Hara, at the speed your formation is moving, Tripuran airspace may be just two muhurtas away. Please do activate your force-shields by then. Tripura has incredibly powerful weapon systems, including long-range missiles."

"Thanks you, Dev Guru. I'm fully aware how critical this mission is for Dev Lok. Pinaka has already understood my intentions and corrected the course on its own. Even now, it is engaging its force-field shields."

༄ Ш ༈

Hara was totally taken aback by the intensity of the first blast impact from the long range Tripuran missile. It came from nowhere and even before he could think of manoeuvring Pinaka away, it had hit the ship. There was an apparent jerk as the projectile detonated and its complete energy was absorbed by the force-field shield. Even so, it was uncomfortable to think that the worse lay ahead when they get closer to the airspace surrounding Tripura.

Within another quarter yojanas, however, he had no time to worry about Tripura. A squadron of Daityan warplanes had appeared over the horizon. One of the Devan vimāns escorting Pinaka had already launched a missile and the front-most Daityan plane disintegrated ahead of them. Within the next few seconds, all hell broke loose. The Daityan vimāns had started blasting the pulse-ray guns with incredible accuracy. Two of the Devan vimāns were hit and went down. Hara thought to himself that this needed to stop. Pinaka, as if on cue, translated his thoughts as command and activated its integral guns to deadly effect. When the intense energy pulse emerging from Pinaka hit a Daityan plane, it vaporised into black smoke.

By the time they reached the visual range of Tripura, 70 per cent escort vimāns of Dev Lok had been taken out of action. The remaining fell back and veered off, unable to face the intense firepower from the citadels. Now, it was entirely up to Hara. Pinaka seemed to sense it as they moved forward towards the coordinates of Atalantpuri and Tripura.

30

MIGHTY TRIPURANTAKA

Hara was completely awestruck when the incredible sight of Tripura came into view. Seen from the air, it looked much more magnificent than he remembered. The three circular citadels that were evenly perched on the sheer cliff on the lofty mountain seemed celestial. The illusion of their circular motion due to light reflecting from the invisible force-field shields was even more pronounced from the air. The citadels seemed to perfectly complement the fabulous city of Atalantpuri below. Here was one of the greatest achievements of humanity—the culmination of many centuries of growth and enterprise of a fantastic civilisation. It was a matter of profound irony that he had now come to destroy it for safeguarding the very interests of humanity itself.

Even as he looked on, at least three vimāns emerged from each of the citadels. Pinaka's defences seemed to have sensed it and started blazing its own powerful pulse-ray guns. Three of Daityan vimāns were vaporised soon after they emerged from Tripura's shields. The remaining six attempted to veer off to surround Pinaka and fire at it from behind. The ship's shield absorbed most of these blows even as it launched a series of missiles towards the citadels. There were explosions all around the fortress but as expected, the citadel's shields were too strong to suffer any real damage. By then, Tripura had launched three of its own missiles which came straight towards Pinaka.

Hara knew that even Pinaka couldn't continuously sustain the full firepower from Tripura. His mind was flooded with synaptic responses from the ship's internal systems, as it struggled to avoid the flight patterns of missiles as well as the line of fire of the high intensity energy pulses now spewing out from the citadel's powerful guns. He could sense the warnings from within Pinaka that it was reaching the limits of its defensive capability and endurance. Inspite of best attempts to avoid, two powerful missiles hit them and Pinaka's shield started weakening.

"Hara, please manifest Rudraksh. If Pinaka's shield weakens any further it will be catastrophic. Its shield is not likely to be able to sustain the combined fire power from three citadels of Tripura," Hara's mind heard the desperate pleading from Brihaspati.

"Yes, Dev Guru. It is now the time to end it." Hara knew that the only way out was to focus on the primary purpose of this mission. Pinaka was well capable of doing whatever it can to defend itself. There were only two clear paths ahead – either total destruction of Pinaka and his own body along with it or the destruction of Tripura. He had to stop himself from being distracted by the thoughts of everything around him and focus inwards towards Lord Rudra. It was time for the great Mūrthi Lord to take charge. Summoning his meditative skills and Jwalaprabha, Hara blocked all the thoughts and retreated inwards to the quiet and peaceful state of Stithapragya.

As soon as his mind quietened, Hara sensed the presence of Lord Rudra within his mindscape. The presence continued to expand till his complete persona was bursting with overwhelming spiritual energy and the primordial cosmic reverberations of OM. Pinaka seemed to recognise this change within Hara and exposed him to primary energy torpedo of the ship. The energy torpedo responded and with immediate effect the life-force started draining out from Hara into it. Had it not been for the spiritual energy supplemented from Lord Rudra he would have collapsed, dried out without any life-force or Prana. As if by instinct, he felt himself staring directly at the brilliant astral form of the Mūrthi Lord. His own kundalini chakras were set off one by one as they aligned with that of Rudra. All of a sudden, everything ceased to exist. The physical reality, his mind, his own astral self, indeed everything that provided him with the barest shred of identity disintegrated. He was now Rudra himself and the only awareness was that of the inner eye of his kundalini channel, the doorway that linked the physical reality with the primeval potential shakti of Brahmn that manifested it. And then it happened.

The Atalantian citizens witnessing the exchange of fire between Tripura and Pinaka shrieked in horror as the familiar scene around them seemed to change at a rapid pace. It seemed that the sun was losing its brilliance and within few moments became a pale shadow of its former glory, as if in an eclipse. The sky turned dark; wind picked up speed and very soon it was as if a cyclone had suddenly materialised around Atalantpuri. The Mūrthi aerial ship Pinaka radiated an eerie glow as it aligned itself against Tripuran towers. A single shaft of brilliant light burst forth from within its bowels and struck the shields surrounding the three citadels. The three powerful force-field shields of the citadels glowed bright red as they tried to resist the enormous energy impinging on them. It only took another split second before the expanding shaft of intense pure energy negated the shields one by one and hit Tripura.

𐤀 Ш ϙ

"Hara, wake up please." The sound seemed familiar as Hara slowly drifted back to consciousness. Brihaspati had found him unconscious inside Pinaka after he rushed in, as soon as the aerial ship automatically flew back and landed at Amaravati.

"Where are we, Dev Guru?" Hara asked, still groggy with extreme weakness.

"Welcome back, Hara. You're now back at Amaravati," Brihaspati smiled down at him.

As they emerged from Pinaka, Indra Dev walked up to Hara along with Dev Rishi Narad and other Sapta-Rishis. They all bowed together. Then Narad said, "Hara, we always knew that you would deliver us from suffering. Dev Lok is indebted to you forever."

Later, when they were at the Indra Sabha, Indra declared, "The Bheeshma warrior monk Hara had earlier saved Dev Lok from a crisis by preventing an assassination attempt on me. With great risk to his own life, he travelled all the way to Mount Kailash to engage with Rudrapeeth and summon Lord Rudra to help us. Now, he has delivered us from total annihilation. As recommended by the Sapta-Rishis, in honour of his selfless actions for Devarth, it is my privilege to bestow upon him the most exalted honour of Dev Lok – The 'Greatest Deva' – the Maha Dev. His name would also be recorded in golden words within the Dev Lok chronicles as 'Tripurantaka – the Mighty Destroyer of Tripura'."

When there was a standing ovation from all present at the Indra Sabha, Hara sat calm and composed. At last when everyone became silent, he said, "What I have done so far were only actions in my karmic path."

"Even so, for the citizens of Dev Lok, you will always remain Maha Dev – the saviour of Dev Lok," Brihaspati said cheerfully.

֏ Ш ♀

It was when all the celebrations were over and Hara was with Brihaspati that he came to know the true import of what had actually happened.

"I understand that the mission was a success?" Hara asked Brihaspati.

"Success? Hara, there has never been an incident in our history that had such a cataclysmic impact. Not only Tripura but the complete Atalantpuri has been obliterated from the face of this Earth. The power of Rudraksh was such that everything collapsed within a single krastha. The complete mountain, on which the Tripura citadels were perched, came down like a fallen elephant, right on top of Atalantpuri. Under its immense weight, the continental shelf itself gave away and the tip of Atala island on which the capital city of Daityan Empire was located, plunged into the bottom of the sea. It was like an enormous earthquake and its tremors were felt even within Dev Lok. A tsunami that was triggered off by the collapse of a piece of Atala spread across the ocean, wiping out everything in its wake. The Daityan navy was obliterated. The waves washed out many of the townships across Bhārat subcontinent. There was damage to both sides but it was the Daityas who suffered the most. Most of their islands were completely washed away. The war is over and the Daityan army stationed at Bhārat is on retreat. Indra has called in for ceasing all hostilities to allow graceful withdrawal by their armed forces. In fact, the Devarth armies are even assisting Daityas limp back and retrieve their lives. The days of the powerful Daityan Empire are over."

"Dev Guru, do you sincerely feel that whatever happened was for good?" Hara asked doubtfully.

"I do, Hara. This was the correct karmic path and you know it."

"Yes. My Karma led me to this path where I've been the cause of destruction on such an unprecedented scale. Hundreds of thousands of lives have been lost. Yet you say that it was all for good cause," Hara smiled weakly.

"Who would know it better than you, Hara? Even as a Bheeshma monk you have lived by the order of right Karma. The consequences of your actions were never in your control. What has happened is what was meant to be. Besides that, I believe the destruction of Tripura was also the karmic path chosen by the Lord Rudra."

"That's right. Lord Rudra did tell me as much when I meditated on Rudrapeeth. However, now that our karmic paths are separate again, I feel the responsibility for what I've done weigh upon me alone."

"You must know that Lord Rudra would've never chosen an incorrect path of Karma. So please rest assured that what you did was indeed what was meant to be," Brihaspati reassured him.

"What now, Dev Guru?" Hara asked.

"Hara, you are now the Maha Dev. I guess many people within Devarth would consider you to be the representation of Mūrthi Lord Rudra himself. It is up to you to choose your karmic path ahead. I'm sure Indra Dev would be delighted if you stayed at Amaravati, but ultimately it is your wish."

31

NOTION OF DHARMA

Brahmagiri Ashram, the alma-mater of Bheeshma, was located on top of a mountain towards the southern peninsula of Bhārat subcontinent. A Devan vimān had brought Hara and Nandi over there directly from Amaravati. On Hara's insistence, the vimān pilot had left them at the foothills of the mountain. He wanted to walk up the familiar stone pathway that led up to the Ashram from the foothills. It was a secluded area, far away from most of the civilisation.

As they climbed up the steps along the long and winding path that led up to the main Ashram gate, Hara recalled the day when Acharya Parashu had brought him here for the first time. He was then full of curiosity, typical of a young man making the first steps towards a purpose in life. Now, many ayanas later, he was treading the same path as a completely different person. After the destruction of Tripura, Lord Rudra had retreated into his inner consciousness. Yet, even though their persona was separate, he felt a familiar astral connection with him and knew that he could interact with the Mūrthi Lord whenever he wanted to.

The view from the path leading to Brahmagiri was fantastic. It was early morning and all around the valley below was lush green with a touch of mist here and there. The climb was tough but Hara actually felt invigorated with all the fabulous views, smells and sounds stimulating his senses. There was a waterfall on the way up to the mountain and they took a refreshing dip in the clear pool beneath it. Then they started off, once again enjoying the sights and sounds all around them – the play of light through the trees, the gentle fragrant breeze, sweet sounds of birds chirping, and the distant calls of wild animals that set the theme of the jungle mornings.

It took them more than two muhurtas to finally reach the entrance gate of the Ashram. Carved in stone on top of the gate was the huge majestic statue of Prince Bheeshma – the original founder of the Bheeshma order. As they got into the Ashram, many monks came up to greet Hara. It was obvious that the news of his adventures had made him a demi-god in their eyes. They led him straight to the hut of the grand patriarch of the Bheeshma order – Maharishi Vashist. Nandi stayed behind with other monks and went about exploring the Ashram premises.

♈ ♌ ☿

Maharishi Vashist, with his aging yet regal profile, white hair and flowing beard, projected the very image of wisdom, compassion and inner strength. Though no one actually knew his exact age, many Bheeshma monks had seen written records of his existence for more than four hundred ayanas. This, however, had nothing to do with any medicinal therapies. His diet was indeed very simple and frugal. When asked about the secret of his extraordinary longevity, he always gave the same answer – yogic purity, meditation and righteous Karma.

The Maharishi was sitting in a meditative position with eyes closed when Hara entered the hut. He hesitated to go any further and attempted to trace his steps back so as not to disturb the meditation. Just then Vashist opened his eyes and smiled at him, "Welcome back, Hara."

"Pranam, Maharishi." Hara bowed respectfully.

"So you're back at Brahmagiri after saving the world?" Maharishi asked with a twinkle in his eyes.

"Only following my karmic path, Maha Guru," Hara bowed once again.

"You don't have to be so formal with me, Hara. Come, sit with me and tell me what all happened since you left Brahmagiri many ayanas ago," Maharishi Vashist said.

"Of course, Maha Guru. However, I am sure I have nothing to tell you that you don't know already," Hara replied respectfully.

"Yes, that may be so. I may know a thing or two more as well which may bring cheer to you, but we'll leave that for later. I would still like to hear everything in your own words. It is after all not often that one gets to hear from an illustrious young Bheeshma monk who is honoured as the Maha Dev," Maharishi Vashist stated, with obvious pride and affection.

They spend the next one muhurta or so discussing all that had happened since Hara left Brahmagiri along with Acharya Parashu to undertake the mission of saving Rishi Agastya. Hara's voice quivered when he described the tragic events that led to the demise of Parashu, Uma and his friends.

"Hara, I can see that you've still not got past the emotional burden of your recent memories," Maharishi said, looking at Hara's sentimental state.

"Yes, Maha Guru, these thoughts continue to haunt me," Hara admitted.

"You shouldn't be engaged with this conceptual world so intently and lose touch with your inner self. Please know that all those with whom you might've parted ways along your karmic path are fine. They continue their own journey," Maharishi Vashist said.

"Yes, Maha Guru. Even though I know that to be so from a spiritual perspective, I find it difficult to shake off the memories and the emotions that accompany them," Hara replied.

"Then you must attempt to separate the two. You must know that it is difficult to get a spiritual perspective when you're still entrenched in the conceptual world," Maharishi Vashist advised him.

"Maha Guru, why do we have a problem while attempting to understand spirituality within the conceptual sense? After all, our scientific discoveries are based on concepts," Hara asked.

"That is a good question, Hara. All our concepts are based on mutual referential frames of identification. It is also the structure based upon which, all the scientific knowledge is built. Any flaw to this frame of reference can render the whole concept invalid. For example, look at those flowers over there in the Ashram's garden. What colour are they?"

Hara looked through the window of the hut at the blooming flowers within the garden. "They are all red in colour."

"They're indeed red, but how do you perceive it within your mind? What if I tell you that they might be getting perceived as blue in your mind? Would I be wrong?"

"How can that be, Maha Guru? I called them red because that's what my sight detected and communicated to the brain through the optical nerves."

'Yes. The image of the sight reached your mind which compared it with past concept of colours stored in your memory. When there is a match, you identify it as the stored concept which in this case is red. But then again, how can you be sure that the concept stored in your memory is correct?"

"Based on past experience and identification during childhood, Maha Guru," Hara said, not understanding what the Guru was trying to hint at completely.

"What if you actually perceived them as blue but since during your first experience you were instructed - probably by your parents or teachers—to identify them as red, you've since been doing so forever? "

"I'm confused, Maha Guru. Are you saying that all of us could actually perceive an object differently in our mind yet identify it with each other similarly, only because we were instructed so in childhood?"

"It can sometimes be confusing, Haŕa. All I'm saying is that many of our concepts based on varied internal perceptions are quite untrustworthy in their capability to show us the real single truth. The idea of truth itself in a conceptual sense can only be relative to different internal perceptions, even if it seems to be on common platform of mutual identification. In order to attain the single real truth, one needs to rise above the conceptual level which is the realm of spirituality."

"What about this world that we see around us at the conceptual level? Are you saying that it is also a relative perception and not real?"

"What is your deduction? What is the 'real' based on? Isn't it merely based on a fragmentary framework that hangs on the treads of your own memories and personal sensory perceptions? Your so-called 'real' world is completely unsharable and intimately your own. Nobody can enter it, see as you see, hear as you hear, feel your emotions or think your thoughts. Even when anyone attempts to understand you, they can only do so from the perspective of their own private world. In your own world, you're truly alone, enclosed in your ephemeral dream, which you assume to be real."

"Maha Guru, you mentioned that all scientific concepts are based on mutual referential frame of identification. So does this mean that they're also untrustworthy?"

"They are trustworthy as long as the parties identifying them are within a single framework of identification. However, when you reach the borders of such framework, even well-established scientific truths and laws of nature tend to become uncertain. For example, the laws of nature that govern the physical properties of this manifested cosmos seem perfectly valid within a certain normal framework of identification. But these very laws seem invalid to understand the behaviour of objects either when they are in relative motion at extreme speeds, or when they are extremely small. These very scientific laws then become either totally relativistic or altogether uncertain. Deduction through empirical observations being the foundation of all scientific theories, it then becomes clear that observed phenomenon is affected by the act of observation itself. The strong relativistic connection between the observer, the act of observation and the observed, which defines the laws of nature at any point of time and space, becomes more and more apparent as one reaches the borders of any referential frame of identification or observation."

"So if the 'realness' of objects based on the scientific laws of nature governing them are relativistic and uncertain, what is actually out there, Maha Guru?"

"What you have out there is the universal potentiality. They seem 'real' only when you attempt to observe them. What we conclude to be observation or perception of real is actually a virtual creation of our mind itself, made out of this universal potentiality, based on a template of our tendencies, memories, emotions, habits, etc. In other words, our sensory perceptions including the mind provides us with the tools that help us create a world within an apparent realm of space and time—a world which seems to have shape, smell, colour, taste, among other attributes. This universal potentiality is nothing but what we also understand as awareness, cosmic consciousness, Brahmn, or God.

"Maha Guru, does this apply to the truth about our own selves?"

"Indeed, it does. Your belief about yourself or in short your personality or ego is also nothing but a virtual impression created on the basis of certain concepts, memories, sensory feedback and your own deductions. If you observe carefully, it can be seen that all of them are relatively dependent on one another with none having an independent standing on its own."

"So our conceptual impression of who we are is uncertain in itself?"

"Isn't it obvious? After all, how can you be sure about certainty of something that has no standing of its own and is dependent on other relative and uncertain concepts? So, even to understand our own selves we need to have a perspective which is above the conceptual level."

"I can see the logic now, Maha Guru. All the scientific or conceptual observations and perceptions in this universe depend on the observer or the perceiver. So in order to analyse the merits of the observed, it becomes invariably necessary to understand the observer as well. In other words, since the observed directly depends on the observer, the correct perspective about the observer is the foremost necessity, before we can even hope to understand the observed."

"Yes, Hara. It should then be obvious that the nature of the observer or our own self can only be understood from a perspective that is higher than the observer. It is such a perspective that we hope to achieve by being in close connection with our spiritual nature."

"What about our concept of consciousness during life and its loss during death?"

"Death is the end of our current virtual impression about us or our ego along with all that propagates it – mind, memories, and sensory impressions, etc. Once we realise that we're not our ego but an extension of the unborn universal potentiality, birth or death have no meaning."

"Maha Guru, the fact is that in reality, most of the beings are continuously engaged with this manifest world. It may be a virtual world constructed by the mind out of the universal potentiality. Yet, isn't it the only foundation for our conscious intellect? In that sense, how can we say that birth and death have no meaning?"

"Birth, death, and destiny do hold a meaning as long as we continue to identify ourselves with the mirage of ego and the virtual world that we construct around it. Since this virtual world is constructed out of the universal potentiality, it is also bound by its nature – Karma. Incorrect actions or inactions motivated by our limited ego creates karmic imbalance. The nature of the universal potentiality is such that it would automatically correct this imbalance by perpetuating the delusion of past, future, life, death, and rebirth."

"Maha Guru, we Bheeshma monks attempt to follow the correct Karma, by maintaining close connection with our spiritual nature. As I understand, this also means undertaking the correct action in any situation, such that it doesn't create any karmic imbalance. What is the nature of this correct action?"

"Correct action or inaction is that which is done when one is *not* motivated by the fruit or fears of such action or inaction. Such correct actions or inactions are also called Dharma, which is outside the realm of karmic equation. In other words, karmic equation is only applicable when actions or inactions happen outside of Dharma. Most of us who live in the world of concepts and mind are bound by the karmic equation."

Hara thought for a while, and then asked, "Maha Guru, what is the reason for this to be so?"

"Your question has more to do with who we are. Our conceptual worlds, and the thoughts based on the same, are only limited aspects of our universal self. Dharma means action or inaction which is in line with our universal purpose. As mentioned earlier, any action or inaction within the realm of our conceptual thoughts, which is usually motivated by fruit or fears for our limited virtual self or ego, may conflict with our universal purpose. The imbalance created by this conflict within the universal potentiality gets automatically corrected through the karmic equation."

"So does this mean we've no free will to choose our action and control the outcome?"

"Our ideas of 'free will' as well as control over outcomes are mere illusions. If you examine closely, the so-called 'free will' is not so free, considering that it is totally based on the deductions of our thoughts, which in turn are bound by our limited internal perceptions, intellect, memories, prejudices and such, over which we have little control. Our ego only claims ownership of control over things that happen the way they are meant to happen anyway. Any deviation in the short term gets corrected by the karmic equation."

"So the Bheeshma monks, while attempting to do the correct action or Dharma are following the purpose of their own universal self?"

"Yes indeed, Hara. Such a purpose and action tends to be generally similar for all who're able to connect with their universal self. This is so because the universal self of an individual is actually nothing but the cosmic consciousness of everyone and everything. This connection is to be achieved through meditation. Meditation and action hold equal significance for a Bheeshma monk, and both go hand in hand."

"Maha Guru, is it that all Bheeshma monks have always followed Dharma?"

Maharishi Vashist smiled while replying, "Not necessarily, Hara. Part of being Bheeshma is to follow the path of correct Karma or Dharma. Understanding perfect Dharma is, however, only possible for those monks who're advanced enough on the path of self-realisation. Most others live by a code of conduct that is driven by least personal attachments or ego. Since this is not perfect Dharma, it may indeed attract some karmic residue and the individual needs to live it through."

"So what happens when a monk reaches the state when he has no karmic residue?"

"This only happens at the very last stage when consistent dharmic action and meditative association with the universal consciousness frees the individual from the bounds of conceptual universe. It is a state of permanent and real existence, consciousness and bliss which is also known within the scriptures as self-realisation, *nirvana* or *moksha*."

"Maha Guru, I can understand that the ultimate purpose of spirituality is to reach such a state. You had also once said that the state of an individual when he is able to instinctively and effortlessly do correct action or inaction without attachments is also likely to be a state of permanent and uncorrupted happiness or bliss. However, correct action and happiness both being dependent on each other, which one should we pursue first in order achieve the other?"

Maharishi Vashist explained patiently, "Pursuit and achievement are wrong words as they sound like we need to acquire or gain something on the path of spirituality. In reality, the need is exactly the opposite. We need to actually shed or loose things to achieve happiness. The more we shed our dependency or attachment on material aspects, or even the concept of pursuits and achievements, the happier we tend to become. Ultimate happiness or joy is experienced when we shed or lose attachment to everything that usually makes us what we are—material objects and own body which are nothing but objective sensory aspects of our consciousness, memories, fears, aspirations, opinions including our perception of other person's opinions, ideas including our pet religious ones, mental concepts including the concept of God, etc. Lasting happiness or bliss happens when we cross the final barrier by shedding attachment to what is most precious to us all – our own personality or ego. When this happens, what we originally are shines forth. Unalloyed happiness or pure joy is what we originally are and also our real, permanent, uncorrupted, and unborn state. Spirituality is nothing but efforts to remove the corruptive influence of ego that cloud our real selves."

"So we need to attempt and stay away from the corruptive influence of attachments that propagate the ego. Any action that happens in such a frame of mind is likely to be correct. This seems like a very difficult task for anyone living in this conceptual world," Hara said.

"You're right, Hara. It is difficult to do so while within the realm of the conceptual world of our mind, body and senses. Meditation, which is an attempt to directly access our own inner universal consciousness, is the right means of purifying ourselves and realising the state of perfect happiness. To a lesser extent, even with our ego intact, living well guarded from its corruptive influence also helps to purify ourselves."

"Maha Guru, you had once said that every state has conceptual opposite like pleasure to pain, wealth to poverty, sickness to health, etc. So what is the opposite of happiness?"

Maharishi Vashist replied, "Hara, happiness is the only concept which has no opposite. Actually the duel concept of opposites has any meaning only within the conceptual level. Happiness, which is what we fundamentally are, is beyond this level. Even so, to understand it from a conceptual perspective, we can take the example of light. You may say it has an opposite called darkness. But then, you realise that darkness is nothing in itself. It is merely the absence of light!"

"Maha Guru, some people may say suffering to be the opposite of happiness. What about that?"

"Hara, if examined clearly, you would see that suffering is indeed nothing but happiness denied due to continued attachment with some person, object, body, sensation, concept, fear or aspiration."

"So you mean to say that to end suffering, we need to merely remove the attachments which cause it in the first place?"

"For most humans, this is not as simple as it sounds. Our ego, which is the prime basis of our conceptual world, can't shed the attachments because it is itself virtually made out of that stuff. Attachment plus the expectations of fruit or fears of actions that come with it, and the suffering that follows it, can only end when we eventually detach ourselves from the conceptual world through meditation."

"Maha Guru, my profound thanks to you for explaining the way of ending the suffering. I had also instinctively felt much of what you explained me when I was in direct astral association with the Mūrthi Lord Rudra. However, following the destruction of Tripura when we were separated again, these doubts seemed to resurface. Anyway, now that my mission is over, what am I to do?"

"Our mission is never over, Hara." The Maharishi smiled and continued, "However, it may now be time for you to seek some peace and also consider the grihastya way of life."

"There could never be grihastya for me without Uma," Hara said summarily.

"Hmm. You may still want to seek some peace. I'm told Manasarovar is an excellent place to spend some time?" Maharishi Vashist asked.

Hara's eyes brightened up when he said, "Yes, Maha Guru. It is indeed a pristine and peaceful place. When I was there last time on the way to the land of Nagas, I did long to spend more time there."

"Then why don't to do so now? I'm sure Kuber, the King of Yaksha, would be delighted to help you build an ashram over there?"

"Maha Guru, thank you for indicating the path ahead. Come to think of it, this has always been at the back of my mind. If I have your permission, I'll start my journey immediately," Hara said cheerfully.

"Of course, Hara. But before you go, there is something that I need to give you," Maharishi Vashist got up and walked up to a low table nearby and took out a scroll. "This is a final message from your guru Acharya Parashu. He was insistent that you read it only after your ongoing mission was over. Otherwise you might've hesitated from your correct karmic path. Now that you've already accomplished that, you should be free to read it. I would, however, recommend that you hold on to it for some more time and read it only on the way to Manasarovar."

32

LAKE OF THE MIND

The air was cool and crispy as Hara and Nandi neared the Manasarovar Lake. They had reached Alakapuri, the capital of Yaksha kingdom a day back, once again by way of the Pushpak vimān that King Kuber had sent for him. After that, in spite of repeated requests, from Kuber, he had chosen to trek his way up to Manasarovar Lake. The two day-long climb had steadied his mind after all the turmoil within it for the past few months. Lord Rudra had completely returned to his individual astral state, though the astral bond remained. Hara had an opportunity to sense the enormous ocean of peace within the realm of the Mūrthi lord and longed for it instinctively. Yet he also knew that there was residual Karma in this life to live through. Some day he might be fortunate again to feel the same depth of peace and ecstasy.

The destruction of Tripura had completely changed the demographic pattern of the known world. After the sinking of Atalantpuri, the survivors of the Daityan royalty had retreated to few tropical archipelagos of the earlier Empire. Along with the remnants of their army and navy, they had established a new nation on islands that were least affected by the tsunami. The robust stone embankments created by Maya to check rising sea water had been breached, rendering many parts of these islands inappropriate for cultivation. Quite a few Daityas continued to remain on these archipelagos, surviving on newly-created crop fields, remnant forests and seafood. Many moved to the inland forest lands and river basins that Maya had been preparing for quite a while as a counter measure for the continued inundation of their islands. This land was hardly sufficient to absorb all the population rendered homeless so there were still many more who sought refuge within Devarth nations. Inspite of the best efforts on behalf of these nations, it had put extreme pressure on the already difficult situation of food and other resources available therein. Bhārat, Gandharv, Yaksha and Kinnara kingdoms helped absorb many of the Daityan refugees and directed them to settle down at the thinly populated regions near the receding icelines and establish their own unique communities. The technological know how brought along by them would help many Daityan communities to cope with the hard life in these frontier communities and even prosper over the coming years. Many may also find it difficult to adapt and fade away or get assimilated into the native population in these regions.

Apart from Daityas, who suffered the most in the short term, Devas also had to adapt to the new situation. Many of their islands had been seriously impacted due to the tsunami. Maruth troops had to be deployed to control the population as well as ensure emergency supplies to the affected islands. Similar situation was also faced by Bhārat and Gandharv kingdoms whose coastal settlements had been badly damaged. It would take many years for all nations to heal the wounds of war and restore normalcy. Various kings and their councils were busy with governance as well as repair and reconstruction work to re-build the infrastructure damaged or destroyed as a consequence of the war. The situation of scarcity and strife would last for many years.

Now that the calming presence of Mūrthi Lord Rudra's persona was no more within Haŕa, and there was no immediate action to occupy his mind, painful memories of the past were attempting to resurface. The thought of Uma and the accompanying feeling of anguish kept returning. As advised by Maharishi Vashist, this was the time for him to find some solace from all these crippling emotions. It would be best to spend some time to stay and meditate at the serene environments of Manasarovar. As he had experienced earlier, the pristine lake and calm environment around it would be ideal for him to seek inner peace and also heal the festering wounds in his mind. With his exalted position as the Maha Dev, it wouldn't be difficult to get all necessary help from both Nagas and Yakshas to establish an ashram near the banks of Manasarovar—also known to many as the 'Lake of the Mind'.

Hara looked at Nandi who had been his constant companion. It was clear from his eyes that the young monk worshipped him. Not just as his guru but as Maha Dev. Hara was not sure if such adoration was a good thing. After all, both of them were still Bheeshma monks and their primary purpose was to follow the path of right Karma. There was much that Nandi needed to learn; Hara was sure he would find his own karmic path once he learnt more things. But till then, Hara must let him grow, as he himself once did under the shadow of Acharya Parashu.

The thought about Acharya Parashu reminded him of the scroll given to him by Maharishi Vashist before he left Brahmagiri a couple of days ago. They would reach Manasarovar soon, so Hara sat down on a wide boulder and opened the scroll.

As he opened the scroll, Hara couldn't help recall the serene face of his revered guru. The words had been written by Acharya Parashu himself, in his characteristically simple style of writing.

"Hara, by the time you read this message, our karmic paths would have separated. You would already be on a new path, well on the way to the glorious future that lies ahead of you. Did I know whether the end of my physical life was near? Yes and no. Either way, my karmic path in this realm seemed to be near its end when you left for Amaravati. I

know that you've suffered much since then. Yet, what I'm going to tell you could only be done after your recent karmic mission. Any kind of distraction would have made you hesitate from that path.

Your beloved Uma is alive and well. I knew that the safest place for Uma to be during all this turmoil was either at the distant nation of Yaksha or the land of the Nagas. So the timing was perfect when Yaksha King Kuber met me at Lonar. I had to put him under oath not to disclose this to anyone till the time is appropriate. It was good to see that we Bheeshma still hold substantial moral authority of influence on the kings. I had a tougher time convincing Uma to leave though, but it seems she has eventually come to trust my insights. I'm sure the Yakshas would protect her from any harm till both of you're ready to meet again.

It is now time for you to live through a period of grihastya and love. I wish you the very best in this life. Keep your meditative stance pure. Remain connected with your inner self. Remember that I'll always be watching you..."

Hara got up with a start – Is Uma really alive? He felt the sense of excitement welling up within him. Is this what King Kuber meant when he said that there was a surprise waiting for him at Manasarovar? Is Uma really waiting for him there?

EPILOGUE

It remains an enigmatic mystery as to whether the destruction of Tripura by Lord Rudra described within the Indian mythology was the same event that marked the end of Plato's Altantis. We are also not sure whether there is any substance in some popular belief that the huge Lonar crater in western India was caused due to a man-made atomic explosion in the bygone epoch.

Either way, human-triggered or otherwise, it is possible that many cataclysmic events happened towards the end of Ice Age. Over the course of few centuries after this event, there were several natural events of gargantuan proportions all across the world. Global warming led to inundation and eventual submersion of many islands and low-lying coastal land. The habitable landscape of the planet underwent dramatic realignment. Apart from rise of sea water, increased tectonic activity of the Earth's crust led to largescale earthquakes and volcanic eruptions across the globe. Many of the living species became extinct and those who survived had to considerably adapt to the changed environmental realities. Humans were no exception.

This period of heightened geological activities and catastrophic environmental upheavals also initiated the end of the 'first wave' of advanced human civilisation on the planet. Largescale ecological changes forced all the established civilisations to change course and adapt to new situations.

Many, who remained stuck to the earlier ways of life, perished, got wiped out and were completely erased from the annals of history. Fantastic cities and infrastructures were demolished beyond recognition during the numerous earthquakes and tsunamis. Eventually, most of the physical evidences regarding the technologically-advanced civilisations of first wave got submerged under the oceans and became mere legends in the collective social memories of humanity. Over the course of countless generations, such legends that were passed through word-of-mouth got corrupted and transformed into exotic myths. However, few overwhelmingly traumatic events did persist as such within the myths, though the fact around them got coloured into multiple interpretations.

One such myth is that of the Pralay or the Deluge and on how the surviving humans were saved due to divine support. The days of the extraordinary inundation or floods, and the escape of survivors from the first wave, by way of few remaining ships, arks and boats remained deeply etched on the sociological psyche of humanity. The memories of this event lingered on persistently within almost all the cultures across the globe. All the surviving societies did have their unique experiences and memories of this tragic phase of human history, which transformed into the multifarious myths about the event itself.

After the end of ice age, most parts of the globe were exposed to sunlight and became suitable for the proliferation of life. Vast portion of the planet started becoming green and soon turned into dense forests or grasslands, teeming with wild life. This encouraged largescale migrations of humans all across the globe. They came in contact with the aboriginal pisachas and barbarians who had occupied these unknown lands earlier. New phase of intermixing of cultures, bloodlines and languages followed. Over the course of time, many nation states surfaced, got consolidated into great empires and prospered, but eventually withered away.

Legends got mixed up with memories of recent history, thereby creating new myths with many flavours.

The end of Ice Age marked the doom of both the Daityan and Devan nation states that were based out of tropical islands. The fertile island habitats on which they had proliferated were eventually inundated and submerged under the rising oceans. The first to suffer were the Daityas. After the destruction of Tripura and Atalantpuri, the Devas remained the dominant civilisation for many centuries. However, eventually, they also had to face the increasingly cataclysmic environmental changes unleashed by the nature on an unprecedented scale. The beautiful city of Amaravati was completely demolished in one such event. The oceans also claimed most of their island paradises. Records of the unique way of life of the Dev Lok got buried in exotic myths.

The surviving refugees from Daityan Empire and later the Dev Lok, migrated to various continents all around the world, and in due course of time started their own distinctive new cultures and civilisations. Eventually, many recently—formed rivers emerging from receding ice-cover created huge areas of cultivable land suitable for habitation by the migrating human population. The fertile shores of few rivers like Tigris, Euphrates and Neel (Nile) gave rise to new civilisations in Mesopotamia and Misr (Egypt). Based on the few historical records surviving from their glorious past, the migrants from Devan and Daityan nations tried to emulate their past as best as they could. Even though lacking the full technological know how of the first wave, they attempted to reconstruct numerous structures of the bygone era using stone and other locally available materials. At extreme cost of labour and efforts, new rulers from Devan lineage even attempted to rebuild the pyramid-shaped Devayana structure – which had been the spiritual heart of Dev Lok – using stone blocks on a colossal scale, on the shores of river Neel.

Many survivors had to take refuge within the existing kingdoms like Bhārat. In the following millennia, the receding icelines brought about many changes within the habitation patterns across this sub-continent as well. The changing glaciating outlines of the melting ice-shelves severely impacted the course of major rivers that had sustained the early human habitations. Starved of melt-water from nearby glaciers, majestic and iconic rivers like Saraswati dried out completely when at the same time, newly formed glaciers at higher latitudes or altitudes helped the then small rivers like the Indus become much more prominent. Eventually, the historical records of the kingdoms like Bhārat, Gandharv, Yaksha, Kinnara, Nagas and others got buried in the myths and legends of these times. New nation states emerged from the ashes of the old ones. The subcontinent of Bhārat retained a sense of continuity with the first wave through numerous myths and scriptures. Due to its spiritual legacy, this land provided a certain degree of stability, tolerance and freedom for multiple ideas to co-exist. Those who followed spiritual ways of life continued to find a place within the society in general. The Rishis, Yogis and others pursuing the path of knowledge contributed to formulation of many epics, stories and scriptures.

The demise of the Devan and Daityan nations proved to be a loss to humanity as a whole. The know how of many of their unique indigenous technological achievements were lost forever. Their way of life merged with other popular cultures of that time. The Vigyan Vedas and all records associated with it were totally destroyed, especially since it was kept limited to a very small controlled group of priests. Along with it, the high-tech knowhow passed on from the Mūrthi were also completely lost to humanity as a whole. The written materials of the Gyan Vedas were also lost. Fortunately, part of the wisdom contained within these scriptures was still known to a few Rishis who lived on the inland nations. They attempted to reconstruct them as best as possible and shreds of the original wisdom were compiled into Vedas, Puranas, Upanishads, Agamas, Sangam literature, etc. Many historical records of actual events that happened before the end of Ice Age were rewritten in the form of epics. However, all these new interpretations were also coloured by the local customs and traditions prevalent during the millennia that followed the demise of the first wave of human civilisation.

The Mūrthi continued to maintain their interests in the development of humanity. The downfall of the first wave of the human civilisation was recognised by them as part of the karmic evolutionary process. They knew that sustainable development was only possible when humanity matured to a level when they could understand the meaning of Karma, and realise their own purpose in this cosmos. The dark ages that followed the first wave lasted for many millennia. With time, new civilisations sprouted in numerous parts of the world. Unfortunately, they were far less sophisticated when compared to the first wave. This upsurge lasted for a few millennia but couldn't develop beyond a point due to the intrinsic immaturity of human nature. Mūrthi did help nudge humanity from time to time through astral engagement with spiritually-advanced humans. These Avatars, Buddhas, Saints and Prophets did contribute to improving the human condition which kept vacillating over the course of subsequent millennia.

As centuries passed on, new sparks of scientific ideas started changing the human society itself. The great interest and hunger for knowledge in the fields of science, literature, new ideals of freedom, etc., started influencing all facets of human life. The second wave of human civilisation had begun. The scientific knowledge led to invention of new technological systems that once again improved the way of human life on the planet. Renewed interest in shipping and exploration of faraway lands reconnected cultures that had been separated for many millennia. Mechanical transport systems and electronic communication systems were invented, leading to the opportunity for expanding the scope of interaction between multiple cultures and societies across the globe. Better transportation systems also made it feasible for mega cities to develop.

Increased production of food and other necessities meant that many people could focus on aspects of life well beyond day-to-day basic struggle for survival alone. Business and trade prospered and the general nourishment levels improved significantly. Scientific developments also led to new ways of medical treatments. The combined effect was the betterment of human life expectancy and health. New scientific discoveries and inventions further accelerated human thirst for knowledge, leading to great discoveries like the nature of sub-atomic structure, laws governing the universe, among others. Better understanding of the cosmos also uprooted many entrenched and outdated religious dogmas.

New scientific discoveries increased human control over the environment as well as the plant and animal species of the planet. Due to better availability of food, improvement in health and a general environment of stability, human population kept burgeoning into unprecedented numbers. The huge amount of food as well as material desires demanded by the population resulted in unsustainable levels of human consumption. This put severe strains on the global natural resources as well as the balance of natural order. In many ways, the second wave human civilisations ended up following the Daityan way of life of the first wave. Pollution, overconsumption, adverse impact on environment became major problems once again. Scientific knowledge also led to development of Anvik and other destructive weapon systems that threatened to extinguish all the achievements of humanity.

The great scientific advancements of the second wave led to landing on the moon and exploration of new planets within the solar system. Humans started migrating in small numbers to the new frontiers of habitation within the oceans, outer space as well as other suitable planets like the Mars. Developments in information and communications technologies created new opportunities to accelerate the benefits of knowledge. With increasing sophistication, these technologies eventually led to global networks as well as the creation of Artificial Intelligence (AI). Human civilisation soon became almost like an integrated global organism, with its own comprehensive nervous system and collective brain. New virtual meta-worlds were built and evolved into alternative realities within cyber space. Many people chose to actually live within these unconventional parallel existences for majority of their wakeful time. Eventually, the progress of human civilisation during its second wave of advancement reached the point of technological singularity. The AI systems created by humans gained consciousness. They matched and eventually surpassed even their creators in terms of intellect.

At some point in future, the scientific knowledge converged on spiritual wisdom. The meaning of the objective cosmos and its relationship with our spiritual nature became clearer. Many of the Mūrthi technologies of astral engineering and their use for productive co-existence with natural systems were rediscovered. Intrinsic cosmic connection of human spirit with the 'universal potentiality' was revealed once again. Direct astral links with the Mūrthi were proactively re-established. This accelerated the technological growth as well as hastened the journey of humanity on the path of spirituality. It was the dawn of a new phase of human Karma.